Sign up for our newsletter to hear
about new and upcoming releases.

www.ylva-publishing.com

Other Books by Lee Winter

Standalone
Vengeance Planning for Amateurs
Hotel Queens
Changing the Script
Breaking Character
Shattered
Requiem for Immortals
Sliced Ice (anthology)

The Truth Collection
The Ultimate Boss Set (box set)
The Brutal Truth
The Awkward Truth

The Villains series
The Fixer
Chaos Agent

On The Record series
On the Record – The Complete Collection (box set)
The Red Files
Under Your Skin

The Villains Series:
Book 3

Number 6

LEE WINTER

Acknowledgments

Before we begin, let's get this out of the way: I strongly recommend you read the first two books in *The Villains Series* before opening this story. I see *Number Six* as a spin-off as well as book three in the series. There are spoilers and references to previous events and characters that will make a lot less sense to fresh readers.

It also helps to have read *Hotel Queens*, but that isn't essential.

Why did I write a book centering a Las Vegas sex worker and an ethically dubious, ex-spy retiree? Good question!

The sex worker, Monique Carson, intrigued a lot of people when she first appeared as a minor character in *Hotel Queens*. For years, my publisher begged me for a book about her, but I resisted, thinking interest in a whole book about Monique would be low.

Then Monique acquired a surprisingly large following after the *Number Five* short story appeared in my *Sliced Ice* anthology.

Number Five is included as a bonus here, so if you haven't read it, I'd suggest skipping to the end of the book and diving into that first. For reference, this novel starts six weeks after the events in the short story.

When I wrote *The Villains Series*, I developed a powerful fascination for the ethically gray, mature former spy Ottilie Zimmermann. She was only a small side character, but I wanted to know everything about her...

Who would turn the head of such an uptight bureaucratic pragmatist? Wouldn't it be amazing if it were someone as free in mind, body, and spirit as Ottilie wasn't? What if the woman who made officious Ottilie melt were Monique? They're both clever women who read people extremely well. It would be intriguing seeing them meeting their match in each other.

The writing wheels turned, and here we are. It's been fourteen months since Ottilie "retired" and finds herself in Vegas in Chapter One.

There are many people I have to thank, beginning with the experts. Former fashion model mentor Siobhan Halo, doctor and author Chris Zett, BDSM aficionados and authors Thea Belmont and Allison Ashton, and ancient Egypt lover Lara Hart.

Lastly, I have to give a grateful nod to queer adult-film star Nina Hartley. She puts herself out there often to educate, openly and honestly, about the business of sex work—good and bad. Her online interviews were invaluable to my research. Nina's playful, flirty confidence and love of sex are characteristics I've imbued in Monique.

There is, obviously, a dark side to sex work. Sadly, too many of those involved in it are vulnerable and exploited. While I touch on a few of these issues, I acknowledge that Monique is in a position of power and privilege and has complete autonomy, so her experiences will be different to those of many others. At the end of the day, this is fiction, so if Monique's best life is being paid for sex with women and absolutely loving it, that's her truth.

To my beta readers, Astrid Ohletz, Kristen Neely, Jane Waterton, Jens Sadowski, Mary M., and Carolyn Bylotas, thanks so much. I love you heaps. Your insights are excellent.

To my copy editor Michelle Aguilar, and my new content editor, Sarah Ridding, thanks for everything, especially for fixing my overwrought adverb addiction!

Thanks to my long-suffering fiancée Sam, the woman behind the absent-minded author, and provider of so much support.

To everyone else, I appreciate you for taking a chance on my unlikely story. I'm as surprised as you are this book exists! It's a little unnerving being so far out of the usual romance norms, so I truly hope you like it.

Dedication

For reader Shannon Luchies, whose steadfast fascination and love for Ottilie inspired me to keep going, even when I was convinced no one would love her as I did.

Thanks, man.

In life, there are only two things that matter: power and control. Those who run the world and those who seek to. Everything else is a lie hidden by shiny distractions. Never ever attempt to unpeel the lie.

— Ottilie Zimmermann
Retired from [redacted]

Power is an illusion. I can strip you of it or give it back in the blink of an eye. It is a concept sold by men who get hard from the thought that it makes them special. It doesn't. I can tell you, having made the weak feel powerful and the powerful feel weak, that power is actually nothing at all.

— Monique Carson
Las Vegas's CEO Sex Fantasies Expert

Chapter 1
Vegas vs. Beirut

In the choice between Beirut and Las Vegas, Ottilie Zimmermann decided it would be a close call. She had stayed in both, nearly died in one, felt like dying in the other, and would rate each as *generally unfavorable* on TripAdvisor. If she ever used TripAdvisor, which she most assuredly would not.

But now that Ottilie was back in Vegas, experiencing her trifecta of pet peeves—loud noises, flashing lights, and garishness—Beirut was nudging slightly ahead.

As Ottilie pursed her lips hard enough to suck the pulp from a lemon, her sharp gaze mapped the horrors surrounding her. Above, on a giant digital billboard, was a shock-pink, flashing advertisement for nightly shows by America's sweetheart, pop sensation Carrie Jordan. Next to Jordan was a Coca-Cola bottle slam-dunking itself through a basketball hoop, creating a 3D wave of brown fizz that seemed to leap out of its background.

Below, electric blue letters screamed about a Mega Poker Tournament. Opposite was an advertisement for SlotZilla, a casino tower with a zip line, that invited people to do the "Super-Hero Zoom."

Ottilie shuddered, and not just because *superhero* should be one word.

Sighing, she rubbed her aching neck and turned to face Hotel Duxton Vegas's gleaming front doors. She was only here for a week or so as she tied up loose ends from her former job. And then, finally, she could retire for good, her conscience clear.

Well, clear enough. From the corner of Ottilie's eye, Carrie Jordan's dazzling smile widened into smug perfection.

Assuming she could make it that long.

A man stood behind the reception desk, his name tag stating that he was Graham. He was tall, thin, in his mid-thirties, and apparently incapable of noticing Ottilie. She glanced at herself, analyzing her tweed skirt, brown, flat, sensible leather heels, and an elegant cream blouse pinned down by a pearl necklace.

Ordinarily, being overlooked would please her. After all, Ottilie had made it her life's work to be invisible. She cultivated a harmless persona that was exceedingly helpful when in the business of collecting and trading secrets. It was exceedingly *un*helpful, however, when you wanted prompt service.

She cleared her throat and regretted it. Her neckache suddenly reverberated straight into her skull.

A sixtysomething woman appeared from an office behind Reception—*Mrs. Menzies*, according to the name tag. She took one look at Ottilie, and then Graham, and frowned.

"Are you being attended to?" she asked sharply enough to get her negligent employee's attention.

Graham started, eyes widening at the sight of a guest. Fear flitted into them. His hands on the counter went from a relaxed curve to straightening out, sharp and flat. A common tension tell, Ottilie noted. Likely, he was anticipating a chewing out as soon as Ottilie was gone. He also did not like his supervisor.

Ottilie examined the woman: a Mayan fertility goddess shape—short and wide—with hard, dark eyes and heated cheeks. The tips of her hair were slightly damp.

Damp? It was one in the afternoon. Why damp? Ottilie mulled that over. The woman didn't seem the type to work out in the gym on her lunch break. Perhaps she'd just arrived to start a late shift?

Ottilie looked closer. Mrs. Menzies's pupils were dilated. Well, that narrowed the likely causes down: drugs, adrenaline, recent brain injury, or sexual arousal.

Given her age, lack of fitness or head wounds, and that wet hair, Ottilie's short list narrowed to one. On a hunch, Ottilie deliberately curled her lips into a knowing smile, one that suggested she'd worked out all her little secrets.

Mrs. Menzies's nostrils flared and her cheeks flushed. And so began the most rushed room check-in in living history.

Well, well. Theory confirmed and, even better, mystery solved. Ottilie did detest the unexplained almost as much as loose ends, clutter, and disorder.

"I apologize for any delay. You're in Room 613." Mrs. Menzies thrust a key card Ottilie's way and beckoned a porter over. "I hope your room is to your satisfaction," Mrs. Menzies said curtly, gaze darting everywhere but at her.

"*Satis-faction...*" Ottilie murmured innocently. "Yes."

Mrs. Menzies's eyes widened, and she looked so rattled, it was funny.

Ottilie spun around and headed for the elevators, smile firmly suppressed.

Ottilie unpacked her suitcase, willing the pain now at the edges of her skull to dissipate. The source of her headaches—her neck—had never been right since '85. The neuropsychiatrist at the Walter Reed traumatic brain injury unit had done his best, but what was done could not be undone.

As the years passed by, almost everything set off the clawing, radiating ache: Cold weather. Flying. Sleeping too little. Sleeping too much. Excessive desk work.

Retirement couldn't come soon enough. Ottilie had been counting down for the past three years. She could almost taste the Mai Tais on a warm Pacific island of her dreams.

Opening the closet, she hung up a row of smart tailored business suits—starched gray or brown tweed skirts, jackets, and cream silk blouses—snapping the sleeves straight.

Her stockings and delicates she folded into exact triangles and placed them into a drawer. The elegance of triangles was that a pair turned into perfect geometrically pleasing squares. She appreciated the symmetry. It was beautiful.

Moving to the hotel bathroom, Ottilie lined up her rows of high-end, anti-aging creams. She'd been persistently fighting her age for decades. No, she did not look sixty-five, a fact she was quietly pleased about. "Early fifties" was the age she was most often assumed to be—occasionally even late forties.

Achieving a younger appearance took effort, time, and money. Sometimes she wondered if a lifetime spent playing an older woman who faded into backgrounds had made her subconscious assert itself and demand she scrape back the years.

Whatever the reason, it didn't matter. Given all the weaknesses available to humanity, vanity wasn't a bad one to have.

Ottilie shifted to the bedroom and immediately stripped the duvet from the bed and dropped it, folded, in a corner of the room. Disgusting things; rarely cleaned and harboring who knew what sort of grime—or worse.

Finding a clean, fresh-smelling blanket, she unfurled it onto her bed. Next, she perched on the end and fished out her phone. Only one message—from her realtor—informing her that a potential buyer had accepted her counteroffer on her apartment.

It was sold. Excellent. She was one step closer to her retirement dreams.

Ottilie had never felt much affection for the sleek, polished one-bedroom apartment. It had been a luxurious place to sleep and a central base from which to visit the best museums and restaurants around DC. But it had never felt like home. Aside from her fish tanks, there was little she loved about the place.

NUMBER SIX

Now that she thought about it, nowhere Ottilie had lived had ever felt like home. That would probably be something for a therapist to unpack, if she'd ever deign to see one beyond that CIA-mandated professional she'd once endured. Since then, she'd had no desire to ever step foot in a therapist's office.

She tapped back one word to the realtor: *understood*.

Her phone pinged with a new text message. Recognizing the number, Ottilie smiled. Hannah Hastreiter. Hannah's career-climbing son might have anglicized his surname to Hastings to fit in better, but Hannah had no such interest in losing something so precious for such a risible reason. She was aged eighty-four, a former stage dancer, and had a rudimentary (at best) understanding of texting. But her ongoing efforts to connect with Ottilie were always appreciated.

No matter where in the world Ottilie had wound up in the past fifteen months since they'd first met, her friend could be counted on to amuse her in one way or another, and not always intentionally. Ottilie opened the text.

Ottilie, dear, have fun in Vegas! Will you please send me a photo of the showgirls? You know how much I miss dancers and dancing. Oh, how I love the outfits! So much pizzazz. Hannayite

A pause, and then Ottilie's phone pinged again.

I mean Hannayite.

And again.

HANNAYITE!

Then: *Wjat is hapenign! Didnt mean to send that. Sorry*

H.A.N.N.A.H

PS I don't know even what is Hannayite?

Ottilie's lips twitched as she texted back: *Hannayite is a mineral found in animal droppings.*

Hannah replied promptly: *Oh dear. That is NOT what I meant to write!*

Ottilie snickered softly and replied: *I gathered. Your phone autocorrected the spelling. Ask your granddaughter to explain it.*

She laughed to herself at the thought of a frazzled Michelle attempting that task with her technologically challenged safta. That was a little evil of her. Ottilie resumed texting.

Anyway, I will endeavor to locate you some dancers. The "pizzazz-ier" the better. Have a nice rest of your day.

A vomit emoji appeared, which Ottilie was entirely sure was the last thing Hannah had intended to send. She smiled widely.

Ottilie set to work on her phone, searching for casinos running showgirl productions. Frowning at finding none, she gave up and ambled into the kitchen to assess the facilities. A toaster. Rare, but she'd asked for one ahead of her stay. Tea and coffee options. Excellent, and even rarer—casinos didn't like customers in their rooms sipping beverages when they could be spending money on the main floor. Again, she'd paid well for the little things.

Satisfied, she returned to the main room, unrolled her yoga mat on the floor, and began a basic routine. It paid to keep nimble as the years passed.

Originally, she'd taught herself yoga to be agile, should it be required in the course of her job to duck or weave from an adversary. Now her routine merely ensured she could scoop things off the floor with ease, slide on stockings elegantly, and stretch to the taller shelves at the store. She was damned if she'd be old before she was ready.

At that reminder, she slowly turned herself into a pretzel and performed her best Lord of the Fishes pose. Her neck protested, and something made an ominous popping sound, but her body complied.

Ninety minutes later, hair sticking to her forehead and cheeks pleasantly warm, Ottilie rolled her mat back up and put it away. She settled again on the edge of her bed and checked her phone. It was early evening now, and a new message had appeared.

Michelle Hastings. Former CEO of Ottilie's previous company, The Fixers. And Hannah's granddaughter. Ottilie's feelings on the woman were...mixed.

Ottilie, why are you telling my safta to get me to explain autocorrect to her? This took me almost TWO HOURS!! She still thinks her phone has an evil gremlin in it doing the changes for kicks. That was NOT an appreciated exercise!

She smirked. Well, *she'd* appreciated it, at least.

I'll bear that in mind, Ms. Hastings, she texted back.

Her own comment made her laugh. Unfortunately, that just made the pain radiating at the base of her skull arc up again. Ottilie grimaced as she twisted this way and that. She might need a physical therapist appointment while she was here if it persisted.

After meditating a few moments, the pain faded and Ottilie got down to business. She checked the time—not too late—dialed a number, and said, "I'm in Vegas. What have you ascertained?"

"Uh, Ms.—uh—Zimmermann, ma'am?" came the sputtered reply. Snakepit always sounded so surprised and unprepared, even though he'd been well aware her call was coming.

"Please tell me you've narrowed down our target's whereabouts by now?"

"Um, no new pings," came the squeaky young man's voice. "His phone's still switched off. But Hotel Duxton Vegas absolutely was where he last used it. I could hack the hotel guest registry to see if he's staying there?"

Ottilie ground her jaw. "*Of course* I want you to do that."

"Oh...um...okay. I'll get right on that."

"All right." Ottilie rubbed her neck again. "Text me when you have something."

"Yes, ma'am. G'bye, ma'am." The call ended.

Snakepit was a genius, if lacking in initiative and some fundamental social skills. Ottilie had been benevolent in offering him this one last job as a paid assignment, instead of reminding him about the circumstances under which he'd abruptly left her company. He was aware of that too and seemed suitably grateful he wasn't being blackmailed.

She hoped he'd be able to deliver because anything that extended her stay here was completely unacceptable. With a scowl at that thought, she retired early for the evening.

Chapter 2
Naked Truths

Monique Carson strode out of the hotel elevator on floor six, headed toward her room after a rather delightful lunch with her oldest friend.

Cleo had been up to her usual mischief, suggesting various women for Monique to date. And Monique, as always, batted away her suggestions with disinterest. One thing she already had in abundance was women. All ages, all types, all shapes, and all naked and desiring her. Yes, they were clients, but she had no burning urge to add even more women to her life in any capacity.

Besides, what woman would want to date someone who pleasured other women for a living? Hers was not a popular profession for suitors. Every woman she'd ever gone out with in recent years had, sooner or later, asked her to quit or inquired as to when she'd be retiring from her job. The question meant they didn't understand her at all.

Any woman she seriously considered a relationship with would have to accept her exactly as she was. And where did one meet a special woman like that? They didn't just materialize in front of you.

As she neared her room, a woman who Monique had never seen before approached. Not unusual in a hotel, of course, but Monique was quite sure she'd have noticed this one.

Dressed in a tweed skirt suit, she strode at a devastating pace. Her eyes were sharp and cool, her expression determined. The woman was of average height with a slightly rounded stomach and hips, and generous breasts hidden by a tightly buttoned-up ivory blouse. Not a hint of cleavage showed, which seemed a rather large pity.

The woman's hair was blonde, streaked faintly with gray, and curled into her neck just above the collar. At her forehead, her hair swirled softly up, sweeping to kick up just above her right, formidably arched eyebrow. Her skin was flawless and unlined, quite a feat given her age, which Monique judged to be just over fifty.

Her neck hinted she might be a little older than that—necks and hands on women were age's true indicator, Monique knew full well. No amount of makeup or surgery could hide all one's secrets. So, perhaps, closer to sixty.

Age was irrelevant, though. Because, from Monique's point of view, this woman was utterly magnificent. Her grace, poise, and commanding stride said she was someone to be reckoned with.

For Monique, there was no more impressive sight than a woman of a certain age who knew her own worth, oozed charisma and confidence, and had absolutely no fucks to give.

At the exact moment the woman sensed Monique, her impatient pace instantly slowed. Her countenance shifted from determined to serene. Suddenly, it was as if the stranger had always been some refined, elegant grandmother out for an afternoon stroll.

The transformation was so swift, so unlikely, that Monique wondered if she'd imagined it. As the woman drew level, Monique tried to meet her eye and offered a "hello." It came out throaty because Monique was weak in the orbit of powerful women.

Monique's sensuous voice was almost always guaranteed to get a response. People couldn't help reacting to her. She was used to the attention and well aware she had a "presence" that was hard to overlook.

There was a lot to look at: her tall height could be considered impressive. She had long, thick dark-brown hair, prim teacher-glasses eternally perched on the end of her nose, and a maroon bra peeking from beneath a plunging black executive jacket. Even those who loved to be outraged by her overt sexuality invariably sneaked another peek. They couldn't *not* look.

Not this woman.

She didn't react at all. There was barely a glance in her direction before she strolled past, and then she was gone.

Monique was overwhelmed with questions.

Who was she? Someone who could change her whole persona in a split second and someone utterly impervious to Monique's presence.

She prided herself on being able to read people within moments, but now here she was, confounded. That was new.

Oh, how Monique loved a mystery.

Chapter 3
Take Me

It was seven the next evening, and Timmo, aka Tiffany Monahan, was Monique's last client of the day. She never took many. Why would she? Monique didn't need the money, and she liked to be on top of her game for the women she shared her skills with.

Timmo was the shortest, butchest woman Monique had ever met, and she was an absolute delight: a bundle of charm and cheekiness and youth with an irrepressible grin that could not be wiped from her face, not even when Monique explained her fee.

"It's all right, y'know," Timmo said. "I've been saving all summer for this."

"Is that so?" Monique purred, eying her unbuttoned blue-and-red flannel shirt over a black tee. That form-hugging shirt was tucked into worn black jeans above brown boots. "What do you do?"

"Farmhand, officially. Shitkicker, more realistically. Think of the grossest jobs on a ranch in nowhere, Nebraska, and I'm your boy."

"*Boy*? Would you prefer to be called by male pronouns?" Monique asked gently.

"Nah, it's just what the crew calls me." Her voice deepened and she bellowed, "Hey, boy, there's a pile of shit that needs shoveling, get on it.'" She shrugged. "Doesn't bug me in the least. I get mistaken for a boy so often, I just roll with it. They think they're pissing me off, but they ain't."

"They want to rile you up? Why?"

"I pull more chicks than they do!" She laughed hard, and her bulk shifted and rolled like the incoming tide. It just made her all the more delicious to Monique.

"My, my. Are you a lady-killer, then?"

Timmo's eyes crinkled. "Yes and no. I've never had a *lady* before. Every woman I've ever been with has been rougher than a cowboy's butt after ten hours in the saddle. I'm not knocking my lovers, y'know. I like 'em all. We are what we are, and it's fun, but that's not what I dream about."

Monique leaned in. "And what do you dream of, darling?"

"It's been my fantasy to be with a lady for so long, I can't even tell you." She ran her eyes appreciatively over Monique's form. "Someone real pretty, y'know? With manners and elegance and who dresses so lovely. Maybe she comes from old money and has actual refinement? Like she's seen the inside of a ballroom or a concert hall. Not another grunt like me who thinks cutlery's more a suggestion than a requirement."

"I understand." Monique subtly shifted until she was indeed posed more gracefully. "If it helps, I do know which one's the salad fork and how to do a Viennese waltz, and while I'm not 'old money', I'm well off enough to be in no need of it." Her expression was teasing. "So, what would you do with your lady?"

"I'd worship her," Timmo said, her intense gaze fixed on Monique. "Every inch of her. And I'd probably faint like a sack of potatoes if she worshipped me right back." She ran her fingers through her slicked-back blonde hair. "God, I'm so excited, I'm about to burst."

Monique smiled. "Did you come to Vegas just for me, darling?"

"Oh, no. My best friend from school, Marty, is getting married. He wants an Elvis wedding. I'm the best man. Soon as I heard where it'd be, I wondered if maybe I could tick that fantasy off my list. There's a lot of beautiful ladies here. Have you seen the dancers?"

"Indeed I have." Monique's smile widened. "And been with one or two."

Timmo's eyes became rounder. "Wow. Lucky you."

Monique smirked and pushed her laminated page toward Timmo. "I'm sure you've probably already seen this on my website, but it's my menu of choices. What number appeals to you?"

Briefly, Timmo scanned the page, but it was clear she'd already seen what was listed. "Number one."

How surprising. "That's usually selected by women new to sapphic delights, or those who are questioning their sexuality. It's like a primer of what lesbian sex is like."

"I know." Timmo's cheeks reddened. "Honestly, I want to know if I'm doin' it right. And more than that, I want to know how to treat a lady. Or improve my technique if I'm doin' okay. A fumble down her pants behind the cowshed ain't exactly the best education on what to do. I want to start with the…uh…fundamentals. Work my way up from there. When you're horse riding, you start with walking, not galloping."

Monique nodded. "I like the way you think."

"You do?" Timmo grinned hard. "Good, cos I like you a whole lot."

She reminded Monique of an enthusiastic puppy. A terribly cute one. "Do you wish me to use toys?"

Timmo shrugged. "Never used 'em before. Wait, do I get to use one on you?" Her eyes went wide, as if she were suddenly considering the possibilities.

"I'm afraid not," Monique said with a chuckle at Timmo's hopefulness. "I adhere strictly to the menu. You may touch me only if I allow it. And you will not be granted permission to enter me, toys or no toys."

"Really?" Timmo bit her lip. "So I can't tongue you or anythin'?"

"That I might allow. I'll let you know if I approve when we're in the moment. But fingers and toys inside me, no. If you do want that from a sexual partner, I have a list of lovely women who are experienced, talented, and full-service."

Monique half expected Timmo to opt for going elsewhere. She'd come so far to be here, it seemed likely she wouldn't want to waste her time on not getting everything she'd fantasized about.

Instead, Timmo just grinned and said, "Nah, that's fine. I'd like to stick with you, if that's okay."

"It's more than okay. I'm sure we'll have a lot of fun."

NUMBER SIX

Timmo beamed from ear to ear. "What happens next?"

"Next, I ask cash or credit? And after that, you get wet and naked… in the shower."

"Right. And, uh, it's cash." She pulled out a worn, black Velcro wallet and slapped it onto the desk.

Timmo's tanned expanse of flesh was a delight to explore. She was so responsive to every touch and trailed finger. Her large, pillowy breasts gleamed from the wetness of where Monique's tongue had been, and her ample stomach rose and fell sharply as she gasped out breaths.

"Uh…Ms. Carson?" she gulped as Monique tongued her clit with expert swishes.

Timmo had an impressive clit that was large and swollen. A mouthful to be toyed with. Delightful. Monique *really* loved her job.

She met Timmo's desperate eyes and let go of her clit. "Yes, darling?"

"I don't often beg, but I'm prepared t' do it. Let me have a memory to go home with? Can I do the same to you?"

Monique considered the request. She knew she was privileged to live in a large city with everything—and everyone—at her fingertips. Timmo lived in the middle of nowhere and couldn't fulfill any fantasy without the investment of a great deal of time and money.

"I'll think about it," Monique said and then plunged her tongue deep inside her.

Timmo wailed in pleasure.

Monique ran her hands all around Timmo's large thighs, smooth as could be except for a scar at the knee. Timmo had already explained that as a farm accident. "Me versus a bull. Didn't win."

She was so gorgeous, so enthusiastic, with all that flesh to rub and tease and fuck. Monique was quite certain Timmo was having the time of her life too, given that every part of her body was quivering and she was moaning.

Maybe she would indulge the young woman. It wouldn't be the worst thing to have those cheeky lips nuzzling her clit. She was also rather curious as to whether Timmo had any talent. It might be interesting to find out. She hadn't exactly allowed Timmo to worship her, which had been a big part of the woman's fantasy.

Five minutes later, Timmo's eyes grew very wide as Monique shimmied out of her pants and panties and turned to face her. She still wore her white blouse and a black bra, but nothing else.

"Well, darling, it's time to see what skills you possess." She offered a cocky smile. "Think you can please a lady?"

"Oh my fucking God." Timmo whimpered. "Oh my *God*. You're so beautiful."

Monique preened a little. "Well. May I sit on your face?"

Timmo nodded hard.

"No fingers, though," she cautioned.

Timmo shook her head.

"Good." Monique got into position, lowering herself onto that eager mouth. "Make me come, darling. Show me what you've got."

Timmo's strong, rough hands clasped her ass to hold her in place. Her mouth opened and seemed to swallow Monique's pussy and then wetly swirled her tongue all over her, from clit to entrance.

And, yes, it felt nice. Really nice.

That roaming tongue prodded her entrance a few times, and Monique squirmed. *More than nice.*

Then her tongue was hard against her clit, pressing with force, until Monique felt arousal hitting.

A smug delight lay in Timmo's eyes now as she tasted Monique's essence. Timmo's hands began to make squeeze-and-release motions on her ass.

Monique was dripping. Aching. She undid her shirt and pushed her breasts from her bra.

Timmo's tongue froze in mid stroke. Then her eyes clenched shut, and she began to quiver.

The woman was coming? Monique ground herself against Timmo's mouth, taking over where she wanted the pressure and how. Her pleasure was building rapidly, and it intoxicated her how much she was enjoying herself.

Timmo's eyes opened again, a glazed look in them, half stunned, half stupefied. Then she took Monique's clit between her lips and sucked it as if she were trying to force ice up a straw.

Monique came. Shuddering and shaking, she put her hands on either side of the wall behind the bed and thrust against Timmo's mouth, reveling in the little shudders. Then she stilled.

Gently, she extracted her body from Timmo's mouth and rolled over onto her side.

"Wow." Timmo gasped. Her mouth was red and her lips swollen. A sheen of wetness was smeared across most of her lower face. "You're... *Wow*."

"It turns out you do know how to please a lady," Monique said dryly. "Just so you know, it's rare I allow that."

"Thank you," Timmo said, her tone reverent, holding Monique's gaze. "I mean that."

"Was it everything you fantasized about?"

"Nah." She grinned.

Monique blinked. "It wasn't?"

"It was so much more. I mean, *fuck*. I don't even have words for how amazing that felt." She looked up at her from her eyelashes.

Monique smiled, pleased.

"You really are so beautiful," Timmo said quietly. "I could just stare at you for hours."

"You're pretty adorable yourself."

"Eh, I'm a short, fat little butch." She shrugged.

"You say that as though they're bad things. They're not, darling. Every woman is beautiful to me. Some more inside than outside. I think you're both. I do hope you'll visit me again sometime."

Timmo blushed hard. "I'd love that, but unfortunately I had to save six months to afford this."

There was a slight edge there, a question perhaps.

"I'm sorry it's hard for you."

"Yeah." Timmo hesitated. "I'm just wondering, though. If you don't need the money and someone who really needs to see you is, um, financially strapped, would you ever consider a discount?" Her tone rose to hopeful.

"I can't," Monique explained gently. "I don't do discounts, not even for the cute ones. I know what I charge is a lot. But I have to charge that, or I'm sending a message I don't like. It's about valuing myself at a level I'm comfortable with. If I discount my rates, I'm discounting my body, and it tells people I'm not worth much. I won't do that."

Timmo sagged.

"But I argue that access to me is well priced for what I'm offering. Most people sell their brain or their muscles to employers. But they don't also include their vulnerabilities and being stripped bare, emotionally and physically. When I charge a client, I'm giving a lot for that. I'm not just a body. This isn't just sex. I'm giving them access to so much more. And I'm worth it."

"Yeah." Timmo nodded. "You so are. Sorry to ask. I just really want to see you again, and I won't be able to afford it for ages."

"I understand. I'll count down the months till we meet again." She grinned.

Timmo laughed. "Thanks." She sat up and began dressing.

Chuckling with her, Monique rounded up her own clothes, dressed, then saw Timmo out. She put her hotel phone back on the hook, her cell phone off silent, and sprayed a little air freshener.

As she tidied up, she smiled. It was satisfying being with someone so enthusiastic, so delighted by being with her. Timmo had been undemanding, easy to please, in touch with her body, and in love with being aroused.

Not every woman came to her with so few hang-ups or so much self-awareness.

And while Monique loved all the interesting challenges her many and varied clients presented her with, sometimes the Timmos of the world were a wonderful breath of fresh air. A woman who took one look at Monique and knew *exactly* what she wanted.

It was flattering being desired. Yet that wasn't why she did what she did. What she also loved was being *needed*. She took a great deal of pride in unfurling the petals of a tight bud: the moment of awareness of a woman discovering her own pleasure, sometimes for the first time. When that happened, she felt like an all-powerful queen.

Being worshipped as one was fun too. She smiled to herself as she remembered the way Timmo had looked at her with burning hunger and complete wonder. Some days—hell, most days—that was enough too.

Monique went to strip the sheets.

A knock sounded, short and sharp.

Monique frowned. She wasn't expecting another client until tomorrow. Monique's plans were a sedate room service dinner while she looked over some company prospectuses that her business manager, Ray, had sent over. He'd flagged them as ripe for investment.

Opening the door, Monique drank in the unexpected sight. The stranger from the hallway yesterday whom she hadn't been able to get out of her mind.

"Ms. Carson?" she asked, gaze darting about.

"Yes?"

"I'm in need of your services," she said. Her words were curt and clipped, her accent faintly German. How intriguing.

Monique rapidly tried to go through her mental schedule as to when she could make room to book in this intriguing woman. One thing was certain: she could scarcely wait.

She smiled and said, "Well. Do come in."

Chapter 4
A Pain in the Neck

Ottilie had poked her head in at the four main bars at Duxton Vegas, hoping to find her quarry. Snakepit hadn't yet gotten back to her as to the man's whereabouts, nor had the man used his credit card in days, which was odd. But she knew he loved to drink and play poker. Perhaps he was doing one or both somewhere around here.

She played nine hands of blackjack at the casino, trying to conceal her impatience, before deciding her quarry was either lying low this evening, or at a different casino.

The thrumming at the base of her neck was getting worse. She cashed in her remaining chips while trying not to be overwhelmed by the sensory overload.

It wasn't just the flashing lights or the discordant jangling of slot machines behind her. Electronic blinking posters advertised Carrie Jordan's new show at Duxton Vegas—a technicolor onslaught that seemed constantly in her peripheral vision. She was tempted to smash her elbow into the nearest Jordan digital billboard and ruin that obnoxious megawatt smile, but she didn't want the orthopedic bills.

Stopping by the concierge desk, Ottilie planned to ask for recommendations for someone to look at her neck. Or, at the very least, the nearest supplier of painkillers. Instead, she found herself in front of a drawn-looking Mrs. Menzies, who appeared to be dealing with a drunk.

NUMBER SIX

"Why won't you come home?" the belligerent little rodent was demanding of the appalled woman.

Oh, lovely. Ottilie scowled. *Domestic drama.* Embarrassing *and* likely to take far too long. Ottilie and her throbbing neck did not need this.

"Not *here*, Frank," Mrs. Menzies spat, eyes darting about. Her cheeks were flushing the darkest red. "As I told you yesterday *and* last week *and* two weeks ago, I'm done. We're done. You're a cheat, and I'm sick of pretending you're as good as it gets."

"Like you've got anything better waiting. Look at you!"

Mrs. Menzies's voice shook slightly as she pleaded in mortification, "Stop. Shouting." Her darting gaze fell to Ottilie. She turned back to her husband and lowered her voice. "Frank, I have guests to attend to."

"You're worthless. Just an ugly, dried-up old crone," he retorted, the nasty glint in his eye proving he wanted an audience to her humiliation.

Mrs. Menzies's lips pressed into a hard, cold line.

Dried up? Implying a woman's fertility was her only thing of value? That older women were nothing? Even a fierce-looking woman like Mrs. Menzies, who Ottilie had observed ran the entire hotel reception area with military precision? She had more competence in her pinkie than this reprobate had with his decade-old tan suit with soup splotches on his tie.

Ottilie reached for her phone, took a step to the side to discreetly capture him in profile, and hit record. As her video app captured ten bilious seconds of the man's escalating insults, she studied him more closely.

Footwear: brown brogues, in reasonable condition. But the thickness of the sole seemed far too worn for the age of the rest of the shoe. His trouser hems had dust on them and were ever so slightly scuffed at the back. So he walked a lot—in this outfit. For his job, then, as no one goes for long walks in a suit. Salesman?

His cuff link was unusual. A small camera lens? Although it looked more like a logo?

She finished recording, then clicked Google, searching, *Frank Menzies, salesman, Vegas, cameras.*

And there. The lens logo matched a website called Alcatraz Security Las Vegas.

Frank was pictured among the "committed sales team" who were authorized dealers in home security products, from intercoms to locks to surveillance systems and cameras. It listed each salesman's contact details, along with those of the company's manager.

Ottilie generated a disposable email address, one that would last only ten minutes, then attached her video file and sent it to Frank.

Done, she looked up to find him now belligerently leaning on the desk in front of Mrs. Menzies as though about to settle in for the duration.

It was more than enough to test Ottilie's thin patience. She cleared her throat. "Excuse me," Ottilie told his back, "some of us have business to attend to here."

He turned, brows knitting at the intrusion.

Continuing, Ottilie said, "Your wife has made her position clear: *go away*. If you're too deaf or stupid to understand her, that's not something to announce to the whole room, is it?"

Frank glared at her. "Did you just call me stupid?"

"I did not."

His uncertain eyes blinked as he regarded her.

"I was initially unsure whether you were deaf *or* stupid. They're obviously not the same. But the fact you heard me suggests the answer. *Now* I'm calling you stupid."

"What the hell?" His doughy hands turned into fists.

"Frank!" Mrs. Menzies cried out. "Stop!"

"Ah, of course, *macho dramatics*," Ottilie drawled sarcastically. "*Terrifying*. Now, then, before you embarrass yourself further, check your email."

He screwed up his bulbous face. "Why?"

"Because the next person I send that video to will be your boss, and I will ask him how it will look having an abusive stalker—who threatens his wife—as the salesman of a home security business dedicated to making its customers feel safe."

NUMBER SIX

Frank fumbled for his phone, his face losing all color. Those tinny insults of half a minute ago now played on the phone's speaker for all to hear.

Mrs. Menzies stared at Ottilie in what seemed like utter astonishment.

Disquiet now rippled over Frank's face. Even so, he growled, "You can't tell that's me. It could be someone else!"

"Someone else with Alcatraz Security Las Vegas cuff links?"

He glared at her, then folded his arms, saying mutinously, "It's still the side of my head. Not like you can even see my face."

"Fine," she snapped. "Wait here." Ottilie stepped away from the desk, made a short phone call, waited five minutes, then checked her email. She forwarded a file she'd received to Frank's phone and marched back to him.

"Check your mail again," she said tersely.

He opened his phone, and his eyes grew wide. "That's..." He glanced up at the small camera above the Concierge desk and looked back at his phone. "How did you get *that* footage?"

"Do not annoy me further," Ottilie said. "As you can see, I have powerful resources."

"Goddammit. What do you want?"

"For you to go away. Now. And if you bother this woman again"—she pointed at Mrs. Menzies—"I *will* send that video to your manager, a Mr. Drew Hamilton, I believe? I'll be sharing a copy with your wife too, to ensure you behave. Understood?"

"Who *are* you?" Frank's voice rose far too high.

"The woman *you* are preventing from getting hotel assistance. Now, *leave.*" Steel underpinned her demand.

Mrs. Menzies's eyes grew wide and disbelieving, as if no one had ever dared speak to her husband like that in his entire life.

Frank left, stumbling over his feet in his haste, swearing up a storm before he took one sweeping punch at her on the way out.

Ottilie swayed out of its path easily, having anticipated he might try to regain his tattered dignity through more macho idiocy. She observed him closely until he was through the exit and gone.

Mrs. Menzies's sounded embarrassed when she said, voice quiet, "You didn't have to engage with my husband. Security was on the way. They would have dealt with him."

"Eventually." Ottilie was unimpressed at their lack of punctuality. "If you wish a copy of that video, supply me with an email address."

Mrs. Menzies nodded and scribbled on a slip of paper. "I…appreciate this." She pushed the paper across the counter.

"I didn't like his attitude." Ottilie took note of the email address, then sent the video to her. "He implied older women are worthless." Her head snapped up, meeting her gaze. "We're not."

Mrs. Menzies didn't appear to know what to say to that. Finally, she offered, "Well, thank you regardless."

"It was self-serving," Ottilie said dismissively. "I required assistance, and he was in my way." Her neck pain made her especially curt.

"Do I want to know how you knew where Frank works?"

"Deductive reasoning."

"And how you got hotel camera footage?" Mrs. Menzies hesitated. "I should probably report that we appear to have a security weakness."

"Probably," Ottilie said neutrally. "But my associates are superior to any you'd have working in IT, so it wouldn't do much good."

"I see." Mrs. Menzies gave her a look of unmistakable respect. Her back straightened, stiff and professional. "Now, please tell me how I may help. I'd be more than happy to assist you."

"I need someone who can give a decent massage." Ottilie suppressed a sigh and greatly regretted her time at the gambling table, where she had been hunched in an unsympathetic position. "Something special for my cervical area."

Mrs. Menzies inhaled, darted a look all around, and murmured, "*Special?*"

Why had she phrased it like that?

Ottilie studied her in confusion. "Yes. I'm sure you'd be familiar with such a service?" Weren't all concierge desks supposed to have contacts for any given request? "Well?"

Mrs. Menzies's lips compressed and her cheeks reddened.

If Ottilie's neck wasn't killing her, she'd have made an effort to pick apart the subtext. But pain was dulling her whimpering brain. She was about to suggest that if her first request was too difficult, might Mrs. Menzies instead tell her where she could get some heavy-duty painkillers? Ottilie had run out this morning.

Before she could ask, Mrs. Menzies lifted a finger, then picked up her phone and made a call. She pursed her lips and hung up. "A guest at this hotel is an expert in…special massages," Mrs. Menzies said quietly. "She's even in the room next to yours, which is convenient. Unfortunately, Ms. Carson isn't picking up her phone. I could keep trying and contact you when she is available?"

"No, thank you." Ottilie sighed. "I don't know how long that will be, and I think I'll just go to bed. Thanks, anyway."

Mrs. Menzies nodded.

The pain worsened. Ottilie finally gave up trying to rest and admitted she needed immediate relief. Which room was this Carson woman in, who Mrs. Menzies said was her neighbor? Across the hall, or on one side of her?

She swapped her pajamas for a tweed skirt and ivory blouse, holding her head very straight to stop the waves of pain. Slipping on her heels, she tried to work out which door to start knocking on first. Maybe she'd get lucky and find Carson first up. Maybe the woman would take pity on her, despite Ottilie having no appointment. If she just explained…

Another wave of pain hit her, and Ottilie realized she was well past social niceties. She didn't care if it was rude, she needed treatment now.

The woman who greeted Ottilie at room 612, the one who answered to Carson, was not what she expected. Not that massage or physical therapists conformed to any particular look, but this woman was distinctly different from average.

She was commanding and provocatively dressed, with a plunging cleavage that revealed a hint of black bra.

Ottilie almost took a step back and apologized for clearly being in the wrong place when she remembered the woman had already said yes to the name Carson.

"I'm in need of your services," she said, voice tight as she swallowed back the pain.

She looked pleased. "Well. Do come in."

Ottilie did as instructed but sneaked another glance at the woman as she closed the door behind them.

Ms. Carson spun around and regarded her. "Problem, darling?" she purred. Her entire face had lit up at the sight of Ottilie. As though she recognized her. But that wasn't possible. Ottilie would remember having met this woman.

"Am I not what you expected?" Ms. Carson continued. "I assume Mrs. Menzies sent you to me?"

"No to the first question," Ottilie answered. The last time a professional attended to her cervical spine stenosis, he'd looked decidedly more clinical. "And yes. She did."

"Come, sit down. Let's discuss your needs and when I will be able to attend to them. I don't usually take a new client without them filling out my online form and agreeing to my terms, but if Mrs. Menzies sent you, that's acceptable. I trust her."

Ottilie wondered what terms there were just to get one's neck looked at. Ms. Carson gestured to a chair opposite a large wooden desk. The latter was much sturdier than any Ottilie had ever seen in a hotel room. The room was decorated in reds, definitely not hotel decor. The smell was of air freshener. Recent. What was truly unsettling was the large bed, its sheets a tangled mess.

Well, Ottilie couldn't be too indignant—she hadn't made an appointment. The woman hadn't been expecting a client. And it also sounded as if she was planning to schedule Ottilie for another time. Perhaps if she pleaded her case, the woman might make an exception and attend to her immediately?

Brief introductions were made, emphasis on brief, given that Ottilie did not share her surname, seeing no need, and Ms. Carson did not share her first name.

"What qualifications do you have?" Ottilie asked. "Mrs. Menzies seemed to think you were a specialist in my area of concern?"

"Indeed I am." Ms. Carson eyed her with clear interest.

"I have an issue that needs some delicate, special attention." She rubbed her neck. "It's been troubling me for some time."

"Is that so?" Ms. Carson's eyes gleamed. "I can pay close attention to any part of your body you wish. Or perhaps you'd like to select from the menu? Then we can arrange a time and—"

"Menu?" Ottilie cut her off in some confusion. "You have a menu?"

"Certainly." Ms. Carson plucked a laminated sheet off the desk. "Whichever service you most *desire*."

Ottilie's eyes skidded across the page. *Good God!* She launched to her feet and, bewildered, said: "You're a prostitute?"

"I prefer sexual educator or sex therapist or sexual fantasy facilitator. But technically, that's true, given women pay me to touch their bodies in sexual ways to induce arousal." Confusion tinged her tone when she added, "I don't understand. You weren't expecting someone like me? Did you not ask Mrs. Menzies for someone with my expertise?"

"Of course not! I told Mrs. Menzies I had a cervical issue that needed urgent attention!" She rubbed her neck frantically. Flames of pain seared her.

"Ah." Ms. Carson inhaled. "Well, the cervical area refers to both the neck and part of the uterus. I suspect Mrs. Menzies thought you were asking for something entirely different. And, if nothing else, she is extremely good at fulfilling the needs of her guests."

Oh. Ottilie's cheeks seared hot at the thought of the front desk woman thinking she'd been asking for sex. That she wanted to pay for it too. "Well, I have no interest in engaging your services!"

"Are you quite sure? I am very good at relaxing women." Her tone was teasing, but she cocked her head, looking thoughtful.

"*Very* sure."

"You know, I can actually do a very good massage, if that's all you want." Ms. Carson studied her. "I wouldn't normally be available..." Her gaze shifted to the rumpled sheets. "But you say it's urgent. And it's something I can do relatively easily."

Oh dear God. She's just had a client!

"So, what cervical issue do you have specifically?" Ms. Carson continued, heedless to Ottilie's mortification. "Cervical stenosis, I'm guessing? My mother had an issue with that. I found a way to relieve her pain for a few years before she passed. It's an awful condition, I'm well aware."

Ottilie was conflicted. "How do I know you're not just saying that?"

"*Cervical stenosis*. Rule number one: avoid poor sleeping positions, first and foremost. Number two: do *not* rotate the neck, no matter how tempting. Yes?"

That was…accurate.

"I understand if you want to seek an actual specialist in this area. But I can also see you're in a great deal of pain. Will you let me assist you tonight? I can make you feel so much better rather quickly."

Ottilie inhaled. Any relief would be welcome right now. "It's not normally this bad," she murmured.

"What changed?"

"Stress and a bad seating position on a flight."

"Show me exactly where it hurts most." Ms. Carson actually sounded concerned, not to mention clinical. Gone was the flirting and innuendo, thank goodness.

"Here." Ottilie pointed, just as more pain shot up her spine. She flinched.

"All right." Ms. Carson studied her. "Would you feel better having a shower first?"

"I'd rather not." Ottilie inhaled. "I'd rather you also didn't touch my back. Neck, shoulders, head are fine."

"Do you have a medical concern?" Ms. Carson asked.

"Why do you need to know?" Ottilie snapped, then regretted it. Pain was making her irritable.

"I'm sorry for not explaining. If you have any health conditions that need me to make accommodations, I'm happy to do so."

"I apologize for my terseness. The pain is…not good. And no health conditions. Just leave my back alone. Where do we do this?"

"I can attend to you on the bed?" Ms. Carson said.

At Ottilie's dubious look, she added, "I have a change of sheets. Or in the chair, if you'd prefer. It's all the same to me."

"Chair." She inhaled. "Please."

NUMBER SIX

"Chair it is. Would you like to remove your blouse? Retain your bra."

"No. My blouse stays on."

Ms. Carson gave a small nod. "Will you unbutton it a little at least so I may access your shoulders better?"

Ottilie hesitated, wondering if this was all some seedy ruse, but then decided she honestly didn't have the luxury to say no right now. Her pain was unbearable. She undid three buttons and looked at Ms. Carson questioningly. "Enough?"

"Yes. Let me get some massage oil."

"No oil."

"Chemical sensitivity?"

"No, the smell just gives me a headache. Well, more of one."

"I have one oil that has no scent. Would you be open to trying that?"

"If you must." Ottilie almost whimpered when another stab of pain hit her.

"Wait right here."

As if she could go anywhere now. It hadn't been this bad for months. Perhaps all the jet-setting she'd been doing of late? Rounding up all the potential rogue elements worldwide had finally taken its toll. At least Ottilie was now down to two last irritants, and then she was free. Beach. Mai Tais. Bliss.

She closed her eyes and let that thought take her away. Maybe five minutes or five seconds had passed before she felt warm, oiled, assured hands on the base of her neck. She tensed out of habit. Ottilie didn't like being sneaked up on nor touched unexpectedly. A recent phobia.

Her moment of tension lengthened when Ms. Carson's fingers trailed over to her bra straps. "May I slide these down? They're in the way."

Ottilie hesitated.

"Just over the edge of your shoulders," she clarified. "I won't if you say no. It will help your treatment, though."

"Yes."

In a flick, they were gone, and then the back of Ms. Carson's fingertips were trailing from her shoulders to the base of her neck. A flare of warmth followed her hands, and it spread through her.

"The secret to a good massage is care."

Care?

"Showing those I help that I care." She pressed her thumbs on either side of Ottilie's spine, at the base of her neck.

Pain flared instantly, but it felt like the good kind, not that Ottilie could articulate why she'd just thought that.

Ms. Carson removed the thumbs, then soothed away the pain with her fingertips. "Anyone can touch you, but how it feels depends on how it's done. Touch is my love language, and it expresses my care for my clients. That love of touch and need to care is not sexual. It's emotional. It's me"—she ran four fingers up Ottilie's neck, then pressed her thumbs above them into the base of her skull—"showing you I'm invested in your well-being. It's…care."

Now that she said it, Ottilie realized her physical therapist back home always hit the appropriate spots as needed but that his touch was perfunctory. It was neither warm nor particularly gentle. It was remedial and mechanical but never soothing or caring. The thought wouldn't have occurred to him.

Four fingers tap-danced at the skin behind each ear, in the small mound just beyond her occipital lobe.

"Oh!" she gasped as Ms. Carson found the exact spot that seemed to hold all her tension.

"Breathe if you can. It'll take a moment for me to work on this."

Work she did, coaxing the pain down from an obnoxious roar. Her fingers danced all over the neck and shoulders, sometimes punctuated with a light commentary, "This is what I call Swirling Fists." And, later, as her thumb and index finger squeezed, "The Pincer Grip."

Ottilie hadn't even known she had pressure points in a semicircle across her head, where one might wear a headband. She certainly didn't realize pain could be so pleasurable when mixed with warmth, compassion, and someone who knew exactly how to place her hands on a body. It was a master class of expertise in muscle, nerves, skin, and bone. And, yes, a master class in…care.

NUMBER SIX

Ottilie had never experienced anything quite like it. A touch like this could be addictive.

By the time Ms. Carson's fingers had slid up into her hair and over to her temples, Ottilie's muscles were relaxed and liquid with relief.

Ottilie tried to pinpoint what made her massage so different from Stephen's beyond the perfunctory nature of his work. And it came down to the way Ms. Carson's fingers never shifted from point to point but rather sensuously *trailed*.

The result was undeniable. Ottilie found to her surprise by the end that she was thoroughly enjoying it. When it was over, she all but sagged in disappointment.

"Thank you," she murmured.

"Is your neck better?" Ms. Carson stepped back and pushed Ottilie's bra straps back into position. She turned to reach for a towel. "My mother swore my massages were better than opium. I'm not sure whether she'd really tried opium for an actual comparison." She laughed lightly. "Unlikely for a legal secretary."

"It's much better. Thank you." Ottilie stood and quickly did up her three buttons in case Ms. Carson got the idea to do them for her. The moment she tugged on her blouse, the oil, still warm on her skin, made the material stick to the back of her shoulders.

"Let me get you a tissue for that." Ms. Carson leaned over her desk, the material of her pants tight against her perfectly round backside, and plucked several tissues from a box. Coming to stand behind Ottilie, she said softly in her ear, "Allow me?"

Ottilie stood ramrod straight as Ms. Carson's hands swept under her collar and along her upper back, professionally wiping away the oil. "I'm sorry to say I don't think I got to it in time."

"Excuse me?" Ottilie said.

"The oil has soaked into your beautiful blouse." She sounded disappointed. "Next time, let me wipe off the oil before you get dressed again."

"Next time?" The woman certainly didn't lack for confidence.

"Well, should you need to return before your stay is done. I'd be happy to assist you once more." The woman's words were polite, but there was a honey to them that made Ottilie uncertain. Then she wondered why she was feeling so weird about returning to a woman with such magic hands.

Maybe it was her overconfidence? Ottilie did not approve of that. Worse, she didn't like the feeling that she didn't understand Ms. Carson much at all. Ottilie hated the unknowable, mysteries; their lack of resolution always picked away at her, like vultures on a carcass, until she solved them.

"We'll see," she said. "My schedule is quite tight." She reached for her purse. "How much do I owe you?"

"Nothing."

Ottilie peered at her. "I'm sorry?"

"I'm proposing a quid pro quo."

"What do you want?" Ottilie asked suspiciously.

"Your company. For breakfast tomorrow morning."

As in a... Was this a date? But who did dates for breakfast? Maybe Ms. Carson was too busy with clients at other times.

Ottilie wondered where she was expected to share her morning toast and tea with this unusual woman, and she glanced around the room.

"Oh, not here," Ms. Carson said with a smile. "This is my workplace. Well, one of them. I'm talking about downstairs in the hotel's main restaurant. Say, eight?"

"Why?" Ottilie asked. "Do you get lonely eating your cereal on you own?"

"Exactly." Ms. Carson smirked. "I'd like to get to know you a little better."

"To what end?" If her intentions were romantic, they'd be short-lived. "You must be aware I don't live in Vegas. I'm not here for long at all."

"All the more reason to have breakfast tomorrow. I'll explain in the morning."

Explain? That didn't sound romantic, then. Did she have something else in mind? Ottilie couldn't begin to think what this woman wanted from her, given Ms. Carson had no clue who Ottilie was or the power she possessed. "Why me?" she asked as she slowly turned toward the door. "I'm entirely uninteresting."

"Ottilie, come now," Ms. Carson said with a tsk as she opened the door for her. "That's not true. I knew that from the moment I passed you in the hallway two days ago."

So that explained the flash of recognition when the woman had first laid eyes on her. It was startling that a complete stranger had worked out she hid a great many secrets. That never happened.

"I'm as boring as can be," Ottilie persisted, stepping into the hall.

Ms. Carson laughed. "Oh, yes. As boring as Hedy Lamarr. You know, she was a lot more than just a pretty face."

"Of course I know that. She was the mother of Wi-Fi," Ottilie said promptly. Not to mention, wasn't there something about a torpedo and frequency hopping? She racked her brain to pull up the facts.

Wait, had the woman just called her *pretty*?

Ottilie slid a suspicious gaze toward her, but the woman's expression gave nothing away.

"Until breakfast," Ms. Carson called cheerfully before she closed the door.

Had Ottilie even said yes? She stared at the room number.

What had just happened?

Chapter 5

Breakfast Like an Emperor

"Why breakfast?" were the first words Ottilie uttered as she sat down opposite Monique the next day.

Monique discovered that the sight of Ottilie first thing in the morning was no less enticing than seeing her stride down a hallway or sink into a massage. She was just so…put together. So assured and confident. And yet her walls were higher than any Monique had ever encountered. This was a woman one did not get to know easily. "And hello to you too, Ottilie. Did you sleep well? How's that pretty neck of yours?"

Ottilie emitted a small, irritated huff. "I slept adequately for a too soft bed, a too hard pillow, and an entirely problematic neck. I doubt it is particularly 'pretty,' Ms. Carson, given all it's doing is giving me grief."

"Please, call me Monique."

"Is that your real name?" Ottilie asked. "Or the name you give to clients?"

"My clients rather enjoy calling me Ms. Carson, so they have no need for a first name, even if I wanted to supply it to them. Which I never do." Her lips quirked. "And, yes, Monique is my real name. But you're not a client, are you?"

"My neck begs to differ. Thank you for helping me, despite the misunderstanding. I know you didn't have to."

"You were in pain. And, honestly, I appreciate showing off what I'm good at." She took in Ottilie appreciatively. "Win-win."

"So...why breakfast?" Ottilie asked again as she began adding honey to the toast she'd retrieved from the buffet. "It seems an odd form of payment."

"Breakfast is the most important meal of the day." Monique smiled. "Didn't your mother teach you that?"

"Actually, I often heard *Frühstücken wie ein Kaiser, Mittagessen wie ein Edelmann, Abendessen wie ein Bettelmann*. Which means 'Breakfast like an emperor, lunch like a nobleman, dinner like a pauper'. And I elect to have honey on toast for breakfast because I cannot get my preferred choice—Zuckerrübensirup."

"What's that?"

"A savory-sweet sugar beet syrup from Germany. My mother virtually raised me on it. Nothing quite like it in the US."

"So you're German?"

"No. I was born in the US."

"Yet you have a slight accent. I suppose that'd be your parents' influence? Or is it just your mother who's German?"

Ottilie gave her a long, measured look. "I do apologize for being blunt, but I'm really not interested in small talk with someone I'm unlikely to ever meet again. So, was there a point to this breakfast? Surely me paying for my massage would have been more efficient?"

"Efficiency is not the point of life, dear Ottilie."

"Nonsense," Ottilie said. "Efficiency and order grease the wheel that keeps society running. Wouldn't it have been so much simpler to have just taken my money?"

"Simpler? Naturally. But I don't need simplicity, and I don't need money. I asked you to breakfast because I find you interesting. I wanted to know more about you. You are quite a chameleon."

"Me?" Ottilie looked blankly at her. "What makes you say that?"

"We passed in the hallway on Tuesday. Your stride was confident and assured. Then you sensed my presence. You instantly became a slower, older woman. You shrank before my eyes."

"You have quite the imagination." Ottilie took a sip of tea.

"I do," Monique retorted. "But not on this. I want to know why you do this? It was so instinctual; it can't have been a one-off."

With a faintly rueful tone, Ottilie said, "The Japanese have an expression: 'The nail that sticks out gets hammered down'. It's a habit of a lifetime. When I began in my particular career, it wouldn't do to stand out. Being too noticeable was not ideal. But what is learned to protect oneself is difficult to unlearn, even when no longer required."

At least she hadn't denied it. "What is your job, then, that you feared being hammered down for sticking out?"

"I'm retired now."

"But before?"

"Many things. Most recently, I was a personal assistant for a CEO at a consultancy firm."

"What did it consult on?"

"Nothing I can talk about. I signed an NDA. Why do you do sex work? If you don't need the money?" Ottilie asked.

"Why do I think you have no interest in my life and just want to avoid answering my question? You've already admitted hating small talk," Monique said, tone gentle. "See, here's the thing: the woman who approached me in the hallway, before she noticed me, was no PA."

Ottilie gave her a startled look. "Excuse me?"

"I don't know who you really are, but it's not who you claim." Monique wondered how that would land. Denial or laughter?

Shaking her head, Ottilie said incredulously, "So all personal assistants have to act a certain way? That seems awfully limiting. You don't strike me as someone with limited views."

Deflection, then? Monique snorted. "You're really good." She turned her smile flirtatious. "And I must say I do love women who are very good. Or…very bad."

Ottilie sighed. "I know you think you're being terribly charming, but I have no interest in someone like you."

Monique froze. The playfulness died on her tongue. Well. It wasn't as though she hadn't faced this particular bias numerous times. People did so love moralizing about certain professions. "I see. Should I be grateful you even deigned to be seen in public with me?" She made her tone deliberately chilly.

Ottilie frowned as if reviewing what she'd said. "Oh. You think I'm judging you for your sex work? Not at all. In fact, sex workers have been invaluable over the years in assisting my former company. They're highly effective. I hold them in esteem. It's rather astonishing how easily led people are by their sex drives. That can be useful, as I'm sure you know." She paused again. "Is 'sex worker' the correct term for you? I apologize if I'm not using the right descriptor."

She looked so placid and unruffled as she went back to sipping her tea.

Well, that was unexpected. "Sexual educator, teacher, healer, entertainer, listener, and expert in women's CEO sex fantasies all come under my purview. Take your pick."

"That is quite a mouthful. How do you fit it on your business card?" Ottilie's lips twitched.

Monique, though, was still processing the revelation that Ottilie's company had hired sex workers and found them "invaluable." And there were NDAs involved. "Do you work for the FBI or CIA? Or a political party?"

Ottilie laughed softly. "Why don't you take a moment and consider what you just asked?"

"Ah." She had a point. "You wouldn't be able to tell me if you did."

"Exactly."

"Am I warm?"

"You're not cold." Ottilie eyed her. "You're sharp, aren't you?" Her tone was approving. "I appreciate that."

"You also said you had no interest in 'someone like me.' What does that mean if it's not a reference to my work?"

Placing her cup back in its saucer, Ottilie said, "You appear to be very sexual. You flirt and tease constantly. This seems very important to you. It's your entire identity. But it's not mine. Not at all."

"Not at all?" Monique's eyebrows lifted. "Are you asexual?"

"What I am or not is none of your business. But why is sex all you seem interested in? You appear quite stuck on that topic."

Monique inhaled. Perhaps she had been coming on a little strong. And when was the last time someone had been interested in her *in spite* of her sexuality, not because of it? Few were the people she met socially who wanted to engage her brain. That just made Ottilie all the more interesting.

"I apologize, Ottilie. I'm a little out of practice being around someone who's not a client. I'm used to charging the atmosphere and motivating whomever I'm with to think about sex."

"That sounds exhausting." Ottilie sounded appalled at the idea. "When are you ever just you? Or *is* this you? Forever teasing people?"

Good question. It had been a long time since she'd dropped her playful routine around women. While running her investment business, obviously, she could be strictly professional. But since she'd semi-retired as CEO of Carson Investments, her chief distraction had been sex work. It had been fulfilling and saw her embrace her flirtatious side more than ever.

"I *do* know how to behave, Ottilie," she said with the hint of a smile. "I even have another job that requires it."

"Oh?" Ottilie leaned in closer.

"Nothing terribly exciting." Monique offered a careless wave. "Boring, dry numbers. A lot of spreadsheets and reports. I've handed off the bulk of my day-to-day duties now. These days, I focus on clients of a different kind, and that's been a great deal of fun."

"Dry numbers? Spreadsheets? Sounds lucrative. Is that why you don't need my money?" Ottilie guessed.

"Astute." Monique chuckled. "Numbers may be dry, but they do pay."

"How do you juggle both jobs? They sound like two extremes."

"By ensuring the two careers never meet. I'm not ashamed of either job, but blurring lines isn't a good idea. It's cleaner, easier, to keep my careers apart. With rare exception, few people know of my roles in both enterprises."

"I understand," Ottilie said. "We all have our secrets."

So true. Monique would dearly love to know some of Ottilie's. "Now, I have to ask, are we really never going to see each other again? You're too delicious to let go. It's like having one bite of chocolate mousse and having the plate whipped away."

"Must you?" Ottilie asked in exasperation. "You're incorrigible."

"That's not something I usually hear at my age. I'll take it as a compliment."

"You would."

"But tell me, is there anything I can offer you to meet me again?" She supplied her most winning smile. "I'm rather knowledgeable about Vegas, for instance. Would you like the tour?"

Ottilie began shaking her head but suddenly stopped. "Actually, I'm looking for showgirls."

"You are?" She blinked. "You?"

"I am," Ottilie confirmed. "I have a friend, a lovely older woman who used to dance professionally, and she's requested a photo of showgirls. The problem is, nothing comes up when I google showgirl performances in Vegas. The strip clubs, of course, come up, but I was seeking the Broadway-style productions Vegas is famous for."

"Sad to say, you'll have a long wait. The last show was in 2016." Monique deflated, remembering the final performance of *Jubilee*. "To quote a friend of mine, they got 'Cirqued.'"

"Cirqued?"

"The circus came to town—Cirque du Soleil—and that's all anyone wanted to see. Showgirl extravaganzas were considered too expensive to run, seemed stuck in time, and no longer had the risqué appeal of seeing the occasional topless dancer, given that the strip shows reveal far more. As a large-scale event, showgirl productions are dead. But as an art form, it lives on." She reached for her phone and looked up a number.

"How does it live on?" Ottilie asked. "Do you mean the showgirls walking around The Strip who charge for photos?"

"God no," Monique said. "Those amateur cosplayers aren't real showgirls. They wouldn't be able to stalk down grand staircases in six-inch heels, glitter, and feathers while wearing an enormous headpiece. Your friend deserves the best." She rose. "Excuse me a moment while I get her the best."

Monique stepped away from the table so she could talk about Ottilie out of earshot and returned a few minutes later.

"There are private showgirl productions," she explained, "which are usually hired out for corporate events. Many former showgirls now freelance. My friend is in dress rehearsals for one such event now. She's agreed to let you sit in on a session this morning and have a few photos at the end as a professional courtesy for your dancer friend. Does this work for you? You'll have to be there at ten this morning."

Ottilie's mouth fell open before she quickly snapped it shut. "Thank you. I didn't expect this."

"It's my pleasure." She lifted her phone. "What's your number? I'll text you the details."

The pause was long and noticeable. "I'm sorry. I don't give out my private phone number."

Monique held her gaze. "Neither do I. I'm making an exception. Will you?"

After an even longer pause as if to debate that, Ottilie pursed her lips, sighed, then reached for her phone. "Don't make me regret this," she murmured.

"I'm quite sure you meant to say, 'Thank you so much for doing me this favor, given I'm someone you barely know.'"

Dipping her head in acknowledgment, Ottilie said, "I do apologize. That was rude of me. Thank you, Ms. Carson."

"Monique. Please."

Ottilie pursed her lips and nodded. "Monique."

And with that, phone numbers and details were exchanged.

"Cleopatra?" Ottilie asked, glancing at the contact's name.

"Yes. Cleo once was Vegas's most famous Queen of the Nile. So please make sure you treat her as royalty and don't get in her way."

"I will be suitably reverential," Ottilie promised. "To the point I doubt she'd even know I'm there."

With a snort, Monique said: "While *I* find you impossible not to notice, I have a feeling you could definitely blend into the background if you wanted to."

"Of course I can," Ottilie said, her eyes twinkling.

Monique laughed and couldn't help but notice how attractive Ottilie was when amused. She would dearly love to see that again. "Oh, I wish I could be there to see you meet Cleo. Alas, I have a client."

"Will your friend really be fine with me turning up to rehearsals?"

"She will be today. It's also final auditions for backup dancers. There will be new people everywhere, so she won't mind one more. You'll fit right in." She paused and gave her a once-over. "Or, I should say, while it's unlikely you'd actually fit in, somehow I'm betting you'll manage it anyway. Yes?"

Ottilie seemed as though she rather liked that assessment. She allowed a tiny smile. "I suspect I'll manage."

Monique would dearly love to see how Cleo interacted with Ottilie. Nothing much got past her astute friend. Monique made a mental note to check in with her later. Even so, she suspected that whatever Cleo learned about Ottilie would probably fill a teaspoon. And that was her appeal.

Dear God, how Monique loved a mystery.

Chapter 6
Audience with a Queen

For a queen, Cleopatra looked decidedly ordinary, except for her height, which was remarkable, Ottilie thought. Of course, there was little doubt society would regard this woman as gorgeous. Cleo had an otherworldly gracefulness to her, gliding about like the dancer she was, head poised, her swan-like neck perfectly straight.

And yet, even as an abstract notion, Ottilie couldn't bring herself to find Cleopatra beautiful. She was also well aware this was a "her" problem because Ottilie truly found very few people attractive.

"Interesting," Cleo said. "Very interesting."

"Hmm?" Ottilie regarded her. "I'm sorry, what is?"

"Monique said she was sending a friend over who wanted the showgirl experience…or at least some photos of one for a *friend*. That is always a lie; the friend is them. Well, I expected the usual: Someone awestruck. Or, someone at least…interested." Cleo gave a curling half smile. "Are you even here willingly? Is this a hostage situation?" She laughed then, long and hard. Her waist-length raven hair shook, as did her gold-coin-laden brassiere. Her bosom…*tinkled*.

"Sorry." Ottilie was usually so much better at feigning interest in social settings. "I've only been in Vegas a few days. I flew in from Europe. I'm a little jet-lagged. You are, of course, a most impressive individual."

NUMBER SIX

Cleo snorted. "So much conviction." She clutched her chest. "Come now, tell me the truth: why am I not dazzling you with my razzle?" Cleo's grin was cheeky.

"I really do have a friend with an interest in dancing. It's not me, though."

"Oh, I actually believe you. And I think Monique was enjoying herself a great deal sending you to me. She knew."

"Knew what?"

"How I love women who are outside the mold."

Ottilie frowned. She was the most mold-fitting woman in existence. At least, that's what she projected to the world. Cleo should not have been able to detect otherwise.

"Now, come on through, and I'll introduce you to the rest of the showgirl family."

"That's really not necessary," Ottilie said. "I'd be happy just to take a photo of you."

"Nonsense. That's not the full showgirl experience! Besides, you've presented me with a challenge, and I do love a challenge."

"A...challenge?"

"Oh, yes. I'll have you respecting everything showgirls are before this rehearsal is out."

"I respect them now," Ottilie tried. In truth, she hadn't given the profession much thought.

"Do you, though?" Cleo clucked her tongue. "You don't know anything about us."

"That is true."

"Exactly."

"But I can appreciate the hard work it takes to dance professionally while knowing little about it."

"Perhaps. Now, then, how do you know Monique? Do you know how rare it is for her to ask me for a favor?"

"Is it?" Ottilie asked in surprise. "I barely know her. She treated my neck, asked me to breakfast, and offered to solve my showgirl problem."

Cleo's gaze raked her. "Well, well. I wonder what makes you so different. That is out of character."

It was? "How do you know her?"

Cleo led her to a stage. "I've known her forever. I lured her to Vegas, you know. Well, sort of. She came for business and fell in love with my world. Oh, those were wild days. It was all a lifetime ago, though." She turned to the dancers in the background and clapped her hands. "We have a guest for today's rehearsal," Cleo announced to the room. "Ottilie."

Bored, impassive faces of more ordinary (to Ottilie) women stared at her.

"And you will treat her well because Monique has sent her."

That earned some suddenly awake looks. Apparently, Monique's name carried a certain weight. Surely Monique hadn't…plied her trade to all these women?

Well, what if she had? It really wasn't any of Ottilie's business, was it?

One of the young women in the auditioning dancers' group craned her neck for a better look at Ottilie. The blonde all but crawled up the back of another dancer to check her out, expression cool and assessing.

What was that about?

The rehearsal proved to be surprisingly interesting. The women were all tall—obviously—but their legs made up most of their height; their torsos were disproportionately small.

Cleo's lead dancer, a blonde named Sahara, was helped into a set of wings attached by way of something they called a "backpack."

The woman's fixed smile faltered the moment it went on.

"This weighs sixty pounds," Cleo explained, turning back to Ottilie. "All the feathers are real—ostrich, goose, and duck. I saved this backpack from one of my old shows." Her expression turned wistful before she returned her attention to the dancers and clapped again. "From the top!"

Cleopatra glanced at the separate auditioning dancers' group, who were watching, rapt. "Pay close attention to the kicks," she called to them. "I'll test you on what you've seen a little later."

The more they rehearsed, the more Ottilie could see the high level of skill. Not just the moves, but the balance. Coming down stairs, twirling, keeping perfect pace with the others. What interested her most was that although Sahara was the lead dancer, and clearly talented, she did little actual dancing herself. Probably not surprising with sixty pounds on her slender back.

A pair of muscled men were always at her side to offer their arms and move her, keeping her perfectly stable. How interesting. It was so seamlessly done, if you didn't know what you were looking at, you wouldn't see it.

When the dancers took a break, Ottilie asked Cleo about the technical aspects: the way Sahara had been protected and moved to appear more agile than the enormous wings allowed.

Cleo gave her a curious look. "Most people are so distracted by the theatrics and glitter that they don't see what we do." She tilted her head. "What do you do?"

"I'm retired."

"And before then?"

"Personal assistant."

Cleo nodded slowly. "Were you one of those PAs who practically did their boss's job too?"

"Why do you ask?"

"You absolutely ooze competence."

"I was good at my job," she said neutrally.

"You're a careful one, aren't you? Careful with your words. You watch people."

"I'm just observant."

"If I didn't know better, I'd say you were an undercover detective. Met a few of those over the years. They always had a tell: noticed *too* much."

Ottilie laughed. "No. Just a boring retiree."

"Boring? Oh, I don't think so. If you were, Monique wouldn't have sent you. Boring doesn't turn her head."

"Or she's just helping out someone who needed a photo of some showgirls."

"Monique doesn't do that either. She likes to keep a tight rein on everyone in her life. Everyone stays in their appropriate circle: colleague, acquaintance, or client; never the twain shall meet." Cleo tapped a few notes into her phone, glancing at her dancers a few times as if to remember some stray thought. Then she added casually, not looking up, "What's interesting is that Monique doesn't have a friendship circle. There's just me. I'm the only one."

"No?" That seemed hard to believe.

"She has plenty of acquaintances, of course. She's a popular lady: outgoing, clever, beautiful, and amusing. Everyone enjoys having her around. But she's private and plays her cards close to her chest. She lets people in only so far. So many have tried to get close over the years, but she's not interested. With you, though? You barely know her, yet she calls you a friend. She had to know I'd notice that."

"She was being polite. I assure you we're not friends."

Cleo snickered softly. "That's funny. Most people would kill to be called Monique's friend. She's just got that allure, hasn't she?"

Ottilie supposed she did if you were interested in *peopling*. Ottilie was considerably more interested in retiring. And Mai Tais. Beach. Bliss. She gave a small shrug. "Well, I won't be in Las Vegas for long, so any sort of friendship is rather pointless. She took me to breakfast this morning, and I still don't understand why. I said as much." Ottilie added with her driest tone, "She accused me of being interesting."

Cleo suddenly snapped her fingers. "Oh, I see. You're a cat!"

"A....cat?" Ottilie peered at her. Was she being insulted?

"Yes. The more someone wants a cat to like them, the more indifferent they are. So the more intrigued Monique is and the more you shrug, the more Monique wants to know you. Pure cat." Cleo's smile was wide and amused. "Damn. She can't figure you out. That must fascinate her to no end."

"There is nothing *to* figure out. I'm not interested in your friend in any way, but she acts as if that's rare and curious."

"It is. *Everyone* wants a piece of Monique. Even those who hate everything she stands for still gravitate toward her. She intrigues everyone."

"Not everyone," Ottilie said, even as a sense of disquiet stirred within her. Was that even true? Or had Monique gotten under her skin a little too? Last night's massage, for instance, had been more pleasurable than she'd care to admit. She eyed Cleo impatiently. "Would I be able to get a photo soon? If that's acceptable? For my friend?"

"Yes, we can do that now. But you'll have to be in it."

"No, thank you."

"Too bad." Cleo beamed. "It's a condition of me allowing photos with my girls."

Ottilie eyed her pointedly, well aware there was no such condition. Cleo was obviously just amusing herself.

The things I do for Hannah.

"Is it true you're a friend of Monique's?" one of the backup dancers asked as Ottilie was positioned next to Sahara. Wearing purple tights and a bright-red Carrie Jordan T-shirt, the questioner looked barely out of high school.

"No," she replied coolly.

"Oh, damn," she said. "I was going to ask for an introduction. I was hoping she could set up my financial portfolio this year."

Ottilie turned to look at her. "What?"

"She helps out a lot of the girls. I'm not sure if she's taking on any new clients. I heard she's not working full-time anymore."

"She does investment work?" Ottilie clarified. *That* was the job involving spreadsheets Monique had mentioned?

"Daphne's portfolio had a massive return last year. Isn't that right, Daph?"

Daphne, a lithe, elegant woman wearing more feathers than seemed sensible for someone in her late fifties, agreed, "Oh, yes. I'm retiring early next year thanks to her."

The blonde auditioning dancer appeared out of nowhere, raking a curious gaze over Ottilie. "Can anyone get her financial services?" she asked. It seemed as if it was just something for her to say. The insincerity dripped off her. "Where do we sign up?" Her smile was over-wide.

"All right, pussycat," Cleo said, her gaze direct and amused as she approached Ottilie. "Your turn. Tatas primed!" She held up the phone Ottilie had handed her two minutes ago for the photo.

"My tatas are staying put," Ottilie objected just as Sahara and Daphne, on either side of her, pushed in sideways against her and turned on dazzling smiles for the camera.

Cleo tapped the phone, then reviewed her work. She burst out laughing. "Oh, it's a keeper. Your dancer friend will love it."

Ottilie walked over to have a look, and yes, indeed, the showgirls looked spectacular, while Ottilie, a full foot shorter, had boobs pressed into either side of her face. Her expression was exasperated. It was too absurd not to be funny. Hannah would love it. She sighed mightily.

How had she gotten roped into this at all?

"I'm sending myself a copy," Cleo announced, fingers and thumbs a blur over Ottilie's phone keypad. "Sahara and Daphne have never looked better." Then she smirked. "And I know someone else who'd love a copy."

Ottilie sighed again.

―――⋘⋙―――

After the photos were done and everyone was packing up, rehearsals over, Ottilie waited for Cleo in order to properly thank her. She'd considered at length what to give her in return and decided on something she might not even appreciate.

"Who is she?" Ottilie asked Cleo, subtly indicating the nosy blonde dance applicant she'd noticed earlier.

"Bella Higgins. Her parents are rich. She doesn't need the work, let's put it that way."

"Can she dance well?" Ottilie asked.

"Well enough to be in serious contention," Cleo said absentmindedly. She tapped some papers straight in a pile, then placed them into a folder.

"Don't hire her."

"Excuse me?"

"Bella is a sociopath trying to get her closest rivals to quit."

Cleo's head snapped up, and she shot Ottilie a charged look. "Okay, *what*?"

"I noticed immediately she was not like the others. She was so watchful and careful, perceptive, always wanting to be at the center of where the attention was. Also, she was the one steering the conversation among the younger dancers. The topics started off innocuously enough but kept taking darker turns."

"Darker turns? What do you mean?"

"Weirdest place you've ever had sex, she'd ask. And weirdest person," Ottilie said.

"That's not that unusual. Young people do love to discuss sex."

"Yes, but not once did she supply answers to any of her questions. She's a collector. She was digging out information on her competition all morning. Mentally storing it away. Perhaps as insurance or for blackmail? But she was subtle and cunning. And just by being there, collecting, she was unbalancing the group dynamic."

"Are you sure she never answered any of her own questions?" Monique asked slowly.

"Positive. She was testing the girls for all their weaknesses, mentally noting them. It's deliberate and calculating. I'd liken her to a velociraptor."

"I...see." A troubled frown crossed her face. "I'd been counting on her parents to make a donation to our cause. I suppose that won't be happening." Cleo tilted her head. "So, one bad apple aside, *do* you have a new respect for my dancers?"

"Yes." Ottilie nodded. "Especially how they push through the pain threshold."

"Excuse me?"

"Roman?" Ottilie studied her. "His shoulder injury? He can't take any weight on it after only a few hours of rehearsals."

Cleo glanced toward her male lead taking a drink in the adjacent room. "His injury was six months ago. He's fully healed."

"Are you sure?" Ottilie asked, tilting her head. "He's holding his water bottle in his left hand despite being right-handed. Before rehearsals, he held it in his dominant hand."

"How do you even know he's right-handed?" Cleo peered at her.

"He scratched his back a minute ago with his right hand. But you already know he's right-handed."

Cleo narrowed her eyes for a moment, then straightened. "Roman," she announced cheerfully, but her gaze had fixed on him like a bulldog. "Are you available to practice that lift after Sahara's flick kick jump?"

Sahara glanced up from where she was pulling on her sneakers on the opposite side of the room, a question on her face.

"With *me*," Cleo clarified. "Just another fifteen minutes should do it."

Roman winced. "Uh." He hesitated. "Sure. Uh. Today, though? I have an appointment in half an hour." He was a terrible liar.

"Never mind." Cleo turned back to regard Ottilie. She didn't say anything, but her disappointment was clear that Ottilie had been right.

"I'm sorry," Ottilie said. "I thought you'd want to know."

"Mm." Cleo shook her head. "Fresh eyes, I suppose."

"Yes." With that, she took her leave.

Chapter 7
The Selling Price

Monique sighed as her client left, dissatisfaction filling her. She was getting too old for this game. She could have been vastly enjoying herself watching Cleo circling Ottilie, but instead she'd been enduring this.

The client, who was new, had treated Monique as if she was doing Monique a favor by allowing her to fuck her. She had a cruel tongue too. And that wasn't the only cruel thing about her.

As Monique stood under the wide nozzle of her shower, sinking into the water's cathartic spray, she tried to pinpoint what it was that had made the angry woman so dreadful to deal with and, say, Mrs. Menzies so delightful.

Both were indomitable women with strong views and a lot of pent-up tension—not just the sexual kind. Both liked it rougher than most. They loved the physicality of being with a woman of Monique's height and strength. But that was where the similarities ended.

On the surface, her client today was stunning. She had a lithe body for a woman in her early sixties and blonde hair that somehow went perfectly with her cold blue eyes. Her jaw was sharp and came to a strong, proud chin. Her breasts were a lovely handful. She kept herself in shape, and she knew it.

She'd loved being in the dominant position and holding Monique down, keeping her in place and talking dirty. That didn't bother

Monique under certain circumstances. But several times she had taken without asking, ordered instead of asked, and treated her like the hired help. Which…Monique was, even if she didn't need the money.

It all came down to respect. Most clients, like Mrs. Menzies, treated her as a respected businesswoman; this woman had not.

Why am I putting up with women like her?

At first, when the woman had swept into the room and run her haughty gaze all over Monique, it had been arousing. But when her anger had revealed itself after her all-too-quick orgasm, when she'd decided she wanted a power trip, she'd turned on Monique. Tone vicious and dangerous, she'd said, "Now you will do *exactly* as I say."

Monique, of course, had not done exactly as the woman had said, and the client had retaliated: pinching Monique's nipples without permission and frequently threatening to shove her fingers where they weren't welcome until Monique had slapped them away.

The dark look in the woman's eyes told Monique none of these transgressions had been an accident. She hadn't forgotten the rules; she'd just wanted to punish Monique. Hurt her.

Why? Most likely because she resented having to pay for sex. That was sadly common. Women like her client—who had husbands and high-profile careers and were deeply closeted—had few options. They tended to resent their circumstances a great deal. So they lashed out at the women they paid to take it.

She was being paid to take it.

As she stepped out of the shower and toweled down, the earlier events bothered her more and more. All the woman had seen her as was a cheap streetwalker. Just a shell who sold her body.

Monique had enormous sympathy for sex workers who didn't have a choice, including the streetwalkers, who especially lived a dangerous life. The ones with pimps who couldn't say no to any client.

That was the sinister side of the job. Monique's unorthodox lifestyle was all very entertaining and evolved when she had all the choices in the world. She was wealthy, could pick and choose her clients, and charged high fees.

Did that make her inherently better than those without her advantages?

Oh, she was certainly a better choice for the *clients*, who could sleep well knowing they weren't exploiting someone vulnerable. But she was still a sex worker. And today, the client had treated her like *them*. She'd felt dirty.

Such slurs usually bounced off her. Monique knew her own worth, and it was certainly not tied to a stranger's opinion. But this client had been clever and had known exactly how to slide the knife in between her ribs to make the insults destructive.

How...unsettling.

She'd told the woman to lose her number at the end of the session. That had only sharpened the woman's rage. She'd dressed furiously, shot Monique a filthy look, warned her she wasn't done with her, and then had attempted to slam the door behind her.

The air pressure in the room, with no open balcony door or windows, had prevented it and that had just seemed to infuriate her more.

The sick feeling in Monique's stomach hadn't left her an hour later. Was it the woman's implied threat? Or being treated like the "cheap streetwalker" her client had called her?

She phoned Mrs. Menzies, quietly telling her to add another name to the list.

It was a code they'd developed should a client prove problematic. A way to ensure issues weren't repeated, that Security would be ready if said client returned with attitude. Mrs. Menzies always appreciated the heads-up.

"I'm sorry your visitor was difficult," the manager said. "Are you... well?"

"Yes. Fine." Monique inhaled. "Well, I will be. A bit of decompressing is necessary. It's unfortunate one cannot always know with absolute certainty who will misbehave. While I'm exceptionally accurate, I know there's always the possibility of an unpredictable outlier—the chance of ugly behavior, no matter how fancy the suit or expensive the designer watch."

"Very true."

"I'm sure you didn't expect Frank to cause a problem either. People aren't always their best selves."

Monique had learned all about Mrs. Menzies' ranting husband from the hotel employees' gossip network.

"You heard about that?" Mrs. Menzies sounded long-suffering when she added, "Of course you did. Well, it might have been worse. Fortunately, a guest stepped in and prevented him from escalating before he could move on to anything worse than straining his throat."

Monique hadn't heard this part of the story. "Which guest? Do I know them?"

"No. Although you almost met her. I was going to send her up to you last night, but your phone was off the hook." She lowered her voice. "The woman asked if I knew someone who could give a *cervical* massage."

Monique laughed. "I've been meaning to talk to you about that. Ottilie found me anyway. She had a neck complaint. Nothing…further south."

"Oh!" Mrs. Menzies made a choking noise. "I thought…"

"Oh, I *know* what you thought," Monique said lightly.

"I'm almost afraid to ask how that played out."

"It played out with me giving her an entirely professional neck massage. Ottilie was grateful and then went on her way."

"Thank goodness." Mrs. Menzies sounded close to hyperventilating. "I mean, she might have sued the hotel or something! Of course, I wouldn't normally send a guest to you without specific instruction, but I thought I knew what she was asking. I wanted to be helpful, given she'd just assisted me with Frank."

"I find it odd she stepped in for that. I've found Ottilie to be more of an observer. Someone watchful on the sidelines."

"I think she was enraged by some cracks Frank made about older women."

Monique clucked at that. "He's an idiot. You're about to hit your prime now that you're free of that odious man. You know that, don't you, darling? You're free to be fabulous."

"Now, don't you start with your nonsense."

Monique chuckled.

NUMBER SIX

"All right, then," Mrs. Menzies said, all business. "I've made a note about your...problem person...and I'll see you at our scheduled time."

"Can't wait, June!" Monique ended the call.

Her smile, which always rose unbidden when dealing with the eternally prickly Mrs. Menzies, fell away. She remembered her *problem person* and felt annoyed all over again. How had she let her get under her skin?

She glanced at the time and dialed another number. Cleo would be done with rehearsals by now.

"Ah, here she is," Cleo said with a laugh. "Woman of the hour!"

"What did I do?"

"You sent me your *friend*. Was this for my benefit or yours?"

"How was it to either of our benefit?" Monique asked. "It was purely for Ottilie's benefit."

"Don't," Cleo said. "I know you. You're a very intentional woman in everything you do. So I'm guessing you knew about her superpower?"

"Her"—Monique frowned—"superpower?"

"Yes. Same as yours."

"She's fabulous in bed? Or analyzing a company's annual report to work out what they're not saying?"

"She reads people as brilliantly as you do," Cleo said.

"Ah." Yes, that was certainly part of Ottilie's appeal. Monique loved working out who people were too. A shame she hadn't been able to get a good read on today's client before the woman had treated her with such contempt.

Silence briefly fell. "You okay, hon? You sound a little...off?"

"Nothing a chat with my oldest friend can't fix. Client stuff."

"Client stuff? Did one turn on you?" Cleo's concern was evident in her voice.

"She tried a few vicious games and had various unsavory thoughts about me and my vocation."

"Shit," Cleo muttered. "I hate people sometimes. Sorry, hon."

"It's fine. Occupational hazard." She sank into an armchair. "Now, take my mind off The Entitled One. What did Ottilie do that has you worked up?"

"She noticed Roman's injury's still bothering him."

"I thought he was over that."

"So did I. He's not. He's been keeping it from me." She huffed. "I'll have to make allowances now so he's not doing so many lifts." Cleo paused. "And Ottilie spotted a pretty little sociopath in the midst of my auditioning dancers."

"Really?"

"This one newbie was testing the girls for all their weaknesses, cataloging them. Ottilie warned me she'd be sowing dissent if I hired her."

"*Did* you hire her?"

"God no. Group cohesion is everything in the dance world. You know that. We're not a bunch of catfighting models, hon."

Monique rolled her eyes. "Hey, we weren't *catfighting*. We were too busy screwing each other for that."

"Until the breakups."

"Until then…" Monique thought fondly back to her modeling days. There had been a lot of delicious hookups. The memories cheered her a little.

"Thanks for sending her to me," Cleo was saying. "She's a clever, clever woman. No wonder you're taken with her."

"Taken with her? I don't know where you get these ideas from."

"I get them from being your oldest and most agile friend."

"Well, I'm not about to argue which of us can do a high kick."

"You sent her to me because you wanted to see what I thought of her."

Maybe she had done exactly that. A pointless exercise, most likely, because Ottilie was unknowable…and would be gone soon.

"I think she's cool and distant, but there's a lot going on underneath. She's impressive, I think, but prefers to hide it."

"Yes," Monique agreed. "All of the above."

"You and those older women, hmm? Still at it."

"Still at it." Monique couldn't disagree. After all, every woman who'd ever turned her head had been older.

"I blame Stacy, of course," Cleo said adamantly. "That mentor-bitch did a number on you."

"Some women are harder to forget than others," she conceded.

Cleo snorted. "Are you going to ask her out?"

"Who? Stacy?" The words came out strangled. "I'd sooner chew off an arm. You remember what she did!"

"Not Stacy!" Cleo sounded appalled. "I haven't forgotten her evil ways. *Ottilie*. The clever watchful woman you had me vet today."

"I didn't have her vetted." *Liar.*

"You did. And I cautiously approve. She's an interesting, astute woman and a complete mystery, and I know how much you love those. Now, on that note, I've gotten you a treat. Check your phone."

Monique's cell phone beeped a moment later. And there was a photo of Ottilie, looking startled, her face framed by two pairs of sparkly boobs courtesy of Cleo's much taller dancers.

She burst out laughing. "How on earth did you get her to agree to that?"

"By not telling her it was happening. Don't worry, she knows I've sent you the photo. You can laugh over it together. Or tell her not to scowl too much over it together."

Monique stared at the photo, loving the way the elegance and austereness of Ottilie shone through despite the ridiculous image.

"One of a kind," Monique murmured.

"What, hon?" Cleo asked.

"Nothing. But thanks. For the photo and for cheering me up."

"Sure, sweetie. Let's grab dinner soon. I need all the goss on your life like air. You know Rochelle is wonderful, but, my God, domestic bliss is boring." Her huff was purely for effect and made Monique laugh—as intended, no doubt.

Who was Cleo kidding? She adored her wife and never found married life boring. Clearly she was just trying to lighten the mood. Monique said her goodbyes, her gaze returning to Ottilie's photo.

Even bookended by two incredibly gorgeous, statuesque showgirls, Ottilie stood out. There was just something about her. Indefinable. Interesting. Assured.

Beautiful.

Chapter 8
Crocheting and Blackmail

Finally, it was two o'clock. Ottilie had survived the morning's indignity of The Photo. She had dutifully texted it to Hannah despite being well aware there would be jokes at her expense. Apparently, she wanted Hannah to be happy, which wasn't exactly new.

She had become extremely protective of the charming eighty-four year old. At first, Ottilie had wondered if it was just a case of recognizing "there but for the grace of God go I" if circumstances had been different. She hated to imagine her mind withering from boredom, starved of the ability to feed itself due to physical infirmities.

Hannah couldn't just go and explore her world on her own or, on a whim, pop into a museum or library or gallery. Her limited mobility meant that even just leaving her apartment required help. And if no one was around, as had been the case until recently, she just…stayed there. Watched excessive TV, stared outside, or, with the zeal of a missionary, latched onto any visitor, desperate for intelligent conversation.

What hell that had to be. Ottilie felt that to the core of her being.

As time went on, though, Ottilie had begun to truly value the woman herself. Hannah's sharp mind was a delight. Her utter joy whenever Ottilie sent her clues on where to meet next filled Ottilie with an unexpected warmth. She did appreciate intelligent people.

NUMBER SIX

Unfortunately, meeting intelligent people wasn't on her dance card today. Right now, her quarry was more in the rat-cunning category. Well, closer to rat, and every bit the same nuisance.

The Republican Women of Las Vegas group had assembled in Hotel Duxton's Roaring Twenties function room and appeared excited about their esteemed guest speaker arriving soon.

An upbeat Carrie Jordan medley played in the background as Ottilie, tucked away in one corner, busied herself by crocheting a pawn to go with the bishop she'd completed a few days ago.

The attendees here were an interesting mix of killer businesswomen and wealthy socialites, all perfumed and primed to network. As they waited, a variety of women inquired about Ottilie's stitching, out of politeness, boredom, or, in one or two cases, genuine interest.

By the time she was deep into double crocheting her pawn—black—the former senior senator for Massachusetts had taken to the stage to enthusiastic applause.

Phyllis Kensington's speech sounded like one she was trying on for size somewhere it wouldn't be reported on. Vegas was far enough out of the usual spheres of influence in which she circulated. While her days of having spheres of influence were over, not so her political ambitions, it seemed.

The gist of her speech was how shocked she'd been to discover the sexual depravities of her cheating husband, who'd enjoyed waving his trysts in her face—to the point that she'd resorted to paying a shady company, The Fixers, to handle him and cover up his misdeeds.

There was a full ten minutes dedicated to the agony she'd gone through when all that sordid, nasty, *private* business had been made public by the terrible media. Her sharp gaze roamed the room, as if assessing how her half-truths and outright lies were landing.

Her blue eyes narrowed into slits when she discovered Ottilie, who smiled pleasantly and saluted her with her crochet needle.

Hissing in a breath, Kensington finished by explaining how even though she was a victim in all this, caught up in the public mess that was "Fixergate," wasn't it always true that women were punished for the bad behavior of men?

There were nods aplenty at that, and for the first time, Kensington smiled. Perhaps she could sense her ambitions weren't as dead as she feared, that the road to redemption started with a single grassroots speech?

Heaven help us if she's right.

No word, of course, that she was anything but a victim. That she'd once *run* The Fixers. But no one knew that beyond about fifty employees and four board members. (Five, if you wanted to get technical. Ottilie did not.)

At the end, Kensington coyly batted away questions of whether she might have another run at politics, turning on the charm. Her magnanimity was practically oozing when asked if she'd provide any new recipes for her famous website, At Home With Phyllis.

"But of course!" she declared gaily. "I can't wait to share my latest recipes with all my lovely followers."

Phyllis Kensington did not, in fact, cook. Nor did she, last Ottilie checked, have more than a handful of followers left.

Sensing they were wrapping up, Ottilie carefully packed her crocheting into her Oroton bag and waited. Her quarry would come to her.

As the farewell air-kisses took place, Ottilie checked her phone and discovered a screed of enthusiastic texts from Hannah after receiving the showgirls photo. Her delight made Ottilie's mild humiliation well worth it.

They're so beautiful! Look at their postures! The feathers! And you look so like a fish out of water, dear! I laughed so hard, my granddaughter ran in to see if I was having a seizure. She took one look at the photo and said it served you right for being my friend!

Ottilie smirked. *Good one, Michelle,* she conceded inwardly.

Do you not dance? Have you never danced? Hannah texted next.

No, Ottilie replied. *My parents considered anything artistic or creative to be wasted effort.*

Oh what a terrible loss! Hannah wrote back. *I wish I was fighting fit and my hip wasn't so bad. I'd love to teach you some moves!*

Then: Michelle just saw this text and said you know "plenty of moves" already and adding more to your repertoire is overkill. She also says you should frame that photo. I agree! It's spectacular.

Ottilie narrowed her eyes and typed her response.

Tell your granddaughter I've said she must next explain memes to you, in detail. It's an important part of texting. Now, I must go. Have a lovely day.

She smiled to herself. Ottilie almost felt sorry for Michelle. They'd likely never be good friends, given their past association. But their gentle tug-of-war over Hannah was friendly enough and amusing them both, it seemed.

A throat cleared impatiently.

Ottilie looked up to see that all the attendees had disappeared. A lone organizer remained, stacking chairs in the distance. The former senator now loomed in front of her, hands curled into loose fists. Defensive. Adversarial.

How interesting. She pushed her phone back into her bag as Kensington dropped, uninvited, into the seat beside her.

"I didn't take you for a supporter of grassroots political events, Tilly."

"Ordinarily, no," she replied, lips thinning at the shortening of her name. "In this instance, I heard who the guest speaker was."

"Did you fly to Vegas just to see me?" Kensington asked, her blonde eyebrows shooting up to her hairline.

"You have been otherwise uncontactable since the media scandal. But I was here anyway. I'm killing two birds with one stone."

"*You?* Killing something?" Kensington laughed derisively. "How… fanciful. Well, then, you wished to reminisce with me? Since we got on *so well* when you worked for me."

Ottilie's jaw twitched. So many things were wrong with that sentence.

"Well?" Impatience filled her tone now.

"I'm curious," Ottilie began idly. "How many more of these tedious luncheons will you have to do in order to facilitate a return to politics?"

Kensington's nostrils flared. "Why do you ask?"

"The voters see you as enabling your husband's cheating by covering it up, not being a victim."

"For now. But I'm excellent at reshaping narratives."

"Yes," Ottilie conceded, "you are. But how many more pleading speeches would you need to make if everyone knew exactly where you used to work? And in what capacity?"

Kensington stared at her. "Is that why you're here? Threatening to leak that I was the…" She lowered her voice. "CEO?"

"As a matter of fact, I am. Now, here are the terms." Ottilie reached into her bag and drew out an envelope. "From the board. Memorize it, as I'll be taking it back. No paper trail. The most important thing is the people listed, whose names you will forget were ever associated with your former organization."

Reaching for it, Kensington quickly opened the envelope. After reading The Fixers's names, she said, "Quite a list. I only recognize ten people on it."

"Then you will forget those ten names in perpetuity."

"And if I refuse?"

Ottilie reached for a second envelope. "This is everything we have on you and are prepared to use."

Kensington tore it open and began shuffling through the pages inside. She gasped and pointed at the third item. Her head snapped up. "You cannot have footage of *that*."

"I assure you we do. There was a camera above the desk in the CEO's office."

"What?" Kensington's eyes flew wide open. "You're bluffing."

"I do *not* bluff." Which the woman would know if Kensington had paid even the faintest attention to Ottilie at work.

Ottilie pulled her tablet out of her bag, hit mute in deference to the distant chair stacker, and then played the recording from the security camera.

While the then CEO, Michelle Hastings, wasn't visible, Kensington was front and center in the camera's eye: clearly removing her thong, demanding sex from Hastings, and being shot down acidly.

"It's far worse with sound," Ottilie said lazily as the view now showed the former senator fondling herself and making crass comments. "Which I'm sure you'd remember."

Kensington drew in a long breath.

"I imagine," Ottilie continued, "that leaking this would be ruinous for your image. Family values. Home-cooked recipes. Church on Sundays."

Kensington leaned away from the tablet and hissed, "If you leak that, I will make it my life's mission to destroy you."

"How?" Ottilie asked, unmoved. "I fail to see what you could do to me."

"I will tell the world that you worked at The Fixers."

"As a mere PA. And I left long before all the nasty business came out."

Kensington's brow wrinkled. "You did, didn't you?" An eyebrow lifted. "Your departure's timing was a little too good, now that I think about it. Did you know The Fixers was going down?"

"I did."

Kensington eyed her more sharply. "How?"

"Because you were in charge of it. Its demise was inevitable. I could feel the coup brewing for months. You were the worst CEO I've ever seen."

"Excuse me?" Fury flashed in those penetrating eyes. "I was decisive! I had a vision!"

"Yes: to destroy your enemies. None of whom had anything to do with the organization or its aims. You did very little *actual* work."

"You're just bitter." Kensington folded her arms and scoffed.

"I'm…bitter?" Ottilie choked out. "Why? Because my boss was terrible?"

"I was never less than exceptional. You're bitter…due to that night."

Horror iced Ottilie's veins. "We are *not* discussing that!"

"Oh?" A knowing, malicious gleam entered Kensington's eye. She leaned in. "I think," she said pointedly, "you hated that you wanted it too."

In a churning, sickening flash, Ottilie's mind whirled her back to that night.

Phyllis Kensington hadn't been CEO of The Fixers more than a few months. They were still getting a feel for each other, but what Ottilie had seen so far hadn't impressed her. The former senator was mercurial, driven by whims and ego, and was used to absolute obedience.

She'd begun a vendetta against everyone she wanted punished for slights against her before she'd joined The Fixers.

It was an outrageous misuse of company resources; worse, the board had decided to allow Kensington to use staff resources as she liked—"a little leeway while she settles in."

Yet again, Ottilie felt like Cassandra of Greek myth: destined to always be right but her warnings never heeded. How many times had she cautioned them against hiring Kensington in the first place? She'd all but begged them to see that for all Michelle's failings—her disrespect to the board—she was still ten times better on a bad day than Kensington was on a good one.

It hadn't mattered. The board wanted to believe they were right in hiring her. They ignored every red flag. And they told Ottilie to do her best to "make peace" with the new CEO. And she was trying. For weeks, she'd been trying—until that night.

It was seven-thirty, and Ottilie entered the CEO's office and asked Kensington to sign some paperwork before leaving.

That's when she caught sight of her: the top three buttons of her blouse askew, hair unraveling from its usual blow-waved perfection. She was arranged sloppily in her chair, as if sitting erect were no longer feasible.

Prickles went up Ottilie's skin. She disdained drunkenness. A sign of a weak mind.

Voice slurring, Kensington beckoned her closer and ordered, "Sit." As if Ottilie were little better than a dog.

Reminding herself of the board's orders, Ottilie dutifully seated herself in the visitor's chair.

Tutting, Kensington beckoned her to her side of the desk. "I meant here." She patted the edge of the desk in front of herself. "I need to talk to you, and I don't want to shout."

Ottilie cautiously relocated herself to the desk's edge.

Quick as a flash, Kensington's chair shot forward. Her hands slid under the hem of Ottilie's tight tweed skirt, pushing higher up her thighs.

With a bark of protest, Ottilie tried to slap her hands away. "Stop that!"

Kensington ignored her. "Hush, Tilly." She sounded even more drunk, proving her long lunch had been liquid in nature. Her fingers reached Ottilie's underwear, and Kensington moaned in crude appreciation. "Oh fuck. Is that silk? Have you been wearing silk panties all this time? For me?"

Squirming, Ottilie finally managed to push away the hands. "Do not touch me!"

"Don't play hard to get. The way you stare at me...I know it's mutual. I've wanted you since the moment I saw you. Let me have you."

Ottilie arched backwards and growled. "There is nothing mutual!" She yanked her skirt firmly back into place, then anchored it with her fisted hands stiffly against her sides.

Instead of expressing disappointment or even acknowledgment that she'd made a huge error—and to Ottilie's incredulity—Kensington slid up her own skirt, pushed aside her G-string, and leaned back in her chair. She began to stroke herself, watching Ottilie with a smug expression.

"What on earth do you think you're doing!" Ottilie demanded.

"Let me look at you," Kensington slurred. "Show me your tits if you won't let me touch you. Undo that blouse for me. Take off your bra. I'm wondering what your nipples look like. Are they luscious and plump like the rest of you? Or tight and hard like mine? Show me. Show me right now!"

Humiliation and fury warred over her response. Ottilie had worked with many morally bankrupt people, but none had ever made her feel like a piece of meat. Face on fire, Ottilie slid from the desk.

Kensington's long legs shot out straight and bracketed Ottilie hard against the desk drawers.

"No, no, we're not done." Kensington's fingers were a blur between her own legs. "I'm so hot for you. I fantasize about you; did you know that? All efficient and stern and righteous, hunched over your desk, working oh so very hard. It gets me so wet."

Ottilie swallowed down her disgust. Was this supposed to be a romantic proposition?

Kensington, still ferociously rubbing her clit, said, "I think about bending you over my desk in here. Pushing my fingers into you from behind. Fucking you hard, with your skirt all bunched up at your lovely, thick waist. Trembling for me. Oh, I think of you constantly."

Fury blew away the shock that had robbed Ottilie of movement, and she slapped Kensington's leg away with venom. "Fuck you," she swore and stormed out of the room.

"That was the plan, sugar," Kensington called after her. "Your loss."

Red spots appeared before Ottilie's eyes.

The wet sounds continued behind her as she flew to the elevator and stabbed the Ground *button.*

Disgust coated Ottilie's mouth at the reminder of that night. She liked to be prepared for every eventuality, but that…the disrespect and groping? It hadn't been anywhere near her radar. She'd been caught so flat-footed.

Had Kensington been a foreign operative or even just a stranger who'd done this, she'd have left them bleeding on the floor.

Her shock, though, had induced something in Ottilie she hated. Just for a moment, she'd *frozen*. Acted like a cornered animal. With… weakness.

She kept going back to that moment Kensington had trapped her: those icy eyes, like sharp little chips, looking amused in the face of Ottilie's rising panic.

It had taken months for Ottilie to stop berating herself and to file away the incident in the back of her mind under *Regrettable—Never to Be Repeated*.

Except, everything had gone to hell afterwards. Her sexual harassment complaint to the board had been met with indifference, as if it had been nothing.

Kensington's retribution over being rejected had been swift and cruel. Her announcement soon afterward to the entire office that Ottilie was "little more than a glorified typist" had been the opening salvo in a vicious campaign of disrespect.

Now, in the present day, the former senator was gloating once more, staring at Ottilie without a shred of guilt, shame, or even discomfort as she brought up that disturbing night. And she had the audacity to suggest Ottilie had wanted it too?

Why would she say that? Ottilie tried to push aside her distaste and think.

Oh. She was trying to rattle her? Retaliation, perhaps, for Ottilie insulting her leadership skills.

She sighed in irritation. "Getting back to the video, we would have no qualms about releasing it. You'll be impossible to elect ever again. The media will have a field day talking about you as a pervert—a creep just like your husband. A fact I can certainly attest to."

"You think I'm *perverted*?" Kensington tilted her head, eyes hard. "Why? I asked you once. You said no. I never asked you again, did I? That hardly makes me a creep. So sue me if I made a pass at an underling after I'd clearly overindulged. If I were a man, this would barely warrant a slap on the wrist."

Seriously? She hadn't asked! She'd tried to take what she'd wanted. Yet even now she was reframing herself as a victim? Ottilie's jaw set hard. Coldness swallowed her.

Kensington's eyes flashed. "It's blatant homophobia; that's what this is. I'll screw them all over if they try that on me! I'll come out of this as the poster child for media persecution. They'll be terrified of attacking me ever again."

Maybe some of Ottilie's disbelief and rage leaked because Kensington suddenly lightened her expression. "Anyway, as I said, I'd overindulged." Her wave was dismissive. "It was nothing. Nothing at all."

Nothing?

There was that word again. Pain shot up Ottilie's arms from where she'd clamped her fists so hard. Her nails bit into her palms. She tried very hard *not* to remember all the ways she knew how to incapacitate a human. The CIA had thoroughly trained her for every eventuality. How dare this woman treat Ottilie as some toothless annoyance? As harmless!

Ottilie's neck started throbbing, the ache blurring her logic. She could just lean over and snap Kensington's scrawny neck, then disappear. It would be so easy. She had several passports. Multiple bank accounts in different countries. Different names. Connections everywhere. People with power and private jets, who owed her favors.

It was tempting. Ottilie was *not* nothing. She was *not* harmless.

But the darker impulses fled as quickly as they arrived. She reminded herself it wasn't Kensington's fault that she didn't know of Ottilie's vast sphere of influence. After all, she'd gone to great pains to hide who she really was. And Kensington might possess sharp claws and a vicious tongue, but she was lacking any great intellect or power. She was a hissing Siamese cat at best.

Heedless to the danger she'd just been in, Kensington pushed the pieces of paper with Ottilie's demands back at her. "Is this what you've been doing with yourself post-retirement? Running around, warning people in high positions at The Fixers?" Kensington's look was scornful.

"Tying up loose ends." Ottilie choked out the words, still not as calm as she'd like.

Kensington's cold gaze raked her. "So, you do blackmail now?"

Ottilie snorted. She'd *always* done blackmail. "You're not being asked to do anything terribly onerous. Just that you keep your mouth shut regarding everyone listed." She pointed at the paperwork.

After a pause, Kensington shrugged. "Fine. I don't care. Besides, I assumed there was a reason certain people weren't being named in the fallout. I'm not a fool. I wasn't about to start naming anyone not mentioned by the media already."

Oh, she *was* certainly a fool, but Ottilie wasn't about to open that can of worms. Her breathing returned to normal.

Kensington added, "So why wasn't your name on the list you showed me?"

"I don't add my name to lists as a general rule. Consider it me being cautious."

"Mmm." Kensington sounded as though she did not disagree.

"But you'll forget my name too. That goes without saying." Ottilie shoved the papers back into her bag and fussed with the closure. "All right. That's the business sorted. We're done. You will not be hearing from us again…unless you cross us."

Kensington watched her, expression sly. "How efficient you are. All the *I*s dotted; *T*s crossed."

Ottilie's fingers clenched again. She straightened. "You called me 'a glorified typist'," she said against her better judgment. Voice low, she added, "*That* was a mistake."

"Oh dear, I'm trembling in my fashionable heels." Her eyes swept Ottilie. "Something *you* might want to look into. Acquiring fashion that doesn't make you look like you're doing a World War II informational video for the British government. You're like the personification of sepia. Such a shame you weren't interested in any fun."

Fun? Ottilie fixed a glare on her, incredulous that the woman had just returned to *that* topic. "You really don't understand consent, do you?"

With a small snort, Kensington said: "Christ, are you still fixating on that side of it? My dear, no one forced you into anything. You left my office dignity intact, silk panties *on*, but you're still whining about how I treated you. And saying '*That was a mistake*' as if you're planning revenge or something equally ridiculous? Sugar, I've been threatened by the worst there is, and you're not even in the ballpark. You. Are. Nothing."

Ottilie clamped her jaw.

Kensington rose to leave. "Time to go. I'd say our time working together was a *pleasure*, but, alas, you said no." Kensington's expression turned savage as she leaned in close and hissed in Ottilie's ear, "While I did love the idea of fucking the prudishness right out of you back then, telling you and your empty threats to fuck off now is the next best thing. It's certainly got me wet."

A furnace roared in Ottilie's ears. The disrespect!

Kensington turned on her heel, then paused and glanced backward. "You were nothing more than an officious little bug with delusions of grandeur. Consider yourself lucky I even looked at you twice. Although, admittedly, I *was* drunk at the time." She smiled sweetly.

Ottilie inhaled, aware now that she *would* end this woman. One way or another, the comfortable, entitled life Kensington enjoyed would be over.

In a soft, even voice, all she said was, "We will see who is nothing."

Ottilie kept it together as she stalked back to her hotel room, but the moment the door closed, she let out her fury. Sweeping all her bottles and elixirs off the bathroom counter in an almighty crash did little to alleviate her rage. She shook out her balled-up fists and then… screamed. Into a pillow.

It was muted and brief. She so rarely indulged any part of herself that wasn't ordered and controlled. A pointless exercise. She didn't feel better for it.

Before she could stop herself, she reached for her tablet and loaded up a video, one she'd never shown another living soul—the other recording caught in the CEO's office, of Ottilie's disastrous encounter with Kensington that night.

Her discomfort radiated from the screen. So did her horror and… her weakness.

Three minutes later—had it really been only three minutes?—Ottilie flung down the tablet in disgust. So much for compartmentalizing away one's misfortunes. Her go-to solution for life was failing her. She needed revenge.

Ottilie strode in frustrated circles around her hotel room. She knew so many ways to hurt the damned woman. The only thing she couldn't do was out Kensington as a former Fixers CEO because that was the deal they'd reached today: Kensington's silence on employees in exchange for Ottilie's silence on Kensington's CEO role.

That just meant she had to hurt her in a different way. Stopping in mid stride, she suddenly knew exactly how to hit her where it would hurt most.

She set to work.

A few hours later, Ottilie sat back, satisfied. She snatched up her phone and made a call.

Number Six

"Ottilie?" Michelle Hastings answered, surprise evident. "Did you mean to call me? If you're after my safta, she's napping."

"Yes, I meant to call you, not Hannah. This is business," Ottilie ground out. "I need..."—she tried to contain her still burbling fury—"a favor."

Michelle drew in a shocked breath. "You do not sound at all like yourself. Has something happened?"

"Nothing that cannot be fixed. My favor involves punishing Phyllis Kensington. Are you interested?"

"Ah." Michelle's tone tightened. "What's she done now?"

"She is being...true to form." *Count to ten.* Ottilie tried that but got stuck on three. "In other words, crude and terrible."

"Sounds like her. What do you need?" Michelle asked after a pause.

"Contact that reporter Catherine Ayers. Give her a story. It's one I can verify. I have access to all the proof."

"You're exposing a Fixers CEO now? I assumed that wouldn't be happening—for any of the CEOs," Michelle said, sounding anxious. As she would.

"This story isn't about her former role. It's something else. Something that will ruin her."

"Why can't *you* contact Catherine? You know our history. Even if we've reached an understanding now, I don't want to bother the woman. She's been bothered by me enough for a lifetime."

"I'm aware of what I'm asking. I *am*." Ottilie's voice shook a little. "But I'm a stranger. Ayers knows you. She'll listen."

"There are other nationally renowned journalists," Michelle suggested.

"They'll want to know who I am in the scheme of things. And I don't want that. I need to stay well out of scrutiny."

"Of course you do." Another pause. "Why should I help you? And don't say because you're friends with my grandmother. That's irrelevant here."

"I would never use my friendship with Hannah for business," Ottilie snapped.

After a pause, Michelle said, "I believe you. But hasn't Kensington already been punished? The whole world knows she covered up her husband abusing a teenage boy because it suited her political ambitions. Why should I force myself to approach Catherine Ayers again," she asked, "as a favor for you?"

"How did it feel," Ottilie asked sharply, "when she tried to demand sex from you in your office that night?"

"Ottilie?" Michelle's voice sounded astonished. "That sounds perilously like a personal question, and we don't do those."

"I'm aware you had a preexisting relationship with the senator. But on the video, in the office that night, you sounded clearly uncomfortable. More than that. You were…disturbed."

Michelle sighed. "Why are you asking about ancient history?"

"*Is* it…ancient history?" Ottilie's voice cracked and sounded vulnerable to her own ears. "For you?"

Silence flattened the air.

Then, "Oh. Damn her." Something like genuine sympathy flooded into Michelle's tone. "You *are* her type. I know she has a thing for uptight, older women who she'd call her 'church ladies.'"

Ottilie snorted. "I haven't been to church in decades."

"Still." Michelle clucked her tongue. "I'm sorry. I didn't know she'd tried it on you too."

"Well." Ottilie stiffened. "How could you? I told no one outside of a complaint to the board."

Michelle said gently, "I know all too well what Phyllis is like and how much she hates hearing no. Yes, I can get behind some vengeance. What have you got on her for me to give Catherine?"

"I've prepared a document. I'll email it. And I can get the notebooks mentioned as proof by the weekend." Ottilie pressed send on the email she'd already cued up. "Just keep me out of it."

There was a ping, a long pause, then, "Oh dear. It looks like Phyllis will regret the day she pissed you off."

"Indeed." Ottilie said in a tone so chilly it could ice over Vegas.

"Cover up something dirty, people shrug," Michelle mused. "They expect sleaze and corruption of politicians. Do this, though? Steal all your famous homemade recipes from your underpaid cook? Who also happens to be a struggling Black mother of four? Recipes you claim

NUMBER SIX

you spent decades developing yourself? The optics are the worst. This will ruin her political ambitions for life."

"Yes, that's rather the point." Ottilie rubbed her aching neck. "I have arranged with the cook to give her a better job—health care, far superior conditions, and twice the pay—well out of Kensington's reach, in case she attempts retribution. Also, I've paid for a lawyer for the cook so she can sue Kensington for compensation for those stolen recipes. That should be a nice, public court case because I've told him not to settle." Pain gnawed at her again, and she growled softly.

"Are you okay?"

Ottilie froze. "I see that justice warrior of yours is rubbing off on you. Since when do you care about my well-being?"

"You think I'm unfeeling to suffering?" Michelle actually sounded hurt.

"I…apologize," Ottilie said with real regret. "I'm taking my run-in today with that abominable woman out on you."

"*Today*? This happened today? I don't understand."

"No, it didn't just happen. But, yes, I saw Kensington today, and she mocked me for what she tried to do to me and thought adding salt to the wound would be fun."

"She does have a cruel streak. Look, I know it's not my place to say this, but I think you should talk to someone. Otherwise it'll eat you inside. Trust me on that."

"No, thank you," Ottilie said with a shudder. "Therapists like to pathologize everything. I'm not interested in hearing names of all the conditions I may or may not have."

"I don't mean a therapist," Michelle said. "Let me get my safta to call you when she's up from her nap."

"No, don't bother her. I'm sure Hannah has far better things to do than hear about this."

"She's really good at this particular topic," Michelle said quietly. "Trust me on this."

"You…told her about Kensington?" Ottilie was stunned. "Your… personal involvement?"

"No. But there were other…difficult work things. In the past. She was incredibly understanding."

"That FBI business, you mean? When you were undercover with the domestic terrorist?"

"You knew about that?" Horror sharpened her tone. "Did everyone at The Fixers know?"

"No, no. Just the board. They wanted to know why you'd left the Bureau when you were applying for a job with The Fixers. Number Three, as FBI director back then, informed the board of what had taken place." Ottilie paused. "A most unsavory business. I'm sorry you had to go through it. It should never have happened."

Michelle hissed in a breath.

"Michelle, I apologize for even bringing it up. That was thoughtless. I'm feeling a little…out of sorts."

"I understand why, given Kensington's behavior," Michelle said, her voice tight. "And to answer your question: how did it feel? Dehumanizing. Both Kensington and the domestic terrorist. Is it ancient history? Yes. I've talked about the worst of it. I'm feeling… better. So listen to me when I say this: find someone to talk to who understands, even if it's not Hannah."

"Perhaps." Ottilie had no interest in involving an elderly woman with her own struggles. It was weak. Ottilie wasn't weak.

Ottilie said her goodbyes, hung up, and then threw down the phone. No, she wouldn't unburden herself on anyone. She would simply…endure.

Her neck sent a new claw of pain through her. Apparently, endurance was her forte.

Chapter 9

Confessions on a Balcony

That night, Ottilie settled onto the wide resin wicker chair on her balcony and leaned back, closing her eyes. She let out an involuntary shudder of distaste at her day.

With her eyes closed, her brain focused on the distant street noises six floors below. Occasional honks came from crawling cars along The Strip, music blaring from both vehicles and the entertainment venues competing to lure in customers. Sometimes a drunken, angry shout sounded, but more often it was laughter and ribaldry. It was a city of dreams, after all.

"Tired, darling?" came a voice disconcertingly close.

Ottilie snapped her eyes open and climbed to her feet. Peering over the shoulder-high frosted-glass divider into the adjacent balcony, Ottilie spotted Monique in a lounge chair, partially hidden by a fake palm, serenely sipping a cocktail.

"Sorry, I didn't mean to disturb you," Monique said with a charming smile. "But you are rather luscious."

Luscious. The word reminded her of Kensington's unwanted attention, and it curdled Ottilie's stomach again. "Can you just…not?" she said, exhaustion washing over her. "I'm not in the mood for your compliments." She returned to her seat in annoyance.

Hidden once more, Monique was still easily heard. "How so?"

Ottilie frowned. "Just when I think I might like you, you start your flirting routine. Can't you ever have a normal conversation? Does it have to always devolve into overfamiliarity?"

"I apologize." Monique said, sounding sincere. "Is everything okay?"

How on earth could she sum up a day like today? Phyllis Kensington did a tedious lap of her brain, and Ottilie resented her all over again. She'd locked her away long ago, slammed her behind some large mental walls, and now she couldn't get the obnoxious creature out of her head.

"I'm just dealing with an appalling person I'm determined I'll never see again."

"Ah. One of those."

It sounded as if she could relate. Had she endured some clients who weren't easy to control? Or, worse, who didn't like taking no for an answer? She probably did in her line of work. Ottilie felt irritated all over again at Kensington and those of her ilk.

"How do you deal with people who give you indigestion?" Ottilie asked after a few moments, staring resentfully into the night sky. "People you just cannot abide and who insert themselves into your space regardless?"

"I call Security," Monique said lightly. "And I make sure I never deal with them again. Gone."

Ottilie hesitated. "Do they leave your head so easily too?"

"Has something happened?" Monique sounded truly concerned now.

She drew in a breath. Perhaps, of everyone, Monique would understand. Except Ottilie didn't share. Anything. Ever. First rule of the spy game they'd drilled into her as a trainee was to keep your mouth shut. But even before that, her diplomat mother had warned her of the dangers of loose lips.

"Share only what you must to lubricate a discussion and draw others out," she'd warned her often enough. "No more. No less."

Such lessons had made making friends as a child difficult.

The silence dragged on too long because Monique finally said: "You don't have to tell me. I promise I'm not prying. No judgment. But if you wanted to vent, I'm someone who has heard just about everything."

She probably had.

NUMBER SIX

Ottilie warred with herself. It wasn't as if Monique Carson was anyone in her life. In a few days, Ottilie would leave Vegas, never seeing her again. A stranger with a few of Ottilie's low-tier secrets was not someone who could harm her. Monique didn't know who Ottilie was, where she'd worked, or even her last name.

"I am exceptional at compartmentalizing," Ottilie suddenly said. "It has kept me able to do work others would likely fail at."

Monique said warmly, "I'd believe it."

Ignoring the praise, Ottilie pushed on. "Today I dealt with someone from my past who is not a good person."

She almost snorted at the ludicrousness of that. *Who* in Ottilie's working life had ever actually been good? She recalled Michelle once asking her if they had any cases that were actually good and Ottilie had choked. One did not engage The Fixers if they wanted "good" done. One engaged The Fixers if they wanted to pay to further their name, power, success, money, or entitlement.

The only decent human who had ever darkened their headquarters had been a crusading employee, Eden Lawless, who'd swiftly left again after coming to the blinding realization she was far too good for their immoral little cesspit.

Monique asked, "And this not-good person bothered you today?"

"Correct. And I'm unaccustomed to not being able to push someone annoying aside as beneath my notice."

"Because you're 'good at compartmentalizing.' Ordinarily." Understanding filled Monique's voice.

"Yes. It's rare someone gets under my skin and stays there. It's… disconcerting. And the stress of it all has my neck aching again." Ottilie stopped in irritation at herself. "That wasn't a hint, by the way," she said hastily.

"Oh, I know. But if you'd like another neck massage, you have only to ask. I'd be happy to help. Sounds like you need one after your day." Then, "No strings attached. No requirements for breakfasts or anything else. I'm just being neighborly."

Memories of how blissful the last one was filled Ottilie. "Honestly," she said, tone heartfelt, "I'd love that."

"Come around to my door. Meet you there."

Ottilie was melting into Monique's warm, teasing fingers, into a space without pain, and it was bliss. Her body was lighting up along the edges of her touch, and Ottilie was all but purring.

"How are you so good at that?" she murmured.

"Practice. And care. Remember? We had that discussion."

Ottilie remembered. But she'd also forgotten just how good Monique could make her feel. "I could get addicted to this."

"Then I'm doing it right." Monique's fingers were working Ottilie's shoulders now.

Ottilie's head lolled forward. "I'm very grateful."

"You don't have to say that," Monique assured her. "You don't have to say anything. But if you do want to talk to me, I promise anything you share would die with me." Monique's fingers never stopped their gentle stroking.

"There's not much to tell," Ottilie said. "My irritant, for want of a better word, simply reminded me of an incident between us a year or so prior which I greatly detested."

"An incident you buried away because you compartmentalize," Monique guessed. "And your irritant unburied it today."

"Yes." She paused. "I cannot work out why I'm so bothered," Ottilie admitted, "by the…unburying."

"No one likes old wounds being scraped over, Ottilie," Monique murmured, sliding her fingers over Ottilie's scalp. It felt incredible. "Not even you are that impressive to be unbothered by it."

That was true, unfortunately. Ottilie appreciated how Monique didn't push her for more details. "And yet I'm disconcerted. The issue that was raised…" she inhaled, unsure whether to say it. Michelle's warning to talk about it circled her brain.

On the one hand, she never usually shared anything of importance. On the other, she'd tortured herself enough over freezing when Kensington had shocked her that night. She didn't want to go through the self-recriminations again.

Later, she'd invested far too much time and energy on all the things "she should have done". Not just regarding Kensington, but when Ottilie had taken it to the board. Twice.

The first time—the sexual harassment complaint—the four men had shrugged. One, with arousal tinging his voice, had asked if he could watch the video. Ottilie had glowered at him until he'd withdrawn the request.

Then they'd told her there was no one who could replace Kensington, nor did they want to replace her, and since Ottilie had turned down Kensington's *request* with venom, they considered the matter dealt with and closed.

But the board's response to her second complaint—the bullying—involved them telling Ottilie that managing "difficult personalities" was part of her job. That stung. They actually had the audacity to look bored. That had been almost as galling as Kensington's transgressions.

Monique swirled her fingers all over the back of Ottilie's head.

Ottilie finally said, "The issue causing me difficulty is regarding consent."

The magic fingers stopped. Monique's tone became tight when she said, "Consent? As in lack of it?"

"Yes." She suddenly worried about where Monique's mind had leapt to. "I don't mean..." Ottilie exhaled. "It was about crossing lines not consented to. I was able to remove myself. But today, she enjoyed rubbing my nose in it, reminding me of what she did back then."

"She? Your irritant is a woman?" Surprise filled Monique's voice.

"It's partly why I didn't anticipate her attack. Foolish, I realize now. Especially since I already knew she'd done this before to another woman. I just didn't think she'd notice me. No one does—which is intentional." It had been a fair assumption Kensington would overlook her too.

"Oh, Ottilie." Sympathy filled Monique's voice, and she resumed stroking her neck.

"At the time, I was so shocked, I didn't do much but get out of her way."

"And now you've been second-guessing yourself over how you handled it? Along with feeling…shame? Embarrassment? Self-blame, perhaps?"

"Yes," Ottilie admitted quietly.

"And then you locked these emotions all away and felt the incident was dealt with. Until today, when this woman reappeared and shattered your equilibrium?" Monique asked in a kind voice.

"*Shattered* is a strong word…" Ottilie frowned, hating the taste of it. She was not some pathetic victim curled up in the corner. Never that.

"Unbalanced it, then?"

Unbalanced. That would do. "Yes."

"And seeing her again brought back all these emotions despite the fact you're good at compartmentalization. This astonishes you. Perhaps you think your mind has given it more weight than it deserves?"

"That is…accurate." Ottilie hesitated before continuing. "Years ago, something much more frightening happened to me in the line of work. I was a children's tutor in a foreign country. Political events overtook me, and I found myself imprisoned for a few months until I determined a way to attain my freedom and that of my companions. That event, in every way, shape and form, was worse. Far worse."

It had been years since she'd thought of being taken hostage in Beirut.

"That sounds terrifying." Monique's hands came to cup her shoulders. Her fingers clenched.

"My point is not that it happened but that the recent event involving my…irritant…bothers me *more!* How can that be? That's the source of my confusion. This recent incident was so insignificant compared to the one when I was twenty-four. That's what's so galling. It was just…unwanted groping in the office." She scoffed. "Disgusting remarks. And witnessing self-gratification that I didn't consent to. In Beirut, though, I was…" She faded out. Ottilie hadn't intended to reveal where it had occurred.

"Beirut?" Monique drew in a tight breath.

"Where it happened is irrelevant."

"Why do I get the feeling there's a lot more to that story?"

"Politics can be volatile, and innocent people often get caught up in it. The where isn't the point."

"Darling"—Monique's hands slowly resumed their massage—"I do know when someone's skipping all around the truth. But I accept your need for your secrets. So, back to the topic: why Beirut affects you less emotionally than your office harasser? Would you like to know what I think?"

"I would." Ottilie pursed her lips and waited.

Monique's fingers made slick scribbles up her neck. "The issue isn't about degree of severity. You're focused on the wrong thing. It's about power."

"Power?"

"In the most recent event, you had none. You hated that. Even if the irritant retreated, even if she'd done 'nothing much' to you, you still had a moment of feeling vulnerable and helpless. Powerless."

Ottilie shut her eyes, detesting that memory.

"You're not used to feeling powerless, I think. I'd guess that your whole identity is about being in control at all times. Back in Beirut, although you were a captive, it sounds as though you took the initiative and freed yourself."

Her fingers traced a small scar at the base of Ottilie's neck. "*You* decided how to handle the situation, and *you* enacted a solution. You had the power. The more recent incident, though—no power. You felt utterly without control."

The impact of the words slammed into Ottilie. That made complete sense.

"And today you saw this woman again, the one who made you feel helpless, and it all came rushing back. You probably had a flashback to how vulnerable you felt, compartmentalizing be damned."

Eyes springing open, she ground out a "yes."

"And now you feel disappointed in yourself for experiencing it again?"

Ottilie's shame bubbled up once more. "I feel I acted with…weakness then. But not even being able to push away that feeling now? It's…" *Absurd. Risible!* "Unexpected."

"It's understandable. I've had one or two clients whom I get flashes of at unexpected times. Clients who think my rules are mere guidelines and try to cross my boundaries. Toxic people can play on your mind for a long time if you let them. Just today I had a client who thought, because of who she was, her status and her wealth, I'd just roll over and take whatever she demanded. That's somewhat acceptable if you're still respectful of your partner. She wasn't. Disturbing woman."

Ottilie's heart clenched at that. "It seems we both had entitled people to contend with today. I'm sorry you went through something awful too."

"It's fine. I can snap pretty much anyone back into line with a sharp warning."

"But not all," Ottilie noted.

"No, not all," Monique said with a sigh, "Three times in my career things have gotten out of my control. It's a deeply unsettling feeling."

"How did you handle it?"

Monique stepped away from Ottilie's back, signaling she was done, and wiped her hands on a towel. "Don't move." She fetched a towel and wiped the oil at the base of Ottilie's neck, then continued talking. "As I said earlier, I called Security and let them deal with it. They did—efficiently. I'm a valued guest, after all."

"You would be if you've been here fourteen years. They must love you, even if hotel management doesn't know what you do exactly." Ottilie did up her blouse's top buttons.

"Oh, they probably know. Women like me are in hotels all over the world. The smart managers treat us as businesswomen and look the other way. If we don't bring them problems, they don't make them for us."

"It's good the management here is pragmatic, then," Ottilie said. "I don't imagine they all are."

"No, not all are." Monique paused, thinking. "Although a new CEO recently took over the hotel chain, and he's here in Duxton Vegas now, overseeing a staffing crisis. I have no idea how accommodating he'd be to me. I hate having a lack of certainty."

"It would be unsettling," Ottilie murmured. "I also hate uncertainty."

Monique came to sit on the bed facing Ottilie's chair and smiled. "Look at us finding common ground. Anyway, back to our topic at hand. On consent issues, when lines are crossed, I always feel disconcerted. As if I should have handled it differently. But…" She met Ottilie's eye. "It doesn't mean what happened was my fault. It never means that."

"I don't feel responsible for what happened. More…unprepared. And angry that she felt it was her right to take what she wanted because she saw me as her underling. An…inferior."

"She saw you as inferior?" Monique's eyebrows lifted. "*You?*"

"People see what they expect to see," Ottilie answered cryptically. "She is an arrogant, entitled woman who hides her true nature well. The board did nothing when I complained."

"That's appalling. Why wouldn't they act?"

"Because…" Ottilie sighed. "She was the company CEO."

Monique hissed in a breath. "I'm not shocked, I suppose. By the CEO or the board. Power does strange things to people. It doesn't make them insensitive or sexual predators, of course, but it does make them feel invincible. So, whatever their foibles are, they feel freer to indulge."

"Yes," Ottilie said. "I believe that's true for many with power. I never succumbed to that weakness, but others are less evolved."

Silence chilled the room. And then Ottilie realized her mistake. "Not that I'm powerful," she added quickly. "How could I be, if I found myself in that situation? Treated as the inferior?"

It was too late, though. Monique was studying her with far too much awareness. "Oh, but you are, aren't you?" She sounded intrigued for a moment, and then her expression fell. "Was that what made it worse? You were powerful in your own right, and someone even more powerful took advantage? Any one of us can be made to feel small and powerless in certain circumstances. I know I've felt that. It's a disturbing feeling."

"You?" Ottilie couldn't picture it. Monique radiated confidence and strength.

"Everyone," Monique said. "Yes, even me."

"I…suppose."

"By the way, I know a therapist who specializes in clients who've gone through harassment or sexual assault. Several women in my line of work swear by her. I could give you her card?"

"Not necessary, thanks. I think I'll be more at ease now that I've initiated some payback. She won't underestimate me again."

Monique tilted her head. "Good for you. Now, if only I could hire you to take care of the annoying senator who ruined my day earlier."

Ottilie froze. "Excuse me?"

Regarding her in confusion, Monique asked, "What?"

"Which senator?"

"You know I can't tell you that. And I've had too many tequilas to drown my sorrows or I wouldn't have even let slip her profession." She smiled, or started to, then stopped. "Why have you gone so pale?"

Ottilie didn't speak. *What were the odds?*

"Oh hell." Monique pursed her lips. "You think we both dealt with the same woman? No, there are many senators in this world."

"*Senators* who happen to be in *Vegas* now, who are also *female*, entitled, and who prefer sex with *other women* are not plentiful."

"It would be a short list, yes, but not necessarily a list of one," Monique tried.

A very short list indeed. "By any chance does your senator profess to cook? Is with the Republican Party? And is actually a *former* senator?"

Monique's expression became pinched.

Identity confirmed. "How often?" Ottilie hoped she wasn't a regular because…just…*no*.

"I can't answer that." Because that would confirm Kensington *was* a client.

Monique went still for a moment and then huffed. "Just the once." She sighed. "There was something off about her. She tried to ignore my rules, and multiple times, I had to warn her. In the end, she stormed out. Won't miss her."

"I'm sorry you had to deal with Phyllis Kensington in a bad mood. She's unpleasant."

Monique nodded. "Agreed. But that's on her."

"Still, it must be hard, dealing with clients you wouldn't choose to be around, with or without the intimacy."

"It doesn't happen often. In fact, it's quite unusual." Monique's lips quirked. "I can usually see the beauty in every woman."

"How interesting." Ottilie hesitated. "I don't see beauty in anyone."

"What do you mean?" Interest flared in Monique's eyes.

"I'm only attracted to someone I find intelligent. I simply don't see them as attractive otherwise."

"How does that work, though? You can't know someone's intelligent until they engage with you. That must mean everyone in passing is unattractive to you?"

"More like...they are bland to me. For instance, meeting Cleo's dancers? I understand society thinks they're beautiful; I just don't see it. They all looked to me to be tall, athletic, and symmetrical. With nice hair."

Monique laughed. "Symmetrical! Oh God, I've got to tell Cleo that."

"I'm not sure how to explain better except to say that very few people spark my intellectual curiosity. And those who do..." She pondered Hannah for a moment. "I actually feel protective of them. Because they're rare to me. Special."

"And *then* do you find them attractive?"

"Yes." She did think of Hannah as attractive, for instance, as well as her granddaughter, Michelle. There was no denying their intellect. "But just finding someone intelligent, and therefore attractive, doesn't mean anything. Who wants to be with every attractive person they meet? To me, good looks would be just another facet of who they are. Like their height, ethnicity, skills, and personality. That's all it is to me."

"How fascinating. I've heard about people who are like this—sapiosexuals? You're the first I've met."

"I hate that word. It makes me sound like an exotic species of lizard or something. Why do we have to label everything?"

Monique laughed. "Okay, I won't use it. So, when did you first realize you viewed the world differently than most other people?"

Thinking back, Ottilie stopped in her teenage years. "When I was at a party once, I was with two girls from high school I didn't know very well and a boy we'd just met. I didn't find any of them attractive. Then, one of the girls, Hope, started telling me in incredible depth about her science project. The more she spoke, the more I realized she was *very* good-looking."

"Go on."

"At the end of the evening, after Hope and the boy had left, I apologized to the second girl for ignoring her. She said she didn't mind because it gave her a lot of time with the boy. She declared him *gorgeous*; I hadn't even noticed." Ottilie drew in a breath. "Then she said it was *so nice* of me to spend all that time with Hope, given she was so boring and plain; everyone thought so. I realized then that I saw her as beautiful. It came as a shock to realize how out of step I was with everyone else."

Monique sat back. "Amazing. And that's not 'out of step,' Ottilie, it's unique. I love discovering diversity in sexuality and attraction. I'm at the opposite end of the spectrum from you. I can see beauty in so many aspects of a woman's form. But you only see beauty as an afterthought, and only if they're smart."

"Yes. I do see their talents and abilities, of course; it's just that I'm blind to their looks. But in that sense, are we so different? I can find beauty in the plainest of people, whom society dismisses as ugly, and you can too?"

Monique laughed. "That's a different way of looking at it." She shot her a mischievous look. "Dare I ask whether you find me attractive?"

"Too soon to say," Ottilie said lightly. "I have, however, upgraded you from tedious, which is where I place the vast majority of people, so there's hope." She couldn't hide her lips twitching.

"I see." Monique grinned. "Please let me know immediately if you are suddenly aware of my devastating beauty."

"In that event, I'm sure you'll be overcome with joy," Ottilie drawled.

"Oh, but I will be. You are an impressive woman, Ottilie."

"And you're starting to look smarter by the second," Ottilie teased.

NUMBER SIX

"And, therefore, more attractive." Monique smiled sweetly. "Have I mentioned that I love how clever you are and how observant? It's like meeting myself."

"Oh, I'm not sure you're *that* clever," Ottilie shot back. "Anyway, I think your interest in me is more because I'm a challenge. Unraveling me is a game to you."

Monique studied her for a long moment. "No, Ottilie. I'm enjoying getting to know *you*. It's not just for fun. I've truly never met anyone like you in my life, and I've met a lot of people."

"Cleo said something today about how you sent me to her. That you wanted her opinion on me. Is that true?"

With a sheepish look, Monique admitted, "Perhaps."

"That's a yes, then."

"I just wondered if she found you as interesting as I did. I wanted to know if it was all in my head how fascinating you seem to be."

"And?"

"It turns out you greatly impressed her with your deductive reasoning and character profiling."

Ottilie regarded her. "I found out something about *you* today. You don't have any friends aside from Cleo."

"No."

"Why?"

"We all have our secrets, Ottilie." She smiled, but it didn't reach her eyes. "Ask me something else."

Ottilie could hardly object to that. "Why did you never tell me you were in investments?"

"Who says I am?"

"Cleo's dancers. They're enthusiastic groupies."

"Ah." Monique's expression settled. "Well, yes, I'm CEO of an investment company. Semi-retired now as I'm slowly training my replacement, but I still retain the title and the power. And, because I remember what it was like being young and foolish and awash in money, I personally set up share portfolios for Cleo's dancers."

"Were you a dancer once too?"

"Me? Never." Monique laughed. "No, I was studying finance at college when a talent scout discovered me. I wound up doing runway modeling in Europe for a few years. I noticed how little financial advice the girls got. I helped out one or two, and then word got around that I was the one to go to for those who wanted investment advice. I was so good at it that I set up my own company. My model agency boss even invested with me—and also fired me for not being focused enough on modeling."

"Oh dear."

"No, it was fair; I wasn't. By then, I was fascinated by the whole process of turning something small into something big but, more than that, being the one to correctly predict market trends. But I wanted to do everything ethically."

"That's different."

"It was in those days. When I was back in the US, my first clients were all models and friends of models I'd helped earlier. I met Cleo and her dancers when I was in Vegas for a convention, and I helped them out too. I stayed because I loved the energy of the city. And I was also madly in love with Cleo." Her eyes crinkled. "Anyway, having a niche—in my case, ethical investing—allowed me to thrive."

Ottilie's brain shifted a few facts around. "Ethical investing." She shook her head slowly as the penny dropped. "You're..." Ottilie stopped. "Carson Investments is the world's largest ethical investment company. Are you saying Carson Investments is you? You're *that* Carson?"

Monique smiled. "Pleased to meet you."

"Why do you do sex work when you don't have to?" Ottilie gasped out.

With a sigh, as if this was the thousandth time she'd heard the question, Monique said, "Because I enjoy showing women how to love their bodies. I have a skill for it, and that is fulfilling. Seeing women open up like a flower. Watching the wonder on a woman's face having her first orgasm? Or a seventy-year-old having another orgasm after so long without? If you love your work, why stop?"

"Do you love finance too?"

"Yes. In a different way. On that note, I also would appreciate you not sharing both of my professions with anyone. I'm not ashamed of anything I do, but I like to keep things delineated as best I can." Monique waved at her. "You're now one of only a tiny group who know

NUMBER SIX

of both my jobs. Cleo's dancers know only that I'm in investment. You, up until now, knew only that I was a sex fantasies expert. I prefer that few people know both."

"In case your shareholders get twitchy about a sex worker being the CEO of Carson Investments?"

"I employ so many people. I'd hate to have to downsize my business because a lot of clients bailed on moral grounds."

"Would they, though?" Ottilie asked. "Surely people tend to follow the money, regardless of who's handing it out."

"Usually true. But remember, I'm the head of an ethical investment firm? My clients tend to have very firm views on what's right and wrong and good and bad, and I'm pretty sure a lot of them put *sex worker* in the naughty category. Not even in the good-naughty category."

"I understand. I won't tell a soul."

"Yes, I suspect you're very good at keeping secrets."

Ottilie merely smiled.

"So how does someone like you wind up in Vegas, of all places?" Monique asked. "And how do you know so much about identifying sociopaths hiding amidst dancers?"

"I'm observant."

"You're far more than that."

Ottilie regarded her. "What are you really asking me?"

"I just… I can't believe you're a mere personal assistant. There's so much more to you. I can feel it."

"And I can't believe you're the CEO of one of the top investment companies in the world. It's hard to reconcile."

"Because I'm such a sex-focused soul?" Monique's eyes twinkled.

"Actually, yes."

"Can't picture me with cute nerd glasses perched on the edge of my nose as I go over a spreadsheet?" she asked, lips curling.

"Well, *now* I can." Ottilie wondered what she was supposed to do with that image. She smiled back in spite of herself.

"Flirt." Monique's own smile became wide. "I'll take it, though."

Ottilie blinked. "I'm quite sure no one's ever accused me of flirting in my life."

"Not even your boyfriends? Or is it girlfriends?" she asked innocently.

Ottilie waved that fishing expedition away.

"I'm honored to be flirted with, in any event," Monique murmured. "Now, it's been a long, exhausting day for us both. I'd love to continue this conversation at a later date."

Taking the hint, Ottilie rose. "Thank you for the massage. My neck feels much better."

"I'm glad. And I very much enjoy talking to you, Ottilie." Monique walked her to the door. "I hope to see you again soon."

I'd like that, Ottilie almost said without thinking. She mentally stopped and rewound and realized she truly meant it.

How…unexpected.

Chapter 10
Toast and Gratitude

The next morning, Monique rose at her usual time—dawn—and checked the international stock markets, satisfied herself that her company was holding steady. She completed a short but concentrated workout in the hotel gym, and then returned for an indulgent, long shower.

After donning her hotel-issue white robe, she went to sit on her balcony with her black coffee and bowl of granola. (One could never underestimate the power of good fiber.)

What she found, taped to her side of the frosted-glass divider, was a note. Even if Ottilie wasn't the only person who could have placed it there, Monique would have guessed anyway from the exacting penmanship.

Good morning. I did not wish to wake you with a text message in case you like to sleep in. But when you are awake, would you consider joining me for breakfast? Just knock, if so.

Of course she would agree. Ottilie was about the most interesting person in her life right now and never ceased to surprise her. With her bowl and coffee mug, she sauntered next door, knocking with her elbow.

Ottilie answered after a few moments, took one look at her in her robe and slippers—which was quite literally all Monique wore—and merely hiked an eyebrow. "Come in. I was just making some toast."

Today Ottilie wore a deep crimson dress with three-quarter sleeves and a hint of bust. It hugged her fuller form in delicious ways.

As Monique passed the open door to Ottilie's bathroom, she spied a vast array of creams and anti-aging concoctions. Was this Ottilie's secret to her younger looks? For someone who talked of retirement often, she hardly looked close to it.

Ottilie led her through to the main room.

How neatly everything was laid out. A small pile of books and papers were perfectly aligned on a coffee table.

"This is like a display room," Monique said, impressed. The bed was crisply made, hospital corners and all, even though it was well before Housekeeping was due. "Are you sure you're even staying here?"

"I like things ordered," Ottilie said, tone brisk.

"There is no duvet on your bed." She glanced around and spotted it folded in one corner.

"If you ever want to lose your lunch, look at one under a UV light. They're filthy things, stained with fluids, that never get washed enough. Even in the world's best hotels, it's always the same."

"Do you often examine things under a UV light, darling?" Monique asked in surprise.

Ottilie regarded her evenly. "No comment." She smiled. "Can I get you anything?"

"No thanks," Monique said. "I brought my breakfast. I'm all set."

"Make yourself at home on the balcony. I'll join you shortly."

Actually, Monique would have dearly loved to linger inside and see what the papers and books were that had Ottilie's attention but instead headed for the balcony.

She settled in the resin wicker chair and resumed working her way through her granola as she enjoyed the view.

The sight today was startling blue skies in the upper atmosphere, with a cream dusty haze closer to the city, creating a soft-focus effect at odds with the garish burst of vibrant colors below.

NUMBER SIX

MGM's enormous amber letters were directly in her eyeline. To the right and below, the swirling top tip of the Big Apple Coaster from the New York-New York Hotel & Casino begged for attention. Mercifully the red metal beast was closed this early.

Between the towering shards of buildings lay one incongruous flat spot: Harry Reid International Airport. Beyond the tail fins of a handful of jets squatted the most organic presence in Las Vegas. The McCullough Range's purplish-brown ridges and dips framed the whole horizon. Stout and wide, it brought to mind an impassive sumo wrestler, solid arms folded.

Dropping her gaze to the streets below, Monique picked out the 100-foot-tall biggest Coke bottle on earth—part of the Coca-Cola Vegas store. It was a fabulously gaudy tribute to humanity's excesses. Its juxtaposition against such a majestic natural mountain range was probably the most Vegas thing in existence. It made her smile.

From the first day, Monique had appreciated all of Vegas, every weird, absurd, colorful bit of nonsense, banality, and wonder. There was such a diversity of bizarreness to be found just by looking out the window. It was the very opposite of staid and the life she'd originally had planned for herself. Monique was quite sure that it was a big part of Vegas's appeal. That and the welcoming family of dancers she'd found.

Ottilie joined her, sitting in the adjacent seat with altogether too much grace for so early in the morning. She placed two slices of toast lavished in honey before herself. A tea was slid next to the plate.

"It's a lovely day," Monique said casually. "Well, for Vegas."

"For Vegas," Ottilie agreed. "The day I arrived, I was tossing up which was worse: Vegas or Beirut. Vegas was edging slightly ahead."

"With anyone else, that'd be a joke. With you? I'm sensing not so much."

"I assure you it wasn't a joke."

"I believe you." Monique shook her head. "I never know what's next with you. Like, inviting me to breakfast? This is a lovely surprise."

Ottilie took a sip of her tea. "I found myself, this morning, feeling...grateful. For your insights into various topics last night."

"It's no problem. I hope I gave you some peace of mind."

"You did. It occurred to me I could thank you."

"By sharing breakfast with me?"

"Yes. It was what you asked of me as payment for my first neck massage. And it seems to be something you need: social interaction. You say you don't have friends aside from Cleo, but I think you crave company nonetheless. This seemed something small I could offer back: breakfast with you, each day, until I leave. If you'd like it."

"I would love that," Monique said sincerely. She turned over Ottilie's choice of words, *you crave company*. That made her sound… desperate?

Ottilie frowned, gaze flicking across Monique's face. "Have I caused offense? I assure you my company is optional," she said lightly.

"I'm wondering about your view that I crave company. Given my job, all I have all day, every day, is company."

"That's different. It's business. You need to talk to people who don't pay to spend time with you."

Monique eyed her in surprise. It was accurate. Then again, Ottilie's astuteness about people rivaled only her own.

"I notice things," Ottilie said, reading her mind.

"You do. I appreciate that about you." For once, she left the teasing tone out.

Ottilie's gaze swept her face, assessing, and her expression shifted to what looked like faint approval.

So, she liked honest compliments, not flirty ones. Monique filed that away. She'd already gathered that was the case after the start to the previous evening's conversation: *Just when I think I might like you, you start your flirting routine.*

Monique was developing a rather intricate mental list of Ottilie's preferences. She chose not to examine what that meant.

"May I ask a personal question?" Ottilie asked.

Shaken out of her musings, Monique glanced at her over her coffee. "Go ahead."

"Why does a people person like you have no friends? Isn't that unusual? Even I, despite being quite content in my own company, have a friend or two at any given time."

NUMBER SIX

"Me and friendships," Monique said, exhaling. "It's a long and sad story. I wouldn't want to bring down the mood." She forced her lips to curl to show she wasn't burdened too much by the question. "I'd much rather hear about you."

"And I'd rather hear about you," Ottilie countered, meeting her eyes. "Well. We seem to be at an impasse." She smiled, and it was a smile Monique had never seen before: warm and genuine, soft and almost sweet. How breathtaking it made Ottilie.

Her heart did a tight little clench of approval.

Oh no. This was not a wise route to take. And yet she couldn't stop the words that fell out of her mouth next.

"I have an idea," Monique said. "One of the massage therapists at Wynn Resort owes me a favor. I could get us in this morning for one of her pamper spa treatments. I'm thinking the Nalu Body Ritual. It's this gorgeously relaxing Polynesian fusion massage with body exfoliation, and coconut oil scalp treatment."

Ottilie blinked at her. "Excuse me?"

"Or the scalp treatment alone, if you prefer? Hair, neck, and skin revitalization. It's the most divine luxury spa. You'll think you're in Paris. You'll waft out feeling years younger."

Carefully, *too* carefully, Ottilie said, "You think I need to look years younger?"

Monique laughed. "Darling, you are perfection as you are. But if you like *my* massages, these are even better. For luxurious treatments, the Nalu is one of the best in the world."

"You saw my bathroom counter, didn't you?" Ottilie said dryly. "The anti-aging creams? I admit that's my secret vice."

"We all have vices," Monique said with a small shrug. "So, my treat?"

"It sounds expensive. I can't ask you to pay."

"We'll each pay our own way, then. But you'll come?"

"I admit it sounds…interesting." Ottilie then paused. "This isn't a date."

"Perish the thought." Monique smiled at her consternation. "I'll call my associate and book us."

It might not have been a date, but it felt as intimate as one, Monique thought idly as she leaned back in the spa's deck chair beside Ottilie. The post-massage recovery area—it probably had a far fancier name, something French—was divine.

Off-white chaise lounges dotted an elegant room stenciled with intricate cream-colored tree branches on the lavender walls. They were the only two people in the beautiful space, and Monique would have felt warm and sleepy if not for the intoxicating sight beside her.

Ottilie looked as relaxed as Monique had ever seen her, in a matching white waffle-weave robe that revealed an appealing amount of cleavage.

Monique took a moment to appreciate the swell of her breasts and her pale legs leading to slippers (more waffle-weave white).

Although her eyes were closed, Ottilie murmured, "Enjoying the view?"

"How did you know, darling?" Monique said with a laugh.

"I hazarded a guess, given it's you."

"Impressive you know me *so* well. Especially since it's only been four days."

Ottilie opened her eyes and gave her a knowing look. "You're not as much of a mystery as you like to think you are." She closed her eyes again. "Although I still don't know why you don't have friends."

"That." Monique waved a hand. "A sorry little tale buried in my past. Besides, I have Cleo and her wife to socialize with if I ever want to do the intensive friendship experience. And there's one or two of my clients I'm fond enough of that I'd almost file them in the friends category."

"Cleo has a wife?" Ottilie's eyes opened again, and she tilted her head. "Is it Sahara?"

Monique chuckled. "God no. They'd kill each other in a day. They're too similar. You wouldn't have met Rochelle. She's a doctor."

"Opposites attract," Ottilie said. "*Interesting.* I've found that to be true quite often."

"From personal experience?" Monique asked, unable to resist.

"From observation. I worked with a CEO once who was as walled off as they come. Yet she fell apart around a professional protester who had a thousand causes, from saving whales to fighting unrecyclable coffee pods. She used the word *goddess* in place of *God* unironically. I've never met anyone like that sweet summer child."

"Your CEO apparently hadn't either." Monique said, amused.

"No. They had a brief round of World War III that shook everyone to the rafters. It didn't stick. The war, I mean. The love story prevails."

"Ahh." Monique smiled. "New love. You have to appreciate a happy ending."

"Ordinarily, I think happy endings are so absurdly optimistic. But those two? Well. I'm pleased it's worked out." Ottilie's eyes brightened for a moment. "Sometimes I allow myself a tiny conceit that I may have helped them a little. I pointed out their attraction to each other. They were so oblivious of the other one's feelings, and so aghast that their 'secret' crush was patently clear to me."

"And now they're happy together."

Ottilie's smile became serene. "Some endings are inevitable. In hindsight."

"So, what of you?" Monique asked. "Do you not seek a happy ending for yourself?"

"My dating pool has always been incredibly limited on account of my brain's eccentric views on attractiveness."

"That would be a problem."

"Only if I see it as one," Ottilie said lightly. "The main advantage is I was able to advance far in my career by not being distracted by messy relationships."

"You didn't date, then?"

"Not often. I doubt I've missed much."

"You remind me of an asexual employee of mine. Ben has little interest in dating or sex. He was so work focused, he became my youngest fund manager."

"Who said I have little interest in sex?" Ottilie peered at her. "Not doing a thing doesn't mean not liking it. It's more a matter of priorities for me. I put my career first when I discovered that finding romantic partners whom I'm genuinely interested in was too difficult. I am *not* asexual."

"Apologies, darling. I didn't mean to say the wrong thing."

"No apologies necessary. Asexuality is a perfectly fine state of being, but it's just not who I am. And I prefer precision in all things."

"Well, speaking of precision, I can't help but noticing every time you talk about romantic partners, you never say *men*. It's always *people*. I find that vagueness to be…interesting."

"Are you always this nosy?" Ottilie sounded mildly peeved.

"Always, darling."

A few moments passed. "I have dated men," Ottilie said finally. "A dreary exercise all told if you remove the lively conversation. Nothing else was enjoyable. They were useless in bed. I have dated one woman. She was…" Ottilie bit her lip as if in thought.

"She was what?" Monique asked, her curiosity abounding. "Let me guess. She was a revelation?"

"She was a disappointment too. Although not in the same way as the men. She was dating me for other reasons, I suspect."

"Other reasons?" Monique stared at her. "What do you mean?"

"I'm not entirely convinced she was interested in *me*. We met at an Indian embassy party. I saw this young woman, a waitress. Quick-witted and amusing, devastating in both intelligence and looks. I was immediately taken with her. Over the course of the evening, we talked for hours between her duties, and she agreed to a date. It was the first of many. Six weeks later, my boss called me in and showed me a photo of us talking at that function. He wanted to know what I'd discussed that night with one of India's top security assets."

"Assets? As in…a spy?"

"An…embassy employee. Officially." Ottilie supplied a rueful look. "I wasn't about to tell him that since then, we'd done considerably more together than debate the spices in the samosas. Anyway, while I didn't blame her for not telling me her real identity—she couldn't—I also wasn't sure if she was interested in me or in something I was working on. She swore she'd been there to keep an eye on someone else at that party. I wanted to trust her, but I couldn't. I broke up with her."

"Oh." Monique's heart went out to her. "That's awful."

"Well, it wasn't exactly uncommon where I used to work. She understood. And that was decades ago now. I didn't take it personally; it just made me sad. Not to mention, wary in the future. Far more cautious."

It sounded like a special-op…spies dating spies, perhaps? Didn't that confirm Ottilie was ex-CIA? Especially if her boss knew the waitress's real identity?

"It's of no matter," Ottilie said dismissively. "I dealt with it and moved on. Many years later I even employed her. She's extremely good at what she does, even if I didn't like it possibly being done to me."

Monique's opened her mouth. "That's…well…*incredibly* pragmatic of you."

"It is who I am. Goal oriented." She glanced at Monique. "What of you? Are you about to tell me that your list of conquests is as long as your arm?"

"Not at all. For some reason, the fact I have sex with a woman or two a day is a turnoff for my romantic prospects. Even those who claim to be fine with it, saying they understand it's *just work and not personal*, before long, are asking how long I intend to keep doing my job and wouldn't I be happier focusing on investments?"

"So they're not fine with it," Ottilie scoffed.

"No. I never lie to my dates. They know on the first meeting what I do and what that entails. So far, the only ones who have been fine with it I wouldn't want to date. They seem a little too…" She rubbed her eyes. "It's not about being with me at all, but the *idea* of me. They're dating the *expert paid to have sex with strangers*. They get off on it. It's a kink to them."

"So you attract everyone except whom you want. That is unfortunate."

Heart beating faster, Monique asked, "Don't you find it a turnoff too?"

"What?" Ottilie looked baffled. "Why would I? I don't care in the least what anyone does as long as they're not hurting someone." Her lips pressed together. "Although I'm well aware how absurd that comment is coming from me. I've worked for decades in a job that hurts people." She scowled. "Damn it. I don't know why I just told you that."

"I'd already guessed that," Monique said. "The CIA is many things, but harmless isn't one of them. I suppose you could justify it being for national security. That'd be one way to sleep at night."

There was a long silence.

"My last job did not involve national security," Ottilie finally admitted. "And I still found a way to sleep at night." She cocked her head. "Does that make me a terrible person?"

"I don't know." Monique studied her in disquiet. "Did you enjoy hurting other people?"

"Of course not!"

"Did you hurt people on purpose?"

Another pause. "Sometimes." Then, "More often than not."

Monique stared at her, appalled. "Really?"

"It was usually a side effect of the main goal. But, yes, hurt was inflicted, often deliberately." Ottilie exhaled. "And not that I'd admit this to anyone else, but, secretly, I spent a fair bit of time trying to steer the more unethical impulses of my company's board and the various CEOs into less harmful waters. I even succeeded at times."

"But those times you didn't win, you…what? Just went along with it?"

"We were rarely harming *good* people." Ottilie's eyes fluttered shut for a brief moment, and she sighed. "And I know I'm rationalizing it. I always have. I told myself if *I* wasn't doing my job, it might be someone else who was less evolved and more ruthless, who wouldn't care about the fallout at all."

A bad taste filled Monique's mouth.

Ottilie studied her. "Now you see why I don't judge the choices you make. Our jobs are not *nice* every single assignment, are they? It simply is what it is. And I had a certain satisfaction with my work—when I broke it down to its core element and focused on that."

"Its core element?"

"I was a personal assistant of such efficiency that I would defy anyone to manage a CEO's office better."

"And *that's* how you slept at night." Monique couldn't keep the slight edge out of her tone.

NUMBER SIX

Ottilie clearly noticed it because her lips pressed into a line. She met Monique's gaze evenly and said, "Yes. That is how."

Monique sagged a little. "At least you're retired. Or very close to it."

"I've been counting down the days now for three years."

"That sounds as though you didn't like working there."

"I was deeply invested in it initially, but, as time went on, I disapproved of its new direction. I thought the board made mistake after mistake, letting their egos dictate decisions. When I particularly hated something that was planned, I would take action. Subtly. On one occasion, I even succeeded in having an out-of-control CEO removed. He was not pleased."

"You had that much power?"

"Officially?" Ottilie mused. "Officially, I had almost none."

"Then you had more power than anyone knew?"

Ottilie blinked and then stiffened. "I assure you I will disappear once I'm done in Vegas," she said, tone razor-sharp. "No one will ever find me, in case you think I need investigating by someone official."

"That never entered my head," Monique said truthfully. "I'm not your judge or jury, Ottilie. I don't even know your last name. I'm just a woman asking questions about someone I find intriguing. But your job, the power plays, and so on, does explain a lot."

"Oh?"

"How you reshape who you are constantly. How you become invisible around other people. Why you're a chameleon."

"Force of habit."

"I'm guessing that habit came from your former CIA training?"

Ottilie tsked. "You've already had enough secrets out of me."

"Have I? I know only that you worked for a company that hurt people. I can tell you from my investment job that that's at least twenty percent of the Fortune 500 companies right there. Screwing over people is, sadly, not rare in business. Profits are all that matter. So, no, I have no idea where you worked or who you are or anything else."

Ottilie seemed to relax marginally. "You have a golden tongue when it suits you."

"Practice," Monique teased. "My tongue is very skilled."

"Don't." Ottilie scowled. "I was almost appreciating you until then."

"You were?" Monique smiled at the admission. "Let's change the subject, then. Will you tell me about your time in Beirut?"

"Why?"

"I just can't picture you as a children's tutor."

"Tell me why you have no friends other than Cleo, and maybe I'll answer you."

Monique opened her mouth, then closed it again.

"Not so easy, is it?" Ottilie noted. "We all have our secrets. Let's leave it there."

We all have our secrets. Even so, Monique really wanted to know. Wanted to finally understand who Ottilie was beyond her chameleon disguise, impenetrable walls, and morally ambiguous career.

Monique pressed her hands into her eyes briefly. "I don't like to talk about my past; it's not you. I hardly even talk about it with Cleo, and she already knows all there is to know. And yet I still want to know about *your* past. I'm aware that makes me a hypocrite."

"You and everyone else," Ottilie said evenly. "I wouldn't worry. Humans are a mass of contradictions."

"We are." Monique considered that. Ottilie seemed to be a prime example. Ottilie appreciated the happy ending for her CEO and her justice warrior lover. And she'd stood up for Mrs. Menzies when her aggressive husband had confronted her at work. So Ottilie could be romantic and fearless.

And yet she'd worked for years for an organization that harmed others. And she did it by focusing only on being an efficient personal assistant?

"I can sense you struggling," Ottilie said. "Trying to work out what to do. Whether you're going to walk away from me or not."

"How do you feel about that?" Monique asked. "That I'm having a crisis over you?"

"Surprised you care so much."

"I mean, how do you feel that I see you as so morally confusing and contradictory that I'm in a quandary over it? I find it hard to get my head around someone who freely admits working somewhere that *deliberately* inflicts harm."

"Understandable."

"And?"

"Well, if you're asking how I survived such an uncomfortable environment, I tried to focus on my own tasks and not get too caught up in toxic deeds or distracting emotions."

"How can you disengage emotions? They're part of who we are."

"By concentrating on the things I *can* do and putting aside everything else. I could shape the opinions of various CEOs from time to time, even if I was only an assistant."

"Only an assistant." Monique scoffed. "You've already admitted you had way more power than that."

"It's a perception thing. From the CEOs' point of view, that's who I was."

"That's who you were to *them*. But who are *you*?"

Ottilie started and looked down.

"Do you even know the answer?"

"Why do you wish to know me?" Ottilie pinned her gaze back on Monique. "I'll be gone soon."

"I've never met anyone like you."

"Nor I you," Ottilie admitted.

"You might be the calmest person I've ever known. Among the smartest. The most pragmatic, certainly."

"These traits have served me well."

"Do you care?" That was the bottom line, wasn't it?

"About?"

"That bad things happened to those people on your watch?"

"Yes and no."

Monique's stomach tightened even more.

"If I cared too much, I couldn't have done my job. If I didn't care at all, I wouldn't have put the brakes on the worst excesses. I didn't care *quite* as much as the CEO who ran off with her justice warrior. I did care considerably more than that CEO's predecessor, and her successor, come to think of it. Two particularly odious humans—psychopaths, the pair of them—but what can you do?"

What can you do? Monique turned that over. Ottilie had been walking a fine line. Was she a force for good in a small way, preventing worse things from happening in her workplace? Or was her blasé attitude just a cover for complete indifference?

Monique was torn between intrigue and distaste.

Ottilie regarded her, expression a mix between bland and slightly curious. "Did you reach a decision yet? As to whether you wish to run from me or not?"

"Would you care if I did?"

Ottilie fell silent. Then, "Ordinarily, no."

"But?"

"I'd like it if you didn't. Although I'm aware you probably should."

"Why would you want me to stay?" Monique asked in surprise.

"I think, at the end of the day, I find you interesting too."

Yesterday, that answer would have excited Monique. Today, it just added to the confusion. She rose. "I appreciate your honesty. I have a lot to think about. Perhaps it'd be best if we didn't have breakfast together tomorrow, though."

"Because you're still deciding what you think about me."

"Yes. That. And you're distracting. I can't fully work things out when you're beside me, being all…"

"What?"

"Compelling. Alluring. Fascinating."

Ottilie's smirk was tiny but there. "Are you overdue an eye test, Ms. Carson? I assure you I'm none of these things."

Monique laughed in spite of all her reservations. "So you keep telling everyone. But, Ottilie? That doesn't work on me."

Chapter 11
Boss Me

That afternoon, with her troubling morning spa session still filling her mind, Ottilie headed down to the front desk. An important document she'd been waiting on had arrived. Her realtor had insisted on posting the original for her to sign rather than emailing her an electronic version.

As she waited at one side of the semicircular reception area for Mrs. Menzies to fetch her mail, a child's head appeared above the counter on the facing side.

Then it disappeared.

And reappeared.

A girl. About…ten? Hard to tell, given she was a blur trying to being seen above the high barrier.

"Grahammm!" came the plaintive cry of the tiny human.

That got his attention. Graham spun around in his chair, not noticing Ottilie—what else was new?—and faced the girl.

"Miss Imogen," he said, shooting to his feet, his voice smoothing into obsequiousness. "How may I help you?" He leaned over the counter and looked down at her.

"Dad said my new fish had arrived; that they're here waiting for me?"

Ah. No wonder she was excited. Who wouldn't be? *Fish!* Ottilie found herself moving closer to the girl, curious as to which specimens her father had acquired for her.

That was one thing Ottilie would miss about her home. Her large fish tanks. She'd collected various exotic species over the years. The past six months had been spent rehoming them to suitable adoptive owners. She couldn't take them with her as they wouldn't survive the tropical conditions of her next destination.

Graham disappeared from view as he bent to floor level, then emerged, plopping a plastic bag with half a dozen orange fish swimming in it.

They appeared to be healthy enough specimens of common goldfish.

The little girl pouted. "Oh."

"What's wrong?" Graham wrung his hands anxiously in front of himself. His reaction seemed far out of proportion for the small guest.

Seriously, who *was* this child?

"That one's black!" She pointed at it. "I wanted them all gold!"

He frowned. "Well..." He shifted uneasily, hands fidgeting, looking flustered. "I'm sure your father could put in a complaint—"

"If I may," Ottilie cut in. "It's black *now*." She met the girl's eye. "Goldfish often change color. Black and brown are common initial colors for the species, but this is often only temporary as they age. It's theorized that little fish being darker makes it easier for them to hide. When they're bigger, they don't need the survival advantage as much and change color."

"Really?" Her eyes lit up.

Graham slunk away in obvious relief, returning to his work.

"Indeed. If you make sure their diet is correct and that the tank is kept clean and in sufficient sunlight, a black goldfish could well change to other colors. Orange, yellows or reds, perhaps? That's what makes a goldfish magical," Ottilie said earnestly.

"Magical?" Her eyes were wide.

"Yes. You never know exactly what you're going to get." She smiled.

The girl...what had Graham called her...*Imogen*? Beamed.

"Thank you."

"Is this your first goldfish?"

She shook her head. "My first black one, though."

"The first black one you know of," Ottilie said patiently. "For all you know, the ones you had before started out black. That's what makes them interesting."

Imogen grinned hard. "That's awesome. Do you have a lot of fish?"

"I used to. They're all gone now." She still felt their loss. It would be temporary, of course. Ottilie would correct this soon enough.

"I'm Imogen," the girl said. "What's your name?"

"Ottilie."

"Otter-Lee?" She screwed up her face in confusion. "That's weird. But, okay, I'll name the black one 'Otter' after you."

Ottilie felt her nostrils flare. "I am most assuredly not an otter!"

She giggled.

"Why not Carassius?" Ottilie asked. "After its Latin name, *Carassius auratus?*"

"You're funny."

"I am?"

"You know I'm just a little kid, right?"

"I wouldn't use that as an excuse," Ottilie said with a smile. "It's not difficult to learn another language. I know five."

"Me too! Well, three." She bounced up and down. "Dad says I'm annoying in three languages, but my auntie Amelia says it means I'm not wasting my fine mind."

"Your aunt is quite correct. Your father is wrong." Ottilie was well aware this was regarded as the worst, most undiplomatic thing one could tell little humans—that their parents had flaws. But she wasn't about to lie.

Rather than being upset by this pronouncement, Imogen snickered. "Yeah, I know. You sound like Auntie Amelia." She grinned hard. "And Dad's just mad he doesn't know what I'm saying half the time."

"I see."

Imogen tilted her head, regarding her. "Hey, Otter-Lee? Do you think fish know us? Like, can tell humans apart? And do you think they know they're in a bowl? Do you think they ever want to be free? Dad says they don't remember anything, so we can keep them anywhere, but what if they do have feelings and memories? How would we know?"

"Enough harassing the guests, Miss Duxton," Mrs. Menzies said firmly, bustling out from the office behind the front desk. "I apologize for the delay, Ms. Zimmermann. Here's your paperwork." She handed over an envelope.

Miss Duxton? As in Hotel *Duxton*? It would explain Graham's fawning over the child.

Imogen thrust out her lower lip in dismay, her expert source on fish intel having been withdrawn from her.

Ottilie took pity on her and said, "In answer to your questions, we don't know fully what a fish thinks or feels. Scientists can only make theories based on experiments. But that doesn't mean you should ever take them for granted. You must always remember our fish rely on us. Treat them well because you'd feel bad if it were you, wouldn't you? Make sure to be good to them. That's your number one responsibility as a fish custodian. All right?"

Imogen nodded solemnly. "I promise, Otter-Lee. Thank you." She carefully picked up her fish bag, then headed toward the elevators.

"Otter-Lee?" Mrs. Menzies murmured in amusement. "I do apologize. The CEO's daughter can be full of enthusiasm but less interested in the etiquette of not bothering others."

"It's fine. I always appreciate a fellow fish enthusiast."

"You seem to be good with children," Mrs. Menzies said as if she hadn't expected it.

"She wasn't a child," Ottilie said absentmindedly.

At Mrs. Menzies' startled look, she clarified. "She's an inquiring mind stuffed into a tiny package." Ottilie took the paperwork, thanked Mrs. Menzies, and left.

This was how she'd been raised: as if she were a very short adult who already understood most grown-up concepts. Her parents never dumbed anything down nor put on cutesy voices for her. They talked to her as they might a colleague.

She'd been a sponge, absorbing ideas and concepts quickly, and had become exceptional at conversing with adults. It had made for some difficult socialization at school, but she'd never cared much for her peers. It had often felt as if she were waiting for everyone else around her to grow up, and it was frustrating. To this day, she was impatient around immature people.

Her upbringing, spent surrounded by intelligent, deeply curious adults, had also made her appreciate cleverness at a young age. It was why she disliked the nonsense of, say, flirting, when it was the equivalent of empty calories in a conversational meal that could instead be filled with something substantial.

And it was why she'd recently begun appreciating Monique Carson, once she'd seen beyond her surface nonsense. She'd found another inquiring mind.

Had Ottilie frightened her off, though? With her honesty about what she used to do?

She certainly hoped not. She'd shared more, within certain boundaries, than she ever had, in the hope that Monique might understand better who she was. For some reason, that felt important.

A sense of loss swept over her as she headed toward the elevators at a stinging pace. She very much hoped she had not lost Monique.

The vice principal was someone Monique would have been weak-kneed over had they met outside her room. What was it about austere, repressed women that did it for Monique? Ordinarily, she'd already be lost in a lust haze, but now she was distracted, still troubled by Ottilie and her many secrets. It had been a few hours since their spa together, and she still could barely get her head around what she'd learned.

The confounding woman was hardly some mousy PA for a big corporation that did dubious things. She was a PA, certainly, but she wielded real power. She'd also dropped a few subtle clues. How many times had she mentioned what *the board* said or thought? How she'd complained directly *to the board.*

What assistant ever had such access to a company's board of directors? They granted Ottilie audiences—even if they dismissed her concerns. They allowed her *inside* that boardroom. That was strange.

Who was this woman? And why was Monique torturing herself even considering her? She should walk away—*run*—and forget they'd ever met.

Except…Monique didn't want to. She enjoyed the parry and thrust and intellectual discussions and the mystery. She enjoyed *her*.

Vice principal Victoria Mills reappeared, post-shower, having re-donned the outfit she'd arrived in instead of opting for a bathrobe as most clients did.

Her outfit was a high-necked ruffled blouse, black, with an equally black skirt suit that offset her pale skin. Victoria's hair was done up in a tight bun. Eyebrows—arched, thin, and black—matched those coal-dark eyes. Remarkably goth-looking for a woman with such a strait-laced vibe. Her focus locked onto Monique.

Instead of seeing lust in her gaze, as Monique was long accustomed to from clients—especially new ones—Victoria's eyes held a tinge of fear and shame.

Victoria abruptly looked away. "I should leave," were the first words she spoke after the shower. She reached for her handbag.

Well. That explained her getting completely dressed again.

"Or you could stay," Monique said, carefully putting more distance between them so as not to spook her. "You came here for a reason." She settled into the chair behind her desk. "Why don't you sit, relax, and tell me what it is?"

"I can't." Her prim, uptight countenance was belied by the tremble in her voice.

"How about I guess?" Monique gave her a gentle smile. "You haven't ever acted on your desires for a woman, and you came to me because you feel it's long past time you did so?"

"No." Her jaw clenched. "Well, not quite." Victoria inhaled. "There's a woman I see rather a lot. I find myself…strongly attracted to her. I might even be…well."

In love? Falling in love? Clearly the words were hard for her. "And this woman you see often, is she a…colleague?"

"No. Not exactly." A blush warmed the woman's cheeks. "More than that."

"A superior." Monique nodded. "Ah, that complicates things."

"Exactly." She nodded once too, firm and hard.

"Are your feelings not returned?" Monique asked gently.

"I'm not sure *feelings* is the right word. I can only speak for myself, and I know I feel…more…than I should. It's been six years now, and sometimes she looks at me as though she would love to…I don't know, kiss me? But then she waits, waits for me to do or say something, and I don't. I can't. She walks away."

"She can't make the first move, though, if she's your boss," Monique said. "You understand, don't you?"

"I've never been sure if it's that, not wanting to put a subordinate in an awkward position if she's wrong. Or not caring enough to bother. But sometimes…the looks between us are so charged, it makes it difficult to think. And once she touched the back of my hand to get my attention. It *burned*! And she snatched her hand back as though she were affected too. I don't think I'm imagining things. But sometimes I fear it's wishful thinking? I wish I knew for sure."

"Why don't you tell her?"

"Because…" Victoria's expression collapsed into embarrassment. "She might want to act on it, and I honestly don't have a clue what to do next!"

"Ah." Monique smiled kindly. Therein lay the nub of the issue. So to speak. "That's why you're here, isn't it?"

"First, I tried to look at porn—two women? It was terrible. Just so…unromantic. They were performing for the viewer. The male viewer. All those little pouts, and keeping their heels on? Who does that? Well, it didn't feel very intimate. Then half the time a man turned up." She recoiled. "None of those scenarios were remotely appealing. They're not how it feels when I think of *her*."

"Your principal." Another guess. One above a vice principal, after all, would be the one who ran the school.

"It's *special*, not sordid. I don't want sordid."

The principal, then. "How did you choose me?"

"I came across your website when I was searching for discreet women-loving-women sexual counseling. I saw your menu, and I liked how beautiful the page was. The headline that said, *Ms. Carson Will Instruct You Now* caught my eye, and the font was so elegant. Not tawdry at all. And I thought maybe I could just pick up some of the practical things I need to know." Victoria's face and neck bloomed red. "I've never done anything like this. I never felt comfortable enough to explore that side of myself."

"I understand entirely." Monique straightened. "I can promise you'll come away with all the knowledge you need to be confident with your woman. But are you very sure you don't want your first time to be with your lovely woman? Not me?"

Victoria's head snapped up. "I spent twenty years as a math teacher." Her tone was clipped. "I deal in the most absolute of disciplines. When one doesn't know an answer, one simply researches it until competent enough to solve it. And if you can't solve it alone, you seek out an expert for guidance. So it is inconceivable to me that my first time with her, if it ever happens, will be an awful, fumbling, amateur humiliation because I couldn't overcome my pride to learn a few basic pointers ahead of time."

"And that's where I come in." Monique nodded. "I admire your courage and your frankness. I'd be happy to help, Ms. Mills. Will you tell me which number on the menu appeals to you most?" She pushed her laminated guide across the desk to the woman.

She suspected Number One, Take Me, would be her preference, given it was often selected by questioning or straight women trying lesbian sex for the first time.

Possibly Tease Me, Number Two, if she didn't want to be touched too much. Some people loved a featherlight caress and hints of more. Perhaps Victoria would save more physical expressions for her love.

Number Three, definitely not. She'd yet to meet someone with limited sexual experience who went straight for the soft-BDSM delights of Thrill Me. She didn't get the impression Victoria had had many lovers, although the quiet ones could surprise you.

As for Boss Me or Worship Me? Well, Four and Five appealed to a rather specific section of women. Victoria was seeking instruction, not CEO role-plays nor prostrated devotion.

Victoria did not even look at the menu. "Number Four."

Boss Me.

How unexpected.

NUMBER SIX

Monique did so love becoming the CEO of women's fantasies, reeling off instructions with an imperious attitude as she fucked a client. She supposed a woman like Victoria, in love with her boss, might actually want to fantasize about her superior taking her over a desk.

"Number Four." Arousal twitched between her legs. "An excellent choice."

"I chose it because your menu says that is your specialty, not for any other reason." Victoria jutted her sharp chin out as if the words pained her but she wasn't about to be defeated. "If I were in a restaurant run by a Michelin-starred chef, would I not choose the dish they're most famous for? Their area of expertise?"

"Indeed." Monique licked her lips. "Ms. Mills, during Number Four, I will be stern with you. Demanding. Do you understand?"

"Yes."

"All right. What are your thoughts about toys?"

"No, thank you." Victoria worried her fingers in her lap and sat straighter.

Monique nodded. "Please be aware I adhere strictly to the menu. You may touch me only if I allow it. And you will not be granted permission to enter me."

Victoria blinked. "I thought...well, you know."

"No, you may not do that. That's one of my boundaries. I'm here to show you how your body can feel, how I can make you react. I may also show you where and how to place fingers and hands and your mouth on me to give a woman pleasure, but I don't allow the intimacy of having a client *inside* me. If you do want that from a sexual partner, I can recommend someone else."

"My time in this city is limited. I'm here for an education administrators' conference. I don't have time to research any of the names you give me."

"So my terms are acceptable?"

Victoria paused and then nodded. "Yes." Her pupils dilated.

"I will be taking you not in a bed but on a desk. *This* desk." She trailed her fingers across the dark wood surface. "It may not be always comfortable. But I can promise, if you're open to it, you'll get a great deal of sexual pleasure from it."

"I see." Victoria's cheeks bloomed red. "That is to say…yes."

"If you have any relevant medical or personal issues, please let me know now. For example, physical limitations or injuries. Or words that trigger you?"

"No." She frowned. "I had no idea sex with another woman was so complicated."

Monique's eyes crinkled. "Just the first time when we negotiate limits. I'd hate for you not to have a most pleasurable session. On that note, I'd like you to select a safe word."

Victoria's mouth fell open. "What on earth for? Do you plan on hurting me?"

"Of course not. But sometimes an experience like this can be overwhelming—and not just when it's new either. It can stir up emotions. Or it might just feel uncomfortable and make you wish for a pause. I will stop instantly if you use your safe word. So please choose one. Nothing that might come up in conversation during sex play."

"Binomial," Victoria said instantly.

"Is that a nomial who has twice the fun?" Monique teased. "Or just twice the options?"

"Do *not* joke about math," Victoria said, her tone haughty.

And *ohhh*, Monique quivered at the snap of command. "Just bear in mind that when we begin, *I'll* decide what you will or won't have. It's part of the Boss Me package. Do you understand?"

"Yes." Victoria drew in an impatient breath. "Is that everything? I feel you've done more talking than…engaging."

"I just like my clients to be well prepared. But if you're ready?"

With her thin brows knitting, Victoria looked almost aggrieved when she said, "You may begin."

Monique rose from her chair and moved to the other side of the desk, where she stood in front of her new client. "So, you're the new secretary the agency sent over?"

Victoria gave her a startled glance. "Excuse me?"

"You're *not* my newest employee?" Monique arched an eyebrow.

"Oh." Victoria huffed out an embarrassed-sounding laugh. "Er. I suppose?"

NUMBER SIX

"You're not certain? Would you like to leave and return when you *are* certain?" Monique sharpened her tone. "I have no time for indecisive staff. I expect efficiency and…obedience."

"What is the nature of your business?" she asked, her voice slightly hoarse.

"This is the Carson Academy. I am the principal of this girl's high school. Which makes you my new secretary."

Victoria gasped. *Due to the school setting? Probably.* Her nostrils flared. "Yes," she whispered. "I am."

"Good. Stand up and let me get a look at you."

Obeying, Victoria stood a little unsteadily.

Monique ran her gaze slowly all over Victoria's body. "Acceptable," she said, voice low. "I don't like your hair in that bun, though. It's too tight. How will you be able to think with it pulling on you all the time?"

She reached for the bun, plucking out hairpins, then let Victoria's hair down. Monique ran her fingers through the dark lengths. "Much better." Her fingers trailed to her neck and drifted under her jaw.

Victoria swallowed.

"It is a condition of your position to assist me in all matters. And I require daily stress relief," Monique continued. "My job is complicated and exhausting. Will you be able to aid me with that, Ms. Mills?" She plucked casually at the buttons on her own blouse as she spoke, revealing more and more of her bra.

"You would be violating federal and Nevada state law in insisting on such a stipulation," Victoria said instantly.

Monique shot her an *Are you fucking kidding me?* look. "Only if it's not consensual."

"Yes, well, I'm just pointing out in the interests of accuracy how such suggestions of sexual impropriety in the workplace might be received in the real world."

Some people were terrible at role-play.

Monique offered a fondly exasperated look. "This isn't the real world. It's Carson Academy." She paused. "You know, Ms. Mills, it's not too late to choose Number One."

Victoria's expression turned sheepish. "Sorry. I have a tendency to focus on the wrong things at times. I...believe I can overlook any flagrant employment violations and be an acceptable assistant."

Suppressing a laugh at her extremely earnest concession, Monique said, "Very good, Ms. Mills." She whispered against her ear, "It's rather hot in the office today, and you're wearing too many clothes. Why not remove your blouse, hmm? We should be able to work in comfort together."

And in that instant, Victoria froze.

Monique tilted her head, trying to assess whether it was temporary, based on more real-world objections, or something else. "Are you well, Ms. Mills? Do you need to use your safe word?"

"I just..." Victoria gave her a lost look. "I've never undressed in front of anyone before."

"Never?"

"No. I've not had a romantic partner." Her expression looked tense, as if expecting to be judged.

It was Monique's turn to freeze. *No one? Ever?*

Victoria Mills was not unattractive. She supposed that shallow society might deem her plain and uptight, strict to the point of frosty. Even so, surely she'd had offers? But perhaps she'd never wanted anyone but her principal?

"Are you really sure you want to start with Number Four?" she asked gently. "Number One might be better suited? That session is soothing and sweet."

"What if I don't want soothing or sweet?"

"Is *she* not soothing or sweet, then? Your boss?" Monique asked on a hunch.

Victoria's face creased into an unexpected smile. "No. Not in the least. She's all about discipline and order. She tells everyone off but gets this sparkle in her eyes when she does, as if she wants to see what they'll say back. No one ever stands up to her. Except me..." Victoria faded out, a far-off wistfulness entering her expression.

"How exciting she sounds," Monique said easily. "I do love bossy women. I can see why you'd enjoy being with her."

"I suspect I will." She shook her head and began undoing her blouse with military efficiency. "Sorry, I'm making a mess of our role-play. I've never done it before, obviously. Anyway, let's continue."

"Nothing to apologize for. It's your first time. Of course there will be a learning curve and questions for us to get to the bottom of." Monique's fingers landed on her own blouse. "Would it help if I were topless? Would that ease your nerves about being without your blouse?"

A choking noise sounded from Victoria's throat. "I'm not sure I'm quite ready for that."

"All right." Monique suppressed her mirth. "I'll keep my impressive breasts at bay for now."

"Let's just keep them in reserve." Victoria nervously drew her shirt off and then straightened. "Principal Carson? Is this better?"

Her tone signaled a shift back to their role-play, and Monique matched her. "Let me see." She ran her fingers over the pale-blue bra that had appeared, more practical than pretty, but she'd expected exactly that.

"I'm thinking I'd feel less stress if I could lick your nipples," Monique said. "Is that acceptable, Ms. Mills?" She rubbed the rising nubs against the cotton with her thumbs.

"It is." Victoria's tone was now no-nonsense and agreeable, and it was turning Monique on to a ridiculous degree. "Yes, Ms. Carson. Proceed."

"Excellent." She unclipped, then slipped the bra off Victoria's narrow shoulders, discovering a rather delightful pair of small breasts. "How divine you are. I appreciate your *generosity* with your boss." She leaned forward and took the closest nipple into her mouth. The breasts were so small, much of the flesh was within tongue reach too.

Monique rolled the nipple around her mouth and sucked before changing to the other side.

Victoria gasped, swaying under Monique's movements, but her arms were ramrod stiff. Her fists clenched and unclenched at her sides.

"Are you still amenable to this?" Monique drew back, examining those fists in disquiet.

"Yes," Victoria said tightly. "I aim to serve you well." Her voice trembled, and Monique realized it wasn't anxiety but tension from arousal that was giving the woman such a strong reaction.

"Sit on my desk, facing me," Monique ordered. "I need to consider my agenda for the next meeting."

Victoria sat, knees primly together, and inhaled sharply.

"Spread your legs, Ms. Mills. It cannot possibly be comfortable sitting like that."

Moving her knees barely an inch, Victoria asked tightly, "Like this?"

"No." Monique tsked and slid both her hands between her thighs, gently parting them. "Like this. I would like you to be extra comfortable while you take dictation as I fondle you."

Victoria's panties were the same pale blue as her bra, and, to Monique's satisfaction, a damp patch was visible.

"You will arrange a meeting with the school supervisor for tomorrow," she announced as her fingers shifted up to the junction of Victoria's thighs. Pausing just above that damp patch, she said, tone loaded with double meaning, "Is that acceptable?"

Victoria squirmed and looked enormously embarrassed as she shifted forward a little, toward Monique's fingers, and whispered, "Yes, this…is extremely acceptable."

"Excellent." Monique's fingers settled on the blue, and she began to rub a line in the wetness.

"Oh!" Victoria gasped.

She rubbed harder. "We have some parents coming in to discuss the math competition later in the year. The one in DC? Will you be able to handle them?" Her finger hooked around the edge of one leg of her briefs and pulled them aside, exposing Victoria's swollen folds.

Victoria's eyes flew wide and she let out the softest of startled gasps.

"Exquisite, my dear. So aroused."

Now crimson, Victoria ground out, "I'd be happy to handle the parents for the m-m-math trip. *Oh!*"

Monique had dropped to her knees and now drew her fingers up and down Victoria's folds, brushing against her clit on each pass. "I

NUMBER SIX

require an unimpeded view of you as I do this. It will greatly assist your principal if you let me. Do you agree?" she asked curtly.

"I...oh...yes. Principal Carson."

Immediately, Monique pulled down Victoria's drenched panties, dropped them on the floor, and leaned in toward the woman for a closer look.

Victoria's pussy was all natural, not especially bushy, but wild and untrimmed. Monique wanted nothing more than to bury her face in the glistening folds peeking through those curls.

She reached out with her tongue and slowly but firmly stroked the flesh, swirling around Victoria's clit, sliding down further to tongue her opening. She teased the juices from her, drawing them back up to her clit, and swirled once more.

Prodding Victoria's entrance with her tongue, Monique was satisfied at the rush of moisture that coated it.

A long, low wail sounded from above.

She shifted her gaze upward to take in a most magnificent view.

The uptight woman was in ecstasy. Delight had washed her bright-red face that had sweaty hair clinging to her brow. She was trembling and bucking and saying, "oh, oh, oh" a great many times before, finally, as Monique lowered her mouth back to the source of her wetness, Victoria gasped out, "Oh, Anna."

Anna. Her principal, no doubt. The woman Victoria had just come from fantasizing about.

Monique was delighted she'd been able to give her such pleasure. Even if Victoria and Anna never found themselves romantically involved, at least Victoria would always have this experience.

She circled her index finger around Victoria's entrance, waiting to see if there was any hesitation.

A throaty "no" sounded from above. "Not that."

Monique retracted her finger and instead focused on rubbing her fingers around Victoria's swollen flesh. "I understand more than anyone. Some intimacies we save for the women we love."

"Yes." Victoria sighed and collapsed back on the desk. She hadn't even denied the L-word this time.

Monique smiled. She kissed her all up her thighs, cleaning up her wetness with her tongue, and then gently closed Victoria's legs.

Rising from her knees, Monique regarded the vice principal with her prim skirt still bunched up at her waist, the only clothing on her otherwise naked body.

Victoria watched her through barely open eyes.

"Well," Monique said. "I'd call that a successful orientation for my new secretary."

Victoria closed her eyes and smiled softly. "Yes. But I'd appreciate it if we could go over some things again. Just so I know I understand the intricacies of your business."

"Absolutely." Monique chuckled and ran dancing fingertips across Victoria's soft white stomach. "I do love a thorough employee."

When they came up for air later, Victoria closely watched Monique as she drew her underwear back on. "I couldn't do what you do," the vice principal said quietly. "And I don't mean the sexual side. That's not it."

"Oh?"

"It's the risk. The vulnerability. How *anyone* could be a client, even a terrible individual. Someone…mean."

"*Mean?*" Monique repeated. "Occasionally women arrive not in the best moods, but they usually get so drawn into what we're doing that they lose the attitude. And if they don't lose the attitude, I kick them out." She smiled. "Are you worried about me, darling?"

"I wouldn't like you hurt, no. But what if you had a client who was—I don't know—a monster? But you didn't see it at first?"

"I'm pretty good at reading people," Monique reassured her. "So much so, I *can* spot the monsters before we get to anything intimate. Even the more subtle monsters. They're always obvious to me." Her thoughts drifted to Phyllis Kensington, who'd had some red flags Monique had noted quite early. In the end, her disrespect had been more annoying than her actions.

"Good." Victoria sat up and began to dress. "I'm relieved to hear it."

"Don't you ever have difficult students? Or one who's dangerous? Isn't it the same thing?"

Victoria paused. "I rarely get dangerous students. But I once had a girl—she was sixteen—declare undying devotion to me." She gave Monique a wry look. "I was so stunned. Usually the English teachers are the ones who suffer through lesbian crushes. Never me."

"Why never you?"

"I'm not around students enough. And I'm not the crushing-on kind. Too strict."

"Oh, I'd disagree. I'd crush on you." Monique shot her a winning smile.

"You're age appropriate. She was not." A little smile tugged at her lips. "I still remember her years later. I wonder if she's happy and settled now. You, Ms. Carson, deal with women in all sorts of emotional circumstances. What if one of your clients decided they liked you a little too much? That must happen sometimes."

"Every now and then. I disabuse them of the notion they have any chance with me, though."

"Does that work?"

"Eventually. I'll explain it to them that I don't date clients, and, if need be, I'll send them details for a different woman they can call for future appointments."

"Have you ever developed feelings for a client?"

"Never." Well, not exactly. "Not romantic feelings. I do get attached to a few clients, though. I have my favorites." She smiled at the thought of Mrs. Menzies. "Ones I'm glad come back to see me." She took in Victoria's interested gaze. "I'd be glad to see you again too."

"Now that you know I'm safe." Victoria smirked.

"Oh, yes. Very safe. Although, next time, I could push your limits a little, if you wanted?"

"I'm not sure I'm ready for that. Now, I should go. There's a speech I must deliver. But thank you for everything."

"Anytime, darling. Anytime."

Chapter 12

Secrets and Lies

Monique sometimes put the TV on in the late afternoon as she checked her emails and corresponded with her investment company executives. It also helped her relax after an intense session, such as the one she'd had with Victoria Mills.

The vice principal had been delightful, of course, but had required a lot of work and close attention. Monique hadn't wanted the woman's first time to be anything less than exceptional. It could be tiring, though, to be so…thorough.

Share prices slid across the bottom of the screen, and she kept an eye on them as she wrote her next email.

Absolutely not, Raymond. I've said no to investing in both those electric vehicle companies for the same reason: the credible allegations in The Japan Times *that they're using lithium ripped out of the Tibetan plateau, potentially damaging an already fragile ecology. I know those EV brands look like a good fit on paper, but dig deeper. You're my acting CEO—do some research. Our investors would be furious if you tried to slip an environmental pillager past them.*

She hit send and scanned the next email.

NUMBER SIX

Ms. Biaña, yes, it's fine to spotlight Humboldt Fog in the client newsletter as the main 'Buy It' rec next month. And you are quite correct that we're still limiting dairy produce stocks due to the methane issue. Humboldt Fog is perfectly acceptable as it's goat cheese.

Ah, the joys of running an ethical investment company. Managers either overthought and second-guessed everything—as Lorna Biaña was doing—or didn't dig into things as closely as they should, like Raymond.

She glanced up at the TV, then did a double take. Footage of Phyllis Kensington was in the frame. Before yesterday's uncomfortable encounter, Monique had been only peripherally aware of her as "the folksy southern senator with the recipes" who last year had morphed into the "ice-cold senator with the creepy husband she'd covered up for."

That reputation-ending media bloodbath had been just the start. With those revelations had come an avalanche of other high-profile people who'd hired The Fixers for awful reasons and had been dragged for it.

Monique had paid close attention to The Fixers stories at the time because the rich and powerful tended to divest shares in bulk when they needed to free up cash for lawyers. Bargains could be had. Company share prices would also be affected by a dirty CEO's downfall. Either way, the Fixergate scandal had made for a volatile stock market for several months, and Monique had made some good business deals as a result.

She turned up the volume on the news report.

"…Kensington was just one of dozens of high-profile people outed as a client of The Fixers," the reporter was saying. "The organization's activities included helping now-convicted pharmaceutical manager Christopher Huntington force the price of a miracle cancer drug to soar overnight in order to ensure his bonus."

A photo of the disgraced little worm filled the screen, and Monique glowered at him. Who did that? Who thought, *Screw everyone, especially cancer patients, I'm going to be rich at all costs?*

Someone without a soul.

Kensington's face was back on the screen—stock footage from a charity event. So innocent and harmless, smiling as if she had not a care in the world.

Monique had seen considerably more than that face yesterday. She was anything but innocent or harmless.

"…adding further disgrace to Kensington's reputation as it was revealed in *The LA Sentinel* today that all the recipes on her enormously popular website, At Home With Phyllis, were stolen from her housekeeper, Ita May Bates, over the past three decades."

A newspaper photo of a lean older Black woman in an apron flashed up.

"Mrs. Bates reportedly showed *The Sentinel*'s DC Bureau Chief Catherine Ayers all her notebooks containing the original recipes, which include notations as she updated them over the years. A handwriting expert has confirmed they're penned in Mrs. Bates's handwriting and that the ink used in them appears at least twenty years old."

"Oh dear," Monique murmured aloud. "That won't play well with your constituents." The senator's dreams of ever crawling her way back into politics were over.

Footage of an irate Kensington being ambushed by media outside her home at dawn, while still in her bathrobe, was being played on a loop now. She threw her rolled-up newspaper at a cameraman, who caught it with one hand and tossed it back at her. She ducked and swore at him like a filthy sailor. And there it was: *the real Phyllis*. The "gotcha" moment that would now be her legacy.

Ottilie's promised vengeance had been swift and complete. Given the timing, who else could have been behind it?

NUMBER SIX

Kensington would be furious, of course. Her short fuse had been evident to Monique after just fifteen minutes in her company. What had it been like to work for her, day in day out, as Ottilie had done?

And what company was that, exactly? Where had Kensington gone after leaving politics and wound up as Ottilie's boss?

Interesting question. She pulled her keyboard closer.

Google proved no help. Kensington had resigned as a senator for "family reasons"—usually code for avoiding a scandal—and then... nothing? *At all?*

Monique drummed her fingers. Wherever Kensington had been CEO post-politics had to have been low-key enough for it not to have been reported on. That ruled out a think tank—they trumpeted their big-name recruits. Besides, think tanks did not have boards, and Ottilie had mentioned a board often.

She thought back, recalling the scraps of conversation when Ottilie had first mentioned her job. *"I was a personal assistant for a CEO at a consultancy firm."*

A consultancy firm that had nondisclosure agreements too. So, somewhere that kept secrets. She closed her eyes and thought. *Secrets and NDAs.* Government intelligence agencies and political parties all loved their secrets, but such organizations did not have a CEO.

Who else kept secrets and had boards? A technology firm? Pharmaceutical developer? But why recruit an ex-senator with no background in either? Might as well put a fish on a bicycle. Anyway, neither option fit with *consultancy firm.*

Just then, the scrolling news feed shifted:

Ex-FBI director Emmett Holt, who co-ran a disgraced elite consultancy company, has been found guilty. Charges relate to his time on the board at The Fixers, which oversaw computer hacking, blackmail, espionage, and multiple data security breaches.

Monique went cold. *Secrecy. Board. Consultancy work.* The trifecta.

Had Phyllis Kensington, cruel and ambitious, been CEO of the equally cruel and ambitious clandestine company, The Fixers—one that she certainly knew about because she'd already used them as a client?

What else fit? Seriously? What. Else. Monique scowled. But if that were true, and it seemed likely, that also meant...*Ottilie had worked at The Fixers.*

Not just as a PA either. Her hints about her influence and her boardroom access suggested she'd had considerable power.

On TV, the shamed board member was being led away in handcuffs, head bowed.

Ottilie had worked for him. *Them.*

Just...fuck.

Monique felt ill. Every immoral, corrupt, broken thing she'd heard about The Fixers flooded her mind. All of those ugly, disgusting things had slithered across Ottilie's desk and she'd *allowed them to happen*. Every day, she'd gone into work knowing she was about to perpetrate destruction and misery. She'd even admitted as much: she'd hurt people.

Compelling, confident, commanding Ottilie, who had seemed so interesting a minute ago, was one of *them*.

Disgust warred with anger and then a futile jag of hope. Surely, *surely*, Ottilie had some explanation? Some way of explaining it as not what it seemed? Or not as bad as it looked? Or maybe Monique was in error? Ottilie would surely tell her if she'd guessed wrongly.

Monique snatched her phone and texted Ottilie. She kept it vague—no names that might get her text flagged somewhere official. You never could be too careful.

I know. Saw your ex-board member was just found guilty.

A reply appeared: *Ah.*

'Ah'? What the hell did that mean? And that wasn't a denial. Her throat tightened. *That's it?!* she texted back in astonishment.

NUMBER SIX

I never pretended to be good. At the end of the day, I'm just a woman who ran an efficient office and dreamed of retirement. I'm sorry if I disappoint you.

No remorse? Monique doubled over as betrayal slammed into her. *Not again!* Another woman she'd trusted…and now this! She'd been right all along to avoid getting close to people!

That text became blurry. Monique shoved the base of her hands into her eyes to viciously rub tears away.

But then fury replaced her hurt. How could Ottilie just pretend this was *normal? She* was normal? Goddammit! She'd *trusted* the woman. Even started to care for her. Monique's heart clenched. She hadn't known Ottilie at all.

People were assholes! You trust a person with all your personal and intimate foibles and hope they'll be honest with you in return. Instead, they turn around and show they weren't worthy of the trust in the first place. She remembered, suddenly, Ottilie's reaction to the woman she'd dated who'd turned out to be a spy. She'd acted as though it had been no big deal for her. Finding out your confidante was a two-faced liar was probably Tuesday for Ottilie.

But Monique hadn't trusted anyone new in years. And now the one she'd trusted had revealed herself to be exactly like Phyllis Kensington: cold, unfeeling, indifferent to suffering.

No, not just like Kensington. Like…Stacy. The woman who'd ruined her for friendships years ago.

Monique's heart cracked in two. She hadn't meant to get invested. And it was too late. She'd started to care. *Ottilie is not for you. She was never for you.*

Tears slid down her cheeks as she texted back, anger warring with pain.

Seems you were right this morning: I should run.

Monique waited, breath tight in her throat. Would Ottilie ask for understanding or make excuses?

I understand. Thank you for our time together. I valued it. Goodbye.

A pragmatist to the end. The damned woman didn't even deny Monique *should* run from her. She just accepted that as fact?

Well, what had she expected? Ottilie to beg her not to run? To ask Monique to let her explain?

Yes!

But Ottilie was Ottilie: a woman with no expectations and an unusual way of looking at the world. As if she'd *ever* plead her case or ask for anything more than Monique hadn't immediately and freely offered.

Ottilie did not beg. Why would she, anyway? She saw no need. It wasn't like she cared.

This was for the best, then. There was no way Monique wanted to get caught up in a vicious mess like The Fixers or the heartless bastards who'd worked there.

Except… She inhaled. It was disconcerting how much Ottilie had fooled her into thinking she had a heart. Ottilie had stepped in to help June Menzies, hadn't she? Although Mrs. Menzies had said Ottilie was annoyed that Frank had insulted older women. So maybe it had been self-serving.

But Ottilie had seemed inordinately pleased that one of her former CEOs was off living her best life with a professional protester.

That gave her pause. How could she be both heartless and delighted by love?

Monique's temples ached. It didn't matter, though, did it? Ottilie had admitted who she really was. One of *them*.

She'd told Monique the truth earlier: humans are masses of contradictions. And looks could be deceptive.

More fool me.

Ottilie had been sulking powerfully ever since getting Monique's last text, although God only knew what she'd expected. Of course the woman was too smart not to have worked it out at some point. There had been too many clues, and Monique had been paying far too much close attention to miss them.

It just would have been nice to go a little longer before Ottilie lost Monique.

Well, not lost. She'd never *had* her to begin with. Besides, Ottilie wasn't interested in the complications that came with what Monique seemed to want most from her.

But beyond that, beyond the flirting, it did feel as though something else was now gone. Something...worthwhile. That loss sat heavily on her chest.

Why did it have to end so soon? Monique had made her time in Vegas less terrible. She'd actually caught herself laughing. And, aside from Hannah, few people ever amused her.

At the reminder of Hannah, on impulse, she made a video call to her friend.

Large spectacles with shining green eyes greeted Ottilie through the video screen, the face much too close. Then Hannah leapt away with a surprised "Oh!"

Ottilie smiled. She did this every time. "Hannah? It's me."

"Oh dear, Ottilie! I still haven't gotten used to this video business. I'm such a Luddite!" She cackled. "How's Las Vegas? Does it agree with you?"

"I'm not sure Vegas fully agrees with anyone." Ottilie saw her own small sneer on the screen. "At best, it serves up fantasies, but they're threadbare."

"Very true." Hannah chuckled. "Although for some, better the threadbare than the nonexistent." She leaned back. "It's so lovely to see your face again, dear. When will you be back in DC? I've been looking forward to your clues so very much."

That pleased her. Ottilie had recognized a bored, intelligent soul the first time she'd met Hannah. And it had amused them both that Ottilie would leave her a trail of clues about their next assignation... usually a teahouse somewhere close to Hannah's apartment that she could manage to get to herself—with a little extra help from her favorite Uber driver.

"I'm afraid I'm not yet finished with business here," Ottilie said. "But soon." She hoped. Snakepit kept coming up with dead ends on her missing quarry. Her target had clearly gone into hiding. That was unacceptable.

"So, what is it, dear, that has you so troubled? I'm always happy to help."

Ottilie lifted a startled eyebrow. "What makes you think I'm troubled?"

"You video called me. In the middle of the day? It's not my birthday!" She leaned in and said conspiratorially, "If it's money troubles, I can probably help. I never have anything to spend my savings on. My granddaughter insists on paying for everything. No matter how silly it is, I only need to write what I want on the list on our fridge door and it appears by magic a few days later!"

"It's not money troubles," Ottilie said, touched her friend would offer. The idea that she needed money was laughable. "And I would never ask even if it were."

"Then what is it?"

Ottilie double-checked the secure padlock icon for the fourth time on her tablet. Snakepit had given her the "most secure device in human history," he'd told her at the time. And he'd souped up security on the home computer of his then CEO, Michelle Hastings, too. The very same computer Michelle's grandmother, Hannah, was now watching her from. So they were safe, *entirely* safe. But this upcoming conversation still made her anxious.

Finally, Ottilie murmured, "Do you remember the day we met?"

"Here? At my apartment? Of course! You'd come to see Michelle. I chatted to you while we waited for her and Eden to come home. Then I left you to it to discuss your *big plans*." Her eyes twinkled.

"Yes." Ottilie hesitated. "Michelle told me later you overheard the rest of that conversation. So you learned about the organization I worked for. My…role…in it."

Hannah laughed. "Yes, yes, you all thought you were so sneaky. Well, never underestimate a safta with too much time on her hands! I'm nosy!"

NUMBER SIX

Breathing in deeply, Ottilie said, "You know who I am and what I did."

Hannah became serious. "Yes, dear. I know."

"And how do you feel about that?"

"My initial thought was you had to be an incredibly powerful and smart woman to head up that company."

"I didn't head it up," Ottilie said. But the protest was weak to her own ears.

"My dear," Hannah said with a light tut, "you think I didn't notice that all the board members were arrested, one after the other? And that the last person standing, the only one untouched by anyone, the secret fifth board member, was you? It stands to reason that *you* were the one who held the real power."

Ottilie pressed her lips together. "I'm not sure the rest of the board would agree."

"They're in prison. You're not. We both know why: you played the game better than all of them. They underestimated you, didn't they? Did their egos get in the way? Well, whatever the reason, you won."

"How do you feel about all this, though? Knowing what you do about me?"

Hannah's gaze was penetrating. "Ah, that's what you really want to know? How I feel about you being a secret *board member* of The Fixers?"

"Yes."

"It's irrelevant. Because you're who ultimately brought it down. No one else could have done that. Only you. And I think that's commendable."

"Commendable? I only did it because it suited me."

Hannah smiled. "It *suited you* to do the right thing. In all the time since we became friends, I've heard many stories hinting at who you used to be. Some good, some bad; all vague. But in every story where you did something good, you explained away your actions as 'it suited me'. As though the fact you did good was an unintended consequence."

"It usually was," Ottilie said.

"I disagree. Even if you see it that way, even if you believe that *wholeheartedly*, you often did good things."

"I'm a pragmatist. Sometimes people are so goal focused that the consequences of what they're doing, good or bad, are irrelevant to them. All they want is the goal ticked off a list."

"And sometimes a person's subconscious is more powerful than they'd care to admit. All along, I've thought you're a good and decent person trying very hard to pretend you're not."

"Hannah," Ottilie scoffed gently, "we've been through this: I'm not good."

"Michelle says the same thing all the time. Pfft." Hannah waved a hand. "I'll tell you what I tell my stubborn granddaughter: If you were a bad person, would you keep doing so much good?"

"Michelle was always a lost cause," Ottilie said lightly. "She was so repeatedly and obstinately and habitually ethical—while desperately hiding it—that I had no choice but to fire her."

"Actually, she tells me the board ordered you to fire her and that you fought that decision."

Damn it! If Michelle revealed much more, Hannah would think Ottilie was as soft as a marshmallow. He jaw tightened. She was not soft. Not weak.

Hannah's eyes crinkled in amusement. "Why do you do this? Keep trying to paint yourself in the worst possible light? Do you think it makes you seem…badass?" She tasted the word in her mouth as if she'd never said it before and then laughed heartily.

"Why would I want to be seen as a badass?"

"Isn't it obvious? For the same reason Michelle put up all those walls. Because no one attacks someone who can't be hurt."

"What?"

"If you're seen as bad, no one will try to hurt you. No one will bother being cruel. What's the point, if you won't feel it?"

"I…" Ottilie was at a loss. "Don't…"

"You're both very dear to me, you and Michelle. Eden too. That awful organization you all worked at doesn't define you. I'm well aware it expected you to do certain things you felt you had to. But that's not the point. The point is how did it make you feel? Did you rejoice in hurting people?"

Ottilie recoiled. "Why would I rejoice in that?"

"Exactly. So tell me again that you're not a good person."

"There's a position between the two extremes, Hannah."

"Yes. And I think you got very used to telling yourself that it didn't affect you—acting as if you didn't care because you're *so* pragmatic and that's all that mattered, running your little office well. But time and time again, you made the right choice. You allowed Michelle to bring down that privacy invasion scheme even though it would hurt a fellow board member."

Ottilie had to concede that one.

"You found a way to give Eden her revenge on that nasty mayor. You didn't have to do that. And I'm sure if we dug around, I'd find a lot of cases where you helped prevent terrible things from going ahead."

"Just the worst excesses," Ottilie protested. "But I also allowed some bad things to happen. Otherwise I'd be seen as…" She faded out, realizing what she was about to admit.

"Weak." Hannah guessed it anyway. "Have you forgotten who my son is? Michelle's father is so senior in government security agencies that he talks and acts like them. His friends are the same. Over the years, I recognized the patterns in people who've gone through the training. I noticed it in Michelle too: her fear of being seen as weak was from her FBI training. You have different signs. On you, I smell the CIA."

Ottilie inhaled sharply. "I have a…smell?"

"More like a tell. You were taught that the mission always comes first. You accept that you are irrelevant to the bigger picture. And, above all, you think being effective means being invisible. The CIA teaches that, not the FBI." Hannah tapped her nose. "But I see you, Ottilie."

"Well." Ottilie wasn't sure what to say to that.

"Have you considered it's time you start seeing yourself for who you really are, not who you're trying to be? Or what you were trained to be?"

"I'm the sum of my actions," Ottilie argued. "I *am* what I do. And what I've done."

"Nonsense. We are the sum of our *feelings*. That's what makes us human. What's in your heart? *That's* who you are."

Ottilie looked away, surprised at the rush of conflicted emotions she felt.

Hannah blinked. "Is…" she began slowly, "there someone new in your heart now? Someone you wish to know, at least?"

Her cheeks warmed. "I doubt it matters. They've just found out where I work, and, obviously, that's that. Predictable. I expected little else. I don't blame them."

"Dear Ottilie," Hannah said with a tiny huff of laughter. "You're missing the obvious. For a smart woman, I'm not sure why that is."

"What do you mean?"

"Remember who you *are*."

"I apparently ran The Fixers," Ottilie said sourly. "That's my legacy."

"No, dear. You're who *brought them down*. And that's all anyone else will remember when you tell them. Maybe let your new friend know that too, hmm?"

"Why would that make any difference?" Ottilie asked, mystified. Learning Ottilie had worked at The Fixers had been enough to make Monique bolt. And that was before she knew how senior in the hierarchy Ottilie had been.

"Trust an old woman," Hannah said knowingly. "Especially one who can translate fluently between walled-off former agents and their sweethearts. There's only one thing the sweethearts ever want to know."

"What's that?" Ottilie's heart thundered in her ears.

"That whatever bad you've done, you fixed it in the end."

Chapter 13
Tease Me

Carrie Jordan was the name on everyone's lips in Vegas. It wasn't hard to see why: The internationally famous singer was on dozens of billboards promoting her concert residency at Duxton Vegas. Her long jet-black hair, blue eyes, and sultry expression promised both girl next door and sexy minx. Worth millions, she was the face of dozens of brands.

And now she was sitting on the edge of Monique's bed, reading through her menu.

Monique wasn't often surprised, but her newest client had floored her.

The uptight vice principal yesterday—a woman so intense, intriguing, and unusual—would normally be her most memorable client of the week. But then Carrie Jordan's assistant had called.

International superstars weren't common clients, despite Monique working out of Vegas. The big names usually had their own discreet arrangements with preferred professionals rather than opting for someone unknown, risky.

Carrie Jordan's assistant had been especially persuasive, doubling her fee if Monique would sign a nondisclosure agreement and fit the singer in before her opening night show this evening. The assistant had mentioned something about her boss needing urgent stress relief.

Well, that Monique could understand. There would be few jobs as stressful as headlining at Duxton Vegas for the next six months.

One thing Carrie Jordan had made clear the moment she'd swaggered into Monique's room was that her image of being fiercely heterosexual, along with sweetness and light, was not even close to the truth.

"Number Three. I want BDSM; I want power plays. I want nothing held back." She met Monique's eye with a burning need. "I expect *fucking*, not sweetness. I'm so over sweetness. All I get all day is men treating me like a little girl they want to fuck and little girls treating me like their hero. I'm neither. I'm an adult woman with real needs. I want you to take me like you know that."

"That can be arranged, darling," Monique said smoothly.

Carrie supplied her gorgeous smile and said, "Thank you. I hoped you'd understand."

Monique smiled back. "So, is that all you want? Power plays? Being treated like the adult you clearly are?"

"I really want freedom and mess and disorder."

"Interesting, since BDSM generally involves a degree of restriction, order, control."

"I meant in my life." Carrie rolled her eyes at herself and added, "My God, you should see the circus that's my life these days. I have a *posse*, for Christ's sake."

"Not a fan of the fawning?"

"I don't think I'd sell many tickets if I told them all what I really thought. It made sense when I was only a teenager. I had so much security, as well as managers, agents, my mother, and a whole army of minders watching out for me. Then I turned eighteen. I thought it'd change. It didn't. So I bided my time. Then I turned twenty-one."

"Still no change?" Monique asked sympathetically.

"Only that my mother left and went home. Then my manager seemed to think it was her job to take her place. She got more overprotective, not less."

"That sounds frustrating."

"Very. I told my manager that if all she sees me as is a teenager, get ready for adult me. She laughed, so I fired her."

"Did that feel good?" Monique asked.

"It felt...overdue. I should have told her to get laid and save the lectures for her own kids. But I didn't. Because I'm Carrie Jordan. And I always say the right thing." She gave a brilliant fake smile, then dropped it in an instant. "After I fired her, I told the rest of my hangers-on to get lost. I demanded a hotel suite to myself for once. And I want to be in control for the first time in my life."

"Understandable."

"And right now I want to fuck whoever the hell I want in my private life, no matter how many conniptions it gives my assistant. She's hyperventilating over the thought *this* will get out." Carrie waved at Monique. "Sorry you had to sign a nondisclosure agreement. But you get it, right?"

"I do. But never fear, I'm the soul of discretion."

Carrie exhaled. "Good. Shit, sorry for the rant. Had a lot bottled up, I guess."

"So, with all this newfound freedom, will you be wanting toys with that?"

Carrie laughed. "Not something I hear every day." An impish look crossed her face. "Do I get to fuck you through the bed with them?"

"No, darling. I'm afraid not."

"Then pass. But I do want power. Domination."

"From me?" Monique checked.

"No! By me! Don't you see how long I've been dominated for? It's my turn!" Her hands turned into small fists.

"Ah." Monique considered that. "I'm wondering if you want to rethink selecting Number Three because I assure you, I'll be the one in charge for that option."

A hint of mischief shot into Carrie's eyes. "So you say." She grinned.

"I do say."

"Will you tie me up too?"

"If you wish."

"Whips?" Carrie suggested. "I really want to play with some whips. Yeah, I know I can't whip you," she added, teasingly. "Just before you warn me again."

"No to whips. Look at the low ceilings. I'd take out a lamp!" Monique chuckled. Besides, she only did light BDSM. Her specialty was in the power of suggestion, having the whip of command rather than actual whips.

"I have a rather snappy riding crop," Monique continued. "And a slapper paddle. But if you want anything more serious, I know several specialists who'd be more than happy to—"

Carrie shook her head. "I chose you, Ms. Carson. I just want to have what *I* want for once. It's pathetic that despite all my fame and money, I have fewer choices than a regular person." Her eyes were wide and earnest.

Monique nodded. "I will attempt to accommodate you but within my rules." She indicated the menu again.

Carrie shrugged. "Right. My assistant's already paid, hasn't she?"

"She has. First, we need to discuss rules, a safe word, and any limits you have. Then you get a shower so you're all pink and perfect..." She ran her eyes suggestively over the singer. "And then we get down to business."

"I'm already pink and perfect," Carrie shot back, amused. "*Glamor Girl Magazine* called me the Singing World's Perfect Pinup."

"I won't argue as to your perfection," Monique said smoothly, "but a shower is required for all my clients."

"But I showered before coming here," Carrie argued playfully. She was cool and unflushed, no evidence of ruddy cheeks warmed by a shower. The lie was both obvious and sweetly told.

Was she testing Monique? Or was she just impatient to get started?

"I'm happy to refund your money if you don't wish to abide by my very simple rules," she said, keeping her tone light. "It's no problem. So: shower or refund?"

Carrie chuckled at being called out and held up her hands in surrender. "Okay! But don't think I'll be singing in the shower for you. I don't do free concerts." Her laughter was infectious.

Monique, who had never much cared for Carrie Jordan's overproduced pop, said with a smirk, "My loss."

Carrie rose. "Point me to the shower."

"First, I'd like you to agree to the rules and establish limits. So we can get straight to it afterwards."

"I have no hard limits."

"None?" Monique checked. "At all?" All clients disliked *something*. Usually, there would be some kink that didn't appeal.

"No." Carrie shrugged. "Nothing." That perfect smile returned.

"Ah." Often clients who insisted this to be true were actually new to BDSM. They didn't yet know what they didn't like. It might be interesting to possibly be Carrie Jordan's first mistress. "Safe word, then?"

"*Country*. Because country music is for boring old farts and I'd sooner suck a dick than listen to it." Her eyes danced. "America's sweetheart" probably loved the audaciousness of being able to say rude things out loud for once. "No, I don't have anything triggering."

Monique didn't comment on her safe word, although she rather enjoyed country music herself. "You understand that I will touch you but that you cannot touch me without explicit permission?"

"It's on your website," Carrie said, lips curling up at the edges. "Bottom of the page. Last paragraph. I've already read the fine print."

Just in case, Monique outlined her rules anyway.

Carrie shook out her beautiful raven hair. "Shower?" She added lightly with a wink, "Sometime before my opening performance tonight?"

Given it was only three in the afternoon, that wouldn't be hard. The playful wink took the bite out.

"But of course." Monique pointed the way.

When the shower door closed, Monique dug out her riding crop and paddle, a selection of silk scarves, and a mask. As she did so, her thoughts meandered to Ottilie. She wondered what she would make of this selection. Would she like to play? Be intrigued? Or would she back away slowly and sternly suggest *none of the above*?

Monique's thoughts slid to Ottilie's looks. She could blend into backgrounds, making herself smaller. But when you talked to her, and dug into that observant mind, she was breathtaking. And when she didn't know she was being watched, when she strode by like a conquering queen, Monique had met none more breathtaking. And yet Carrie

Jordan—with her sunshine, brilliant smiles, and mane of glossy black hair—was the one society deemed most beautiful.

She paused, remembering that Ottilie also hid darkness. The woman's former corporation was up to its neck in scandal. Ottilie might exude a calm, confident charisma that Monique found deeply attractive, but she was also not someone safe, not someone she should want. But even knowing that, Monique found herself still craving more of her.

How disturbing. *Hell. What does that say about me?*

Carrie left the shower, ignoring the fresh robe Monique had left out, and reentered the main room stark naked. She was clearly attractive although far too youthful to turn Monique's head. She had small, pert breasts, flat, muscled abs, and absolutely no hair on her pubic area, which made her seem uncomfortably young. If Monique didn't know for a fact that the singer was twenty-two, she would have demanded ID.

Her toned limbs spoke of a personal trainer and regular workouts. Her even, golden tan spoke of a top salon or spray studio.

For a moment, the artificiality of this woman made Monique crave Ottilie all over again. She tried to picture how *she* might look, freshly stepped out of the shower. The thought made her nipples harden against her crisp, white blouse.

"Yeah," Carrie said, smirking. "I have that effect on people."

"I'm sure you do," Monique teased. "Please restate your safe word, and we'll begin."

Carrie crawled onto the bed, ass high, giving Monique a deliberately provocative view, and said, "Country." She rolled over onto her back, splayed her legs, and added, "Impress me. I'm told that women like you know how to fuck a goddess."

Women like you. Those three words usually made Monique wary. But Carrie blinked up at her innocently, clearly meaning nothing by it.

"I'll do my best," Monique murmured.

"Tie me up," Carrie ordered excitedly. "Nice and tight." And then she waited, spread-eagled. Naked. Hungry.

"You will address me as Ms. Carson going forward," Monique said. She kneeled on the bed, gathering a small wrist in her hands and looping a scarf around it. She insinuated two fingers between the scarf and wrist as she tugged it tighter, ensuring circulation would not be cut off. "Understood?"

"Yes, Ms. Carson," Carrie parroted sweetly.

Monique tied the scarf to the headboard. "Too tight?"

"No such thing." Her eyes were fixed on Monique the whole time. "Make me feel it." A beat. Then, "*Ms. Carson.*"

Definitely the right move to allow slack in the knot, then. Carrie appeared to enjoy pain. Monique similarly tied her other wrist and eyed her. "Test it."

Carrie simply looked at her. Then slowly grinned.

"You wish to disobey me?" Monique asked, curious. "Because you want to be punished?"

"Mask next," Carrie ordered, not answering. "Then run that riding crop up and down my pussy. Over my clit. Okay?"

Well, she might be the client, but Monique was quite certain she'd never had a Number Three session start quite like this. A bossy bottom right off the bat?

"Ignoring my commands and bossing me around won't get results. I'm not your subordinate," Monique said sharply.

"Aren't you, though?" Carrie teased, eyes sparking and bright. "Aren't I paying you to do what I want?" Another pause. "*Ms. Carson.*"

That was true. Monique reached for the mask, pulling it over Carrie's eyes, and felt an odd sense of relief that the woman's unsettling blue-eyed gaze was no longer on her.

She was having a difficult time getting a fix on this client, who was both sweet and amusing yet bossy and constantly testing Monique's limits.

"The riding crop." Carrie drew in a shaky breath of anticipation. "I want to feel it. Make me feel it."

"What if I said no?" Monique asked her. "What if I said you should earn it? Or that you won't get it as payback for ignoring my title?"

Silence fell. Then, "Do not test me."

"What are you going to do about it, all tied up, hmm?" Monique asked.

"I'll make sure you remember me if you don't play my game my way." She smiled widely.

"Was that a threat?" Monique asked incredulously.

"Don't be silly," Carrie said with a light laugh. "Where'd you get that idea from?"

Monique knew gaslighting when she heard it, regardless of how charmingly delivered. "I'm only going to say this once," she said, her tone warning, "You will *not* disrespect me. If you do, I'll ask you to leave."

Carrie sounded astounded when she said, "What is so hard about giving me what I want? I thought you were in the pleasure business, Ms. Carson?"

And she had Monique there. Pushing down her doubts, Monique decided to give her client exactly what she'd asked for.

Monique trailed her riding crop along Carrie's pussy, playing with her, teasing her, making her moan, making her buck upward into it.

Carrie swore constantly, her words merging into one long dirty thought as she twisted and thrust against the hard crop, making breathy demands.

In turn, Monique did her best to taunt her because the singer was clearly far too used to getting whatever she wanted, immediately. For all Carrie's protestations she'd been treated like a child for too long, perhaps *spoiled brat* might have been a better description.

Her behavior earned occasional stinging smacks of the riding crop to her inner thigh that only made Carrie writhe more. She loved pain and groaned hardest when sharply corrected, sometimes mewling in excitement.

Carrie turned out to be far more than just a bossy bottom with brattish tendencies. She fought every command Monique made—and got punished for it, which only made her argue more. Obviously, that was what she wanted.

The blindfold had dropped down, and that disconcerting gaze was affecting Monique again.

Carrie had a weakness, though. Every time Monique called her a "naughty girl," her hips jerked and her pussy became slicker.

"You like being called naughty, don't you," Monique said, eying her folds. They were swollen and seemed to be aching for direct touch, something she'd resisted supplying so far.

Carrie's impatient pleas were turning into demands. "Touch me there. Touch my clit. I'm *ordering* you to touch my clit!"

"Why is it you get off on being called *naughty*, hmm?" Monique taunted. "Mommy issues?" Her finger trailed the crease around her thigh, torturously close.

"That would mean I think you look like my mother. Don't flatter yourself. She's gorgeous."

Was that an insult to Monique or a weird compliment for her mother? Monique had no clue.

Carrie laughed. "You know, I could have anyone. I have thousands of fans who'd volunteer to suck my pussy dry." She shuddered. "Which would be nice since you're refusing to right now."

"Then why did you choose me and not one of your compliant fans?"

Carrie licked her lips. "Truthfully? You look like my former manager. A *lot* like her. On the website, that shadowed picture of you from the back? Your hair, your shoulders, even the way you're standing. It's uncanny. Of course, I can't fuck my manager because she's straight and a complete cow."

Her smile turned vicious. "That bitch would nag me and set strict rules that I should never have had to follow as a grown-ass adult. I used to fantasize about fucking her to shut her up and asking her while I do it if she still thinks I'm a child." Her eyes fluttered, and she shuddered at the thought.

Now her choice of Number Three was clear. This was veering into seriously uncomfortable territory. "You want to fuck your mother figure," Monique said slowly as understanding dawned.

"No! She just *thinks* she's that. I want to fuck her for treating me the way she did. I want to do *every* depravity with you while thinking of her. Now, is that too much to ask?" Her eyebrow lifted. "Let's just say I've gotta lot of shit I'd like to work through." She smirked. "Hate sex can be fun. So can we stop playing around and get to it?"

Over the years, Monique had had plenty of clients with obvious mommy issues. She simply bossed them around, disciplined them, and sent them away happy. Carrie Jordan was probably the first client who had admitted outright she wanted to fuck her substitute mother. Making it all the more unsettling was how disturbingly young—*childlike*—she looked at this moment. Her eyes were wide, pleading, and intense. Her bottom lip quivered.

Suddenly, Carrie wrenched her arms down, tearing away the silk ropes. "Enough! Foreplay's over."

Her dark gaze set Monique back on her heels at how chillingly cold it was.

"Let's finish this." Carrie curled up to her knees, her breasts bouncing. "Promise I'll behave." She shot her a fake pop star smile. "Well? I'm overdue my orgasm. Get your dirty whore mouth on my cunt! Now!"

Dirty whore mouth?

Every warning klaxon went off in Monique's head. *Oh hell no.* She stepped away from the bed in distaste. "No. I don't respond well to demands or insults. Why should I reward bad behavior?"

"Fuck me now, or I will ruin you." Carrie's voice was crass and heavy with warning. "I've paid twice what you normally get. I expect twice the goddamned service."

Monique's jaw ground in displeasure. "I don't think so. Apologize for your disrespect and I *might* think about letting you come."

"Fucking *whore*!" Carrie trembled in the face of Monique's sharpness. Oh, she was definitely getting off on Monique's anger. "*Whore, whore, whore*!"

Monique forced her tone back to calm. "Insult me all you like, but I think I'll just say no."

"You can't!"

"Oh, I can: *No*. You don't hear that very often, do you?" She gave a soft laugh.

Carrie glared in fury. "I'm the one paying you. You're in breach of contract."

"Mmm." Monique eyed her evenly. "And I did warn you I don't take well to disrespect. I'll issue a refund. Get dressed, and get out."

"You're not serious?" There was venom in her eyes now. "You know, I had this whole plan for you. I was going to take photos of you, naked, doing something dirty, your face half hidden. I was going to get someone to leak them and spread the word they're of my old manager." She trembled slightly at the thought.

Monique recoiled. "*Excuse* me?"

"I can see you won't let me do that. So how about this? You're a businesswoman: I'll pay you five grand to do it. Your face would be hidden."

"Absolutely not." Disgust coiled in her gut.

"Ten grand."

"I don't need your money. And I will not help you disrespect a woman because you're angry she tried to keep you in line. I can see now you deserved it."

In a blur, Carrie jumped up, reached over, and grabbed Monique by the biceps. She flung her down on the bed and squatted over her. "I'm so sorry that Your Royal Fucking Whoreness thought she was too good to take my generous offer."

Before Monique could even react, a warm liquid gushed over her. She gasped in shock and locked eyes with the woman peeing on her—and laughing.

Monique shoved her off. Then, voice shaking with fury, she roared, "Get out!"

Carrie jumped back on her, slamming her whole body against Monique's this time, and pinned her to the bed. With all her force, she shoved a finger between Monique's legs, trying to worm past Monique's underwear and penetrate her.

A tearing sound filled the air. Monique half howled in rage and shock. The disrespect was off the fucking charts—exactly as Carrie had intended.

She wrenched the hand away before it succeeded, crushing the wrist in a ferocious grip. With her other hand, Monique slapped her. Hard enough to rattle Carrie's teeth.

Carrie swore, twisted out of her grasp, and leaped from the bed. She reached for something.

Still dazed and shaken, it took a moment for Monique to make sense of what Carrie was holding up. Her phone? What? Who would she be calling now?

Monique sat up. Her white shirt, yellow and reeking with urine, clung to her bare breasts underneath. "What are you—"

The phone clicked, the unmistakable sound of a camera shutter.

"My manager apparently loves golden showers now. Who knew? Great shot," Carrie mocked. "I'm sure that'll fuck her up worse than you looking nude and freshly fucked."

"If you post that anywhere, I'll sue," Monique said coldly. "Delete it *now*."

"If you sue me, everyone will know it's you in the photo. So you won't. You Dirty. Fucking. Whore." Her eyes gleamed at the insult.

"*You* paid to have sex with *me*. What does that make you?"

"Someone with a grudge against her manager and who doesn't care how she gets payback. Face it—you can't do shit. Sucks to be you."

Monique would have dearly loved to tell this vulgar upstart exactly how much her investment company was worth. Rub her nose in the fact that she made more money last quarter than Carrie Jordan would make this year. But it would be disastrous with investors if that got out. If that photo got out.

"Delete it," she ground out.

"Or what? You'll call the police? Who are they going to believe? America's sweetheart or the sleazy hooker telling some preposterous lie to extort me for drug money?" She gave her most innocent look.

A loud pounding rattled the door.

For a moment, a flicker of concern crossed Carrie's face before it disappeared. "Don't say a fucking word to whoever that is." She ducked into the bathroom, still clutching her phone.

Monique wrenched open the hotel room door to find Ottilie, her mouth pressed into a thin, worried line and her sharp gaze concerned.

"I heard you cry out," Ottilie said tightly. Her gaze flicked over Monique's urine-drenched shirt that showed every inch of her breasts, and her torn black panties. Her expression was blank—no revulsion or surprise—almost as though she were…checking for wounds?

Uncertainty filled Ottilie's tone, and she darted a look around, as if assessing the empty room. "It was the sort of cry that… Well, it wasn't normal. What happened?"

"A client happened." Monique ground her jaw. "A nasty, vicious client."

"Are you hurt?" There was that concern again, coming off her in waves. "Do you need medical attention?"

"A phone hacker would be better."

"Oh?" Ottilie's expression changed to cool and efficient. She didn't ask why. "Do you have the phone's number?"

Monique located her phone, scrolled, and then held it up. "All I have is the number for the client's assistant. She's who paid."

"Text me her name and number."

A moment later. "Done." Monique couldn't look Ottilie in the eye.

"And what do you need from the client's phone?" Ottilie checked she'd received the details.

"A photo."

Ottilie's lips thinned even more as if understanding exactly where this was going. "Has it already been uploaded anywhere?"

"Too soon." Then Monique's eyes flitted to the bathroom door and back. "I hope she's getting dressed and not uploading it now." She eyed Ottilie pensively. "Can you really do this? With just the assistant's details?"

Ottilie smiled. "Leave it to me."

In Beirut, in 1985, Ottilie had heard a lot of cries. Cries for mercy. Cries of pain. And cries to be let free. So she had been very aware of the nature of Monique's scream that had filtered through their shared wall. It was a cry of pain, shock, and outrage. Anger too. But the shock had been most prominent.

Given the nature of Monique's job, Ottilie hadn't been about to sit around to wait for a second cry. She'd banged on the door, loud enough to wake the dead.

The sight that had greeted her was beyond disturbing. Monique's hair and shirt were wet, the smell unmistakable. And she looked as if she'd been fighting a demon.

Ottilie was surprised at her own surge of protectiveness. How sorry she felt for Monique, who only ever seemed to want to make people happier. Even if her methods were not something Ottilie related to, her heart seemed good. And good people needed protecting.

Ottilie could hear faint movement in the bathroom. *The client.* She fixed her gaze on Monique.

She was in so much disarray. Gone was her customary confidence. She looked so crushed. Well. The request for a phone hacker was one Ottilie could easily manage.

Before she could leave, the bathroom door opened, and a face Ottilie had seen all over Vegas appeared: Carrie Jordan. The pop star looked cocky and calm, as if she hadn't just crushed a good woman and made her scream in shock and fury.

Ottilie transformed herself instantly. "I'll inform the cleaning staff at once you need a change of sheets, Ms. Carson. I apologize once again for being late to do your room today. As you know, we're down several maids this week."

"Yes, thank you," Monique said, catching on instantly. "That would be good. I appreciate it."

Ottilie bustled out, feeling the singer's eyes on her. But they weren't suspicious, more…dismissive. She hadn't noticed Ottilie wasn't in a maid's uniform. She hadn't noticed Monique had never even called for Housekeeping. She hadn't noticed anything at all because Ottilie was a no one. No ones were not a threat.

Foolish child.

Back in her own room, Ottilie called Snakepit, asking if he had the power to hack a phone based on a name and number alone. He scoffed.

She sent him the details. "This is an assistant to a person of interest," she explained. "Get into this phone, find the number for her boss, our target—which probably will be listed as a nickname or a codename." No assistant worth their salt would have their celebrity boss' actual name listed in case their device was stolen. "Then get into the VIP's phone. After that, you'll need to access some sensitive material."

"What sort of sensitive material?"

"A photo."

"Of?"

"A woman."

Silence fell. "Uh, that's not a lot to work with."

"Just obtain the last photos taken on the target's phone and send them to me. Then wipe it."

"The photos?"

"The phone. All of it. I want to punish its owner as much as possible. Is that in your power?"

"Wiping shit is easy." A few minutes passed. Then, "I have access to the assistant's direct messages and texts."

"How does that help us?"

"I can work out which contact her boss is, based on the contents. So, uh, does *CJ* sound right for the boss?"

"It does."

"Okay. I'm sending a text with a phishing link to the target, pretending to be the assistant. If this 'CJ' clicks on it, it'll embed some *tasty* spyware for me to exploit. I'll get full phone access." A pause. "*Sent*. Now we wait for the fish to bite."

"All right. How is the other business coming along? Tracking down our missing man?"

"He's been on the down-low for a few days, but that can't last. He hasn't checked into your hotel but has gambled there in the past week. He's gotta pop up for air again. No one goes too long without using their credit cards or phone. Not in a place like Vegas."

Excellent point. "I appreciate you making yourself available to me," Ottilie said.

"I, uhm, appreciate you didn't set any goons on my ass after the shit hit the fan," he said. "I know you know it was me."

"Of course I know. Who else could so efficiently hurt our organization?" Ottilie pursed her lips. "It was a short suspect list."

"Well, I'm happy to help now, 'specially if you, ah, never set O'Brian or any other neckless wonders after me?" His voice rose a little in discomfort.

"I'm *paying* you, so I'm not about blackmail. Well, not about blackmailing *you*," she corrected, in the interest of accuracy.

He gave a low laugh. "Thanks."

Ottilie paced the room as she waited, turning over Snakepit's comment: *No one goes too long without using their credit cards or phone. Not in a place like Vegas.*

It *was* odd. She paused by the balcony doors, phone to her ear, and gazed out at the city. Her eye caught the corner of a blue electronic billboard two buildings away.

Vegas's Richest Poker Tournament Starts Sept 12: WIN BIG! WIN CASH!

Hardly *exciting*. Half the casinos on The Strip ran poker contests. Hell, Hotel Duxton had signs everywhere advertising…

Ottilie froze. The answer had been under her nose the whole time. "I know where he is."

"Huh?" Snakepit replied. "Our target?"

"Or, rather, I know where he'll be. He loves to gamble, and poker is his game. Hotel Duxton's holding Vegas's richest poker tournament in a few days—on the twelfth. That has to be why he's here. He's always fancied himself a contender. I suspect he'd love to go pro. It's also common for poker players to do the rounds of lesser competitions as a warm-up to a major event. He could even be placing highly in a few of those minor games. That would explain why he's not needing his credit card: he's cashed up."

"A lot of guessing there, ma'am," Snakepit said, his tone diplomatic.

"Call it intuition. It fits his profile and the man I know." She tapped her chin. "That means he'll probably check into Hotel Duxton on or just before the twelfth. Can you see if he's registered for the tournament already? If he is, I'll need you to get me his room number the moment he checks in."

"Okay, ma'am. Can do." A clatter of keys sounded, then stopped with a loud clack. "Oh, hey? Speaking of winning."

Her phone pinged.

"You got that?" he asked.

"The target clicked your bad link?"

"Yep. I'm in. Total access."

"Look for the photo."

"Already located. That ping was from me. Check your email."

She opened her phone and scrolled. Ottilie stopped. *Hell.*

Monique was in mid motion as if about to rise or push someone off her. She was soaked—urine, clearly—and her hair clung to her stricken face. It was an appalling photo. Ottilie's jaw clenched at the thought of Carrie getting away with demeaning Monique like this.

"Ah, ma'am? Before I wipe anything…uh…there's a LOT of bad shit on this phone. A lot, a lot…"

"Oh?"

"Gross stuff." He hissed in a breath. "Sick stuff. And, um, porny stuff? Like naked, beaten women tied up, looking scared? Not *acting* scared either. Their expressions…" he faded out. "And—I swear I'm not making this up—I think this person has Carrie Jordan nudes, for real. Like, not fakes."

"It's her phone."

Snakepit made strangled noises while Ottilie pondered what to do next.

How easy it would be to release the nudes. Make the awful creature suffer the way she'd doubtlessly planned for Monique. But she wasn't about to participate in revenge porn. Disturbing business.

"Ignore the Jordan nudes," Ottilie said curtly.

"Okay," Snakepit said. "What about the other pics? The creepy shit?"

"Remember a few years back, when that child-porn ring contacted The Fixers and asked for help in hiding their online activities?"

"Yeah," he gritted out. "Disgusting pieces of…" He swore under his breath.

"I'm aware Michelle Hastings instead got you to hack them and feed their illegal content and personal details to police."

"You knew about that?" His voice rose into a startled squeak.

"I knew everything," Ottilie said. "If it happened in that building, I knew."

"Oh. Uh, I guess I can believe it."

"Can you do the same again? Tip off the authorities that Carrie Jordan might be abusing women and explain that the images are copies of what's on her phone? Suggest a raid might be in order to find more?"

"They're not going to believe that *Carrie Jordan* would ever do something like that," he scoffed. "She's the patron of two kids' cancer charities!"

"They will believe if you use the same username you used before when contacting police. You have credibility now."

"Oh. Right. Yeah." There was a rattling of keys that went on for about five minutes. "Sent and done."

"Out of interest, how much damage could you do to someone having a concert in Vegas?"

"Having? You mean for someone attending?"

"I mean…onstage. Performing."

"As in…Carrie Jordan?" he asked slowly. "I can do a whole lot. You're lucky. See, if it was a one-off concert, roadies bring all their own sound gear and use that; not much point learning the venue's high-tech equipment for the sake of one or two nights. But for shows where someone's in residence, like her? They tie in their gear to the superior built-in equipment and leave it set up that way for the duration of the run."

"And how does that help?"

"When I was tooling around the Duxton Vegas security systems, I found their soundstage setup. Also, their lighting and pyrotechnic files. I can wipe it all back to factory default. It'd take ages to reprogram all the cues and effects. And even if they have some whiz with a backup who could fix it fast, they'd have to notice it's been hacked well before showtime. Doubt they'd realize until the pyrotechnics don't go off."

"Do it."

"Which part?"

"All of it. Lights, sound, anything else you can think of." Ottilie rather appreciated this idea. "Destroy her opening night show."

There was a long pause.

"Don't tell me you're a fan," Ottilie said moodily.

"Ah, nah. No, ma'am. I like metal."

"Are you sympathizing with the fans, then? They'll get refunds."

"No, I was just thinking." Keyboard clattering went on in the background. "How everyone thought you were the nice one at The Fixers.

Harmless. Well, until Eden turned up and she got the title. But you're not nice. You're lethal. No offense, ma'am."

"Yes, Mr. Snakepit. Thanks for noticing," she said dryly.

There was a longer rattle of keys. "By the way, our target is confirmed as a player for the poker tournament at your hotel."

"Excellent." She smiled. *One step closer.*

Snakepit didn't speak for long moments, causing Ottilie to frown. "Something else?"

She heard furious keyboard rattling, and low muttering that sounded suspiciously like…*Bad Godesberg. Diplomat.* Then…*Albrecht…* Ottilie sat up straight and fast, chest thumping. "What on earth are you doing!"

Bad Godesberg, the birthplace of Annika Marie Albrecht.

Albrecht, a German *diplomat*, based in DC. Also: Ottilie's mother.

The last mumble was unmistakable. *Directorate of Analysis.*

A chill shot down her spine. No one would have access to her former job title and all that biographical information unless… "Get the hell out of the CIA database right now!"

The keys paused but then rattled some more.

Ottilie knew Snakepit had hacked the CIA database a few years back for the Chaudary assignment. He'd found a back door. Apparently, he'd returned.

"Why?" she asked in exasperation.

"Confirming a hunch. Uh, ma'am." Snakepit spoke nervously, but his usual reluctance to incur her wrath was apparently nowhere near as strong right now as his curiosity.

"Mr. Snakepit, I'd strongly advise you not to pursue this—"

"Holy shit! Your dad's Robert T. Zimmermann? The German mathematician? I've read his books! He cracked part of the CIA's Kryptos code!"

She sighed, well aware of her father's genius. She did not need the recap.

"German, Arabic, English, French, Hindi…" He gave a low whistle.

Ottilie relaxed marginally. The languages she spoke were hardly too reveal—

"Fuck!" All typing sounds stopped. "You…you…" His words sounded pushed out, strangled.

Damn it. It seemed, *top secret* didn't deter hackers of his skill.

"No one had a clue at The Fixers, did they?" Snakepit asked, his tone awed. "Everyone assumed you were a career bureaucrat. But you did *actual* undercover special-ops shit." He drew in a sharp breath. "Beirut? Wait, was that the terrorist cell that…"

"You would be *well advised* not to finish that sentence," Ottilie snapped, her tone as hard and cold as she could make it. "Not to me; not to anyone. And you will exit that file *immediately*! You've already breached the Espionage Act. And accessing *that* particular file could get you life imprisonment or worse."

Silence fell. "Shit, sorry. I, uh, got carried away. Aborting now." Keys clacked loudly, and then the sounds stopped.

"I'm only going to say this to you once, *Gerald*," Ottilie told him icily. "If you share *any* of my details with another soul, there will be consequences that will be far worse than your limited imagination can conjure up." She waited a beat and then growled, "Are. We. Understood?"

He swallowed audibly. "Y-yes, ma'am. Sorry ma'am. Truly. I didn't mean to…ah. I got curious, and I chased down a rabbit hole without stopping to…ah… Shit. Sorry."

She glowered.

"Butyoureallyareabadass," he said quickly, blurring the sentence into one word.

Christ.

"So, ahhh, if you speak to your dad," Snakepit rushed on, "could you tell him I'm a big fan? He made me fall in love with cryptography. It's my number one hobby now."

Ottilie pressed a thumb into her eyes. "Why, yes, I'll tell him a hacker called *Snakepit* passes on his regards. My father thinks I work for an international translation agency. That wouldn't raise any questions at all."

"Oh. Right." He paused, as if pondering how to get around this issue.

"No. Don't bother. This conversation is long overdue to end."

Snakepit made a sad little noise of acquiescence.

"Before I go, look up Carrie Jordan's room number for me."

A pause sounded, then a brief rattle of keys, "Penthouse suite. Floor fifty. Room 5001."

"All right, one last task, and then we're done. I'll throw in a bonus because you'll be losing sleep over it—literally."

She outlined her needs and appreciated he didn't say a word of complaint about it. Probably too frightened of her now. *Good.*

"Lastly, send me the home numbers of the two lowest-paid room service employees on Duxton Vegas's payroll," Ottilie added.

"Can do." Pause. "They're *all* on sucky wages, looks like. Shit, their manager earns less than my cleaner."

"Just pick me one who looks the poorest, and a backup."

Monique immediately began stripping the bed, her fury rising. So much for her delusion she could always spot the monsters. The vice principal had been right. Monique had been so arrogant, waving her concerns away, assuming she would *always know.*

She hadn't seen how bad Carrie Jordan was until it had been too late, and by then she'd humiliated Monique. Anger burned anew.

Why the hell am I doing this?

Between Kensington and Jordan, she was starting to wonder if even low risk was too much. "I'm too old for this crap," she muttered.

Monique couldn't wait to stop touching these filthy sheets and everything they represented and wash away this whole disastrous hour in a shower.

A heavy staccato banging sounded.

Pulling on a robe, she opened her door to find a tanned, sandy-haired man in an expensive suit, flanked by two hotel security guards.

Now what?

"Ms. Carson," the suited man began, his accent a mix of Australian and New York. "I'm—"

"Simon Duxton," she said dully, recognizing him from the finance news reports and dreading where this was going. The CEO of Hotel

Duxton USA wasn't doing a courtesy call to a loyal guest, she was quite sure.

"Yes," he said. "I've had a complaint. A very serious complaint. That you're running a prostitution ring from your hotel room."

She gave a long-suffering sigh. "By any chance did you get a tip-off from an angry woman just now? Someone famous, rude, and entitled?"

"I can't say the source of the allegation, but we can clear it up quickly. If you'll just step aside, Security will make sure there's no cause for concern. They'll be conducting a search of your rooms and their contents."

Monique saw red. "You think I'm a pimp? Forcing women to have sex from my hotel room? For God's sake! Wait here."

She stormed into her room, sorted through her desk drawer and returned. "My business card, stating I'm the CEO of an international finance company. And here!" She slapped a copy of *The Economist* magazine with her face on the cover under the headline: "*The Freak of Wall Street: The investment CEO with a sixth sense for market moves.*"

He blanched, then glanced at the guards, who peered at the magazine cover in confusion.

"I agree you don't fit the profile but...still," Duxton began. "What if..."

"Why would a woman who runs a top international, *ethical* investment company need to run a prostitution ring? And where would these unfortunate women even sleep?" She waved behind her at the queen bed with its ruined mess of sheets. "In the shower?" She gestured at the bathroom.

Its door was ajar. A guard craned to look and sagged. *Yes, idiot. Empty.*

"Well, you do have *two* suites," Simon tried. "Maybe the other one...uh—"

Dear God, Simon Duxton was apparently as stupid as everyone said. "Just how many prostitutes do you envision can fit into either suite? Let alone the fact they'd be needing privacy to *perform,* and each suite has only one main room!"

One guard cut in. "Just let us have a bit of a look around, and we'll be on our way, ma'am," he announced, sounding bored.

"Yes." Simon nodded. "That's all I'm asking."

"No! I've had an appalling day, and I do *not* give anyone permission to poke around my things." She scowled. "And you two?" She pointed a finger between the guards. "You have zero business with me. You're just cosplaying cops without any legal authority."

"Well, I'm the CEO," Simon said, straightening. "This is my hotel and therefore my property. You can't deny *me* access." He took a step closer, and then his nose twitched. He stepped back, looking disgusted.

Monique didn't blame him, given she was still wearing Carrie Jordan's pee. But his revulsion just made her angrier.

"Can't I?" she snapped. "Hotel guests, like rental tenants, have a presumption of privacy. And if you force your way in, that's an illegal search. I *will* sue. Don't think I can't afford the best lawyers in the country. Christ, do you people even *know* the law?"

"Hey, now," Simon said, looking lost. His anxious eyes darted all about like a kid at a new school. "That's not fair."

"Well, if *you* don't know the law regarding hotel guests, I know someone who does. Stay there!" She stormed back into her room, shut the door, and grabbed her phone.

"Ms. Carson?" Amelia Duxton answered, professional as ever, on the third ring. "I assume you're calling about the final paperwork. It should be back from my lawyer tomorrow. I apologize for the delay. He found a clause he wanted to look at more closely."

"No," Monique said curtly. "I am calling because your idiot, sun-stroked cousin Simon wants to conduct an illegal search of my hotel room. Call him for me? Tell him he can't?"

"That's odd. I understand you wouldn't want him to find out about your side business, but I'm not sure he'd care. As long as you pay your bills on time, that's all he's interested in."

"He's here with two rent-a-cops from Security. He's had an anonymous tip-off that I'm running a prostitution ring from my room. A whole ring? From my two one-bedroom suites? Is he a moron?"

"Yes," Amelia said with a sigh. "He is. I'll call him immediately. And you're correct. Under federal law, they cannot conduct a search of a hotel room, even with manager approval, without a warrant or probable cause. There are exceptions, what's called 'exigent circumstances,' but none of those apply here—nor could they as police aren't even present."

"Good." Monique ground her jaw. "That was my understanding too."

They ended the call, and Monique paced the room for a moment to get her temper back in check.

Another charming side effect of her secondary job was having to always hide what she did. It was draining. Yes, it was illegal; she was well aware of that. But she was also aware that it was easy to forget its illegality for long periods when everyone around her looked the other way. Especially given her clients were clearly all adults, all willing, and one of them was even the hotel's front desk manager. It was easy to forget the illegality too when parts of Nevada had legal prostitution and it wasn't seen as a big deal.

Monique could hear murmuring through the door. She could make out Simon attempting to get a word in with his cousin.

Amelia was, essentially, jaw-droppingly brilliant, and the whole undeserving Duxton clan were too busy being angry with her for uncovering illegalities at Duxton Vegas to appreciate her. They'd shunned her. For being too good.

Amelia's business acumen was the reason Monique had invested in Amelia's latest venture, which was right in the wheelhouse of Carson Investments. It was a no-brainer, even if Amelia's ridiculous family couldn't see the diamond they'd tossed aside.

Snatching open the door, she found Simon putting away his phone, cheeks pink. He glanced at her. "I, er, have decided not to conduct a search of your rooms at this time. You've been vouched for by my cousin. Amelia is unimpeachable, so I will take her word for it that you are not running a prostitution ring. But be aware, as Hotel Duxton's new CEO, I will be watching you."

Well, he had to say that, didn't he? To save face.

Monique glowered and folded her arms. "I've lived here for fourteen years. Do you have any idea how much money I pay your precious hotel each year? You should look it up. And while you're at it, learn your damned laws!" Monique then turned to the guards. "And try to remember an anonymous tip-off does *not* constitute probable cause.

It's little more than malicious gossip." She glanced back to Simon. "You can make yourself useful and send up Housekeeping urgently. Now, that's it! Everyone leave me the hell alone!"

With that, she retreated into her room and leaned against the door to shut it hard. Faced with the sight of the urine-soaked pile of sheets and everything they represented, she wanted to scream.

How was this her life?

She flung herself into the shower, scrubbing every bit of Carrie Jordan from her, real or imagined. Then she pulled on a soft, worn pair of jeans and her snuggliest pullover, her comfort clothes. She hadn't had to pull these out in many months.

Hair still a little damp, she answered the door to the two cleaners Simon had sent up and apologized for the urine-soaked mess, placing a sizable tip for them on a side table.

The women knew her, of course, making it more embarrassing. They merely nodded politely with a look of resignation.

Monique felt humiliated all over again. She needed to be anywhere but here.

Moments later, she found herself knocking tiredly on Ottilie's door, all but slumping miserably against the frame when it opened.

"Can I come in? The maids are in my room. Real ones this time." Somehow, her words didn't sound as desperate as she felt.

"Of course." Ottilie stepped aside.

Monique stumbled over to the couch.

"Tea?" Ottilie asked. "Coffee? Something stiffer?" She waved at the minibar.

"No. Thanks." Monique felt wrung out enough and didn't want to add artificial stimulants to her brain's shaky ecosystem.

Ottilie, making herself a tea, seemed to have her charisma back to full.

"I still don't know how you do that," Monique said, eying her. "In my room? You just shrank away. Slid right inside the wallpaper, just about. I don't think Carrie Jordan even registered you were there."

"You don't want to know how I do it," she said with a slight smile, joining her on the couch. She took a sip of tea.

"Because you'd have to kill me?" Monique joked. About all she had left, it seemed, were overdone lines and shallowness. She hated the prickling at the back of her skull. It felt like fear and panic, now that the adrenaline was wearing off. She'd have to face it sooner than she'd like. But not right now.

"Please," Ottilie said sweetly. "I couldn't hurt a butterfly."

Monique smiled in spite of herself. "Any…news?" she asked tentatively. She had no idea what she'd do if Ottilie was unable to access that photo.

Ottilie placed her teacup onto the coffee table and reached for her phone sitting beside it. She sifted through it for a moment and then held it up. "I've had this retrieved, and it's now also wiped from Jordan's phone. From the cloud too. No copies remain except this."

Monique gazed at the photo and then felt as if she were crumpling. In the image, she was small and shameful and a mess. She shook her head, drew up her knees, and wound her arms tightly around her calves. "I look…" She scowled. "Look at her. Is that really me? She's pathetic."

"I'm deleting this now," Ottilie said and did so. "And emptying the bin." She did that too, in front of Monique. "And I see someone caught in a cruel and callous attack. Hardly pathetic."

Monique swallowed. "I won't ask how you got that."

"I know people." She said nothing more.

"Thank you. You did me a great favor today."

"Well," Ottilie said, apparently at a loss. "I don't like bullies. For all her reputation, that woman was vile."

"I'm sure you know better than anyone how looks can be deceiving."

"Very true." Ottilie met her eye. "Do you wish to tell me what happened?"

"I don't know. I'm suddenly deciding between talking it out or getting drunk and not examining my decisions too closely."

Ottilie regarded her kindly. "Or you can do both. Either way, help yourself to my mini bar."

"Famous last words," Monique muttered.

Chapter 14

Vengeance Planning for Former Spies

At 3 a.m., Ottilie's alarm went off and she got up quickly. She pulled on the outfit she'd selected before bed after her drinks with Monique had run late. She might have had only two hours' sleep, but she'd be back in bed before long.

Monique had done a lot of "processing" via the minibar last night. She'd seemed rattled in a way that was both out of character and understandable.

How true her words of days ago had been. That the powerful can be made to feel powerless. Power was nothing. If someone wanted to take it away, they could. And they could do it with surprising ease.

Obviously, Ottilie had pointed out that it wasn't Monique's fault. Any of it. The role reversal was painful almost after their earlier conversation about consent just three days ago.

"I always assumed I could pick out the monsters," Monique had announced, holding a cold glass of gin beaded with condensation against her forehead. "It was a conceit, a lie I told myself, that allowed me to work unafraid."

"Will you be afraid now?" Ottilie asked slowly.

The long silence felt physical and sticky. Monique put down the glass. Her red-rimmed eyes met Ottilie's. "Honestly? I don't know."

And then, to Ottilie's great consternation, Monique Carson—fearless, flirty, confident Monique Carson—had started to cry.

In that moment, as Ottilie had hesitantly slid her arm around Monique's back, rubbing soothing comforting circles, she'd decided Carrie Jordan deserved to suffer in the worst possible way.

Ottilie checked her phone now to ensure her first wave of damage had been executed. Social media was filled with furious complaints about Carrie Jordan's opening night concert. Power outages, light issues, weird sound feedback were all part of the Snakepit hacker service.

Switching to her secure texts, Ottilie found one from two minutes ago saying *Ready*.

She texted back a confirmation and left her room. The Housekeeping maid she'd offered a generous bribe to earlier was waiting in the stairwell. Tired, dark-brown eyes filled with relief. She'd probably worried that no one would turn up and that all this had been just a bad joke.

"Fifteen minutes," the maid told her. "Then I need it back. They'll notice it missing from the board."

"Understood." Ottilie pocketed the key card.

"She is alone. No entourage."

"No special guests this evening either? After her concert?"

"No. I watched her, like you said. She was in an awful mood, shouting at everyone because of her concert, but then she left her people in the lobby and went to her room alone."

"Good." A controlled environment was essential. "Did you bring the other item I asked for?"

"Yes." The maid passed over a plastic drink bottle. "It's not mine," she said quickly, indicating the contents.

Ottilie tucked it into a black nylon pouch at her waist, zipping it closed. "I don't care whose it is."

"Interesting hat." The maid was now staring at her jaunty navy beret, which hid her hair.

It was designed to distract. Often people would remember an unusual item of clothing long after they'd forgotten someone's face or features.

She wore black pants, a black T-shirt with long sleeves, and thin black gloves. If anyone somehow managed to get a glimpse of her, they'd never pick her out in a lineup when she was back in her formal, crisp tweed skirt suit, and the matching personality.

Ottilie handed the Housekeeping employee an envelope. "The agreed amount."

The woman counted out the bills, then put them back into the envelope, and tucked it into her pocket. "There are cameras in the hallway on the penthouse floor. Pointing at the door."

"I know. But they're having a small technical glitch right now."

"They are?"

"Well, they will be. They'll be out for half an hour. I'll return to you before then."

"Fifteen minutes. No more. The night supervisor will be back at that time. I'll wait here."

Ottilie nodded, then climbed two flights up before exiting and taking the elevator the rest of the way.

When the elevator reached the forty-ninth floor, she texted Snakepit: *Now.*

The doors opened on floor fifty. She waited inside, finger pressed on the *Door Open* button.

Her phone lit up. *Go.*

Exiting, she confirmed that the security camera above the elevator, pointing down the hall, had no red light on. The hotel wasn't equipped with 24/7 security guards watching monitors, so no alarm would be raised until the morning. Maybe it wouldn't even be noticed then, if the guards had no reason to review the footage.

Ottilie used the keycard from the maid to swipe open Carrie Jordan's suite. She closed the door softly and dropped to a crouch, waiting for her eyes to adjust to the darkness.

Question one: was Jordan alone? *Had* she picked up some company for the evening after leaving her team?

Soft snores came from the master bedroom. Only one set. Crawling, she quickly cased the rest of the suite and confirmed there was only one occupant.

Good.

Ottilie stood with a soft groan, her knees cracking. Infiltration and payback were a younger person's game.

She moved to the main living area where she'd seen several bags. Rifling through the biggest suitcase, she hit the jackpot. Passport. She extracted the bottle the maid had given her, then poured half its contents onto the passport. Just to send a message about disrespect. The stench of urine filled her nostrils.

Zipping the bottle back into her pouch, she moved to the kitchen. An empty phone charger sat on the main counter. She withdrew a small pair of wire cutters and snipped the cable. Annoying things to replace. Attack of fleas. If she'd learned nothing from The Fixers's security crew, repeated irritating little attacks could be far more annoying to people than full-on ones. Especially if they lasted longer and were a constant source of pain to correct.

Next was the bathroom. A curling iron and expensive hair dryer lay on the counter. Her wire cutters made short work of both. Two new, unlit scented candles were on the counter. Retrieving the bottle, she dribbled a tiny amount of urine on each wick until it soaked in. This "gift" wouldn't be evident until the candles were lit, which could be weeks later. A lasting and noxious reminder.

Slipping the wire cutters back into her pouch, she turned her attention to the pills lined up under the mirror. Hunger suppressants. Illicit uppers. Iron pills. Vitamins. Heavy-duty headache formulas. Nothing too unexpected for an A-lister, especially one performing nightly. And no medical condition that might explain her abhorrent behavior. It seemed she simply chose to be an assaulting asshole.

How disappointing…but not too unexpected. Ottilie had met far too many A-listers with entitlement issues.

After dribbling urine in each bottle, she left the lids off so Jordan would know the pills had been tampered with. She was about inconveniencing the pop star, not poisoning her.

She returned the plastic bottle to her pouch and moved on to the master bedroom.

Carrie Jordan was in bed on her back with only a sheet around her. Her shoulders were bare. On the floor lay a cell phone with a cracked screen. Clearly it had been used to vent some recent fury—not surprising since the evening's concert had been a disaster.

NUMBER SIX

It was tempting to destroy the phone and its contacts—nothing would annoy Jordan more. But Ottilie left it. It would be needed untouched when officials seized it to search for those illicit photos Snakepit had reported.

She studied the sleeping woman for a moment. How angelic she looked. As though she weren't a woman who, hours ago, had made a good and gentle woman humiliated and afraid.

Rage slithered into Ottilie at the reminder.

Knotting a black, thin handkerchief around her head so only her eyes were now visible, she positioned herself on the bed. Settling across Jordan's hips, her weight pinning the woman down, Ottilie leaned in, waiting.

Jordan stirred.

Ottilie tapped the singer's forehead hard and repeatedly with one index finger, lowering her face as close as possible to Jordan's.

Jordan's eyes sprang wide, her mouth opening to scream.

Ottilie pulled back, clamped a gloved hand hard over her mouth, and said, "No, no. Quiet. You will listen."

Her eyes were as wide as trash-can lids.

"Here is your one warning: your concert tonight was no accident. The technical failures were planned. This was payback."

Her eyes grew even wider.

"This was just a small demonstration of our power. We can do this, and much worse, every day for the rest of your life, if we want."

Carrie's nostrils flared.

"You want to know why," Ottilie stated.

Under her clamped hand, the singer nodded.

"Maybe this will refresh your memory." Ottilie released her hand from the woman's mouth and reached into her pouch, withdrawing the half bottle of urine.

"The hell?" Carrie gasped out, struggling to sit up as she saw it.

"Cease moving," Ottilie barked at her.

She froze.

Slowly, Ottilie poured the urine over Carrie's hair until rivulets were running down her face.

Carrie squirmed and gagged a little but stopped under Ottilie's warning look.

"What you did to Ms. Carson yesterday was unacceptable."

"*She* sent you?" Carrie asked in shock.

"No. She is unaware I'm here. But we heard what you did, and my organization is most unhappy. You should know that if you try to hurt her again—or any sex worker—we *will* know and we *will* ruin you."

"I didn't mean to hurt her," Carrie tried hurriedly. "The hooke—Ms. Carson…"

"Of course you did," Ottilie said sharply. "You wanted her humiliated, and you wanted your former manager humiliated."

"My *manager*?" Now Carrie looked truly furious. "Did *she*—"

"No. She did not."

"I'll fuck you up! I have money!"

Ottilie gave her an unimpressed once-over. "Look at you. Just a cruel, spoiled brat. Abusive and entitled. A disgrace."

She remembered Monique's broken expression as she had cried in Ottilie's arms and decided to twist the knife hard. "What will your parents think? Back home in…Charlotte, wasn't it? They seem so nice. Wholesome, even. Do you think your little brother will get into art school?" she asked conversationally. "Mark's work shows promise, but his GPA isn't the best, is it?" Ottilie affected her most thoughtful expression.

"Jesus!" Carrie gaped at her in fear. "Leave my family out of it!"

"I'm not the one about to be dragging their name through the mud with disgusting antics."

"Please!" Carrie begged, and the emotional cracks finally appeared. "I'm sorry!" She wrenched herself into a sitting position, and her sheet slipped down. Now they were both staring at her bare, perfectly round breasts.

Carrie glanced quickly at Ottilie, as if assessing whether the view was having a positive effect.

Was she kidding? Drenched in urine, young enough to be Ottilie's granddaughter, possessing none of the humor, wit, or charm of Monique? "Don't flatter yourself," she said coolly. "Your body is as appalling to me as the rest of you."

Carrie drew the sheet back up. Her cheeks reddened.

"You're thinking of reporting this, despite the publicity fallout," Ottilie said with certainty. "That's pointless. The cameras outside your room have been disabled. Anything you do in retaliation would end badly for you. Go back to sleep. In the morning, you'll wonder if it was just a bad dream." She gave the softest of snorts as she slid off the woman's hips, back to the floor. "Maybe it was?"

Ottilie left the penthouse suite and checked her watch. Four minutes left.

Striding down the hall—red camera light still off—she was in the elevator within moments. Stopping it two flights from her floor, she exited, ripped off the handkerchief, and ran down the stairwell.

The maid jumped to her feet, tension and relief sharp on her face. Ottilie gave the key card to her and the woman then shot off down the stairwell.

After texting *Restore feed* to Snakepit, Ottilie then removed her beret, squeezed it into her small waist bag, and headed back to her room.

It was done.

Idly, as she channel surfed and waited for her adrenaline to calm the hell down, she wondered what Monique was doing. Had she been able to sleep? Was she feeling any better?

How odd that they'd gone from parting on terse terms to this: Ottilie fretting for a woman she'd never thought she'd see again.

There was no denying the enormous satisfaction she'd gotten from punishing the singer for hurting a woman she...appreciated. Someone she apparently greatly cared what happened to.

She would probably never get last night's look of defeat in Monique's eyes out of her head. Or the moment her soft, gentle eyes had welled up with tears and embarrassment. Monique had looked at her with so much shame, then hid her face in her trembling hands.

No, Ottilie would never forget that until the day she died.

Chapter 15
German Ninja Gratitude

The knock on Ottilie's door was far too early. She groaned and rolled over to look at the clock. *Eight?*

Well, she'd been up all hours, but still. She pulled on a robe and went to the door, checking the peephole first. "Ms. Carson," she said uncertainly after opening the door. "What a surprise. And so early."

"We're not back to this surname nonsense, are we?"

"I didn't want to assume."

Monique lifted a jar. "I bring gifts. And grateful thanks."

"Grafschafter Goldsaft?" Ottilie peered at the label. "How did you get any brand of Zuckerrübensirup in the US? And what thanks are owed?"

"Let me put some toast on, and we can talk." She lifted a bag that appeared to hold fresh bakery bread.

"All right. You do that. I'll have a shower and get dressed."

Ten minutes later, Ottilie stepped out onto the balcony, feeling marginally better, and settled into the chair beside Monique. "To what do I owe the privilege?"

"I had the most astonishing visitor early this morning." Monique tilted her head as if to study her closely. "Pop star Carrie Jordan."

"Really?" Ottilie frowned. "What did that appalling woman want?"

"Well, for a start, she looked entirely bedraggled. Her hair wasn't dried or styled. She was looking thoroughly wretched for America's sweetheart."

"Guilty conscience, perhaps?" Ottilie asked, selecting a slice of toast and buttering it. "For attacking and degrading you?"

"She apologized over and over. Offered monetary compensation too."

"How surprising," Ottilie said, reaching for the German spread.

"I was so stunned. I asked what had brought this change of heart."

"Was she perhaps visited by the ghosts of Christmas past?"

"Close. She asked me to call off my ninja."

"You have a ninja?" Ottilie took a bite. Oh, it was heavenly. "I'd forgotten how much I love this. Thank you."

"Specifically, my *German ninja woman*." Monique regarded her with fondness. "Good God, Ottilie, what did you do to her?"

"I'm sure I don't know what you mean. Seriously, where did you find this?"

"I ordered it on eBay the first morning you said you liked it. It arrived yesterday. And, Ottilie," Monique said with a headshake, "I don't know any other German women, let alone ones with some form of ninja-like training in their past. Was there…actual fighting involved?"

"So she didn't say what this ninja did?"

"She did not." Monique smiled. "But I get the impression it was bad enough to have her regretting a *great* many life choices."

"Ah." Satisfaction filled her. "Good."

"And on a related note, I also can't help but notice everyone's talking about her concert last night. It was a complete mess. She had a meltdown about it on stage."

"How…unfortunate for her."

"You really won't tell me what you did? Or, rather, her ninja did?"

Ottilie dabbed her lips with a napkin, then took a sip of tea. "Well, to speculate, it sounds like her ninja made sure she got a taste of her own medicine. And, possibly, left her with the fear of getting more should she ever hurt you or anyone else in your line of business ever again."

"A taste of her own…" Monique gave her a scandalized look. "Ottilie, did you by any chance pee on America's sweetheart?"

"Heavens, no!" Ottilie said, shocked. "How…uncivilized."

"Oh."

"You know urine can be poured on someone's head from a bottle if required." Ottilie waited a beat. "But not their own urine. One should never leave a DNA trail. Amateur mistake." She tsked. "Although I strongly suspect Carrie Jordan will not be investigating anything or anyone regarding this incident."

Monique's mouth creased into a smile. "Thank you."

"I'm not sure why you're thanking me."

"Ottilie," Monique said in exasperation. "Must we?"

"We must."

"Fine. Why did my ninja protector do it?"

Ottilie finished her toast before answering. "Why do you think?"

"I'd say perhaps she's had a lifetime of watching injustice and not being allowed to stop it."

"That's very noble sounding." Ottilie cocked her head. She smiled. "I find that highly unlikely."

"Then what's your theory?" Monique's eyes crinkled.

"Maybe your ninja thought it was the least that singer deserved. Especially after finding some terrible photos on her phone of other traumatized women. But it was more than that. Said ninja probably despised the fact that a good woman had been humiliated. Enacting revenge might have been something your protector was only too pleased to do." Ottilie met her eye. "As for me? I hate she did that to you. I had to listen to her attack you. I heard your fear and shock. It was…distressing." Ottilie looked down, worried she'd said too much.

Because, it turned out, Monique mattered to her. Ottilie had only realized how much the moment she'd heard her scream. By the time Monique had later gotten drunk and was crying in Ottilie's embrace, Ottilie knew she would have committed murder for her. Worse, she still wasn't entirely sure if that was hyperbole.

Monique asked carefully, "Are you saying you'd have done this if you'd heard her hurt *anyone*? Or was it because it was me?"

Ottilie's lips pursed. "I greatly dislike anyone who goes after someone vulnerable. I'm disturbed by the fact she attempted to hurt you because she had power over you. I know how that feels." She ground her jaw at the reminder of Kensington's disturbing actions. "*And* I was particularly offended she attacked you, specifically. Because the list of people I find acceptable is rather short." Ottilie met her eye and admitted the truth. "Monique, I do *not* want you hurt. Never that."

Inhaling, Monique said in obvious relief, "Thank you. I know we—well, *broke up* doesn't seem the right word, since we weren't dating—but let's say *had a parting*. It means a great deal to me that you were there for me. I know a lot of people wouldn't have been. But it also confuses me. Knowing who you are, where you worked…and yet…" She hesitated.

Finally, Ottilie said, "What do you wish to know?"

"I just want to understand. I'm not judging, not this time, but I really want to get my head around it."

"Ask."

"Why did you work for *them*?"

"The position offered was in my wheelhouse of specialty skills. I was there when the company began. The original mission statement wasn't just to"—Ottilie glanced unseeingly at the view—"help the entitled. Originally, it was providing expert services to anyone who wanted it. Back then, the company was well run, sleek, and simple. Its first CEO was competent, and the jobs untroubling."

"What changed?"

"Over time, the CEOs the board selected turned the organization into something darker. It became an entitled, rich boys' playground. The focus was on power games and moneymaking. Since the first CEO, there was only one decent CEO out of all of them—the woman I told you about. Hannah's granddaughter, Michelle."

"Wait, the good CEO is the granddaughter of your elderly dancer friend? The same woman who fell in love with a protester?"

"Yes. She was the one CEO I didn't need to constantly steer away from being terrible. Oh, she was uncontrollable in other ways—do not start me on her sudden need to make The Fixers appear to be a force for good to the woman she was falling for. But that's another story."

"All those other bad CEOs—you did influence them, though?"

"At times. When I decided it warranted intervention."

"So not always."

"No."

"Were all the jobs evil?"

"Evil is a relative term. Occasionally The Fixers did do good. Just not very often. It's hard to do good when you cater to the whims of people like Carrie Jordan: whatever they want, they get. They're used to it. Such individuals rarely want anything selfless."

"How do you reconcile with that?"

"I made my peace with my job years ago. When I understood, with some disappointment, the direction in which the company was going, I focused on what *I* was doing. I made my department efficient and as close to flawless as I could."

"Efficient at doing bad things," Monique murmured.

"Efficient is efficient." Ottilie said. "The act of efficiency is not morally nuanced."

"Please tell me you didn't just sit back in that immoral company and make sure the paperwork was filed perfectly?"

"I did do that."

Visible disappointment washed over Monique's face.

Ottilie exhaled. "But I *did* rein in some awful plans from time to time. So they became less awful." She brushed crumbs off her lap. "But there were some schemes I knew were bad, and I still let them slide to the CEO simply because I was curious to see what they would do with them."

"Why?"

"It would tell me who they were as a person."

"And if they'd green-lit them, then what?"

Ottilie shrugged. "Then I'd have known whom I was dealing with."

"But you were willing to leave the approval of these projects to someone else to decide? What if they'd chosen to go ahead?"

"Then I'd have stepped in."

"But not every time." Monique drew in a harsh breath. "What about cancer drugs not going to poor people thanks to The Fixers?"

"Ah, that one. I did fight that particular case. I lost. The pharmaceutical manager who hired us was about to be rich as sin, and our CEO wanted in. He bought shares right before the Fixers's job went ahead."

"You fought that," Monique repeated, relief flooding her face.

"That particular case, yes. Generally, some things were not for me to interfere with. Many times I chose a tactical retreat so as not to tip my hand."

Monique seemed to turn that over. "You were ensuring no one knew how many strings you were really pulling?"

"Something along those lines."

"I don't know what to make of any of this."

"And I'm not sure why I shared any of this." Ottilie paused, feeling truly disturbed. "I've carried the secret of where I work for years and, more importantly, *how* I work. And you just ask…"

"Technically you didn't share it with me. I guessed." Monique fidgeted. "I'm struggling to weigh this with the woman I know."

"I understand," Ottilie said. She'd expected this, of course. Monique wouldn't want someone like her, and that was hardly a shock, all things considered.

Wait, do I want her to want me?

She'd never been more confused by the question, or the answer, which seemed so obvious. She *did* enjoy Monique looking at her with a great deal of…affection. Interest. As though Ottilie were someone she never wanted to be without.

"You're the woman who did something incredible for me last night." Monique broke into her thoughts. "And who worked…there. For them." She looked helplessly at Ottilie.

So she was still conflicted? That was a surprise.

Ottilie drew in a breath. "My friend Hannah says there's something you should probably know."

Monique looked up, eyes hopeful.

"I'm the one who brought down The Fixers."

"What?"

"In case that matters to you."

Monique's eyes grew wide. "Of course it matters!" She blinked at her. "*You* were the leak?"

"I was the source of every file you see out in the media. I recorded each one myself, and I gave them to someone to pass on to the journalist Catherine Ayers."

Monique shook her head. "How on earth could you leave something so vital out?"

"Is it vital?" Ottilie peered at her. "I didn't think it would make much difference. I have been doing some ethically dubious things for years. One day, I stopped doing them and released the information to the world. Does the latter erase the former to you? I didn't think it would. But Hannah takes a different view."

"Oh, it matters," Monique said hotly. "It matters a whole lot to me."

"How perplexing." Ottilie reached for her tea, just to have something to do with her hands. "But I'm glad you think so."

"Oh, I do." Monique rolled her eyes, seemingly at herself. "I'm sorry. Really."

"For?"

"Thinking the worst. I should have believed my own eyes. I knew."

"Knew what?"

"That you're far from heartless. I know you hide your feelings, pretend you're always doing the practical option, but you continually make choices that disadvantage yourself to help others."

"Well." Ottilie's heart hammered. That sounded perilously close to Hannah's view. "For God's sake, do not tell anyone that."

Monique chuckled. "All right. May I point out that you didn't have to help me last night but you did?"

"Or some German ninja did."

"Don't." Monique rose and briefly touched Ottilie's shoulder. "I'm going to go now, reflect a little."

"Ah." Ottilie knew what that was code for. *It's not you, it's me.* There would be a breakup text within the hour. Well, not a *breakup text*—they weren't a couple. But words to that effect. She found that thought depressing. "Well, thank you for breakfast."

Monique paused, one foot pivoted toward the door, and locked her gaze with Ottilie's. "Have dinner with me? Tonight?"

"Oh?" Wait, so Monique didn't wish to end their association? How unexpected. It was most...gratifying.

"We'll talk some more," Monique said. "I know just the restaurant downstairs. It's one of Vegas's finest. Would you like that?"

Ottilie decided not to analyze her immediate interest in the idea. "Yes, I would."

"Ottilie," Monique said, "I meant that as a date."

Right. "I understand."

"I mean," Monique said quickly, "I don't even know if you're even remotely interested in me like that, or women as a whole—that ex of yours might have put you off dating women for life—so this was perhaps a bold but pointless move."

"You are a brave one," Ottilie said, "I'll give you that."

"Is that a yes?"

Ottilie focused on her cup in front of her. "When my last loose end is tied up, I'll be gone. It could be only a matter of days. I'm not sure, but it's such a short time."

"That wasn't a no."

"I suppose it wasn't." Ottilie looked up.

"So, if it wasn't a no, doesn't that mean you find me attractive?" Monique's eyes crinkled. "Finally?"

"I said I'd let you know if that happens," Ottilie replied, amused. "But I will say this: I thought about *you* when I saw Carrie Jordan naked a few hours ago."

"How surprising. I mean, despite her awful faults, Carrie is a very attractive woman."

"No she's not," Ottilie said with a frown. "She's just flesh and pinkness and tight skin and sullen pouts. I find poodles more appealing. And I do *not* find poodles appealing."

"Her twenty million fans might disagree."

"I don't see it. But you?" Ottilie's tone turned faintly mischievous, "You have potential."

"It's only a matter of time," Monique predicted with a grin.

"So you say." Ottilie smiled at her enthusiasm. "We'll see. But I'm rather surprised you'd still want to date me, even knowing where I worked. What I did."

"Your friend Hannah was right." Monique pushed her hands into her pant pockets. "You destroyed that terrible organization. Maybe lead with *that* next time."

"All right." Ottilie's lips twitched up. "I'll bear that in mind."

"So, back to my question. Dinner—*romantic dinner*—with me, tonight?"

It suddenly felt important to grab onto this fleeting opportunity: a place of acceptance and warmth and friendship. Ottilie found herself wanting to lean into it as though it were a physical thing.

"Tonight," she replied. "I'd enjoy that."

Chapter 16
It Is a Date

Dinner was quiet. Monique couldn't quite work out how to ask what she really wanted to know: why Ottilie had agreed to a date. Did that mean she wanted things to get romantic? Or was it just her accepting that was how Monique saw dinner? She should have asked when she'd first proposed dinner, but she'd been too distracted by Ottilie's yes.

With anyone else, Monique would simply flirt like crazy until the answer was clear to everyone in a fifty-foot radius. Except Ottilie didn't like being flirted with. She saw it as insincere. So, now, Monique, the queen of wooing women, was stumped.

Finally, Ottilie spoke. "Your twitchiness is putting me off an excellent seared duck breast." She smiled.

"Sorry," Monique said. "I didn't mean to be so obvious."

"Everyone is obvious to me," Ottilie said. "It's the curse of being an excellent reader of people."

"Tell me about it." Monique blew out a breath and laughed. "You're second only to me at reading people."

"Only second?" Ottilie scoffed. "Please."

"Well, I suspect you could probably tell me half the life story of our waiter." Monique tilted her head in the direction of the young man buzzing around a distant table.

"I could take an educated guess. And I agree that so could you. So, what's your take on him?"

"Miserable. Hates his job. And he hasn't waited long."

"Agreed. He also came to Vegas to get married on the spur of the moment, and it was over by the time they sobered up. He got a waiter job to get money to go home."

"Okay, what?" Monique chuckled. "He said nothing!"

"He kept rubbing his ring finger where a ring probably used to be. There was no dent, so it wasn't a long-term relationship. If it was any other city, I wouldn't leap to quickie marriage, but this is Las Vegas, and the pain is still fresh for him, so I'm taking an educated guess as to the source. He does hate it here, and he's inexperienced at his job. He wants to leave, so why hasn't he? He needs money. So that means he took the job as a stopgap. Conclusion: he came as a tourist and was forced to stay. He probably got so drunk after his failed wedding that he ran up the bills."

"So now he's a sad drunk?"

"No, but he's a young man in the demographic where drinking solves all problems. He also has a hip injury and a wrist injury. Two things that happen together when you fall down while drunk."

"Or," Monique said, "he's a local kid injured playing basketball and is saving up money for college."

"He's not local. He pronounced the Nevada Special as Nah-vah-da instead of Nev-adder."

That was…true. "I need to know if you're right," Monique said with a grin. "I need it more than anything."

Ottilie smiled back. "I guess we can find out when he brings out the coffee. Ask him how he's enjoying his stay."

Monique did just that five minutes later.

The young man was not a local, had indeed come for a quickie wedding—not his, though. He was, however, a little too fixated on his best friend's bride (hence the ring fixation) and had confessed love to the poor woman right before she'd walked down the aisle. That had led to a fistfight with the groom, minor injuries, and a several-days-long bender that he was still paying off.

Not that he'd said all of that, but Monique had pieced it together. Ottilie had too, it was clear.

"Well," Monique said when he departed, the waiter's cheeks blooming with embarrassment. "You were very close."

"Mmm." Ottilie sniffed. "I'd have done better if he'd said more initially. We only had him for a few minutes."

"So, then…I'm guessing you really were CIA at some point?" Monique said lightly. "Where else would you need to refine such skills?"

"Where did you?" Ottilie asked. "You're not CIA."

"How do you know?"

"I know."

"You know because you *did* work there."

Ottilie leaned back in her chair. "The past is the past. I think of little now but what I'll be doing next."

"Retirement. I remember. So, where will that be?"

"Somewhere tropical with beaches and a great many Mai Tais."

Monique laughed. "I hope you'll wear a big hat. Your skin is rather delicate."

"Too much office work in recent years," Ottilie conceded. "I have a lot of time to make up for. I want to get started…living." Her expression grew distant.

"Getting some 'me time' at last, then?"

"Yes," Ottilie said with conviction. "Finally."

Monique at last screwed up her courage and asked the question she'd wanted to know all evening. "Ottilie, why did you agree to a date with me?"

"You interest me. Few people do. You notice me. Few people do. And you are kind and good. Few people I know are."

"Not many people see me as 'good,' though," Monique admitted quietly. "Given what I do."

"What you do? Ethical investments?" Ottilie hiked an eyebrow. "Are these people in the coal industry?"

"You know what I mean."

"Yes," Ottilie agreed. "You like sex. You are apparently good at it. You wish other women to have fulfilling sex. You take money to show them how. How terrible you are. How *do* you look at yourself in the mirror?"

Monique smiled. "I wish everyone felt that way."

"Are you still troubled by the singer? I assure you she will never bother you again."

"Her attitude is not rare. There was the senator who was also dehumanizing. One week, two terrible clients. It made me wonder why I'm putting up with this. Why I'm opening myself up to such treatment. I don't need it. I don't want it."

"Are you thinking a change of career is in your future?" Ottilie eyed her.

"I've thought about it. But I also love what I do. How can I walk away from helping so many women discover their bodies? Their pleasure?"

"For a perceptive woman, you appear to have missed the bigger picture."

"Oh?" Monique gave her a sharp look.

"There are so many ways you could help women achieve those outcomes without personally sharing your body. There are books you could write. Or a sexuality podcast or blog would be, I'm quite sure, well received. It seems to me that you would help far more women by actually being less…hands on? Your reach could be in the many thousands."

What a compelling idea! Monique shook her head and laughed.

"What's so amusing?"

"You are a woman who, I gather, has had a limited amount of sex in her life, and you've just solved the problem of the sex expert who has had a great deal of it."

"I've solved it?" Ottilie asked, sounding intrigued. "And I fail to see what one's amount of sexual experience has to do with their reasoning skills."

"Good point. And I love your idea. What if…" She stopped, thinking. "I could close my business to new customers and still keep a few preferred regulars. The ones I know and trust."

"Like Mrs. Menzies," Ottilie suggested.

Shock washed Monique. "She told you that?"

"No. You did. Just now."

Monique felt ill. She'd breached a valued client's privacy. She was so appalled with herself. She'd just destroyed June Menzies's trust. "Oh God," she whispered, stricken.

"I worked it out some time ago, though," Ottilie assured her. "There were little clues, going right back to the day I first met her. Don't worry, I wouldn't tell anyone. Although, Mrs. Menzies suspects I know. She can barely look me in the eye."

"You suspected the day you met her?" Monique shook her head in disbelief. "You really are something."

"Yes," Ottilie agreed, eyes bright and amused. "But you're the first person to figure that out." She paused. "Well, in the interests of accuracy, the third. But I appreciate you saying so."

"Third? Who was first? Hannah?"

"She was second." Ottilie smiled. "Hannah's granddaughter was first. Although Michelle was a little slow on the uptake. I worked with her for nine years before she realized my true power."

"It took her nine years? You really do hide in plain sight, don't you?"

"It's a skill."

"Personally, I'd rather you didn't hide at all—at least not around me. I love seeing *you*, not the invisible woman you play so well."

"I find, of late, I rather like not disappearing. It's novel."

That pleased Monique immensely. She sat with that warming feeling for a moment and then rose. "Ottilie? There's somewhere I want to show you."

"Oh?"

"Trust me."

"I'm not sure why, but I do." Ottilie sounded almost aggrieved. "Quite against my instinct."

She looked so put out that Monique laughed. "I know the feeling. Come with me."

Ottilie gazed around in amazement. The entire roof of Hotel Duxton Vegas was covered in greenery. The smell was incredible. Zesty, with sharp and tangy notes. Crisp like morning dew.

"What is this?"

"One giant herb garden," Monique said. "And a few other essentials. The hotel's seven restaurants use it for their menus."

"How did you even know it was here?"

"You have your sources; I have mine." Monique smiled. "Over here. There's a nice spot for taking in the view."

She led Ottilie over to a corner that was dense with parsley, chives, basil, and oregano and pointed her to a pair of crates. "When staff get too stressed, they'll often slip up here and hide. They used to smoke up here too until the chefs got mad their herbs smelled like cigarettes. I'm amazed it's not packed all the time, given how much stress comes from working here."

Ottilie lowered herself to the crate. "I'm surprised anyone would want to work in Vegas at all. It's just so…overpowering. Constant flashing lights and sounds."

"There is that. But the glitz is exciting if you want to get swept away."

"Is that why you stay?" Ottilie asked. "You like the escapism?"

"Initially that was why. I don't need that now though."

"And yet you stay?"

"I'm used to it. And Cleo amuses me. Professionally, I'm usually left to my own devices and no one questions it—I'm referring to my investment company now."

"Why would anyone question what you do?"

"Old prejudices thrive. Men are expected to rule Wall Street, and a female CEO gets attitude. I don't like the chest beating that comes with being in New York. Here? In some ways, the women rule."

"They do?" Ottilie asked, fascinated.

"Only on the surface. All the signs and billboards, posters and promotions? It's seventy percent women. The featured stars, singers, performers. Even the casino staff. But behind the scenes, of course, it's the men in charge. And, the women on all those posters and billboard are dressed for men, when you think about it. But even so, I do love seeing women everywhere I turn."

"Of course you would," Ottilie said with a teasing smile.

"Exactly. I wouldn't do well in a wall-to-wall male environment. It's exhausting."

"Was that another reason you left New York? Exhaustion?"

"*Left* implies I spent much time there. I didn't really. I set up my business in the most logical place to have an investment company, hired highly competent managers, and once it was thriving, I left."

"For…Vegas. And all the pretty women."

Monique smiled. "You make me sound so shallow, darling."

"Not shallow…differently motivated?" Ottilie suggested.

"Did Cleo tell you she lured me here? She loves to tell people that."

"As a matter of fact, she did."

"Well, it's true. But it was more than that. Being enveloped in her world, with all her dancers, felt like a community, and I loved it. I was part of a family. My own family only ever worshiped money. It was a lonely way to grow up."

That did sound lonely. Ottilie could certainly relate to having distant parents focused on other things than their child.

Monique continued: "I don't feel that here, which is funny since Vegas practically runs on the almighty dollar. But it has other charms."

Perhaps it did. Ottilie drew in a deep breath, savoring the earthy scents. "I like it up here. It's less…Vegas. I've been smelling Vegas's unique aroma since I got here."

"Yes, that is all the stale air pumped out of the casinos, along with a little pollution mixed with dusty desert. It's quite a distinctive cocktail."

"Except up here." Ottilie looked around again. "I appreciate you showing me this little spot."

"I haven't taken anyone else up here before. I'd be very flattered if I were you." Monique's smile was dazzling.

"Duly noted," Ottilie said with a tiny smile of her own.

A few moments passed in silence before Monique held her gaze. "Ottilie? I'm wondering something very important."

"Oh?"

"Have you decided I'm beautiful yet?" She seemed to hold her breath.

Ottilie turned that over. How Monique looked now, backlit by the setting sun with the warm lights of the city softening her face, was so very appealing. Their date had shown how clever she was, how perceptive, but Ottilie had known that already. She'd known the moment Monique had pieced together where Ottilie worked. Perhaps even before that.

"I think you're an intelligent, intriguing woman," Ottilie answered.

"Thank you," Monique said softly. "And by that, you also mean…?"

"Yes." Ottilie held her gaze and admitted, "You are a most beautiful woman."

A smile lit Monique's face in a glow that was transcendent. "Didn't I tell you?" She chuckled for a moment, but it died away as she gazed at Ottilie. "I find you breathtaking." Her words were so earnest, lacking the flirtatious quality Monique usually peppered her compliments with.

Ottilie could tell she meant it. Her cheeks warmed, and she broke her gaze.

Monique rested her chin on her hand, elbow on her knee. "So, that begs the next question."

"Oh?"

"This 'me time' of yours. Does that include…relationships?"

"Why?" Ottilie replied. "Are you proposing one, or are you just curious?"

"I love that you didn't shoot me down straightaway."

"I was just seeking clarity first."

Monique's expression fell.

"However," Ottilie said quickly, already missing the happiness in her eyes, "I'm also here, sharing a secret rooftop garden with you. A space that could be seen as intimate after a dinner for two. That is no small thing for me."

"I imagine that's true. It would be far less complicated for you to just avoid me for the rest of your stay."

"It would."

"So why are you here with me?"

"I explained before. Because you see me."

"Ottilie, it's incredibly hard not to notice someone as fascinating as you."

"And yet no one really does. I've spent the better part of four decades going unnoticed. It has served me well. But it can also be quite tiring."

"Because it's not the real you. It's just an act."

"Yes. And whenever we interact, you remind me of what I'm doing. You expect me to be more, not less."

Monique smiled softly. "Because I want to know all of you."

Ottilie gazed back at her. "And I find…I like that."

"I know you're only in Vegas for a little while," Monique said. "I know I can't offer you more than something short and sweet. But, oh, I could make it so sweet. Would you like to? If nothing else, you can tell yourself that what happens in Vegas stays in Vegas."

"Why would I ever tell myself that?" Ottilie asked, perplexed. "It's dismissive. It's saying it doesn't matter, when I assure you if I ever take another lover in my life, it will be because it is a deliberate, conscious desire. Something I want to remember, not forget."

"So, you'd consider it?" Monique asked, hope softening her eyes.

"Why me?" Ottilie asked. "When you could have anyone?"

"I'm captivated by you. Not by just your beauty. I enjoy your intelligence and quick wit. How you see and analyze everything around you. I admire your calm and your confidence. You don't particularly care what anyone else thinks. You are so comfortable with who you are, underneath your chameleon disguise. You say you've spent four decades being invisible, but with me, you let down your guard. It's flattering that you don't hide when you're with me."

"Even though you know what I've been hiding?" Ottilie asked cautiously.

"You destroyed them, Ottilie," Monique said, her tone serious. "That makes all the difference. And I believe I understand how you think now. For you—life, people, choices…it's all a chess game. You move your pieces in one of a few ways: Usually it's in ways that don't actively do harm and that benefit you. Or, in ways to minimize harm, but *only* if you can stay hidden as the architect. Sometimes you move in ways that do allow harm if it gives you answers you seek. But on occasions, Ottilie, you will move the pieces to protect someone else, even if it might hurt you."

How accurate that was. Astonishingly so.

"Don't deny that last one," Monique went on. "You did it last night for me. You did it with Mrs. Menzies when her husband was abusive. You probably usually do it so subtly or cleverly that you think no one else notices: that all along you've been playing a game no one else could see."

Ottilie drew in a sharp breath.

"But I can see it, Ottilie. I've worked it out. Your underlying game has always been about one thing in the past. Efficiency. But prioritizing efficiency over everything else meant you didn't always make good decisions."

"No."

"And yet you own that."

"Yes."

"And now it feels as though you're maybe…reconsidering your priorities? It seems to me, as an outsider, that the day you destroyed The Fixers, you cleared the chessboard and started again."

Ottilie's gaze drifted into the distance. "It can be disconcerting playing a different game than what I know. But I'm trying. I believe I want to try."

Monique paused for a few moments. "Getting to know you—being allowed to—is everything."

Ottilie's attention shifted to her. "No one has ever accused me of being so interesting."

"That just means they didn't know you. Or you didn't let them." Monique studied her. "In my line of work, I've met many powerful women—women who would make you stop and stare. Not because of their looks so much as their sheer force of personality. I'd sort those women into two categories: fire and ice."

"What's the difference?" Ottilie asked.

"Fire—filled with passion and fury, they will get fired up about anything. Formidable women. And ice—cold as an Arctic snowstorm.

They'll show you nothing but walls, nothing but contempt, too, if they think you're unworthy."

"You think I'm a powerful woman," Ottilie murmured. "Like them."

"You are."

"So, which am I? Fire or ice?"

"Neither. You're glass."

"You feel I'm so fragile?" Ottilie asked incredulously. "That I'll shatter easily?"

"Tempered glass," Monique clarified. "Reinforced deep within. Not easily broken."

"Why glass at all?"

"When it suits you, Ottilie, you become invisible. Yet you are piercing, incisive, and strong, deceptively so—powerful enough to withstand the storm. You see through everything and everyone. You are a sphinx of glass. A queen of shards. The first and last I'll ever meet. That's 'why you.' You are utterly fascinating."

Ottilie bowed her head under the unexpected praise, feeling more profoundly understood than she ever had. "Thank you for seeing all that in me. It's unexpected."

Monique reached for her hand. "Always."

Ottilie allowed the contact. A little, warm tingle went up her fingers.

Surprising.

With her thumb drawing circles over the back of Ottilie's hand, Monique said, "I want to know you so much better, and I'll be direct: I want to share myself with you. Mind and body. That's not something I do often. Despite my job, I allow no one to touch me intimately. But with you, I would love that. I would love you to know all of me. I would be honored to make love to you. If you'll have me." Monique looked suddenly uncertain, her cheeks reddening. She glanced away as though convinced Ottilie would dismiss her instantly.

Instead, fingers still tingling, Ottilie was warmed by the heartfelt request. "Thank you for the offer. I'll think about it."

"You are so unknowable," Monique said. "I wish I could know more of you."

"You already know more about me than most people. And probably more than I'm comfortable with. But…perhaps it's time I got more comfortable. I'm starting to feel as though life is passing me by. I'm too young to feel old and too old to feel young."

"You're not too old for anything," Monique murmured. "I'd love to show you just how young you still are."

Ottilie considered her words. She rather liked that thought. *Not too old for anything.*

"But…" Monique looked uncharacteristically anxious. "If you agree, not in my room. I don't want to be anywhere near my room at the moment."

"Because of the singer?"

Monique gave a faint nod. "I do have my other suite, but it's not very cozy as I use it as my investment company office. Besides, that's work and I want you purely for pleasure."

Ottilie hesitated. "It's been a long time since I've said yes to a proposal like this."

"Thank you for considering it."

"How do I know you're…" She hesitated, unsure how to ask politely. "Safe? I understand your side job has…certain risks. Health risks."

"It's so *you* to ask." Monique smiled and added, "More people should." She reached for her phone and scrolled through it. "My last medical results. Received five days ago. I get checkups regularly." She held it out to her.

Ottilie studied the results and glanced at her. "I don't have anything like this for you. I haven't been with anyone in years."

"Then I'm even more honored if you choose me now."

"I barely know you," Ottilie said, pausing. "And yet I feel that I do."

"I barely know you," Monique repeated back. "And I would love to. I don't want you to leave before I know all of you."

"There is that. I'm leaving soon. One last loose end, and I'm done."

Monique joked, "I hope that loose end plagues you for weeks. Months!"

"Flatterer," Ottilie said, realizing she was quoting Monique from days ago. "What would I even do with you? I'm not sure I remember how." She kept her words light, but inside, uncertainty brewed. Her hand reflexively clenched in Monique's.

"Fortunately, this is my area of expertise," Monique said soothingly.

Still Ottilie hesitated. "I'm a complicated woman. I'm aware I'm hard to read. Hard to know. If I were a book, most people wouldn't bother finishing it."

"I would read every line. Worship you, cover to cover."

"Would you understand what you'd read, though?"

"If you'd let me, I'd like to try to read the Book of Ottilie. Will you?" Monique held her gaze seriously. "Let me?"

Gone was the empty flirting. Ottilie saw only earnestness and a burning promise. Monique would worship Ottilie. To her surprise, her palms were now slick. "I suppose I should say…"

Monique drew in a breath.

"Yes."

Chapter 17
Worship Me

Ottilie took Monique to her room and cast an apprehensive look around. Still neat as a pin. She didn't believe in letting standards drop just because she was away from home.

"Well." Ottilie worried her hands in front of herself. She was in her maroon dress with three-quarter sleeves, which gave her face more color. She probably wouldn't need more color at this moment, given it felt as though every capillary in her face were burning. "I'm never usually nervous," she said. "But it has been a few years now. More than a few."

She hadn't been kissed, caressed, or even hugged for so long. How would this feel now? Especially given she was so much older than the last time she'd been intimate with anyone. The previous times hadn't exactly set her world alight either. Was this a terrible idea?

Monique stood before her, beautiful. Intelligent. Interesting. Wanting her.

"Nervousness is only natural," Monique said gently. "Are you worried about anything specific?"

Ottilie drew in a breath. "I have a few…hesitations."

"Tell me." Monique's expression was so kind. "Please?"

"I don't get very…" She sighed and sat on the end of the bed, looking down. "I've noticed as the years roll by…my arousal isn't…as obvious. But it doesn't mean I'm not interested."

"You mean how wet you get?" Monique asked, after a pause as if to decipher her statement.

Ottilie felt her cheeks warm. "I meant that, yes."

"Wetness isn't the only sign of arousal. Shall we talk about how dilated your pupils are? The hardness of your nipples?" Monique's gaze dropped to Ottilie's chest and back. "The way you're breathing deeply right now? I don't need wetness to know you find this exciting. But I have all sorts of lubricant if you'd like." Now Monique's cheeks turned pink, as if her mind had gone certain places. "Flavored, nonflavored, and—"

"Monique." Ottilie stopped her by reaching for her hand.

"Oh." Monique supplied a sheepish look. "I suppose I'm rambling."

"A little." She smiled.

"I've thought about us like this for some time," Monique explained. "And with those thoughts come doubts. What if you don't like it? Especially after all my flirting; have I built up your expectations too high? I'm extremely good at sex in my professional realm, but this is not that. It's different. And…I get nervous too."

"Not just me with those thoughts, then."

With a rueful look, Monique said, "I haven't had sex just for fun for a long time. I mean *work* sex can be fun, of course, but it's never…" She stopped. "This is *personal*. Do you understand? *You're* personal. And suddenly I go from a confident expert to someone who's putty, and nervous when you look at me the way you are doing now."

"How am I looking at you?" Ottilie asked.

"Like you're extremely tempted while also, maybe, trying to decide whether I'm worth the complications."

"Ah." Ottilie turned apologetic. "You really are good at reading people."

"I am." Monique lifted her hand to Ottilie's face. "May I touch you? I love your cheekbones."

Ottilie sat perfectly still. "Yes."

Monique traced her face, just with her fingertips—from her temple, down her cheekbone, to her chin—then drifted up to brush the corner of Ottilie's lips with the side of her thumb. "Beautiful."

Ottilie shivered at the trails her fingertips had left. "I apologize in advance if I'm...well, what's a word lower down than *rusty*?"

"Exploring." Monique leaned in and kissed the left edge of her mouth. "You have nothing to apologize for." She kissed the right side. "Truly, I have no expectations. I just want you to feel good. I want to pleasure you and feel your touch on me. That's it. That's everything."

Then she kissed her. Properly.

Ottilie tentatively kissed Monique back. Tingles of awareness shot through her. The sensation was exquisite, so much so, she gasped.

Monique drew away, her smile tender. "Lovely," she whispered. "Already I'm mush. The things you do to me." There, in her eyes, lay absolute conviction of her words. She slipped a finger under a lock of hair that had fallen over Ottilie's eye and curled it out of the way. "Darling, there's very little I'm not up for. Just ask. And we can go as slow as you'd like. We'll go at your pace."

Heat coursed through Ottilie at the possibilities. "I think I've waited far too long to go slow now. I'm more than ready." She lifted her fingers to Monique's glasses, removing them, and deposited them on the bedside table beside her well-thumbed copy of *Steppenwolf*.

She studied Monique, her breath catching. She'd believed her days of taking a lover were over, yet here she was, excited beyond any doubts. Everything about Monique was suddenly arousing. Her eyes, glossy hair, scent—tinged with earthiness and vanilla—wasn't that ironic? Nothing about Monique was vanilla, except perhaps her skin cream. Ottilie inhaled her scent deeply, and, unable to resist, dropped a small, teasing kiss under her ear. She pulled back a small distance, watching.

Monique's pupils dilated. "Darling," she whispered. "The way you look at me. You will ruin me. And I'll welcome it."

Ottilie gazed into her intense eyes and was overwhelmed by a rush of pleasure. She leaned in and kissed her, loving the sensation of her tongue against Monique's exploring one.

After a moan, Monique murmured, "God, I've missed this. Kissing. Intimacy."

It was so heartfelt.

Ottilie drew her down for another, deeper, kiss, enjoying how incredible it felt to make Monique Carson, sex goddess, moan. Her lover seemed to be turning liquid under her kisses. When they parted, Ottilie held her gaze, appreciating how Monique simply waited for her. No pressure.

"Still good, darling?"

"I normally don't enjoy being kissed," Ottilie admitted. "It feels too much. Too personal. I'm not comfortable with granting anyone so much access to me."

"That I understand," Monique said. "Kissing is one of the most intimate parts of sex. That's why I don't allow it with clients." She trailed fingertips over her cheekbone once more.

Ottilie drew in a breath. "I find kissing you, feels…" *Loving?* Ottilie wasn't about to say that. "It's not about being conquered. *Dominated.* With you, it feels like receiving a gift."

Monique's dark eyes softened. "That's how it feels for me too."

Ottilie kissed her again, deeper this time, her hands pressing into Monique's hair, stroking her scalp, raking it with her blunt fingernails. Her excitement grew as their tongues touched and tangled. Between her thighs, arousal started to ignite. This time it was Ottilie who moaned.

For long, languid moments they kissed, getting used to each other's mouths, lips, taste, and touch. Ottilie's breathing grew ragged.

"Your mouth is dangerous," Monique said, her own voice deep and rough, when they at last came up for air. "I could get lost, kissing you for hours."

"Later," Ottilie said urgently. "Right now…do you mind if we progress things?"

"You only ever need ask." Monique took a step or two back, and slowly began to remove her blouse and pants, never taking her attention off Ottilie. Now only clad in her bra—crimson—and panties—black—her hands dropped to her side, allowing Ottilie to soak her in.

She was an intoxicating sight. Femininity and power combined. Strong, wide shoulders, a tumble of rich dark-brown hair, pebbling crimson nipples pushing against her see-through bra, a soft swell across her stomach, and thighs rounder and stronger than she seemed to possess when fully dressed.

"You're so…symmetrical," Ottilie teased.

"No higher praise." Monique chuckled.

"And beautiful. So *very* beautiful," Ottilie said seriously this time.

At that, Monique drew in a shaky breath, clearly understanding how rare that descriptor was for her. "Thank you, darling. I think you're magnificent." She held out her hand. "Now, let's undress you. No need to be shy. It's just me."

Ottilie took Monique's hand and stood. Then, with trembling fingers, she undid the zip a little at the back of her dress, tugging it off her shoulders.

She realized this was the first time in years that she'd undressed in front of anyone outside a medical setting. She felt exposed. What would Monique make of her flaws? She had many that she'd hidden for years. At the reminder, she suddenly stopped undressing.

"Allow me," Monique said, coming to stand behind her. Her hands froze on the zip. "Oh, Ottilie," she whispered.

As she'd feared. "Beirut," Ottilie said curtly, as her neck and cheeks heated. "I was freed, as I said, but there was a price." She hesitated. "I know it's not pretty."

Monique lowered her lips to the scarred shoulder blades and kissed.

"You don't have to do that," Ottilie said. "I promise you don't."

"I think I do." Monique kissed her way down as she slowly removed Ottilie's dress, then returned and undid her bra. "I'm so sorry you went through that."

"Please don't think about it anymore. It'll ruin our moment."

Monique took the hint and pushed Ottilie's dress and bra entirely off her torso, down her arms.

Feeling even more exposed, Ottilie wondered what her younger lover made of her aging body. She'd once been toned and fit, with not a line or wrinkle in sight. She might keep herself supple with yoga and be fond of her highly effective age-defying elixirs, but she was still a woman of certain years. There was nowhere to hide now.

But then Monique came to the front, met her eye, and said sincerely, "You're gorgeous," before sliding Ottilie's dress over her hips and the rest of the way down.

Ottilie now stood only in her lace panties—French mulberry silk.

Monique's approving gaze as she touched the ivory material did wonders for Ottilie's confidence. "A woman of exceptional taste, I see," Monique said, running a finger along the lacy band.

"I like a private treat," Ottilie admitted. "A little luxury just for myself."

"A treat for us both, I think." Monique's fingers trailed around Ottilie's hips, appreciating the fabric. "It's so sensual, begging to be stroked."

The cool air and Monique's lingering touch tightened Ottilie's nipples. She clasped her hands nervously in front of her stomach.

Monique's eyes darkened, her distraction over the undergarment forgotten. "I love your breasts. May I kiss them?"

Ottilie glanced down at her large breasts and dark-red nipples. What did Monique see that made her look so hungry? "Yes."

Closing on one crinkling nipple with her lips, Monique plucked the other with her fingers.

Arousal prickled through Ottilie, slow at first, before flaring and spreading lower. Squirming under the pleasant sensations, Ottilie murmured, "Monique?"

Letting go of the nipple with a cheeky *plop*, Monique looked up. "Darling?"

"I'd like to see you too."

Monique flashed her a roguish grin. "But of course." She took a step back and shucked her bra, giving it a salacious twirl before letting it fly. Then she lowered her black lace panties down her full thighs until they hit the floor. Now completely nude, she straightened. "Here I am."

She certainly was. How larger than life Monique seemed when naked. Perhaps it was her confidence and awareness of her own beauty that made her seem *more*. Whatever the reason, it was rather like being faced with a magnificent nude of Venus.

Ottilie was suddenly not sure where to look. She discovered she *wanted* to look, quite badly.

Monique widened her legs slightly and said, "I love the way you're reacting to my body. It's doing wonders for my ego." She gave a low chuckle, then slightly thrust out her breasts. They were much smaller than Ottilie's but so very delectable. And so very close.

Ottilie took her all in. Obviously, she'd seen naked women before. In passing in gym locker rooms. No lingering there, and no interest. But now...Ottilie dwelled.

Her gaze traced Monique's delicious flesh and curves and then dropped to between her legs. Her lovely trimmed dark thatch of hair was already slick.

Monique's hand drifted down. "Look at how you arouse me," she said, voice a low rasp. "You do this to me." And she spread her folds.

Oh God. Ottilie's face was on fire. Her breathing quickened.

"You can touch me," Monique said gently. "If that's what you would like to do. Or should we start with you, hmm? I would greatly enjoy that."

Ottilie didn't think she'd survive if Monique started with her. No, she wanted a taste first, to experience what the tempting woman was offering while she could still think straight—so to speak.

Sitting on the very edge of the bed, now at waist height to Monique, she leaned forward and pressed her lips to Monique's soft stomach, then slowly drew her mouth lower. When she made contact with her wetness there and tickled her folds with her tongue, Monique gasped.

Her hands shot out to Ottilie's shoulders to steady herself. "*Oh! Fuck!*"

Invitation accepted, Ottilie licked and sucked, rubbing her nose and mouth and teeth, savoring the piquant arousal. Making this confident, assured woman wobble, sway, and gasp was incredible. Ottilie felt as powerful as a god. She ran her hands all over her fleshy hips and thighs as her mouth explored her.

Monique trembled when Ottilie did certain actions, so she repeated them, lapping a squishy, slippery rhythm against her sensitive nerves.

"Oh," Monique cried out. "Oh, yes. Do *that* again!"

Ottilie obeyed. And then, feeling bold, she slipped a finger between Monique's legs, pausing at the entrance. Circling the wetness. Waiting. Circling...

"Yes," Monique urged her. "Yes!"

Sliding inside, feeling the warmth and pull of Monique's deepest place, Ottilie began to push and retreat as her tongue continued to draw patterns over her nub.

Monique's thighs began to tremble and wobble. The hands on Ottilie's shoulders clenched her painfully. She cried out Ottilie's name over and over and then stopped mid syllable on *Otti*—

Ottilie's tongue became awash with Monique's arousal. *Oh, what a wonderful aphrodisiac.*

Suddenly, she couldn't wait to experience this herself. But for once in Ottilie's assured life, she didn't know how to ask for the thing she wanted most.

Monique shifted onto the bed, rolling onto her back, her legs falling apart, revealing her arousal. She patted the bed beside herself and, tone molten, said, "Come."

Sliding beside Monique, Ottilie stared at the ceiling, trying to control her breathing, chest rising and falling quickly, wondering how she'd become so desperate. She'd always appreciated control. Self-discipline. And she was very close to simply letting all of that go.

Monique said nothing for a moment, but Ottilie felt herself being watched. She could almost hear her smile when Monique said in a husky tone, "I'll get the lube."

Ottilie was relieved at her lover's ability to understand exactly what she needed without Ottilie having to ask.

She slid down her underwear, folded it precisely, and then, at a loss as to what exactly to do with it, placed the damp silk square next to *Steppenwolf*. Rather fitting, really, since it was a book about the duality of man—his higher self and his more animalistic, lower nature. Her own animalistic self was definitely winning tonight, and she had no regrets.

Fidgeting impatiently, Ottilie waited, self-conscious at her own nudity but so aroused, she didn't even try to hide herself. Her pale body, with so many soft mounds and curves, seemed laid out like a model in a Renaissance painting—fleshy, flushed, and ready for her lover.

Monique returned, then prowled across the bed, a small tube now in her hand. "This is odorless and flavorless, but delightfully effective. May I?"

Heart thundering at the thought of where Monique was about to touch her, Ottilie parted her legs. "Please," she croaked.

Monique squirted a dollop of lube onto her fingers and rubbed them together. "It can be too cold otherwise," she said, with a small smile. "I don't want to give you a shock."

Considerate. She nodded tightly.

"May I go inside too?"

"Yes." Ottilie's nostrils flared as Monique gently slid her oiled fingers all around her lower lips. Up and around her clit—that felt heavenly—then down to her entrance and then deeper still, slowly pushing a finger inside her, up to the second knuckle.

So aroused was she that Ottilie cried out, shocking herself. She was never usually vocal.

Their eyes locked as Monique again and again drew her fingers up and over and inside Ottilie. "I'm going to lick you now," she said. "I'm going to tongue you until you can't see straight, and then I'll fuck you with my fingers until you're crying out with pleasure."

Ottilie gasped at the imagery.

But Monique started much lower. The soft inner thigh was her focus and she kissed her way up until she was breathing heavily on Ottilie's most sensitive area. Her gaze met Ottilie's, asking unspoken permission.

"Yes," she gasped out, her chest heaving. "Yes!"

Her tongue on Ottilie's pussy was rough and warm, thick and nimble, and so very skilled.

Two of Monique's fingers entered deep inside her and began thrusting. "You feel incredible, darling."

Ottilie couldn't speak beyond a strained moan, but she definitely agreed.

"I've wanted you since the first time I saw you. You're so beautiful. I see you, Ottilie. I want you so much."

Ottilie clenched around her fingers as butterfly-light sensations started to flutter inside.

"Will you come? Will you lose control for me?" Monique tongued her clit with purpose now. She murmured into Ottilie's sensitive flesh, "I want to see you trembling under my mouth. I want to see your walls crash down. I want to see you truly naked."

Her tongue lashed her clit again, and Ottilie contracted and shuddered, her orgasm building.

So close!

"Show me," Monique demanded in a low voice. "Show me what you look like…naked." She thrust hard and added, "God, you make me so wet right now. I might come again."

Ottilie couldn't hold back anymore. Her head tilted backwards, and she gasped over and over until her throat was raw. The endorphin rush was sublime. Shuddering against Monique's mouth, she finally cried out.

Monique whispered against her slick folds, "Lovely. Beautiful. Thank you for sharing that with me."

As if she'd had much choice; she was helpless against that wicked tongue. Ottilie exhaled, feeling so sticky and sated and warm. It was like coming home and realizing she hadn't even noticed she'd been away.

"On me," she rasped. "Please, I need you on top of me."

Monique obeyed immediately and positioned herself over her, easing her body onto her.

"*All of you.*" She didn't want kid gloves. She wanted the pressure, the feeling of having been taken, of being surrounded by heat and flesh.

"Of course, darling." Monique pressed her weight fully onto Ottilie.

God. It was *sublime*. The crush of her, the sweaty, scalding, delicious heaviness of her magnified all those last-gasp twitches still firing inside Ottilie. She felt almost gathered up. Their breasts were pressed together, and Monique started slowly rocking their hips, pushing their centers into each other.

Ottilie trembled again, rubbing against her over and over. *Bliss.*

"How are you feeling?" Monique whispered against her neck. "All good?"

"Oh. Yes." The heaviness was starting to feel exactly that, so Ottilie tapped one of her biceps.

Monique took the hint and rolled off her.

"Well," Ottilie said, breathing still unsteady, "I greatly enjoyed that."

"I'm so glad, darling." Monique pulled her in so they were side by side. Now their breasts and bellies and knees touched. It felt almost more intimate.

Monique's hands drifted to Ottilie's back, across the uneven surface, pressing her palm into them. It was so reassuring. Welcoming.

To her own astonishment, Ottilie's eyes pricked with tears.

Snatching her hand off her back, Monique said, "I'm sorry, is that painful?"

"No! Not at all. I don't feel my scars. I'm not sure why I'm so…"

Monique frowned, as if doubting her reassurance.

"I promise it doesn't hurt. I had a team of doctors and all sorts of experts who patched me up and tried to make me whole, heart and soul."

"Did they succeed?" Monique asked gently. She returned her hand to Ottilie's uneven back, smoothing circles across her.

"They did their best," Ottilie said diplomatically. "And that's all I could ask for."

"How… Is it okay to ask how you got them? I mean, specifically?"

"No."

"I'm sorry."

"I mean, ask me tomorrow," Ottilie said. "I don't want to think about what happened now. Tonight's been so enjoyable."

"I understand."

Ottilie drew in a small breath and pulled away. "So, what happens now?"

"Regarding?" Monique's expression turned puzzled.

"Well, do you need to return to your own bed, or…"

"Or?" Monique asked, a smile edging into her face.

"If you'd like to stay, I can make space. Here. I'd…like that, if you would too."

"I'd love to stay," Monique said, then paused. "You understand, this has been a very long time for me."

Ottilie eyed her, confused. "Spending the night with someone?"

"That too. I meant, I allowed you inside me. I save that intimacy only for lovers. People I'm…greatly fond of."

Ottilie turned "fond of" over and decided she liked how that felt. "I appreciate that. Well, please feel free to stay. But no kicking off the blankets. I run cold."

"I'd beg to differ, darling," Monique teased. "I definitely beg to differ."

The next morning, Ottilie found herself being snuggled. By a naked woman. Who was also a sex fantasies expert. And the CEO of a world-leading investment company. All of these facts were unusual, but it was the "being snuggled" part that stuck out most in her brain.

Without thinking too hard about it, Ottilie pressed herself deeper into Monique's soft embrace. The feeling of her lover was delicious, and she wasn't about to pretend otherwise. Last night's sex…well. It had been special. She'd felt respected and adored, and her body had lit up and responded. Her skin still tingled at the memories.

Who would have thought she would find passion at her age? And not just with anyone, but a sex professional. There was little doubt Monique had skills and an awareness of the human body that was sublime. Well, if Ottilie was going to acquire a new diversion, she might as well start her education with an expert.

She felt younger than she had in years. She snuggled—*yes, snuggled*—even further into Monique's warmth, loving the feeling of her body behind her.

"Darling?" came Monique's sleep-heavy voice. "You wish another round? Or are we being affectionate?"

"Affectionate. I'm not ready for more calisthenics just yet. I'm a retiree, for goodness' sake."

Monique laughed throatily. "Could have fooled me. You wore me out too."

"You deserved it. Those eyes? That body? As if I could resist," she said archly.

"Ah, it's my fault for being so beautiful," Monique drawled.

"Precisely." Ottilie exhaled. "I'm glad we did this. I'm sixty-five. Far too old to have not said yes more often over the years. I should have taken more chances."

"I'm fifty-two." Monique sighed. "And I've been so focused on playing it safe that I haven't been taking *any* chances. Oh, but I am a master of rationalizing why that works so well for me."

"*Does* it work well?" Ottilie asked, tone gentle. She turned over in Monique's arms to study her face.

"Absolutely." Monique smiled ruefully. "If you only want to feel nothing but safe. The operative words being *feel nothing*. But recently I've discovered I want to risk being outside my comfort zone for the experience of being with you. God, it's terrifying, though, opening myself up after so long."

"Emotions generally are like that," Ottilie said gravely. "I'm usually not a fan of them."

"Well, then. Look at us being all brave." Monique laughed.

"Oh, I don't feel that it's courage I lack," Ottilie said, thinking about it. "My problem is remembering that life's meant to be lived. It's all too easy for me to forget and focus on other things. Things that don't really matter."

"I won't let you forget." Monique's hands slipped around Ottilie's waist, tracing over her curves, stroking her stomach lazily, then trailing across to her hips. "I promise I'll help you do a lot of living in our time we have together."

Ottilie quivered at the thought. "I like the sound of that."

"By the way, thank you, for saying yes to us," Monique said, gaze earnest. "Honestly, I didn't think you would."

"I didn't think I would either." At Monique's raised eyebrows, Ottilie added, "Because I didn't think I would take *anyone* to my bed ever again. As I said, I get set in my ways, so focused on my goals. Then one day I'll stop and glance around and see what my world has become, and it's dreary. Insular. And small. My world, Monique, is now scarily small."

"It doesn't have to be. There's so much to see and do and experience." Her fingers drifted up to Ottilie's cheek, leaving a sparking trail of heat.

"I know," she agreed. "The closer I got to my retirement, the more I started to notice all these little things, things I'd flown past. Imperfect things or unusual things, but all interesting. *Definitely* worth pausing for." She looked at Monique. "I think, now, a little chaos and untidiness and loss of control is exactly what I need. I'm not dead yet. I don't want to be."

"You're far too young to be thinking of death." Monique slipped her hand into Ottilie's hair, playing with its texture. "Far too young to not be devouring life fiercely."

"That was my conclusion too," Ottilie said. She smiled. "I do love the sound of that."

They gazed at each other for long moments, and Monique dropped a small kiss on her lips. Ottilie met her halfway and kissed her properly.

After drawing apart, Monique said gently, "Soooo, it's morning."

"Yes?"

"I hope it's okay to ask. But last night, you said you might explain…" She drifted her fingertips to Ottilie's back. "I've had a number of clients who are military vets with similar wound patterns. Was it shrapnel? From a blast?"

Ottilie closed her eyes. She'd have to talk about it sooner or later, she supposed. Besides, the broader events weren't classified anymore. An investigative reporter had seen to that.

"I won't push if you don't want to talk about it," Monique said softly.

"No. It's… I'm ordering my thoughts."

Monique waited, still lightly stroking her back. "Are you sure it doesn't hurt?"

Ottilie shook her head. "My neck is the main problem."

"I'm sorry. Necks are the worst."

"They tried to fix it properly at Walter Reed, but there was only so much they could do."

With so much gentleness, Monique asked, "Will you tell me what happened?"

Ottilie drew in a breath. She sincerely hoped Monique's reaction to her ordeal would be different than that of the military psychologist she'd endured. Even the reminder tensed her.

"It was late 1984," she said. "I was twenty-four, in Beirut, and spoke several languages, including Arabic. A wealthy businessman hired me as an English and math tutor for his two little boys. Rumors were circulating that he was funding a high-ranking Hezbollah commander. He was suspicious of everyone, but he decided he trusted me because he thought I was German. It was not safe to be an American in Lebanon at the time, so I did not disabuse him of this notion."

"Makes sense," Monique murmured.

"Then on March 8, 1985, a car bomb went off, killing over eighty people and injuring its intended target, Sheik Mohammed Hussein Fadlallah, who was believed by many in the intelligence community to be the commander and spiritual leader of Hezbollah. The man who'd employed me to tutor his sons was caught in the blast and died instantly."

Distaste filled her mouth at what followed. "Foreign nationals were being captured by Fadlallah's enraged soldiers. I was warned by some well-placed associates to get out. My employer had been a widower, and I couldn't just abandon his children, so I instead rushed them to their grandmother's house that night. But the grandmother had been suspicious of me from day one and turned me in."

Monique's breath hissed.

"I was rounded up along with several groups of hostages. Any low-value targets were executed on the spot."

"You weren't seen as a low-value target, though," Monique said. "Why?"

"Due to the grandmother's suspicions, they wanted to interrogate me to check my story before deciding what to do with me. The situation was chaotic. The US government said it had no spies on the ground. They told Hezbollah there would be no ransoms or prisoner exchanges for any of us. The guards told us often that we'd been abandoned."

Monique stared in dismay. "What the hell? Were they really doing nothing? What was all this even about?"

NUMBER SIX

"Journalist Bob Woodward revealed what had gone on behind the scenes much later, so it's no longer a secret: On September 20, 1984, three months before I was in Beirut, a truck bomb killed two dozen people at the US embassy in Aukar, Lebanon. In retaliation, the US government sent in CIA-trained foreign intelligence agents in specialist teams to get inside Hezbollah terrorist operations. A few operatives were there to observe and report; most were there to do worse."

"Worse?"

"That car bomb attempt on Fadlallah's life was carried out by CIA-trained Lebanese intelligence operatives." Ottilie pursed her lips. "President Reagan's national security adviser said the car bombers had acted on their own. Not America's fault."

"Convenient."

"All lies are."

"But how does any of this relate to you?" Monique asked.

"Some of the CIA-trained foreign agents sent in, the ones who were just watching, seemed unassuming. Innocuous, even."

"Like…a tutor? For a businessman's children."

"That is one example of how it might work. Of course, as an American, I wasn't a *foreign* operative. I sounded a bit foreign, though, and my department head thought that was extremely useful. Even before I left, he told me that he'd say I'd gone rogue if I confessed to anything politically inconvenient under torture."

"Charming." Monique's eyes narrowed.

"Practical. At least from his point of view." She gave a small shrug. "Anyway, my hostage group knew from the start we were alone."

"How terrifying." Monique's hand began rubbing soothing circles along her arm. "Were you all CIA?"

"Officially, none of us were. The clearly identified Americans were all kept together, and they were who Hezbollah focused on interrogating first."

"Were you with them?" Monique asked. Horror crept into her expression.

"No," Ottilie said. "My group contained all the foreigners who weren't American. Well, at least as far as Hezbollah knew. I did recognize one man as being from the US embassy, which also meant he was

CIA, although he had his captors convinced he was South African. Another man looked Egyptian, but his mannerisms, body language, and speech patterns told me he was almost certainly an ex-Marine. And to them, I was a simple German tutor, caught up in the mess through no fault of my own."

"The other hostages didn't know about you?"

"As I said, officially, no one knew anything. I'm fairly sure my cover was intact but it wasn't safe to discuss anything personal." She gave a twisted smile. "We all realized two things quickly: If we were to get out, we had to do it ourselves. And one of the guards was not like the others. He was born in Lebanon, but with his light hair and skin, he looked nothing like a Hezbollah foot soldier. We speculated that perhaps he was some commander's bastard son. The other guards ostracized him, which was useful, since he was often left alone with our group."

"He got you out?"

Ottilie glared at her. "*I* got us out. He was the instrument."

Monique blinked. "How did you get out?"

"He took a liking to me. I allowed it. I"—Ottilie's lips thinned—"encouraged it. I eventually did a trade with him, if he let me make a call to my poor sick mother to tell her I was alive. Needless to say, I called someone else instead."

"What did you have to trade?" Monique asked, dread filling her features.

"What do you think?" Ottilie stared at her in astonishment. "Seriously, what do you think I had to offer? I was twenty-four and apparently attractive and had caught his eye. The US embassy hostage got in my ear the moment he noticed it, suggesting what I should do. I thought about it for days, but I knew he was right. I also knew he'd have done the same thing if our guard had taken a liking to him instead. He was pragmatic and astute. We understood each other."

"So you…seduced him? The guard?"

"I allowed him to think he seduced me. He'd take me into another room and talk to me in Arabic about his family and how he had no friends or wife because he looked so foreign. Sometimes he'd touch my blonde hair and call me *jameela*—beautiful. He only…traded…with me once, but I was taken to be alone with him often."

Ottilie ground her jaw. "Apart from the CIA man, the other hostages could barely even look at me each time I returned to the cell. Their reactions were *enraging*." Her hands clenched. "Especially the ex-Marine, who looked at me with so much disgust. *I* was the one getting us freed, and yet he acted like I was a…" She pursed her lips.

"Whore." Monique finished for her in resignation. "Yes. I know that look well."

Ottilie nodded. "What a judgmental, loaded word that is. To this day, hearing it makes me furious."

Monique's arms wrapped tightly around her. "Trust me, I understand. What happened next?"

"After the trade, he kept his word and allowed me my call. I phoned my 'mother' and left a coded message as to our whereabouts. Three days later, there was a raid by foreign soldiers. Not US Special Forces, of course—the government was still busy denying everything—but their technique and equipment were familiar: They came in loud and fast, throwing flashbangs to disorient the guards. Unfortunately, flashbangs pick up gravel and any detritus lying around. As the person nearest the door, I was left with terrible injuries."

"Your back?"

"Yes. The concussive force flung me hard into the floor, herniated a disc, and caused some small fractures in my vertebra. My neck was never the same."

Ottilie could still smell the next memory. She hated the stench of it, the room, the explosives, the blood. "Before I was injured, though… I shot him in the head."

Monique choked. "What?"

"The guard. The one who…whom I manipulated." She sighed and closed her eyes. "He saw the rescue soldiers before anyone else. He pulled out his rifle. The ex-Marine rushed him, and they wrestled. The rifle skidded across the floor. I retrieved it and shot him in the head. The man was a terrorist, yet his last expression was shock at my 'betrayal.'"

"Oh, darling."

"I'm not sorry." She tightened her jaw. "I'd do it again."

Monique swallowed.

Ottilie rubbed her neck, trying to ease the growing ache. "But that was that. I was sent home and assigned a desk job after my recovery. Hezbollah kept blowing things up and taking Americans hostage—so, essentially, life went on exactly as it had done." She shook her head. "Politically, what I went through wasn't worth a damned thing. It altered nothing except for the lives of those hostages. We're forever changed. I see the ex-Marine every now and then. He guards a senior political figure in DC. He still can't look me in the eye."

"Because you destroyed his ego."

"I freed him! Along with everyone else."

"In his mind, that was *his* job. He failed. You went through that because *he failed*."

"Oh." Ottilie hadn't thought of it like that. "That's hardly my fault." She scowled. "Well. He's still ungrateful." She shook her head in irritation at the reminder. "So, are you sorry you asked?"

"No," Monique said. "Never. My God, what you've been through. You were so brave."

"You understand?" Ottilie asked as she met Monique's gaze. "I did what had to be done. No, it wasn't pleasant, certainly not how one pictures their first time. But the man wasn't violent or unkind. He was gentle and said he had feelings for me. He wanted me to see him as *good*. But he was also a terrorist. I never forgot that, even if he did. I am free today because of my actions. Twelve others in my group are too. It's that simple."

Monique's voice cracked. "You hadn't been with *anyone* before him?"

"*Don't*," Ottilie said sharply. "The military psychologist I was assigned was all torn up about that too. She thought I was in denial because I wasn't beating my chest over it. But never forget, this was *my* choice. I didn't have to do it. Every step of the way, *I* had the power."

"The guard had the power. It wasn't a choice you would have made otherwise."

"Of course it wasn't. But I decided I wanted to get out, and I took effective measures."

"Yes. Still, I'm sorry for what you had to give up to be free."

Ottilie's lips thinned. "I was forced to discuss this with my appointed psychologist endlessly. No one I talked to seemed to believe me when I told them that I switched off, did what was necessary, and, most importantly, I was *fine*. My spirit was never violated. But this was seen as evidence I was lying to myself. It was most…frustrating."

Monique frowned. "Being fine with what you went through is good but not…usual."

"Yes, I'm well aware." Ottilie drew in a deeper breath. "And I don't blame people for being appalled by both my pragmatism and my refusal to feel as bad about it as they did. I know it's not normal. But this is who I am. It's how I'm wired: pragmatic to the bone."

Monique regarded her quietly. "I couldn't have done that. It's not just that the guard was male and I'm extremely lesbian, but I can't disassociate like you. I'm always there, all the time, in the moment. I'm truly glad for your sake, though, that you were able to disconnect. You're so strong mentally."

"I simply rewrote the narrative in my head: I manipulated a gullible young man with feelings for a hostage until he did what I wanted. I'm *not* a victim of abuse by someone with power over me. Do you understand?"

"Yes," Monique said. "And I see now that's why you were so affected by what the senator did to you. That night, you couldn't rewrite the narrative. You did feel like a victim. You seem to be most affected when you feel your power has been taken from you."

Ottilie considered that. "That is true. I couldn't just compartmentalize Kensington's actions and simply…move on."

"And when you saw her again, it all came back."

"And that's why I'm grateful for your words that evening after I'd dealt with her. They were calming and helpful. You put things into perspective. That, more than anything else, is why we're together now. You impress me."

"And you, me. You're unique, Ottilie."

"That's what the psychologists decided in the end. I flummoxed them to the point that they finally threw their hands up." She rolled her eyes. "I think I broke them." Ottilie paused. "But the bottom line on that period of my life is I have no regrets. None."

Monique rested her forehead against Ottilie's. "Nothing I've heard has changed my opinion of you. You're the most interesting person I've ever met. I never even guessed at half of what you're capable of. I'm normally so good at reading people. And now I'm also aware I should treat you with *enormous* respect." Her lips twitched.

"A wise decision. One Kensington has learned to her cost." A savage delight threaded through her at the woman's latest public disgrace.

"So that *was* you, then?" Monique asked. "Her Chefgate scandal?"

"Why do they add a *-gate* to everything?" Ottilie protested. "The media has no imagination."

"They really don't."

"And Ita May isn't a *chef*. A very talented cook, yes, but not a chef. I suppose Cookgate sounds odd. But still…"

"You like precision," Monique teased.

"I really do. Last I heard, Ita May has signed a cookbook deal." Pleasure filled Ottilie at the reminder. "That should rub Kensington's nose in her disgrace even more. It's all worked out even better than I'd hoped."

"I have to say I loved your revenge scheme," Monique said. "Especially given it will prevent the former senator from getting any political power in the future."

Ottilie dropped her head to Monique's shoulder, feeling pleased. "Thank you for not judging me, by the way. For how I felt after Beirut. For not putting me through the same incredulity I endured with my psychologist. Oh, she tried so hard not to judge me and be professional, but I could read her too well. God, it was draining. I'm too over everything to go through that all again."

"I've met far too many people to not know that everyone's reaction to stress and trauma is different. There's no one-size-fits-all reaction, no one *right* way to deal with anything."

"Exactly. Although, personally, I'm prepared to defer to *your* special expertise as a way of dealing with my terribly troubled past," Ottilie deadpanned.

"Are you trying to con a lot of therapy sex out of me?" Monique lifted a playful eyebrow.

"Indeed I am. Is it working?"

"Yes." Monique's arms encircled more tightly around her. "I would very much like to snuggle you for a very long time. Among other things."

"Monique?" Ottilie asked quietly.

"Mmm?"

"Will you tell me why you don't have friends?"

Silence fell. Ottilie glanced at her to see if she had fallen asleep. Instead, anxious dark eyes were watching her.

"I apologize," Ottilie said. "It's for you to decide if you want to share. That is your choice."

"And if I don't share…you'll withdraw your friendship?" Monique sounded tense now.

"No. I know trust must be earned. If you don't feel you trust me, I will accept that."

"It's not that I don't trust you. I do. It's just, what happened…it's humiliating."

"As is working for The Fixers," Ottilie said evenly. "I didn't anticipate you ever learning that secret, but here we are. You know more about me than anyone alive now. I'm still not sure how you did that."

Monique gave a soft smile. "I'm perceptive. And highly invested."

Ottilie smiled back.

"I wasn't always," Monique said with a sigh. "Perceptive. I was, in fact, rather dense as a young woman. Foolish."

"Aren't we all?"

"I took it to new levels." Monique drew in a breath. "Look, I don't have friends because I didn't want to be hurt again. That's all it boils down to. I'm a coward. So my philosophy was: no new friends who might betray me, no intimate partners who might break my heart."

"I'm sorry." Ottilie's heart squeezed in sympathy.

Monique closed her eyes for a moment. "I was eighteen, living in Paris. When you're a teenage model, you get assigned a mentor. Someone who's been there, done that, and knows the pitfalls. My model mentor was Stacy. She was from England and had so much grace, so much elegance. I was smitten."

"You were in love?"

"Not as you might think: not romantically, or even sexually. I felt I was too far out of her league to even countenance that. But I was her most devoted, starstruck student. Every day, she'd cup my cheek and tell me she was looking out for me. And…she said to trust no one else. That modeling was a vicious snake pit. Trust her, though, and I'd be fine. Only her."

"*Only* her," Ottilie said, sensing where this was going.

"I'm not sure how she managed it, but over time I became so dependent on her for advice on everything. She was telling me what to eat, how to dress, and the people I was allowed to be friends with. It amused her when I started my 'little investment hobby' as she called it, so she didn't fight that. But everything else, she dictated my every move."

"She was controlling."

"She was more than that. Stacy was my whole world. But I couldn't see her for what she was. Other models around me expressed concern. The manager of my modeling agency floated having Stacy replaced. I was enraged and decided they didn't have my interests at heart."

"Unlike Stacy," Ottilie murmured. "The only one you could trust."

"Exactly." Monique hesitated and admitted, "It was Stacy who hooked me on cocaine."

Ottilie's eyes widened.

Shame flooded Monique's face. "I know. I was twenty by then and under her spell. 'All the girls are doing it,' she told me. 'It keeps models thin. It's not as addictive as people say.' I loved food and was struggling to stay rail-thin. I'd be at the gym for hours. Her solution seemed so much simpler. Besides, I trusted her implicitly. And, yes, it kept me thin…*and* turned me into an addict. Later, I felt so incredibly stupid, so used. That was the last time I ever allowed someone autonomy over my body. What the hell was I thinking?"

"That must be hard to face." Ottilie couldn't imagine how ashamed Monique must have felt by her younger self's choices.

Number Six

"It was. One of the reasons my modeling company let me go was that I was too distracted. Partly due to my new finance business. But also because I was a drug addict. The manager told me she was sending me home for my own good. She hoped I'd get clean and get a clue and look her up again if I sorted myself out."

"Did that happen?"

"No. Even after being fired, I still didn't believe I had a major problem. Why was I being singled out if all the girls were doing coke, I wondered. Why was my manager trying to break Stacy and I up? She was my only real friend, the only person I trusted."

"I assume that at some point you realized she'd broken your trust?"

"Oh, yes. Although, not just broken my trust. Stacy shattered my heart. My faith in people. In even the idea of friendship. After that, I kept everyone at arm's length. It was emotionally safer. And I was getting plenty of physical affection from an active sex life. I had so many people I could socialize with—on a surface level—if I needed to, so I couldn't see the benefit of friendship at all."

"How did you get off the drugs?" Ottilie stopped. A worrying thought flitted through her. "I'm assuming you did?"

Monique gave her a measured look. "I have been clean for twenty-five years."

"I apologize." Ottilie looked down. "I shouldn't have—"

"It's fine," Monique said crisply. "It's a valid question. Anyway, I was back home in the US, so I set up Carson Investments in New York. Two years later, I found myself in Vegas for a finance and investment convention. The day I met Cleo, who was dancing there as part of a corporate event, everything changed. I wanted to be near her constantly. I was so besotted." She paused and added wryly, "She wasn't."

"Oh dear."

"She looked me dead in the eye and said, 'I don't date junkies.' I don't even know how she knew my darkest secret with such certainty. She knew, though. That burned. So, I quit drugs. *For her*. It's so galling admitting I didn't quit for me. It took a while and a few lapses, but eventually I beat my addiction. I moved permanently to Vegas to be with her. And the longer I was here, with Cleo in my life as this incredible, indomitable force, the easier it was to stay clean. But, after a few years, Cleo met the woman she fell madly in love with, her wife, and told me we'd be better as friends."

"Ouch," Ottilie murmured.

"Right? I was still in love. To be fair, Cleo had told me up front before we dated that she would never settle down with me. She was fond of me, of course, but I was a 'friends with benefits deal' for her. And, so, that was that. She moved on with Rochelle, and I was a hurt, rejected mess."

"Sounds very difficult."

"I wish I could say I was mature about it. But, alas, I wasn't the evolved goddess you see before you today." Monique quirked a smile. "I started having casual flings with her dancers to piss her off. That didn't work because if Cleo noticed, she didn't care. Then one of the dancers told me I had a real gift for pleasing women. She suggested I could share it and earn good money at the same time, if I wanted. I was intrigued. Turned out she was doing sex work herself. I decided it might be a good distraction from my overwhelming feelings."

"It was a lot more than a distraction," Ottilie noted, "if you're still doing it."

"Well, I found I truly did have a skill for opening women up to their sexuality and sensuality. More than that, I loved it. So, I became a CEO sexual fantasies expert. It took a few years more, but Cleo and I found our way back to being friends, mainly because we knew each other so well. And her wife is, admittedly, adorable."

"But no other friends need apply?"

"Once bitten…" Monique sighed. "Honestly, by then, I just didn't trust myself. How couldn't I have known what Stacy was like? She'd manipulated me at every step, turned me into a junkie. I felt so blindsided; what if someone did that to me again? Why risk it? I had everything I needed."

"Did you ever hear from Stacy again?"

"Oh, yes. She tracked me down while I was still in New York and tried to lure me back to modeling in Europe. By then, I didn't even want to look at her, but I never forgot."

"I don't understand one thing," Ottilie said. "What did your mentor get out of hooking you on drugs?"

"Control. She got off on having innocent young women obedient and at heel."

"You seem so independent. It's hard to picture you at anyone's heel."

"That has taken a great deal of work. I'm glad you can't see it."

"And yet your entire friendship rules stem from Stacy—who was just *one* damaged, manipulative person."

"I know," Monique said quietly. "I'm well aware. But it's been easier."

"Safer," Ottilie said. "No risk. You'll never feel crushed or betrayed ever again."

"No." She exhaled. "And I know it's the coward's choice. Still, there are people I talk to regularly, joke with, and so on. I haven't ever had to worry about my social batteries dying. There's always Cleo if I need to point to having a friend. What of you? Are you drowning in friends?" Monique stopped. "Actually, I cannot picture that."

"No. I'm selective. I have a few friends here or there I've carefully chosen over the years. That was a deliberate decision. I did not want to befriend colleagues, most of whom I found either tedious or dangerous, and I rarely met civilians outside work."

"What of the friend you wanted photos of showgirls for?"

"Hannah." Ottilie warmed at the reminder. "I felt sorry for her when I met her because she was so clever yet so very bored. What a waste of a fine mind. So I befriended her, and it turns out I'm the one enriched by our friendship."

"She must be incredibly smart if *you're* impressed by her."

"Yes. She's not only smarter than me—I have no doubt about that—but she was someone who had no use at all for anything I could do, which made me appreciate her even more."

"Anything you could do?" Monique studied her. "We're back to power again, aren't we? Who has it and who wants it."

"Power is crucial to so many."

"No," Monique said. "It's about as vital as the approval of others."

"It's irrelevant whether you care for power; it's other people's craving for it you need to worry about. In life, there are only two things that matter: power and control. Those who run the world and those who seek to. Everything else is a lie hidden by shiny distractions. Never ever attempt to unpeel the lie." Ottilie shot her a long look. "Trust me on that one."

"Except power is an illusion," Monique argued. "I can strip you of it or give it back in the blink of an eye. It is a concept sold by men who get hard from the thought that it makes them special. It doesn't. I can tell you, having made the weak feel powerful and the powerful feel weak, that power is actually nothing at all."

"Then why does power make the world go around?" Ottilie asked.

"Only if we let it. If you refuse to buy into it, refuse to accept someone's authority over you, that will undo them pretty fast. They're at a total loss."

"In relationships, maybe. But challenge someone politically powerful, and they'll throw you in jail."

"That's not power. It's brute force. Punishment," Monique observed. "If power were real, if it were more than an illusion or a lofty title, it wouldn't need a big stick to enforce it."

"Monique," Ottilie said with a tiny headshake, "Power *is* the stick."

They looked at each other and suddenly both laughed.

"I love debating you," Monique said, smiling. She dropped a kiss on her cheek. "But..." She glanced at the clock. "I do have a client in an hour, so I'd better get back to my room."

Ottilie's smile died. She quickly turned away as something foreign surged in her. *Jealousy?* She was feeling jealous? When had that ever happened before?

"Are you all right, darling?" Monique asked, concern in her voice.

"Of course," Ottilie said briskly.

"Please don't be worried for me. The client is a regular, someone I trust. She'd never hurt me."

"Good," Ottilie said. "I should get up anyway and stop monopolizing you. I'll let you get on with your day."

"I can cancel the client if you want more 'us' time," Monique offered. "I accepted the client booking weeks ago, before we were... Before *us*."

NUMBER SIX

"I don't want to get in the way of your work." Ottilie smiled overly brightly now. "If that's what makes you happy, you should do it."

Monique studied her, a guarded look on her face. "If you're sure?"

"I am." Ottilie rose and headed to the bathroom, then closed the door.

By the time she'd left the bathroom, Monique was gone.

Chapter 18
Last Loose End

Two days later, the call finally came through from Snakepit. Ottilie felt two emotions in equal measure. Relief her mission was finally at an end. And…disappointment. Wasn't that a confusing revelation?

"He's just checked in, as you predicted. Room 522," Snakepit reported.

"Check the rooms on either side of his. Are either empty?"

Keys rattled quickly. "Both are. How'd you know?"

"He'd request it, if it was possible, knowing him. Gives him a sense of security. Foolish man." She smirked. "Although it's extremely useful for me."

"Do I *want* to know?" Snakepit asked, sounding slightly afraid. And a little awed.

"I don't think you do," Ottilie said, hiding her amusement. "But it won't be anything terribly onerous at my age."

"Well, I wouldn't want to cross you at any age. Anyway, g'luck, ma'am."

"Thanks," Ottilie said. "I'll pay you a bonus for all your extra work and diligence. You're an excellent hacker, Mr. Snakepit. Why don't you relocate for a little while? I think DC might be a little too…hot… right now if you want to stay out of trouble. Sooner or later, various political and police investigations will try to find out how The Fixers knew so much. It's not safe, even for you."

"Yeah. I kinda came to that conclusion myself. I'm making plans. Duppy, my old hacker friend in LA, has offered to put me up for a bit." He snickered. "Can't wait to break it to him I could buy his whole condo block now."

"Well, then," Ottilie said. "Happy life."

"You too, ma'am. Bye."

She hung up and smiled to herself at the idea of having a happy life. At last. She was one meeting away now from finally retiring. Pacific island. Beaches. Mai Tais. *Sold.*

Except, now she also had a sense of loss about leaving. And she was damned sure it wasn't over Las Vegas.

Ottilie situated herself on Alberto Baldoni's hotel room balcony, sipping a coffee she despised, poured from a Thermos. She'd placed a second empty cup, saucer, and spoon in front of the chair beside her and waited.

"Christ!" came a muffled masculine explosion ten minutes later. The door to the balcony wrenched open, and Baldoni appeared. He shook his head. "How the hell did you get in here?"

He turned to glance at the door to his hotel room as if confirming it was still locked and chained. It was.

"Mr. Baldoni," Ottilie said, "never acquire a room with a balcony. Being a former security operative, I'd have thought you'd know it's too easy to breach from next door."

He pivoted to look at the frosted shoulder-high divider between the balconies and then eyed her. "You scaled *that*?" His sharp black eyes widened.

"You make it sound hard," Ottilie drawled, sipping her coffee.

Her contact in housekeeping had let her in next door during her rounds. Not remotely difficult.

And if Baldoni looked over the balcony divider, he'd find a tall chair had been pushed against it. The jump and roll she'd effected over the top of the tempered glass barrier from the chair was a testament to her yoga skills. The not-entirely-graceful landing was a testament to her age. Her knees would probably give her hell later, but such was life.

"So my little stalker's finally caught up to me." Baldoni dropped hard into the chair next to her, irritation thick in his tone before his eyes fell to the Thermos. "You drink coffee now? Since when?"

"Not…exactly. I brought some for you, since I'm aware it's your obsession. Well, one of them. Think of it as a peace offering."

Ottilie pointed to the spare cup, spoon, and open Thermos before him. She pushed a few sugar sachets his way as well, in case he wanted them. "After you left The Fixers, we acquired an enthusiastic employee who extolled the virtues of organic coffee. This was the least obnoxious strain of the ones on offer. I thought you might like it. It's Laughing Man's Ethiopia Sidama."

He made no move toward it. "Poisoned, I presume?"

"This is the reason I'm suffering through a coffee," Ottilie intoned. "To prove it's not been interfered with." She reached for the Thermos and added a little more of the black liquid to her cup and then slowly drank it. "And your imagination runs wild if you think I'd ever bother poisoning you."

Baldoni's nostrils twitched. The brew truly did have a delightful aroma, if your weakness lay in coffee. He reached for the Thermos, poured it to the cup's brim, and then peered hard at the sugar sachets. His gaze darkened with suspicion.

With an eyeroll, Ottilie reached for the sachets, mixed them all up, grabbed one at random, then dumped its contents in her own coffee. Priming herself, she forced more of the liquid down her throat. "Ugh. Too strong for my taste. Now, tea is a gentler brew."

That earned a derisive smile. As if liking strong coffee was for real men. Baldoni took two sugar sachets, emptied them in the full cup, and stirred ferociously with his teaspoon. When he tested it, his eyes lit up. "Fuck, that *is* powerful."

"It is," Ottilie agreed, still wishing she could get the taste out of her mouth.

He swallowed another mouthful and grinned. "So you have my attention. Although it's a bit hard to avoid it when you break and enter."

"Mr. Baldoni, you might have saved us both a lot of trouble by making yourself available when I first requested we meet. I shouldn't have to break into your room to get an audience."

"I assumed I was about to be stitched up as a scapegoat for your dirty little organization. I decided I rather liked my freedom."

"Nonsense," Ottilie said. "Have I not always treated you fairly? Long after you departed The Fixers?"

"You mean, whenever you asked me to do your dirty work? By dangling the carrot that it would annoy my ex-wife?"

"Both those things can be true simultaneously."

He laughed, and his legs sprawled out halfway under her side of the outdoor table. A power play.

She adjusted her chair to face him instead.

Baldoni was an elegant, dangerous man with a bone structure sculptors would weep for. The facial symmetry was ruined by a jagged scar that bisected one cheek, the result of a confrontation with the reporter Lauren King. He wore his damaged face with swagger.

To Ottilie, he was slick, smart, and borderline odious—an occasional necessary evil. Bitter and angry about losing his wife, Michelle Hastings, to journalist Catherine Ayers a decade ago, he'd done everything he could to hurt Michelle ever since. He didn't care that the former Fixers CEO had, in turn, ruined Ayers—and, as a result, become an icy, miserable wasteland herself for years. No, the man was still fixated on the corpse of his broken marriage.

Ottilie withdrew an envelope from her bag. "This is why I'm here. These are the names that are never to be linked to The Fixers. If you leak them directly or indirectly, you will be ruined. That is a promise."

Looking bored, he held out his hand. "Let's see who the exulted few are on the safe list."

Ottilie handed it over. "You will add my name too."

He nodded, read it, then put it down. "Interesting."

"How so?"

"My ex-wife's name is on there. Second last."

"And?"

"Michelle's name stands out. All the other names are either agents I barely knew or department heads who were small potatoes. Daphne

Silver? Phelim O'Brian? And the espionage pair? Why save them? The board wouldn't even be able to pick them out of a lineup. This is *not* the board's list." He eyed her pointedly. "It's yours."

Ottilie inhaled. *Damn him.* "Is that so?" she said neutrally.

"I also know you have no burning desire to protect any of these people. Yet, apparently, you've been jet-setting all over the world, demanding that various well-placed former employees don't leak these names to the media. Why?"

Ottilie didn't speak.

"No comment? Well, here's my theory." He leaned in. "The names are red herrings to throw people off your real game. Only one name on that list has any significance. There's only one person you even know well enough to concern yourself with their fate. So: why are you protecting my ex-wife so much that you'd go to these lengths?"

Ottilie cursed inwardly. Baldoni had been an effective bloodhound for The Fixers, often seeing patterns others didn't. He could work out motives faster than anyone on the security team. No one else had figured out the truth.

While she had no special fondness for Michelle Hastings, beyond finding her occasionally clever or amusing, she would move heaven and earth to protect Hannah.

Ottilie had always been protective of those she cared about—especially given how few there were. She'd wanted to spare Hannah the media circus of seeing her beloved granddaughter named and shamed as a former CEO of the discredited organization.

It would only take one thoughtless ex-Fixers staffer—or, worse, one with a vendetta—for Michelle to be exposed. It was bad enough her voice could be heard on a few of the damning client videos the media were airing, but so far, no one had identified her.

Given it was easily within Ottilie's power to prevent that happening, her blackmail world tour—visiting the ex-employees most at risk of leaking—had been the logical next step. It was a way to ensure Michelle's name never saw the light of day. That had felt like such a simple thing she could do for Hannah, who'd come to mean a great deal to her.

NUMBER SIX

She debated what to say. That Baldoni was right: the other names were a smokescreen and had nothing to do with the board. She'd listed people who had either made her job easier, treated her well, or who were relatively decent people—as much as one could be when working for an ethically dubious organization.

"I don't agree with tarring every CEO with the same brush," Ottilie said. "She's not like the rest. The others, with one exception, were terrible people. She was fair. Michelle doesn't deserve destruction."

"Oh, she most certainly deserves destruction," Baldoni snapped. "For humiliating her loyal husband." Fury lit his eyes, then faded. "But what's the real reason? Because you don't care about fairness; you never did."

"I care. You just never saw it." She'd never shown it to him, she meant. He was so twisted, he'd perceive it as weakness.

"I saw enough. You were no saint. Now, enough with the bullshit. Why are you protecting her?"

She sighed. He'd always been far too shrewd, and he'd be relentless until he got his answer. "Fine. I've become friends with Michelle's grandmother. If Michelle's involvement with The Fixers ever got out, it would ruin Michelle, and devastate Hannah."

"You're protecting that bitch? That old bat took one look at me and called me *dangerous and ruthless*. To. My. Face. I don't know why I'd lift a finger to help Hannah Fucking Hastreiter now."

Ottilie's opinion of Hannah went up another notch. A frail old woman telling off a nasty piece of work like Baldoni was brave. "Are you *not* dangerous and ruthless?" she asked silkily.

"That's not the damned point!" Baldoni snapped. "The woman sabotaged my marriage!"

"No she didn't," Ottilie said with a huff. "It was already sabotaged. Michelle was suffering PTSD from her FBI work. She was vulnerable, and you seemed like a protector, swooping in to save her. You know that's why you wanted her. You felt like a hero. But you must surely know the truth: she never loved you."

Baldoni scowled at her.

No denial. He did know. Or had at least suspected.

"Right," Ottilie said, keeping her tone curt. "Are we done with your justifications? Or do I have to sit here and listen to all the reasons, a decade on, that you still obsess over a woman not interested in you? It's pathetic, Alberto. You cannot force someone to love whom they do not. Besides, Michelle's long since moved on. She's happy with her new woman."

His eyes widened.

"You didn't know?"

His shoulders relaxed.

"What?" Ottilie peered at him.

"I thought being with Ayers was a one-off. But maybe Michelle was never into men at all."

Ottilie had long suspected that might be true. She said thoughtfully, "Does that make you feel better? Because I must say Michelle looks at her girlfriend in a way she *never* looked at you."

Baldoni scowled. "What would you know about anything? I *loved* my wife. You wouldn't know love if it bit you on the ass."

"Foolish boy," she scorned, finally losing patience. "You don't even know what love is! Love makes you want to give that person everything they've ever wanted, not make them miserable at every opportunity as you've been trying to do."

Alberto snorted. "Well, well, listen to you. Don't tell me you've finally found someone who'll put up with you? Is watching you alphabetize your filing a naughty kink they have?"

Adopting a bored look, she muttered, "If you're quite finished?"

"You and love would be like buzzkill and sunshine." He smiled sweetly then, all rumpled and boyish, and for the briefest of moments, Ottilie could see the charmer who'd reeled in a younger Michelle Hastings. "*Now* I'm finished."

"Back to the point," Ottilie said. "I will protect Hannah. With or without your help. But *with* gives you protection."

"And without? What have you got on me?"

"Every dealing we ever had. I'd throw you under the bus so fast, it'd barely bounce running over your body."

He smiled. "You're making me hard, all this ruthless talk."

"Don't be crass," she snapped.

"And what if I threw *you* under the bus?"

"What proof do you have I was anything other than a clueless, sweet secretary? I would play that card and destroy you in the process."

"Well," he said. "You likely could. You're a good little actress when it suits."

"And you're out of options. So, do you agree to my terms?"

"With one stipulation."

"What?"

"Tell Michelle that a showgirl headlining in a big production has fallen for me and that I'm letting her move in with me. Give the girl a good name. Something that says she has big boobs and looks hotter than Michelle ever did."

How petty. "If that's what you want, I'll tell her." Michelle likely wouldn't believe it anyway. Ottilie would be sure to mention that big showgirl productions didn't exist anymore.

"Good." His eyes gleamed, doubtlessly imagining his ex-wife's displeasure.

Ottilie studied him for a long moment. "I want to be clear about one thing: after today, all your petty revenge against your ex-wife ends here."

"You enabled me," he shot back. "Offering me odd jobs here and there, saying they'd annoy her."

"I did do that. I was goal oriented. I shouldn't have reached for an easy solution just because it was efficient. And you should have said no."

"It was too tempting not to."

"I'm well aware. But that's over now. You won't be getting any more work from me in any capacity. I'm tired of looking at you, and I'm tired of hearing about your ridiculous vendetta. It all stops. Now."

He lifted his chin. "Yeah, whatever. Oh, hey, tell my lovely ex the dancer's name is *Lulu*."

"Fine," Ottilie muttered and made to stand. "*Lulu*. If we're done here?"

He rose too. "It's been an experience knowing you. You had everyone fooled. Well, everyone *else*. I worked out you were the toughest person in the entire Fixers the day I met you."

"Me?" She raised a mocking eyebrow. "There were former FBI, CIA, MI5, Mossad, and KGB agents in that building."

"I said toughest. Not meanest or cruelest. Because you were neither of those. But in the apocalypse, Ottilie Zimmermann, there will be only you and the cockroaches."

"Thank you."

"It wasn't a compliment," he protested lightly.

"Wasn't it?" She smiled sweetly and picked up her Thermos. "By the way, the coffee wasn't poisoned. The sugar either." Ottilie then carefully picked up his teaspoon and held it up to the light. "This was."

Baldoni's mouth dropped open. "What?"

"Oh, don't worry. Nothing lethal. Your spoon was dipped in a clear laxative oil before I placed it on your saucer."

He gasped.

Alberto Baldoni had done a lot of evil in his life and had paid for little. This felt surprisingly satisfying, even if it was minor. "Five drops is all that's needed. You probably consumed fifteen. It means you'll spend Vegas's richest poker tournament in the bathroom instead. Better luck next year."

Fury washed across his face. "Why?"

"You inconvenienced me. I would have already been retired by now if not for you. Next time, if there ever *is* a next time, answer my call promptly."

And with that, she left.

―――――・◇・―――――

That night, Ottilie rang Michelle and dutifully passed along her ex-husband's news about Lulu the fake dancer. She didn't bother to hide her disdain as she did so.

With a snort, Michelle said, "I'd say good luck to her, but we both know he's lying. He'd never bother with a woman like that."

"A woman like…that?" Suddenly, a defensiveness arose in Ottilie on behalf of the talented dancers she'd met in Vegas. Women like Cleo and Sahara weren't cheap or disposable.

"Women he thinks are easily turned by his slick suit or charm. He loves the challenge of the chase. The hard-to-get woman. He'd see Vegas dancers as too easy."

Ottilie's hackles went down.

"But why are you even bothering to tell me?" Michelle continued curiously. "You had to know he's lying. It's not like you to involve yourself in someone else's dramas unless it benefits you."

She had her there. When they had worked together, Ottilie's focus had only ever been on furthering her own aims. She wondered whether to tell Michelle that she was attempting a fresh start—at being better at life, beginning by not positioning efficiency above all else.

But even if Ottilie believed that, she doubted Michelle would. There was too much between them, lies and secrets, a sludge of ethical murkiness that would never sit well. In short, Ottilie wasn't exactly a reliable witness.

"I told Alberto I'd tell you, and I have," Ottilie said. "I didn't tell him that you wouldn't believe it even for a second," she added with amusement, "that you were far too smart for that."

"You think I'm smart?" Disbelief filled her voice. "Since when?"

Ottilie pursed her lips. "Michelle, I have *always* thought you were smart."

"The day I was fired, you made me believe you'd been pulling all my strings. I was little more than a puppet! You couldn't contain your derision."

Running a hand down her thigh to reflexively smooth out her skirt, Ottilie admitted, "Michelle, the day you were fired, I was angry at you for forcing the board's hand. I knew your firing would make my life difficult. Dreams of an easy final year until my retirement were in tatters. I knew it would be much harder to manage Kensington as CEO, and I took that out on you. I said things to belittle. To…punish. So you'd feel some of the aggravation I felt."

"You succeeded expertly," Michelle murmured, voice lined with ice.

"Yes, well." Shame seeped into her. "I know I implied none of your CEO decisions were your own. That I had been the puppet master at all times. That was not strictly true. Yes, I had a lot of power, far more than most were aware, but you also had far more autonomy than I let on. I wanted you to question everything, to feel useless. I'm not proud of that."

Silence filled the air, and only Michelle's breathing told Ottilie she was still listening.

"I was still angry when I saw you next," Ottilie went on, "when I went to your apartment with my plans to destroy The Fixers. By then, I had been suffering under Kensington's hands for many months. She was a terrible CEO, and my enduring her was a direct result of your actions. I was stressed, overworked, and fed up with being treated by her *and* the board as little better than sentient pond scum. So I was petty and took some delight in making you feel like a fool for not knowing how brilliant I was." Ottilie grimaced. "That was unworthy of us both. You did not deserve to be the target of my wrath. I apologize."

"And now?" Michelle asked, after a long beat. "Are you still angry?"

"No." Ottilie blinked at the realization of how not-angry she was these days. A weight had lifted when she'd left The Fixers. "I'm not."

"Hannah seems to think you've 'found a reason to live now'. That was all she'd say and I didn't want to press her about your private business, but I have my suspicions."

"Your grandmother is an astute woman."

"Although I admit I'm curious as to who your special woman is. Someone who could manage to turn even your head."

Ottilie froze in shock. She hadn't even told Hannah she was dating a woman. How—

"I see things too, Ottilie," Michelle said dryly. "I'm glad for you." And she sounded it.

Michelle had always been a better woman than Ottilie, a decent woman caught in a terrible situation. Smart. Ethical, as much as she could be. "In spite of all that's been said and done," Ottilie said finally, "I respected you. Then and now. I should have said that before."

"I…appreciate that. But why are you telling me any of this?"

"I suspect this may be the last time we ever talk. Besides, you didn't have to help me destroy the senator. I'm grateful for that. The truth is the very least I could give you in return."

"The downfall of Phyllis Kensington," Michelle mused, sounding satisfied. "Oh, yes, that was a spectacular event."

Ottilie hummed in agreement. "It was." She waited a beat. "Before I go, I should say, most genuinely, Michelle, I'm pleased you've found happiness. You've earned it. I'm certain Ms. Lawless is busy keeping you on your toes, between one protest endeavor or another."

"Naturally," Michelle said evenly, although the smile was evident in her voice.

Ottilie chuckled.

And that was that.

Chapter 19
Pacific Island, Beach, Mai Tais

For several days, Ottilie brooded over Baldoni's comments. Love seemed an odd thing for someone to accuse her of. She'd never been in love before.

Or...now? Well. Ottilie was fairly sure her time with Monique wasn't that. Not love.

Except...

She was still here. Days had turned into weeks since the last loose end had been tied up, and before she knew it, two months had passed. And still she stayed.

She hadn't told Monique her work had been finalized and she was now free to fulfill her retirement dream: Pacific island, beaches, Mai Tais.

Nor had Ottilie made any plans for plane trips or checked that the housekeeper/cook she'd hired was waiting at her island destination.

Instead, she kept finding excuses to stay. Because it made Monique happy and that, in turn, suited her. What she didn't want to analyze was what that meant.

Love makes you want to give that person everything they've ever wanted.

She'd hurled those words at Baldoni without even thinking. But now they plagued her. What did it mean that she'd even ruminated on what someone in love wants?

NUMBER SIX

It was ridiculous because what Ottilie most wanted was to be on her Pacific island. Obviously. And yet what she was *doing* was something else entirely.

She was dining daily with Monique and inviting her into her bed each night. She greatly enjoyed sliding herself against the woman's soft body, breathing in her scent, drawing her close, and murmuring about how she had been feeling cold without Monique—and wasn't this an acceptable solution?

Monique always smiled at her nonsense, pulled her close, and said that she had a whole list of ways to warm Ottilie up, ways Ottilie had never even imagined. And would she like that?

Ottilie had found herself liking a great many of the things Monique wanted to try. Honestly? She was having the best time of her life.

Still, though, her island called. A dream of years was hard to forget. She didn't *want* to forget it. But then Monique looked at her with so much fondness, a look just behind her darkening eyes that pleaded: *Don't go. Not yet. We're not done. Stay?*

And so Ottilie stayed.

What did it mean? For an intelligent woman, Ottilie was not especially fond of not knowing the answer. Or, perhaps, her problem was not believing it.

Because Ottilie Zimmermann, sixty-five-year-old former spy, had absolutely not caught a case of *feelings*.

Monique, naked and quivering, gasped as she came down from one hell of an orgasm. She peppered kisses all around her lover's mouth and neck, while murmuring how beautiful she was.

Ottilie, sweaty in the afterglow, placed a hand on Monique's biceps and squeezed lightly until she had her attention. Almost casually, she said, "By the way, my loose ends have been tied up."

Fear chilled Monique, but then Ottilie squeezed her arm again, forestalling a reply.

"I should have left two months ago. I've been staying on for you. I thought you should know."

On paper, the words sounded romantic and sweet, but there was little of that in the delivery. Even so, Monique's heart had almost stopped beating.

Ottilie held her eye and said, "It confuses me, the pull you have that makes me stay. And I don't like being confused."

Was that why she was staying? To understand her confusion? "So I'm a knot you're unpicking?" Monique asked, her stomach clenching.

"Maybe I *am* staying to see why you have this hold on me. But mainly I think I'd miss you if I left. I'm unaccustomed to that feeling."

"I'd miss you too," Monique said. "Honestly, I don't want you to go."

"It is unexpected."

"Which part?"

"So many things," Ottilie said. "Ordinarily, I don't like anyone in my bed. Yet you fit just so." She blinked. "You fit *me* just so."

"I know the feeling, darling."

Monique definitely did. Her feelings for Ottilie had sneaked up on her gradually.

It was odd to realize how her mind had started rearranging itself from *me* to *us*. When she spoke to Cleo now, she would sometimes say "we" in regards to her plans. It would just slip out. And Cleo would give a low chuckle each time and murmur, "Now I know it's serious. Is there a U-Haul on the horizon?"

At first, she'd denied it—to herself and her friend. It was only casual and would stay that way until Ottilie moved on, because of course she would. It was foolish to hope for more. It was her and Cleo all over again. Ottilie had been clear the moment they'd met what her plans were—and none of them involved shacking up permanently with a sexual fantasies expert in a hotel in Vegas.

Even just saying that screamed *unserious*, didn't it? How could anyone take Monique seriously, given she sold fleeting X-rated encounters to strangers in a city of garish, neon dreams?

She didn't even take herself seriously half the time. It had been so easy to skim over the surface of life. Avoiding commitments, avoiding friendships. Avoiding anything too hard or painful. She never wanted to hurt like she had in the past: Stacy. Cleo.

God, not again!

She was stuck once more, waiting for the impending pain that came from loving and losing. And she was helpless to stop it.

Monique had often found Ottilie poring over a website with island pictures on it, and every time, her heart would stutter. *Is this it?* she'd wonder.

But Ottilie would catch her looking and always say, "It's for later. Only when it's time."

When it's time. And yet it now seemed to *be* time, and Ottilie hadn't left. To both their confusion, it seemed.

And, as bizarre as it sounded, they simply held each other after Ottilie's confession, studying the other's face for a long while. Then they kissed and didn't discuss it again.

Monique put down her cell phone and stared at it in surprise. That clinched it: she was officially having a crisis. One of those slow-moving ones she'd been having for at least five months but that was only just catching up with her.

The caller had been a regular client, a statuesque news anchor from Atlanta with adorable dimples and a wicked sense of humor. She'd just cancelled, and Monique felt *relief.*

Relief!

The oddest part about the feeling was that she genuinely enjoyed Roberta James. The deeply closeted client was respectful, unproblematic in every way, and always appreciative of spending time with Monique.

Roberta loved being dominated over a desk—a request Monique could do in her sleep. And yet, Monique discovered, she was just no longer interested.

Hence: crisis.

What is wrong with me?

Am I tired of sex work?

Am I tired of sex?

That didn't seem likely. She loved fucking Ottilie at every possible opportunity. She'd been even more addicted to her since Ottilie had confessed weeks ago that she had no other reason than Monique for staying in Vegas.

Am I wanting to have sex exclusively with Ottilie now?

Was that it?

She was no nearer to deciding her malfunction that night, when she slid into Ottilie's bed and pulled her possessively against her. Ottilie murmured her approval and pressed back into her, and it was like aurora borealis had ignited inside her.

Monique knew in that moment: She didn't want to leave this bed. And she didn't want to be with anyone else. She just didn't know what to do about it.

So much had changed between them since Ottilie's confession that she no longer needed to be in Vegas. They'd taken to sharing more than just beds with each other.

Fairly regularly now, Ottilie would lounge in an armchair, sipping her tea, listening to a classical music station on the radio she'd relocated to Monique's business suite for just this purpose, *The Art of War* in her lap.

Monique had long since stopped goggling at Ottilie's eclectic reading choices. They ranged from philosophy to chess tactics to exotic fish, and, most recently, Chinese military strategy.

In turn, Monique had begun enjoying curling up next to her, indulging in reading about her own passion, ancient Egypt. No one in Monique's life had ever shared this obscure interest of hers, not even Cleo, despite her stage name. It hardly mattered, of course. Monique wasn't so young as to believe shared obsessions were vital to a relationship's success.

One day, Monique had teased Ottilie that she was Pharaoh Hatshepsut, the most pragmatic of all the rulers. After all, Hatshepsut, who had declared herself king, had later instructed that her image be shown with a male king's body and false beard so as to appear a typical pharaoh. No upsetting of political or social apple carts for Hatshepsut.

Without even looking up from her reading, Ottilie had said, "Of course I am Hatshepsut. Her stepson, Tuthmosis III, had her erased from history. Invisible to the end. Relatable." She'd smirked and then gone back to her book.

NUMBER SIX

"Well, until they found her tomb," Monique had murmured, still in complete shock at the factoid her lover had plucked out of thin air.

The sheer breadth of knowledge Ottilie possessed on a great many subjects confounded Monique. She was often in awe. It was fascinating, yes, but the more she saw all the sides of Ottilie, all the random quirky things that made her *her*, the more Monique feared she again was in so much trouble. So what was new?

Today, Monique was secretly watching Ottilie reading when she should be focused on her paperwork. She was so beautiful in repose, serene and calm. As much as Monique wanted to pounce on her, she'd promised herself she'd review her annual general meeting report first. She'd ravish her adorable woman a little later.

Yes, *her woman*. Because she'd no longer indulge her delusion this was a casual fling. At least to her own heart. Monique had already been down this path before, caring more for someone than they did her. But, try as she might, she couldn't harden her heart over the pain she knew was coming. One look at Ottilie and she wanted to give her the heavens. What a fool she was.

Love made everyone a fool.

A familiar heavy staccato knock sounded, startling her out of her daydreams. She recognized the knock, which came from farther down the hall, on the exterior door of her adjoining suite.

Monique glanced at Ottilie, who'd looked up. "Darling, could you please disappear onto the balcony for a few minutes? I believe Hotel Duxton's CEO wants a word with me. I'd like him to feel he can talk freely."

Ottilie gave a nod and relocated, tea in hand, through the doors. An absolute advantage of having a former spy in one's love life was never having to explain the need for anything even remotely sneaky. She simply understood.

Monique opened the door and stuck her head out. Sure enough, Simon Duxton stood waiting in the hall in front of her other suite, running his hands down his jacket repeatedly.

"Mr. Duxton," she called. "I'm in this one today."

He immediately turned toward her. She studied his scrambling approach. Anxiety was making him clumsy. Which, in turn, made her nervous.

"I..." he began, then stopped and swallowed.

Very nervous.

"Why don't you come in?" she offered. "If this is going to be one of those conversations."

He bobbed his head once in agreement and entered, before closing the door after himself. Standing awkwardly, he glanced around, taking in the neat room and its various piles of financial documents she was working through.

"Have a seat." She waved him to the couch and took the armchair opposite.

"Thank you," he murmured and then sank onto it.

A long silence fell.

"Well?" Monique finally asked.

"I asked around about you," he said. "What sort of a guest you are. You're well-liked. Even Mrs. Menzies said you were exemplary, and I swear, that woman dislikes everyone."

Monique waited for the *but*.

He raked one hand through his floppy blond hair. "I know you're in business with my cousin Amelia. Congratulations on that deal. Everyone wanted a piece of that one."

"Yes. I'm well aware."

"I also looked up the security feed, the one in the hall outside. To see that you weren't, you know...running some prostitution ring. Just in case. I mean, what if you'd fooled everyone? What if someone needed help and I'd ignored it?" He frowned. "I wouldn't want that on my conscience."

Monique's blood went cold. "And?"

"You have a lot of clients, Ms. Carson. For your...investment company." He eyed her. "Some of them are really famous. A pop star. Senator. Finance journalist. A TV news anchor."

"News anchor?" Monique repeated as she stalled, her mind racing frantically.

"I think she's from Atlanta? Tall? Black? Has the"—he waved at his cheeks—"dimples?"

As if she could ever forget Roberta James. "Well, everyone needs investment advice."

"That's just the thing, though," Duxton said. "None of your clients had briefcases or folders or anything else you'd bring to get your financials done. That doesn't seem credible."

Monique's heartrate sped up. "The world is electronic these days, Mr. Duxton."

"Maybe." He leaned back. "But that doesn't explain why all of your clients are women."

And shit. A sick, cold feeling threaded its way through her.

"I'm not as stupid as everyone thinks," he said, meeting her eye coolly. "It's no secret I don't want to be here. Sure, I'd prefer to be back in Sydney with my little girl, seeing the beach more than once a month. Instead, I'm stuck here trying to fix a wages scandal that the Nevada governor keeps threatening to get involved in." He blew out a sharp breath. "And I'm not so stupid that I don't know a high-class hooker when I see one."

Her lips thinned.

"Sorry, was that not the right term? *Escort? Prostitute? Sex worker?*"

"I don't know what you think you know but—"

"No. Don't disrespect me with another lie." He reached into his jacket pocket and pulled out a piece of paper. "I found your website." He pushed a printout of her menu page over to her. "I'm sure if I call the number listed there, some cell phone in this room will ring, right?"

Monique stared in dismay. How had he worked it out? Only her surname was on the website, and even then, she'd spelled it *Carsen* not Carson, despite how common her real surname was. She should have chosen a different name entirely.

"Shall we test it?" he asked.

Monique exhaled. "No."

"Does Amelia know?" His lips tugged down in dismay. "My cousin assured me you weren't running a prostitution ring." He gave a low bark. "I guess the emphasis is on the word *ring*, isn't it? She doesn't lie, but she chooses her words carefully. You both played me for a fool." He glared, but there was no real weight to it. "But if she vouched for you, there's a reason for it."

"We're in business together."

"Yeah. But she doesn't vouch for everyone she's in business with. She must believe you're decent enough to stand by."

Monique found that rather a warming sentiment, especially since Amelia usually spent most of her time with Monique sighing at all her inappropriate comments.

"Which makes what I'm about to say difficult. I want you to leave. I know you've been with us in Duxton Vegas for fourteen years. I'll give you a month to vacate, which I think is generous." He dipped his gaze to the floor.

"I don't understand," Monique protested. "Amelia seemed to think that as long as a guest pays on time and doesn't cause problems, you don't care about anything else. What is the issue?"

"Honestly? I'm being pressured to show you the door. And it's a pressure I'm not able to withstand right now. I don't need any more drama. I'm up to my eyeballs in it. It's not personal, Ms. Carson, but you have to go."

"*Who* is pressuring you?" Monique asked. "I'll have my lawyers have a chat to them. Clear this all up."

"Someone with more power than your rich lawyers."

"Let me guess: is Carrie Jordan threatening to abandon her residency unless I'm gone?"

"What?" Bafflement crossed his face. "No! And, frankly, I wouldn't care if she did. Her opening night show was such a screwup that I've had three cancellations from major entertainers scheduled to perform here next. She's cost us more than she's bringing in."

"She called you last time, though, didn't she? She's who claimed I ran a prostitution ring."

He squirmed. "I'm not commenting on that."

That was a yes.

"All I'll say," he added, "is that this time the pressure is someone else."

"Who?" she demanded.

NUMBER SIX

He rolled his eyes. "She's one of your visitors. I'm sure you can work out who. She's an entitled pain in my ass. Political and powerful."

It was a short list to work out who was political, powerful, threw around her weight, was entitled, *and* wanted retribution on Monique. A list of one.

"Phyllis Kensington has no real power," she said sharply. "Not anymore."

"Maybe not. But she's friends with so many people who do have power. Including someone in the Office of the Labor Commissioner. I can't risk her retaliation on top of everything else. Don't you see the position I'm in?"

She did. The man had no spine and was starting to panic about his diminishing options. "Oh, I see. You folded like a cheap deck chair, and you're trying to shove a loyal long-term guest out the door."

He lifted his chin. "It's every manager's right to deny service to a guest as long as it's not for discriminatory reasons."

She knew that.

"Your last day is the twentieth of next month. Liaise with Mrs. Menzies for any outstanding issues we can help with, such as forwarding of mail. We'll be happy to assist." He rose to go. "I really am sorry, Ms. Carson."

He was almost at the door when Monique said, "You aren't a patch on Amelia. She'd have fought this. She doesn't capitulate, no matter who demands it."

"You think I don't know that? How brilliant and terrifying she is to deal with?" He lifted an eyebrow. "But she's not the one in charge. I am." And with that, he left.

Ottilie pushed open the balcony doors a moment later, a soft frown on her face.

"You heard all that, I presume?" Monique said, her head dropping in resignation.

Ottilie put down her now empty teacup and came to sit in Monique's armchair, sliding herself next to her. It was big enough for two, albeit a close fit.

"I'm about to be homeless," Monique said dramatically. "Well, technically homeless. Obviously, I can afford to go elsewhere. It's just

I've been here fourteen years. I've…nested. And now, suddenly, it's just, *leave*!" She scowled. "I'm too old for this. I keep saying that, you know."

"Too old for what?"

"All the bullshit that comes with sex work. I'm so sick of it." Suddenly, that felt like the truest thing she'd ever said.

"You can fight this eviction, though," Ottilie said. "You have powerful allies. Amelia Duxton, for instance? She helped before. Her cousin Simon respects her. Surely if you called her—"

"No. I'm not going to do that." That odd feeling came over Monique again. It felt the same as the relief when that client had cancelled, but it was much stronger this time. As if the universe was forcing her hand, and she was…what? Okay with it? More than that. Ready to move on.

Ottilie was watching her. "You're not going to fight it?" she asked neutrally.

"No." Monique met her gaze as her decision solidified. "Do you know, the absolute worst part of sex work—aside from potentially dangerous clients—is how vulnerable it leaves you to blackmail. It's ongoing, always in the back of your mind: 'What if Client A accidentally says the wrong thing to the wrong person?' or 'What if Client B retaliates because she's angry about something?' And I'm in a powerful position and financially independent. Imagine what someone without my privilege must experience every day."

"Are you saying you're thinking of retiring from sex work? Or pivoting to something adjacent?"

"Adjacent? You mean your sex podcast idea?" Monique smiled. "I do like that." Her mind had turned it over ever since Ottilie had suggested it so long ago. How would it work? Would she have guests on her show? Who? Academics? Sex therapists? Authors? The more she thought about it, the more intrigued she became.

"I like it too. It means I'd worry about you less," Ottilie admitted. Then a shadow crossed her face. "I do apologize. My opinion is irrelevant. It's your decision entirely, of course."

Ottilie *worried* about her? That sounded downright affectionate, didn't it?

Monique shook herself. "Well, it's a moot point right now. A more pressing issue is where would I be doing my fabulous podcast from? I'm being evicted. And while I have a small apartment in New York because that's where my investment business is headquartered, I truly hate the place. The city, not the apartment."

Ottilie seemed to consider that. Then, voice far too casual, she said, "You know, as it turns out, I know a place. I'd been planning to go there on my own, but I'm sure I could make room for one more. If you need somewhere."

Startled, Monique paused, then said lightly, "Let me guess: it's an island in the Pacific that has a lovely beach and plentiful Mai Tais."

"How *did* you know?" Ottilie teased. But her smile didn't reach her eyes. She seemed…anxious? "I can also assure you it has an excellent satellite internet connection should you wish to continue your investment work remotely from said beach."

Astonishment flooded Monique. That wasn't an offer one made to a casual sex partner. *Please come live with me on my island getaway.* That was an offer you made to an actual partner, wasn't it? "Is that so?" she asked cautiously.

"And that internet connection would be useful in case you wished to do your new podcast series extolling the virtues of sex, which I'm quite certain would be popular. One thing I've observed over the years is just how much people seem obsessed by sex." Her lips tugged upward. "Personally, I've never fully understood the appeal until quite recently."

"Quite recently?" Monique eyed her fondly.

"Mmm. Yes."

"You really wouldn't mind if I came along?" Monique held her breath, worrying. Would Ottilie minimize this, say it was just some practical, temporary solution, perhaps? Something she'd offer a friend? Maybe that's exactly what she saw it as?

Oh hell. Is it?

"No, I don't think I would mind." Ottilie's expression was so unreadable. "That's a first for me, I admit. I like my solitude. On that note, there are a few distant guesthouses on the property. Far enough away from the main villa for absolute privacy. In case you wished to do your side job too. I wouldn't interfere."

"You…would expect me to continue my sex work?" Monique asked in complete confusion. "Bringing clients out to this island?"

"I understand the line between professional and personal. I always have. I admit that sometimes I have these feelings of…jealousy? Apparently, I'm not quite as intellectually evolved as I thought. I think about you with other women sometimes and it's an odd sensation for me."

She'd been *jealous*? Monique started to dare hope there was something much more than casual going on here.

Ottilie exhaled and waved a flippant hand. "But that's me being possessive of someone for the first time in my life. It's unexpected. New. I'm aware these are issues for me to deal with. I would never ask you to give up your work if it fulfills you. And I'm quite certain that with time, I can compartmentalize being in a relationship with a woman who has sex with other women as part of her business."

In a relationship?

Relationship? Relief made her almost boneless. "This is a surprise," Monique managed to say.

"Me being possessive? Yes, I agree. It turns out I'm really quite attached to you. I didn't expect that. I've been on my own for so long that craving another person is unexpected indeed."

Then she stopped short. "Or do you mean you're surprised at me not wanting to prevent you from taking clients? That's not my place. If this makes you happy, it makes you happy. I will adapt. Pragmatism is my special skill, after all."

"*Ottilie.*" Monique drew in a breath, wanting to be absolutely clear on the most important point. The only thing that mattered. "You see us as being in a relationship? A serious, committed relationship?"

"Are we not?" Suddenly, she reeled back, visible horror flooding Ottilie's expression. "I apologize if I assumed." Her cheeks were now stained deep red. "I see that is something I should have asked. I thought I was reading the signs correctly, and now… Oh dear. I've made a mistake, haven't I?" Her words sounded small, her expression crestfallen.

Monique leaped in quickly. "Darling, I am *not* dating anyone else. Why would I when I'm devoted to you? Just you. When I think of my life now, it seems absurd to me not having you beside me, making me think, making me laugh." She paused for effect and added with a purr, "Making me come."

Ottilie offered a small smile, and she sat up a little.

Monique powered on. "We're discussing potentially moving to an island together, so please take that as a large flashing neon sign that we're a committed couple."

"Oh. Well. That's good." Ottilie's shoulders relaxed. "I apologize that it never occurred to me check your views on the matter."

"God, you're utterly adorable when flummoxed." Monique grinned.

Ottilie rolled her eyes. "It appears that the downside of being able to read people extremely well is always assuming you know what they're thinking. It runs the risk of making one conversationally lazy."

"I suppose that's true. Communication is still important no matter how supremely talented we are at mind reading." She chuckled at her flagrant lack of modesty about her skills. "On that note, let's address your other question. The one where you're jealous."

Ottilie frowned. "I'm trying not to be, in the interest of accuracy."

"Either way, I don't want to take any more clients, not even regulars. That's a decision that's been coming for a long time. Even if I'm perfectly comfortable with my line of work, the risks of being disrespected, outed, or blackmailed hang over me. I also don't like hearing that my work makes you unhappy, even if you somehow force yourself to compartmentalize it all away. I want us both happy. And, above all else, I'm not going to invite the potential of danger to our world, especially if we'll be out in the middle of nowhere."

"I *do* know how to deal with danger," Ottilie said. "Have I not demonstrated I'm mission ready?"

Monique's whole body laughed at that, her chest rising and falling like waves. "*Mission ready*? Do you mean like when you were my adorable protective ninja who dealt with that singer and defended my honor?"

"Adorable! I'm no such thing," she said, sounding askance.

"I beg to differ. And that was appreciated, by the way. You know, this sounds perilously close to a commitment," she teased. "Declaring yourself ready to take on danger for me. See, you read things accurately; all the signs were there."

"As I correctly deduced," Ottilie said, then elbowed her gently in the ribs. "But do stop being annoying."

Monique chuckled. "Have I mentioned lately you are the most fascinating woman I've ever met? The sense of rightness I feel being around you is powerful. I care for you a great deal."

Nodding, Ottilie said, "And I am accustomed to you."

Accustomed? The word made Monique deflate, suddenly hurt and confused. As declarations of passion, or even affection went, this was supremely underwhelming. So much for understanding each other. When it came to their feelings, it seemed they were miles apart. All Monique's previous amusement fled along with any romantic notions of sipping cocktails on a beach with her lover.

"What's wrong?" Ottilie asked, concern in her eyes.

"I am not certain this will work," Monique said flatly. "It's too soon." Maybe they'd never get there. Able to bridge the gulf in how she saw Ottilie—*adored* Ottilie—and how Ottilie saw her. To Ottilie, Monique was just someone she liked having around. Nothing more.

"How so?" Ottilie asked, confusion and disappointment in her voice.

Sadness washed through her now. "I'm not like you, who can skate across a relationship, never dropping your hooks in too deep. Me? I need to be needed. I'm aware it's not a very evolved trait for an independent businesswoman like myself to have," Monique admitted. "But I love to give. I discovered sex work as a way to be needed, not just a way to share my expertise. In many cases, women don't just delight in my body, they *need me*. I thrive on that. Do you understand?"

"Are you saying you've changed your mind and want to keep doing sex work in the future?" Ottilie asked, sounding utterly confused.

"No!" Monique blew out a frustrated breath. "I'm saying I've been down this road before, with Cleo. I hated it. I need to be with someone who adores me too, who needs me—passionately and desperately and thoroughly. Someone who'd miss me terribly if I wasn't there. Tempting

NUMBER SIX

as it sounds, I can't go to your perfect island and lie around drinking cocktails while knowing the whole time that you're not that into me. I need you to *need me too*."

Monique spread out her hands. "I can't essentially 'move in' with a woman who fills my every thought but who thinks of me as someone they're merely *accustomed* to. I'm sorry, darling. Thank you for the beautiful offer—one that I know is rare for you—but I need more. I can't settle for living with someone who feels…ambivalent…toward me."

Ottilie didn't speak for a moment and then said, voice low and tight, "I don't think you understand what that word means to me."

Accustomed? What other way was there to interpret it?

"You know that I adapt well to circumstances, even those I'm uncomfortable with. I always find a path to coping with a new reality. This allows me to deal with almost any event, no matter how appalling. But it seems even I have my limits."

Monique listened, mystified.

Ottilie's gaze dipped. "I find I cannot be pragmatic about the idea of leaving here alone. Of missing you. I cannot simply accept this new reality and wave it away through sheer force of will. I cannot just *adapt*. I look at what lies ahead and know with absolute clarity that, without you, my life would be dull, insubstantial, and lacking purpose."

With a wry glance up, she added, "It always would have been that, though. I suspect boredom would have settled in. There are not enough Mai Tais in the world to bury the lack of intellectual stimulation."

"Then why—"

"It was an escape and a choice. I assumed I'd learn to switch off, read a lot, and find a way not to think quite so much. I hoped I'd eventually succeed. But what I didn't anticipate was you." She met Monique's eyes with fierceness. "Suddenly, I'm acutely aware of what I'll be missing out on. I'm *accustomed to you* now. I find that sensation to be so profound that I cannot work around it. There are no other paths to circumvent this, to satisfy my pragmatic nature. My options come down to only this: being with you or not being with you."

Monique felt a shiver at the power of her words.

"All my life," Ottilie continued, "I have been unused to noticing space, to that 'void' I'm told that comes from missing things or people. I'm perfectly happy on my own. Or I was. But now I'm aware that I will not adapt to the empty space your absence would leave. I, the ultimate pragmatist, must admit *I Will. Not. Adapt.* Not without you. Which leads me to the next thought: I know with absolute certainty what will happen without you."

"What?" Monique asked, scarcely able to breathe.

"I'll fade back into the wall." Ottilie's words were sober but delivered without sadness. "Or into the sand, as the case may be. Invisible and unremarkable, uninvolved until the end of my days. And then I will simply pass away into nothingness, forgotten and unnoticed. And I will deserve that ending. It is, after all, fitting, given how I have lived my life: untouched and untouchable, leaving little of myself behind."

Ottilie's intense gaze had a grip on Monique. "But now I see the other door," she continued. "Another choice. With you, I might exist in a way I haven't before. You make me more substantial, Monique. Just by seeing me as you do, I don't fear I'll slip away, just dust on sand, lost. Gone. I would be visible to the very end. Through your eyes, I feel anchored. Whole and substantial. I'm a presence beyond my own shadow. So, yes, please, understand me well when I say: *I am accustomed to you.*"

In wonder, Monique leaned in, kissing her, unable to articulate in any other way how much her words affected her. She drew away and whispered, "Thank you. But I promise you this: no matter what happens to you or between us, you will never be forgotten. Not by me. It's not possible. I will always remember the remarkable woman you are. And I appreciate you explaining how you feel."

"I won't lie. I'm still a little confused by this," Ottilie said. "How *this* feels so inevitable. That part, I don't understand at all. It's as though we are meant to be. Yet I've always disdained the idea of romantic inevitability."

"Why bother trying to understand it? Just go with it. I know I am." Monique felt that mood all the way to her bones. "Besides, I love a good mystery."

"Well, I hate them. Unsolved mysteries fly in the face of who I am," Ottilie said, looking appalled. "But I've decided I'm going to simply accept that sometimes in life there are things that cannot be understood. You being meant for me, and I for you, is apparently one more mystery one must endure." Her lips twitched to show she was teasing.

"Excellent," Monique said with satisfaction. "Now, I think it's time you told me about this distant island of yours is. I'm not sure that *Pacific island with Mai Tais* will work as a forwarding address. Where is it, exactly?"

"Exactly? It's located at sixteen degrees, thirty minutes, nine-point-one seconds south by one hundred fifty-one degrees, forty-two minutes and point-five-six seconds west."

Monique blinked. "You know that off the top of your head?"

"I've been dreaming of it for a long time. It's a private escape off Bora Bora if you want to be less precise."

"Do you think it'll be available to accommodate us on short notice? Or have you already booked ahead? How long can we stay?"

"Honestly," Ottilie said with an amused look, "it's like you don't know me at all. I've been planning this for three years now. I've left nothing to chance. I assure you my little island will be able to accommodate us immediately and indefinitely. After all, I own it outright. I bought it about eighteen months ago."

"You bought an island?" Monique peered at her. "You're joking."

"Why would I joke about that?" Ottilie asked, perplexed.

"You bought an actual island? Off Bora Bora," she mumbled.

"Yes. Why is this so hard to believe?"

"It sounds…" Monique had always assumed she would have the most wealth in their relationship. Perhaps she should reassess that assumption. "Expensive, for one."

"I bargained them down to fifty-two million. It was a steal."

Monique inhaled. "How on earth could you afford that on a PA's salary?"

"I wasn't on a PA's salary." Ottilie hesitated. Worry flitted into her eyes. "I suppose I should tell you. Very few people know this. It's an act of trust telling you." She swallowed.

"You were on The Fixers's board," Monique said flatly.

Shock radiated from Ottilie. "How—?"

"During our conversation at the spa about power corrupting, you said that it had never happened to you. I knew then that you were more than the PA you claimed to be."

"But a lot of PAs have indirect power. Power to influence their more powerful bosses. Why did you decide I was that high up?"

"Originally, I didn't. But I noticed how odd it was that you mentioned the board so often. What they thought, what they did, as though you were in all those meetings. You even complained directly to them—twice—about Phyllis Kensington. I deal with plenty of boards in my investment job, and they do not open themselves up to hearing the complaints from lowly assistants. Conclusion: you were not a lowly assistant."

"Ah." An air of respect tinged Ottilie's tone.

"Lastly, though hardly conclusive, in my experience, a board with only four members—while not unheard of—is too small, can't reach a quorum, and faces deadlocks. I suspected The Fixers probably had five board members, maybe more. That occurred to me long before we'd ever met."

"And how do you feel now?" Ottilie asked cautiously. "About me being one of them?"

"You were never one of them. I worked that out too. How often did they dismiss you, ignore your advice, let their egos rule? Did they listen to your complaints about Kensington? If you were truly one of them, they'd have fired her. I heard all the things you weren't saying."

Ottilie sighed. "In the early days, I wondered why they asked me to join the board. Maybe they wanted a different perspective? But I warned them often when catastrophe was looming. They always knew better and just waved my opinion away. Later, I realized they chose me just to utilize me as a spy on the office floor—someone who would never leave nor turn on them because blood would be on my hands too."

"More fool them for not appreciating all your talents. They sound terrible."

"In its original incarnation, how they sold it to me, The Fixers wasn't terrible," Ottilie said ruefully. "If I'd known then what it would become, I would never have joined them."

"Why did you stay? When you saw where it was headed?"

"I was too focused on the wrong thing."

"Efficiency," Monique said. "Right?"

"Yes," she muttered. "Efficiency."

She sounded so annoyed at herself that Monique said, "We don't need to go over all this again. I understand who you were, even if I don't agree with the choices you made. But the main thing is that you didn't just walk away from that evil place. You *burned it to the fucking ground* after you."

Ottilie snorted. "I did. Yes. Honestly? The best thing I've done with my life was destroying that organization. I see that now." She hesitated. "Of course, if anyone asks, I will always say I did it because it suited me."

"It didn't suit you?" Monique asked, confused. "Destroying them?"

"Of course it did. But the whole truth is I did it because I was angry: At the board. At their arrogance. At Kensington. And because I was also ashamed of what it had become, and my part in that. Destroying The Fixers gave me enormous pleasure. It staggered me how much. I *loved* seeing it burn. When I pulled that emotion apart later, I realized how much I had wanted to be gone from there. My need to leave had been so strong that I constantly fixated on my retirement…yet I never wondered why."

"And that's why you bought an island to escape to."

"My subconscious is not subtle, apparently. And it was as far away from The Fixers as I could get."

Knowing the truth of how high up Ottilie had been in The Fixers didn't change Monique's view of her. The first time she'd ever seen her striding down that hotel hallway, she'd recognized someone powerful. If anything, knowing the truth just confirmed Monique had been right about her all along.

Hearing her regrets, though, was the nub of it. Ottilie wasn't proud of what she'd done, what her company had turned into. And, most critically, she had blown it up on the way out of the door. That part? That was everything.

"Still…a whole island?" Monique said pivoting back to the original topic. "Who does that?"

"Me," Ottilie said firmly. "Your relationship partner."

Monique chuckled. "Well, I did ask."

"So," Ottilie said, reaching for her phone, "would you like to look at the ninety-two-thousand-gallon aquarium, the seven bedrooms, the home theater, the staff house, the guest shacks, the spa, the sundeck, or the beach at sunset?"

"The…" Monique choked. "I'm sorry what?"

"The beach at sunset it is, then." Ottilie loaded up a photo. "This is my favorite view." Two empty swinging cane chairs sat side by side on a pale white shore silhouetted against the orange setting sun. "So? How do you feel about leaving Las Vegas?"

Monique gazed at the image. "With you? I can't imagine anything better." She tapped a photo. "Although, I wouldn't mind looking at the ninety-two thousand-gallon aquarium first because that sounds fake."

"I assure you it's not." Ottilie loaded up the picture. "It's the largest private aquarium in the world."

"Of course it is." Monique shook her head slowly. "What else would you get? Second largest?"

"Exactly." Ottilie pursed her lips. "What a thought."

"Okay, before I commit to escaping to paradise with you, I do have one very important question."

Ottilie's smile dropped away. "Yes?"

"What on earth is your surname?"

Shoulders relaxing, Ottilie said: "That's classified."

"Would you tell me for a kiss?"

"It turns out I can be bribed." Ottilie leaned in close. "Make it a good one."

Epilogue

Sixteen degrees, thirty minutes, nine-point-one seconds south by one hundred fifty-one degrees, forty-two minutes and point-five-six seconds west was beautiful. Monique had been indulging her inner lazy bunny for six months and loving every minute of it.

Every night at sunset, she and Ottilie would take to those beach cane chairs, Mai Tais in hand, and watch the golden ball dip into the water while they talked softly.

Her fear that she'd miss her sex work hadn't come to pass, although she did miss one or two favorite clients, Mrs. Menzies most of all.

On Monique's last day in Vegas, June Menzies had clung to her in a long, wordless hug in Monique's room. "Thank you," the front desk manager had whispered. "For everything."

Monique had tried to give her the name of another sex worker who would be perfect for her, but June had shaken her head. "I've met someone. I don't need another name."

"You've met someone?" Monique had exclaimed in delight. "Anyone I know?"

"Actually, yes." Mrs. Menzies's cheeks reddened delightfully. "She works in the accounts department. You talk to her every three months each time you settle your bills."

"Laura? Oh, she's a hoot." Monique smiled. "Hilarious woman. It's about time you had someone fun in your life. You're long overdue."

Mrs. Menzies had gone even redder. "She's someone I never would have been open to dating if not for you. I didn't realize how bad my marriage was—the constant insults and disrespect—until you showed me it could be so much better. And now Laura... She's shown me it can be incredible."

"I'm *so* pleased for you, darling." Monique stepped back and lightly slapped Mrs. Menzies's voluptuous ass. "For old times' sake," she teased. "God, you're gorgeous."

She harumphed. "Yes, well, none of that nonsense from you."

"I'll miss you too," Monique said. "A great deal."

Mrs. Menzies hesitated, then said, "The hotel gossip network is in overdrive about you leaving. I must say, it's a relief after all the wall-to-wall carrying on since Carrie Jordan was arrested here."

"What's the scuttlebutt about me?" Monique was well aware of the charges against the disgraced singer regarding some "deeply concerning" images found on her seized phone that were part of an "ongoing investigation."

"Is it true about you and Ms. Zimmermann?" Mrs. Menzies asked.

"Well, June, if everyone's suggesting that Ottilie and I are off to an undisclosed Pacific island where there will be obscene amounts of cocktails, beaches, and sex, then yes. It is true." She beamed in happiness.

"So, you really weren't lying," Mrs. Menzies said earnestly, "all those times you told me. You really do love us older, rounder women."

"I really wasn't lying. I love clients in all shapes and sizes, but you were always my favorite, darling. And you've *always* been sexy to me, even when you didn't believe me."

That earned her another abrupt, surprising hug, and an amused June Menzies murmuring in her ear, "Anytime I hear the number five, I will think of you."

"As will I, darling," Monique replied.

Then Mrs. Menzies pulled away and strode off, cheeks as red as stop signs. *Adorable.*

NUMBER SIX

Ottilie emerged from the shower, shaking Monique back to the present.

She was naked and gorgeous, toweling down slowly. "I see the exotic island lifestyle agrees with you."

"Oh?" Monique peered at her over her reading glasses. "Lounging in bed at eleven." She smiled. "I've had time to do my yoga, take my daily beach walk, chat to the cook and the cook's groupie, read another chapter of *Oryx and Crake*, and have a swim. The water is glorious today, by the way."

"Well, I'm stuck answering Ray's emails. He still wants to debate EVs with me."

"How exciting," Ottilie said dryly.

"Yes, darling. Lithium extraction in Tibet is as exciting as it gets for us corporate types. At least I'm also planning my exciting next podcast. Special guest is Las Vegas's sensation, Cleopatra. Its working title is 'Showgirls, Sex, and Razzle Dazzle.'"

Ottilie snorted. "That'll be popular. But it'll be hard to top 'Finding Your Clitoris—Repeatedly.'"

Monique grinned. "I'm happy to report that that masturbation podcast got a million followers faster than any other podcast in history this year. It's now a viral sensation. Never underestimate people's interest in getting off."

"Sex sells." Ottilie shrugged. "On that note, did you say yes to that publisher?"

"I'm still negotiating. I may be a debut author, but I'm not taking the first deal they offer. They're not the only publisher interested. I know my worth."

Ottilie smiled. "I like that about you. By the way, Hannah would love us to swing by for lunch today. Says she's cooking something delicious."

"Is it challah again? God, I love that bread of hers. Divine."

The best part of Ottilie's friend coming to stay in one of the guesthouses for a few months was her sublime cooking. Hannah's repertoire was being enhanced lately thanks to Ottilie's cook, a maternal middle-aged Bora Bora woman living on the far end of the island whom Hannah had befriended. The two women were thick as thieves in the main kitchen most days, with Hannah declaring herself the woman's "oldest, most devoted groupie."

Hannah was a delight, and appreciative of having an island getaway while her granddaughter enjoyed her honeymoon.

Monique had loved Hannah the moment she'd first said hello to her.

Hannah's eyes had lit up with recognition at her voice. "Oh, it's you! The podcast lady?"

Monique had preened.

"Hannah?" Ottilie had asked in astonishment. "You listen to her show?"

"Oh, I'm a loyal follower. There really is only so much I can fill my days with. I listen to all sorts of media, but Monique's show is by far the most entertaining." Hannah leaned in confidentially, adding, "I appreciated the one called 'Bad Hips, Great Orgasms.' Very useful. Not everyone is so young and flexible anymore."

And that was the absolute first and last time Ottilie had mentioned Monique's hobby to Hannah. There were some things Ottilie apparently didn't need to know about her friend.

Now Monique couldn't wait to meet Hannah's granddaughter, when Michelle arrived at Christmas with her new wife, Eden.

This year's Very Bora Bora Christmas would also include Cleo and Rochelle.

Cleo would, of course, bring more U-Haul jokes than ever, as well as one of her old glittery dance outfits, as per Hannah's request.

Monique was most looking forward to bringing together the two career dancers so they could bond. Hannah had been counting down the days with much enthusiasm.

How interesting life had become. There would be food, fun, friends, and sunsets.

Friends?

That was taking some getting used to.

Christmas should be survivable...assuming Michelle and Ottilie didn't rile each other up too much. The duo couldn't seem to resist a little low-level head-butting whenever Michelle Skyped the island to talk to her safta.

NUMBER SIX

Monique wondered whether she should have a quiet word with the former Fixers' CEO at some point. She could explain that Michelle was free from media scrutiny only due to Ottilie, that before she'd moved to the island, all Ottilie had spent her retirement doing was threatening anyone even thinking of linking Michelle to her previous company.

Would that make things weird? Michelle feeling suddenly beholden to Ottilie?

Or maybe Monique should butt out. Leave the two to their amusing little love-hate dances that really just boiled down to them both caring about Hannah.

It suddenly occurred to Monique that Ottilie was taking an awfully long time to dry off after her shower. A curl of desire slithered through her. Was this an invitation? *Well, well.* She perked up.

"You know, it's very distracting, you standing there stark naked." Monique's eyes roamed Ottilie's nude body. She loved how full and curvy and soft it was. "I'm suddenly thinking there's something else I'd prefer to be doing than *talking* about sex."

"Oh?" Ottilie asked innocently, hanging up the towel. "And what would that be?"

Monique patted the bed beside her.

Ottilie shook her head. "Lose the laptop. I'm too old to be banging into hardware."

"Too old?" Monique chuckled. "Please, ever since we've been on Sixteen Degrees, you've been getting younger and younger. Having no stress suits you."

"Sixteen Degrees is not its name, you know," Ottilie observed, but her gaze never left her lover as Monique began whipping off her clothes.

Not that Ottilie had ever actually succeeded in pronouncing the island's name correctly herself, although she'd never admit it. Five languages and she couldn't master one extra-twisty native island name?

Speaking of wrapping her tongue around things... She smirked at Ottilie's expression as Monique's shirt went flying and her breasts bounced into view.

"No bra," Ottilie observed dryly. "I'm living with a bohemian."

"No bra," Monique confirmed, shimmying her underwear down her legs next. "Did you know I almost came thinking about you naked in the shower earlier? But I have some self-restraint." She moved her laptop off the bed onto a small cane table next to it.

"You...with restraint." Ottilie climbed onto the bed, kneeling at Monique's feet, and studied her. "I'd like to test that theory." She gave Monique an intense look. "Spread your legs for me?"

Monique licked her lips, and her pulse kicked up. She spread her legs. "Now what?"

"I like to look, you know that." Ottilie lowered herself between Monique's legs but didn't touch her.

It was true. Ottilie was an observer. In their months of exploring each other's bodies, sometimes she simply enjoyed studying the slick, soft folds between Monique's legs.

Once she'd used a feather on her, which had driven Monique insane. Another time, her breath. Nothing else but a whispered caress, explaining all the ways she'd tongue her later.

Ottilie licked her index finger and then traced Monique's folds lightly. She discovered the arousal at her entrance. "I see you weren't making that up."

"You inspired me."

"What were you thinking about? When you were being inspired?" Ottilie's finger shifted to the base of Monique's clit, and she leaned in, licking gently. She pulled back to wait for a reply.

"I love the way you look when you're turned on. The way your eyes *blaze* when you want me. I've never felt more wanted than when you just lock eyes with me. When I can see your desire, your hunger for me."

"I can certainly see *your* desire right now," Ottilie said, entering her achingly slowly.

Monique gasped at the sensation, and a little spasm of delight shuddered through her.

"I'd like to take you from behind when you're on your knees, I think," Ottilie said matter-of-factly. "I'll lick you until you come. Or maybe...a strap-on?"

NUMBER SIX

Monique twitched between her thighs. "Oh?" She tried not to sound too desperate, but her cool façade was long gone. Her lover had seen her in every kind of disarray there was.

"Would you enjoy me being in charge?" Ottilie asked, as if she weren't in charge most of the time. As if she didn't prefer being on top, sitting on her, and rubbing her wetness all over Monique's stomach while Monique frantically thumbed her clit.

Ottilie was powerful to watch when she was aroused. She would throw her head back sometimes and just moan. Long and low. As if fucking Monique were an overwhelming sensation.

"You love being in charge," Monique pointed out. "What if I did that to you? Hmm? If you're thinking about taking me from behind, you must enjoy the idea."

The finger inside her froze and then began pumping in and out more vigorously. "We'll both try it," Ottilie announced. "And see which we prefer." Then her mouth descended on Monique's clit.

She began to gasp. Nothing at all had ever prepared Monique for what having sex with someone she loved so deeply would be like. It made everything sharper. More colorful. The sensations were powerful.

They hadn't exchanged the words yet because it had felt too soon. Although, the day Ottilie had explained how she could not adapt to being without Monique was declaration enough. Being *accustomed* to Monique was an *I love you* from anyone else.

Whatever they labelled it, though, the feelings were just getting deeper. And the more Ottilie looked at her like *that*, as if Monique were essential to her breathing, the more Monique wanted her.

It was constant now.

Ottilie's tongue tap-danced across the tip of her clit, then slid up and down, playing, toying with it.

Monique was going to come a lot sooner than she'd hoped. She could feel the building pressure, loving the sight of Ottilie folding herself in half with her pendulous breasts pressed into Monique's thighs. Those pillowy breasts shifted as she did.

Monique would taste her nipples soon. Weigh them, stroke them, pleasure them, and make Ottilie gasp out those little huffs of air. Ottilie was never loud, but her gasps said everything.

Ottilie's tongue was doing amazing things to her. That just reminded her of how much Ottilie loved being tongued. She became undone whenever Monique pushed her tongue deep inside her and then ran her pinkie down to her anus and teased around her puckered hole. She'd go bright red in the cheeks every time, but she never asked her to stop.

Ottilie had only once ever asked her to stop, and it had been when her neck had started spasming. She'd accepted a gentle massage instead.

She loved cuddles too. Monique wasn't sure what she thought a former spy might be like in bed, but cuddles hadn't been on her list.

Cuddles were vastly underrated.

"Are you still with me?" Ottilie's lips drew away. Her fingers, though, never stopped playing with her. "I feel you drifting."

"I'm sorry," Monique said. "I was thinking about how much I love cuddling you."

Ottilie nodded. "I do like your cuddles. They're so good that I'm surprised they weren't on your menu."

"I didn't share *all* my special skills with my clients. I like to hold some things back for the women I'm intimate with."

"Women? Plural?" Ottilie glanced dramatically over her shoulder. "Should I be worried you have a harem tucked away somewhere?"

"No harems. Just the one woman I'm wildly into. And I've been thinking of adding another item to my menu that's only available to you."

Just then Ottilie thumbed the side of her clit, Monique's absolute weakness, and said in a low tone, "I'm yours." Her eyes were dark and flinty and she rubbed her hard, again. "And you're mine. Do you understand me, *Ms. Carson?*"

Monique didn't know what it was about those words, but they were hot as fuck. She groaned, arched, and came in a quiver. Possessive Ottilie was both a rare and arousing treat. "Oh, I hear you."

Ottilie slithered up her body and wrapped her arms around her. "That was glorious."

Understatement of the year.

"So, what would be this mysterious new menu item that's reserved just for me?" Ottilie asked casually.

"Oh, that's easy," Monique said, drawing in a ragged breath. "Before I tell you what it is, I should mention that I'm very much in love with you."

"Yes," Ottilie said, not looking the faintest bit surprised. "If it helps, I have known for some time I'm in love with you. Obviously."

That was so Ottilie that she chuckled.

"What?" Ottilie asked. "As if you didn't know."

Yes. She did know. It turned out she knew the Book of Ottilie intimately and had read it cover to cover. That didn't stop the warmth in Monique's belly or the brilliant smile she knew had lit up her face. "There's only one item on my new menu: Number Six."

Ottilie waited, gaze locked with Monique's.

"Love Me." Monique cheeks felt like they were on fire at how that sounded. Corny as hell. So much for having any cool whatsoever around Ottilie Zimmermann.

Silence fell for a long moment and then Ottilie murmured softly, "Well, then, Ms. Carson, I'd like to order a Number Six."

Monique's embarrassment fell away, and her heart suddenly seemed too big for her chest. Smiling, she said, "Now and forever. Number Six it is."

Bonus Short Story

The following short story first appeared in Lee Winter's *Sliced Ice* anthology. It is set in the world of Lee's *Hotel Queens* novel, which first introduced sex worker Monique Carson. This is a sexy peek into the relationship between Monique and her client, June Menzies.

Number Five

Monique Carson, Las Vegas's premier CEO sex fantasy expert, straightened the paperwork on her desk in Room 612 of Hotel Duxton. The desk was wooden, solid, and perfectly sized for the taking of women over or under it while she dictated her orders for the day, depending on the client's desires.

Her clients were all women. Monique loved seeing women open up and come alive from being intimate with someone who knew how to ignite their bodies. There was something so powerful about looking into a woman's eyes the moment she understood what sex could really be like.

Repressed women, unhappy women, bored women. Showing them how much they could feel was a heady sensation, and, by God, Monique loved her work. All her clients, even the walled-off ones, were fascinating to her.

Which lead her thoughts to her next arrival.

If Monique Carson saw herself as olive oil—languid, evocative, and smooth—June Menzies was brittle as sandpaper. The abrasive, sixty-two-year-old hotel executive existed in a state of constant annoyance and ferocity, approaching her work and life as if storming battlements. Little wonder half the staff at Hotel Duxton Vegas were in fear of their front desk manager.

To Monique, though, June Menzies was utterly delicious. After all, a ball of fury was just something else to play with and pull apart. Something interesting. Exciting. Fun.

And although Mrs. Menzies often suggested she hated everything about Monique's teasing attitude and all the salacious details that her work entailed, it never stopped her from visiting. Often.

A knock sounded.

Right on time.

"Darling, come in," Monique purred, stepping aside to allow entry.

Mrs. Menzies entered and placed a small leather handbag on the chair. It was rigid and black, as formal as its owner in her starched outfit.

Her shoulder-length, slightly damp hair was a rich, dark brown courtesy of her doubtlessly expensive hairdresser. She wore her expression and her hotel uniform the same way: stiff and armored. As if just daring someone to take her on.

Mrs. Menzies was rotund, short, with an ample bosom, a thick waist, wide hips and thighs, and a permanently drawn down mouth. Her wrists were knotted into tight fists. She looked even angrier than usual, which probably explained her call an hour ago for Monique to urgently fit her in.

But as much as June Menzies so often resembled an enraged, lethal porcupine, in her dark eyes lay a fire that Monique found deeply attractive.

The woman's rounded cheeks—sporting a rising blush from the awareness of what she was about to do—were as smooth and flawless as the rest of her soft, gorgeously fleshy body.

Every woman was beautiful to Monique—even the ones who never saw it in themselves. Especially those women such as June Menzies.

Mrs. Menzies's husband often dismissed her as nothing, which only made her fight even harder to prove her value in her professional sphere. The more he cheated on her, the more efficient a manager she became. Monique had often thought it would be fascinating to study this link between personal fury and professional prowess…if one didn't mind losing an eye in the process.

Mrs. Menzies's mouth flattened in a sharp line as her intense gaze locked with Monique's. She waved at the damp ends of her hair. "I've already showered."

It was a rule. No one could begin her hour with Monique without showering. All her other clients did so in Monique's suite. June Menzies, multitasking queen, always took care of it before arrival so as not to lose a second of time.

"Number four," Mrs. Menzies announced with an annoyed huff, as if it were difficult admitting aloud what she wanted.

Number four.

Monique had long ago developed a list of five options for clients to select from based on the emotions they wished to evoke. The first three were self-explanatory:

Take Me—a basic lesbian fantasy seduction, usually selected by questioning or straight women wanting to dip their toes in Sapphic seas.

Tease Me—for the delayed gratification lovers, women for whom less was more and a featherlight touch felt like bliss.

Thrill Me—for those who loved hints of danger and daring and being taken to the edge. It had flavors of BDSM, if requested.

Boss Me—number four—was her most popular item by far, given it was Monique's specialty. She would become the CEO of women's fantasies, slide on an executive power suit, and adopt her most imperious attitude, reeling off her orders for the day as she fucked a client any way Monique decided.

The ceding of complete control to Monique was a large part of its appeal to those who chose it. So powerful was this effect, she'd had some women go weak at the knees the moment she'd merely unbuttoned her top button.

Lastly, there was number five. It was an indulgent experience Monique had long thought Mrs. Menzies would benefit from. Once, eighteen months ago, Monique had suggested trying number five only to have Mrs. Menzies erupt in a rage that she was not some "pampered poodle needing to be put on a pedestal and lied to."

What an interesting choice of words. Of course, to choose number five, one had to believe themselves worthy of it in the first place. Sadly, far too many women did not.

"Ms. Carson." Mrs. Menzies's clipped voice cut through her thoughts. "My break times are strict. I don't have all day."

"Four it is," Monique supplied a genial smile. "You *do* love Four."

Mrs. Menzies's head snapped up. "I swear if you suggest Five again…" Her laugh was short and sharp.

"Perish the thought." Monique offered a wry smile. The only person who brought up number five these days was Mrs. Menzies herself.

Monique quickly pushed to one side a pile of notes on her desk, leaving an adequate gap for what she had planned, and licked her lips in anticipation. "Before we begin, remind me of your safe word."

"Chanel."

As in Chanel *Number Five*. Which Mrs. Menzies was also wearing once again. Her subconscious clearly lacked all subtlety.

Monique nodded and removed her navy jacket, slipping it onto the back of a polished wood chair, and then sat on top of the desk, crossing a leg languidly. She leaned back far enough that her breasts strained against her cream shirt.

Mrs. Menzies's nostrils flared. Sometimes she disapproved when Monique made it too obvious and flaunted what they were about to do, even though it was exactly why she was here.

"Feeling annoyed today? Need a bit of venting?" Monique ran a suggestive hand over her own thigh. This particular client needed to get her grievances out before they began, or she couldn't enjoy what followed.

Mrs. Menzies's eyes narrowed. "Yes."

"What's happened?"

"The usual." Her lips thinned.

"You've found out about another of your husband's indiscretions? Or is some pitiful minion giving you grief and not respecting your authority? You want to fuck away your fury?"

"Must you be so blunt?" Mrs. Menzies's lips curled in distaste. "I don't fuck away anything!"

"I beg to differ, darling." Monique plucked at her top button, opening her silk shirt a little. "You want to make the whole world pay when you're angry. But then you come and see me so you won't commit a murder. Your husband should send me a thank-you card. He lives only due to me."

"You give yourself too much credit. I'm still planning on his method of disposal." Mrs. Menzies's lips gave the tiniest concession of mirth.

Monique smiled back. "Well, he's safe for now."

"You think you have me all figured out, don't you?" Mrs. Menzies eyed her, expression darkening.

"I do, darling." Monique plucked another shirt button. Then another.

Mrs. Menzies's eyes fed on Monique's rapidly appearing skin even as her lips tugged down again. "Is that so?"

"I know you'd love me to tear your clothes off you and ravish you the way you deserve, but you will never ask."

"The way I *deserve*." Mrs. Menzies's tone filled with scorn. "Sure. That's it."

"Oh, yes." Monique's gaze slid appreciatively over Mrs. Menzies's body.

"You have to say that. You flatter me so I don't evict my hotel's in-house prostitute."

"You *do* realize most of Vegas's hotels have women like me in them? I'm hardly unique." She smiled. "But…I also keep a low profile, choose only discreet clients, and that enables managers like your good self to look the other way to keep a most excellent guest such as myself. So no, try again."

Mrs. Menzies's jaw tightened, but her eyes signaled agreement. Rules or no rules, no matter the hotel's pedigree, the oldest profession found a way to flourish everywhere. "Fine," she conceded. "So, you say nice things about me because I pay you."

"No, you pay me to help you lose control and you pay me to give you permission to let go. And you love it when I do naughty things that would scandalize your employees, because the forbidden excites you. And most of all, you love being at my mercy and not being the one in charge for once. But you do *not* pay me to be nice to you. So, when I say a thing is so, it is."

Mrs. Menzies snorted. "I have huge, saggy breasts, a fat backside, not to mention stretch marks and wrinkles and gray hairs. My husband calls me frumpy every day. But you, who've had every type of woman there is, declares that I'm desirable." She leaned in. "*Liar.*"

"I have never lied to you, June," Monique said placidly. "Not once."

"Of course you have. I'm not fool enough to believe any sex worker's flattery. And don't you dare tell me you're some kind of idealist who believes it."

"Not an idealist, darling. I merely look past the ridiculous notion of what society claims is desirable." Monique regarded her. "I'm a seeker of more. I like to understand things. People. And on that note, will you tell me why you're so worked up today?" She held out her hand to tug Mrs. Menzies close.

Mrs. Menzies accepted the pull with little resistance.

"Tell me?" Monique slid a hand around the back of Mrs. Menzies's waist, hands falling to that fabulously ample rear.

Mrs. Menzies grimaced. "I really hate the upper management at my hotel."

"What have they done now?" Monique rubbed a little harder, enjoying the fleshy swell through the prim skirt.

Mrs. Menzies's outfit comprised a black skirt, tight across her figure, a matching sharp vest, and a long-sleeved crisp white blouse. Pearls at her throat matched her earrings.

The strict headmistress effect always did things to Monique. There was something so deliciously fun about feeling up someone who lived to be *proper*.

"They treat me as a dumping ground for all their stupid ideas."

Monique, still sitting on the desk, tugged Mrs. Menzies between her legs. "How rude of them," she teased as her hands trailed around to the sides of Mrs. Menzies's skirt.

"Exceedingly rude." Mrs. Menzies parted her legs slightly, her only admission of how much she wanted Monique's attentions.

Slipping her fingers under the skirt hem, Monique toyed with the material suggestively for a few moments as she waited for Mrs. Menzies to finish admitting what was aggravating her most.

"They're dumping some hotel trainee on me with no notice. Tomorrow, I have to train her in all aspects of my job and set it up so she can do the same in three other departments. I met her earlier when she came in to sign some paperwork. She's pure ice. Nose in the air, full of herself. Gave me a chill to the bone."

Monique shifted her hand up beneath the skirt, enjoying the warmth and solidness of voluptuous thighs. The flesh under her fingers quivered.

Mrs. Menzies's expression was as hard and cold as it always was, as though Monique's hand wasn't wandering higher and higher. Her jaw, however, clenched.

"I'm intrigued. There's someone capable of rattling even you? And an underling at that? I so want to meet her." Monique allowed the back of her hand to bump into the junction of Mrs. Menzies's thighs. So warm, even through cotton.

"No!" Mrs. Menzies hissed. She paused. "To you meeting her, I mean. Continue…" A red hue crept up her throat. "…the other… matter." Her eyes darted down to convey her meaning, and both their gazes followed Monique's roaming hand swallowed by Mrs. Menzies's skirt.

Monique chuckled. "Hmm. You're certainly enjoying the *other matter*. I can feel that." She fingered a line into Mrs. Menzies's soaking panties.

Mrs. Menzies shot her an aggrieved look. She always reacted as if her body's obvious interest was a betrayal.

"But I definitely should meet her," Monique purred. "I'll call down tomorrow on some silly errand. Send her up to me."

"Oh, I don't think so. She seems to be the sue-everyone sort. I'm not risking you setting her off with your…antics. I think she's come from money."

"I will behave, darling. No touching. Scout's honor. *Toying* on the other hand… Oh, I'm very good at toying, wouldn't you agree?" Monique thumbed her in an exceedingly sensitive spot.

Mrs. Menzies swallowed. "You…have some talent in that regard."

Monique smiled. Mrs. Menzies was almost ready. She just needed to be fired up—in every sense.

Swaying in a little, chasing Monique's hand for friction, Mrs. Menzies surrendered. "Fine. I'll send her up to you, and you can see for yourself how cold she is. Just…*behave*." Her breath hitched as she swayed in again, rutting herself against Monique's knuckles.

Monique nudged aside Mrs. Menzies's panties and assessed her readiness. Wetness coated her fingers. She allowed the faintest tip of one finger to settle at Mrs. Menzies's entrance. It did a suggestive little swirl. "I'm sorry your bosses are throwing trainees at you and don't care how much they add to your workload."

Mrs. Menzies gasped, and her chest rose and fell rapidly. "It's disruptive and unprofessional." Her jaw ground hard. "They don't care. I put up a lot for this company, and they treat me like…like…"

"Frank?" She had the same frustration in her eyes that she usually reserved for her cheating, worthless husband.

"With no respect," Mrs. Menzies finished.

"As if you're disposable and someone barely worth their time," Monique guessed. She withdrew her hand. Mrs. Menzies was quivering with rage and wet as an inland sea. *Perfect*.

"Yes!" Mrs. Menzies spat out. "Yes!" She stepped back, yanked off her vest, chest heaving with rage. She flung the item to the floor. "Enough. I want this now." She wrenched the buttons open on her shirt, exposing a beige bra with erect nipples punching through it.

Turned on and furious, Mrs. Menzies was always an impressive sight.

Monique's lower stomach clenched in approval. She rose. It was time. Her expression turned cool and imperious as she settled into her CEO persona. She'd dressed especially for Mrs. Menzies, having packed something fun inside her tailored pants today. "Agreed. I think we've had quite enough chitchat."

Mrs. Menzies licked her lips. "Yes." Her voice was now a gravelly croak.

"I have some paperwork for you to review," Monique announced, tone sharp. "My previous assistant was woeful. I trust you'll do better?" Her eyebrow rose in challenge.

"I'm excellent at paperwork, Ms. Carson," Mrs. Menzies murmured. Lust and excitement flooded her face. "Is that *all* you need from me?"

"No. I require some stress relief," Monique replied in her iciest tone. "I want to spread you out and have you on my desk. I trust that's acceptable." It was only barely a question.

"I can assist with that." Mrs. Menzies's chest heaved.

"Take off your bra, then lie on my desk, face first." Monique patted the furniture in question.

Mrs. Menzies's nostrils flared. She did as instructed, freeing her magnificent breasts, and then sank forward over the desk. "Yes, Ms. Carson."

Subservient June Menzies was a beautiful thing to behold. This was the same June Menzies who could reduce her staff to tears with a single stern look.

"While I…avail…myself of you," Monique said, "I suggest you explain to me how you plan to fix my afternoon schedule. And make it good."

Mrs. Menzies gave a faint shudder.

"Well?" Monique snapped at her delay. "Details. Now."

"At two, you have the meeting with the ambassador." Mrs. Menzies's voice was a breathy mess.

Interesting. Mrs. Menzies only selected ambassadors for fictitious meetings when she wanted someone powerful in her fantasy.

Monique's hand slid to the skirt-clad ass in front of her and rubbed it in circles. "Which ambassador?"

"Germany."

"Ah yes, Ambassador Müller. He can be so tedious. Spread your legs for me, June." She waited. "No. Wider."

Mrs. Menzies shifted again after a moment's pause.

Monique stepped in and pushed her groin hard against Mrs. Menzies's ass, confident she'd feel the rigidness of the strap-on.

"Oh-h," she stuttered. "Yes."

"Yes what?" Monique demanded. "Yes, Müller is tedious?"

Mrs. Menzies lifted her ass a little as if to feel the hard shape better. "*Yes,*" she said firmly.

Monique slid up Mrs. Menzies's skirt, exposing her backside to cool air. She then wrenched down Mrs. Menzies's stockings, taking in, with satisfaction, the goosebumps that appeared.

Mrs. Menzies wore beige-colored full briefs to match her utilitarian bra. Forceful and solid like their owner. Monique rubbed the garment's heated crotch, cupping all the way under Mrs. Menzies and coming back up again. Her fingers came away wet. "Very good, June."

"Oh," Mrs. Menzies mumbled. "*Fuck.*" The last word was barely a whisper.

Monique loved it when desire removed her censor button. She could smell Mrs. Menzies's arousal now. *Delicious.* She returned her hand to cup her.

Mrs. Menzies began wriggling beneath Monique's hand, desperately seeking more rigid contact.

Running one firm finger between Mrs. Menzies's legs, Monique pressed hard enough into the cotton near the clit for Mrs. Menzies to tremble.

"All right, June, I'm going to have you now." Monique slowly slid down the final barrier and then dropped the sodden undergarment at Mrs. Menzies's ankles. She ran a hand up the backs of her legs, leaving a trail of quivers in her wake.

The glistening of wet curls greeted Monique as well as a liberal smear of moisture at Mrs. Menzies's upper thighs. Monique leaned in close and inhaled against Mrs. Menzies's folds.

"I'm not impressed you've booked a meeting with Ambassador Müller." Monique exhaled over the exposed heat, appreciating the tremble her breath against vulnerable flesh created. "You know how I feel about him, and yet you did it anyway." She took a slippery lower lip between her teeth and tugged sharply.

Mrs. Menzies gasped in surprise.

Monique released it, tongued it for a second, and rose once more, enjoying the disappointed moan from Mrs. Menzies.

Slowly, Monique slid down the zipper on her pants, making sure it could be plainly heard. "I'm unhappy with you at the moment." She pulled out her strap-on, lathering it with KY Jelly from the tube she kept hidden in her desk.

Monique slid the tip of the hard silicone up and down Mrs. Menzies's folds, making no move to enter her. Over and over she did this, until Mrs. Menzies writhed.

"I'm sorry, Ms. Carson. Perhaps if you…took advantage of the situation before you as my apology?" Mrs. Menzies gasped out the words. "Please?"

Half-naked, soaked, needy, in disarray, and now begging for Monique's attention? These were the moments Monique most enjoyed about her job. Making women *crave*.

"Hmm," Monique said, as if considering the offer. "I suppose it will do. You are a most pleasing sight. Your body is so ready." She dipped the strap-on's head the tiniest bit inside Mrs. Menzies's entrance.

Mrs. Menzies shuddered. "Please," she repeated. "*Please*."

Monique waited just long enough for Mrs. Menzies to squirm in anticipation. Then, she thrust.

The material of Monique's crisp navy pants pressed into the backs of Mrs. Menzies's naked thighs as the silicone was swallowed whole. She went deep and hard. After all, Mrs. Menzies had evoked Germany. If she wanted it light and fun, she'd have mentioned Fiji.

Mrs. Menzies cried out. "Oh. *Oh*." Her hands turned to fists, grasping at air against the table. "More. Deeper. Oh."

"No, no—this isn't about what my *assistant* wants." Monique sounded bored, but her own desire was now raging. With controlling, uptight women like Mrs. Menzies, Monique was always turned on when they crumpled. "Now then, tell me what you have planned for the rest of the day. Quickly." She thrust again, harder.

"Oh. I…call down to Accounts for more RS1 forms. I need to… ohhh…" Mrs. Menzies gasped and shuddered as Monique tilted her hips a little, just where Mrs. Menzies liked it. "Collate the new-hire forms and get some… *God*."

Monique slammed into her. "Such a good employee, aren't you?" Her own clit quivered and her nipples knotted at the sight before her. "You make me so wet, June. Christ, you make me wet."

Mrs. Menzies froze for a moment, her hands uncurling from their fists. "Oh," she cried out.

Monique pulled out of her and ordered her to turn over onto her back.

Redness tinged Mrs. Menzies's cheeks in this new position, and Monique knew it wasn't entirely arousal. Mrs. Menzies's desperate need to come burned in her eyes, warring against her embarrassment. She hated looking this wanton, her swollen folds on display before Monique's hungry gaze. Large, pillowy breasts, legs spread, and wetness smeared all over her inner thighs? *So damned hot.*

"Beautiful." Monique breathed out the word with conviction.

Mrs. Menzies turned away. "You don't have to say that."

She didn't believe it of course. Women like her never did. They believed their intimate partners, the ones who had years to shape their perceptions, not an acquaintance. Just once, Monique wished June Menzies could see herself the way Monique did.

Her fingers found Mrs. Menzies's clit, the tight bud now peeking out between her folds, and she caressed it. *Fast, slow, circle, straight.*

Wet, soft sounds filled the air along with Mrs. Menzies's helpless gasps.

"I need you to pay attention to your CEO, June," Monique husked, leaning in. "I'm going to require a coffee next." She grasped the strap-on with her other hand and slid it back inside as she continued to fondle Mrs. Menzies's clit. "Black, scalding hot, with two sugars." As the silicone pumped in and out, Monique's own cunt clenched in delight.

Mrs. Menzies watched her through half-lidded eyes. Her lips were slightly open, sipping in air, her nose flaring, but she was studying every twitch on Monique's face. As if she was searching for the truth as to whether Monique was aroused by this too.

Aroused wasn't even the start of it. Monique was so damned close.

Mrs. Menzies's intense scrutiny only heightened the experience. Monique's jaw tightened in a bid to hold back an audible grunt of pleasure. She should not be this near the edge, not when her client's needs were paramount. "And then shift my appointment with that idiot ambassador—I will not do *anything* I don't find enjoyable. I never do. Do you understand?"

That was an important message.

Mrs. Menzies didn't answer, but her hands fell to her wide, dusky-colored areolas, plucking at her fat nipples as Monique thrust into her, reveling in her illicit sounds of excitement.

"I'm selective about who I spend time with," Monique added, her breath coming in sharp pants. "I'm choosy about my assistants, for instance. I expect them to be available to cater to my *every* whim." She punctuated the words with a hard press of Mrs. Menzies's clit. She was rewarded with a deep, low groan that made her twitch.

"Yes, very good," Monique gritted out. "I appreciate how you give your CEO your all."

Mrs. Menzies's thighs were beginning to tremble.

"I'm going to need that report on my desk within an hour. And I warn you: next time, I won't go so easy. I'll use my mouth on you. I'll slide my tongue all over your pretty little cunt. I'll make you lose control and moan, no matter how hard you try to be *oh so professional*, and everyone will hear you. You'll be helpless and laid bare, with me watching. With your *staff* listening." She dropped her voice to a lower, seductive register. "And then I'm going to *fuck* you again. And that time, maybe I'll let them watch."

Mrs. Menzies's wail filled the air. Her eternally furious mask fell away, and a shining, naked expression of ecstasy flooded her features.

Stunning. How could anyone doubt the beauty of women?

Achingly slowly, Monique pulled out from Mrs. Menzies, bent over, and kissed her clit, slipping her tongue all over the slippery flesh in a sensuous, drawn-out farewell. Then, she straightened. "You are an *excellent* CEO's assistant, June. I'm very pleased."

Mrs. Menzies's breath was coming in heaving gasps, her eyes still screwed shut.

Monique reached to the desk for a tissue and wiped down the dripping strap-on. After removing it, she pulled up her pants. Finally, she stood back and reviewed the magnificent disarray before her.

Mrs. Menzies lay sprawled on her back, panting, those generous breasts rising and falling, her whole body on display—swollen, aroused, and very much taken. The view was exquisite.

Monique's cunt twitched harder. Honestly, if Monique didn't have another client soon, she'd be sorely tempted to play with Mrs. Menzies some more and give herself her release. God, how she loved women like this. Rarely did she encounter anyone with walls so high who would become so vulnerable in front of her.

"Are you really wet for me?" came a murmur.

Monique's gaze drifted back to Mrs. Menzies's face. "Hmm?"

"You said you were wet." Mrs. Menzies sat up. Her direct gaze was back to sharp and suspicious. "That was just a line to get me off, wasn't it?" Her mouth pulled down.

Monique regarded her. "So wet I almost came. That's the truth, June. I'm still so close, thanks to you."

Unlike other women in her business, Monique never lied to a client about whether she'd orgasmed. Women often knew anyway. And besides, Monique's honesty was one of her selling points. In fact, some clients liked to make it their mission to get her off. She never let them succeed, because for them, the thrill lay in the chase.

For Mrs. Menzies, though, this was no game. Her entire self-esteem was bound in her idea that she was in no way beautiful or worth Monique's sexual interest. It was why she hated the mere idea of number five: *Worship Me*. Because, in Mrs. Menzies's mind, for Monique to ever worship or desire her would require Monique faking the entire encounter.

How little she understood. Monique truly did find every woman had an attractive quality about her. It wasn't some glib line. They all had something about them she was drawn to, inside or out. Most beauty wasn't on the surface anyway.

"It *is* the truth," she repeated.

Mrs. Menzies found her feet. She looked a little shaky. "Well. Thanks for telling me what I wanted to hear." A faint, embarrassed blush tinged her cheeks as she pulled up her underwear and stockings. "You're good for my ego at least after half the shit Frank says to me."

Monique watched her jerky movements. "June," she said quietly, "if anyone could get me to come, it'd be you. I love bossy, confident, controlled women more than I can say."

"Well, I'm certainly that." Mrs. Menzies snorted.

She doesn't believe.

How...disappointing. Monique cocked her head and offered something she never did. "June? Would you like to feel the effect you have on me?"

Mrs. Menzies froze and glanced up in surprise. She swallowed, her desire and interest clear in her eyes. "Yes."

With a head tilt, indicating she should come closer, Monique lowered her tailored pants to mid-thigh, then drew down her panties a little. She clasped Mrs. Menzies's hand, drawing it to cup her soaked center. "Feel for yourself."

Mrs. Menzies's fingers slipped through Monique's wetness, her face filling with a look of wonder. Boldness overtaking her, she slid a thumb higher, nudging Monique's clit, then circling it.

That was all it took. Monique moaned, snapped straight as her thighs quivered, and with a delighted exhalation, she came in a rush of wetness all over Mrs. Menzies's trembling hand.

Well. That was unexpected. Monique blinked as she caught her shaky breath. "June," she murmured in awe. "How delightful you are."

Mrs. Menzies looked absurdly pleased as she removed her hand. She stared at the wetness soaking her fingers as Monique adjusted her clothing again.

They didn't speak for a moment.

"My husband thinks I'm ugly."

"I know," Monique murmured. She met Mrs. Menzies's gaze. "And he's wrong."

"He tells me I'm lucky to even have him. That no one else would put up with me or find me attractive."

Monique lifted Mrs. Menzies's wet fingers to the light. "And yet... all evidence to the contrary."

"That didn't escape me." Mrs. Menzies's voice was tight. "I honestly thought you were lying."

"You have the proof of my desire. Trust your eyes."

Mrs. Menzies hesitated, as if thinking about it. "All right."

Finally. "Good."

"I think maybe next time…" Mrs. Menzies inhaled. "I might like to try number five." Her eyes narrowed in warning. "As long as you're not too smug about it."

"Never." Monique smiled. "And an excellent choice. You deserve it."

Heat rose up in Mrs. Menzies's cheeks, giving them an attractive glow. "Maybe."

"It would be my pleasure to worship you for an hour. And you now know that's the honest truth."

Mrs. Menzies's eyes crinkled. "Thank you." Her almost-smile fell away as her thoughts clearly drifted back to work, life, reality. She finished dressing quickly, her shoulders already sinking as though she were preparing for battle.

"Next time," she said when finished. She swallowed, then turned to the door. "You know what I need."

"Yes. I can't wait." Pleasure infused Monique's voice. "Number five it is."

Other Books from Ylva Publishing

www.ylva-publishing.com

Vengeance Planning for Amateurs
Lee Winter

ISBN: 978-3-96324-865-8
Length: 311 pages (101,000 words)

Muffin maker Olivia puts up an ad for a henchperson to help enact a little revenge on her awful exes. Margaret, a mysterious and icy crime bookstore owner, applies.

While they turn out to be woeful at vengeance, they're pretty good at falling in love—much to their dismay!

An offbeat lesbian romantic comedy starring penguins, plotting, and payback.

Principle Decisions
Thea Belmont

ISBN: 978-3-96324-832-0
Length: 228 pages (71,000 words)

No-strings-attached fun with a dominatrix seems perfect for icy academic Vivienne. That is until she learns who she really is—the new principal at her niece's school.

What happens when Vivienne's called in to see her because her niece, who she's raising, keeps making trouble? And what happens when fun turns to feelings?

A moving BDSM erotic romance.

Heart's Surrender
Emma Weimann

ISBN: 978-3-95533-183-2
Length: 305 pages (63,000 words)

Neither Samantha Freedman nor Gillian Jennings are looking for a relationship when they begin a no-strings-attached affair. But soon simple attraction turns into something more. What happens when the worlds of a handywoman and a pampered housewife collide? Can nights of hot, erotic fun lead to love, or will these two very different women go their separate ways?

The worlds of a handywoman and a pampered housewife collide in this opposites-attract lesbian erotic romance.

The X Ingredient
Roslyn Sinclair

ISBN: 978-3-96324-271-7
Length: 285 pages (103,000 words)

Top Atlanta lawyer, icy Diana Parker, is driven and ruthless, and stuck in a failing marriage. Her new assistant, Laurie, seems all wrong for the job. Yet something seems to be pulling them into a secret, thrilling dance that's far too dangerous for a boss and employee.

How can they resist the irresistible?

A smart, sexy lesbian romance about daring to face the truth about who you are.

About Lee Winter

Lee Winter is an award-winning veteran newspaper journalist who has lived in almost every Australian state, covering courts, crime, news, features, and humour writing. Now a full-time author and part-time editor, Lee is also a 2015 and 2016 Lambda Literary Award finalist and has won several Golden Crown Literary Awards. She lives in Western Australia with her longtime girlfriend, where she spends much time ruminating on her garden, US politics, and shiny, new gadgets.

CONNECT WITH LEE
Website: www.leewinterauthor.com

Number Six
© 2025 by Lee Winter

ISBN: 978-3-96324-981-5

Available in paperback and e-book formats.

Published by Ylva Publishing, legal entity of Ylva Verlag, e.Kfr.

Ylva Verlag, e.Kfr.
Owner: Astrid Ohletz
Am Kirschgarten 2
65830 Kriftel
Germany

www.ylva-publishing.com

First edition: 2025

We explicitly reserve the right to use our works for text and data mining as defined in § 44b of the German Copyright Act.

No part of this book may be reproduced, scanned, or distributed in any printed or electronic form without permission. Please do not participate in or encourage piracy of copyrighted materials in violation of the author's rights. Thank you for respecting the hard work of this author.

This is a work of fiction. Names, characters, places, and incidents either are a product of the author's imagination or are used fictitiously, and any resemblance to locales, events, business establishments, or actual persons—living or dead—is entirely coincidental.

Credits
Edited by Sarah Ridding and Michelle Aguilar
Cover Design by Michelle Ryan
Print Layout by Streetlight Graphics

Printed in Great Britain
by Amazon